bird of passage

e. k. king

Copyright © 2010 by E. K. King

ISBN 0-7414-5815-2

Printed in the United States of America

This is a work of fiction. Names, characters, places, and incidents either are the product of the author's imagination or are used fictitiously. Any resemblance to actual events or locales or persons, living or dead, is entirely coincidental.

Published May 2010

INFINITY PUBLISHING
1094 New DeHaven Street, Suite 100
West Conshohocken, PA 19428-2713
Toll-free (877) BUY BOOK
Local Phone (610) 941-9999
Fax (610) 941-9959
Info@buybooksontheweb.com
www.buybooksontheweb.com

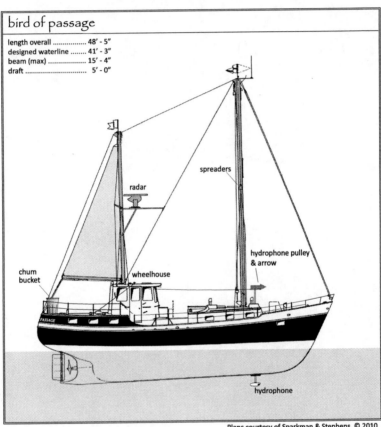

bird of passage

length overall .... 48' - 5"
designed waterline .... 41' - 3"
beam (max) .... 15' - 4"
draft .... 5' - 0"

spreaders

radar

hydrophone pulley
& arrow

chum
bucket

wheelhouse

PASSAGE

hydrophone

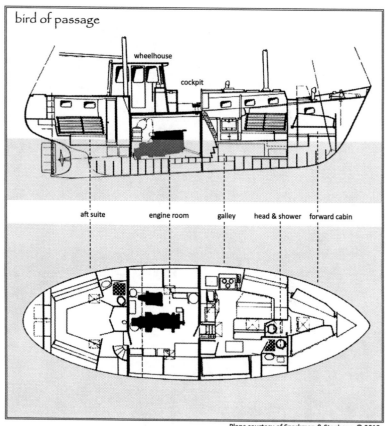

bird of passage

wheelhouse

cockpit

aft suite · engine room · galley · head & shower · forward cabin

For Frank Carey, and Ollie Brazier

...
O, say not so!
Those sounds that flow
In murmurs of delight and woe
Come not from wings of birds.

They are the throngs
Of the poet's songs,
Murmurs of pleasures, and pains, and wrongs,
The sound of winged words.
...

Birds of Passage, Henry Wadsworth Longfellow

*"When you are dead you're dead.
And you're dead for a long time."*
Calvin Landry

Atlantic Ocean

soundings in fathoms

LEG 1

Endless Sun-Filled Days

1

The early morning light of June gave no quarter. The shaft of brilliance from the east blazed through the studio window as bright as a visitation, illuminating the photographs and stacked canvases as it crept with the speed of the earth's rotation towards my prone, disheveled body. The light would soon be upon me as I lay caught between stupidity and the restlessness of reason, watching the particles of dust floating in a slow gravitational descent. My body stiff, my head throbbing from the alcohol, I waited for answers that were not to come but found comfort in the sudden revelation that when you are dead, you don't have to wake up in the morning.

Comforting as it was I remained troubled and haunted with the death of my friend. I thought of loss and friendship and wanted to know why Dave had to die so young leaving a wife, and kids – and me. Never having a chance to say goodbye. These questions were asked during the previous night while I stumbled through the back field of the farm casting dispersions at the stars, speaking to the darkness as if God himself was there to listen.

As the light moved across the morning I knew the questions would have to be asked again and thought maybe the answers could come from the light of day. This day was Friday. Dave and I would often spend this afternoon out in the boat, fishing the rips along the island, enjoying a burger and beers at the bar and later howling at the moon.

"And God saw that it was good." His voice, his face, his spirit was with me constantly. He would stand in the boat at the end of day as we watched the sun go down and marvel at the spectacle. "And God saw that it was good." I can hear him now.

When you are alive, you follow your dreams, your fate, your parental expectations, someone's idea of a productive life, some plan according to a holy book. I was following my bliss, as they say, and my bliss had led me to a loft in an old barn on a farm some friends had rented from a Boston developer who was sitting on the property until the price was right to sell. The rent was cheap, allowing me plenty of time to paint, and the loft was perfect, the light just right.

"Following one's bliss can be a rocky road," Dave had told me once. He always showed excitement in my work, but then, he was always there for me, since we were young. If he wasn't trying to hook me up with some art gallery he was trying to hook me up with one of his wife's friends.

"Brother, you need to settle down and find yourself a good woman" was his come-back whenever I got to feeling low. Now he was gone and I would go back to our haunts and ask him why. I would leave my bliss behind, spend the day on the water, have a burger at the bar, get drunk and hope to find the woman of my dreams. Maybe a good woman would have the right answer. Maybe the right answer would be a good woman. Both seemed hard to find.

2

"What the fuck, Calvin!"

The night had not turned out as I had hoped. The plan was to drink, fall in love for the evening, and worry about the rest in the morning. Sometimes you get lucky, but in a small town like Woods Hole, the playing field is limited until summertime rolls around.

The Lee Side was loud and crowded when I arrived. All the regulars were there and things were as they should be. Pete sat at the bar talking to himself. Chance and his dog held court in the corner. Irene and Teresa were catching up on the recent gossip, their side-kick Harold already inebriated. Nick had a potato chip bag loaded with cosmic mushrooms that he offered freely to anyone interested. Bonnie was still going on about off-shore drilling, and a gang of local commercial fishermen were hunched over a couple of tables planning the evening's activities. There were a number of new faces in the place too. The loud music required lots of yelling to have a conversation and it was hard to hear above the roar of the crowd, but it was good to be among friends, neighbors, and fellow crew members, of the lost and the longing. Those of us who knew him talked of Dave, and at times, I felt the loss and loneliness. But soon the beer smoothed over the rough edges so everything got blurry enough to let go for the time being. But as Dave would say, "Man will you ever learn?"

"WHAT THE FUCK, CALVIN!"

"Sorry, but I don't think this is going to happen."

It took me awhile to summon up the courage to say it. The alcohol helped. "Georgette, this is not going to happen."

She turned down the radio, which was barely audible above the rattle of the old Ford pickup truck. "Why's that, honey?"

"I'm not going to spend the night with you."

There was a long pause as she pulled a cigarette from her flannel shirt, slowly placing it in her mouth, and then snatched a pack of matches off the dashboard. With one hand she bent the match with her thumb, scratched it, and lit the cigarette without looking. She took a long pull.

"What are you talking about, Calvin?" Her Southern accent rose with the rest of her baggage, with her tone of indignation.

"Sorry. It doesn't feel right."

"What doesn't feel right?"

"This."

"What this?" Anger now simmered just below the surface of her words.

"I'm not spending the night with you, and that's it."

We moved about four heartbeats before she slammed on the brakes, and with the jolt, the true Georgette sprang forth. This was the Georgette I had heard so many tales about, the man-eater, swab the deck with your head, tough as nails Georgette who would fuck you harder than a caged monkey.

"What the hell you talking about, Calvin? I thought you were sweet on me?" she screamed, puffing smoke. Bathed in the red glow of the emergency brake warning light, she looked like a Shakespearean witch ready to conjure up the fates. She reached for my thigh but I grabbed her hand.

"I am sweet on you Georgette, but we're not sleeping together."

"Why the fuck not?"

"I don't know."

She pulled another drag on the Camel. The truck, now stationed in the middle of the road, idled roughly. She mumbled, "What? You queer, Calvin? Is that it?"

I was going through my options and realized my chances of getting a ride home were slim after leaving my car with Chance. So we just sat there, two lost souls coming unhinged. I said nothing.

"Get out," she said flatly.

"What?"

"Get the fuck out asshole!" she screamed. "Goddamn it! This is my big night out, and you blow it."

I opened the door and jumped out as she threw the truck into gear and managed a three-point turn in seven tries, throwing all kinds of epithets at me as I stood there at the edge of the road.

"I'm going back to get me a real man, shithead! Goddamn artist fagot!"

She was grinding the gears of the old Ford, searching for second gear in the vehicle that it struck me was as beat and battered as she, as used and abused, and just as pretty and shiny as she must have been at one time. But now, both the truck and its driver were down and dirty. I was not sure what had gotten into me. Maybe it was my good Catholic upbringing. Usually, with enough alcohol in the equation, anything goes in this type of situation; but then, I always believed that myth about seeing your entire life pass before your eyes when you were about to die, and the prospect of envisioning Georgette drunk and naked and in the throes of sexual abandon as I passed through the white tunnel to the final destiny disturbed me. I could have been totally wrong about her, but my instincts told me to run, and so I ran.

When she got the truck turned around, she raced the engine grinding the gears, intent on heading off in the same direction from whence we came.

"Georgette, wait!" I shouted just as the pickup leaped forward. "Wait!"

She hit the brakes, bringing the tangle of fishing gear in the bed of the truck crashing forward into the back of the cab.

"I'm not going to give you a ride," she shouted as she leaned out the window.

I approached slowly, catching my breath barely able to see her as I stood at the door. "I'm sorry."

"Fuck you, Calvin."

"No, I mean it, Georgette. I'm sorry if I hurt your feelings." She said nothing but looked forward down the road into the darkness. "I'm just hung up on somebody."

"You're not seeing anyone, Brillo said. You haven't been with any of the girls since that hippie chick walked out on you. Who you hung up on?"

She had me there. "Me, I guess."

"Brillo said you were strange."

"Brillo said *I* was strange."

There was a pause, and then we both started to laugh. Then she started to sob.

"Goddamn it, Calvin. I just wanted some fun tonight before I went back out. I hate fishing. Goddamn fish. I don't smell, do I? Fuck!" She paused. "I drink too much. Do you think I drink too much, Calvin?" she asked softly.

"I think you're asking the wrong person."

She threw the cigarette onto the road and a small orange sparkle flared up as it hit the pavement. "I think I drink too much," she repeated. "I think I'll go back to the boat and drink some more." She then popped the clutch and the truck lurched and stalled with a clank. "Goddamn piece of shit truck." She cranked it over a good long turn. It didn't catch and she hit the dashboard hard with her fist. "Damn it!"

"You wanna push?"

She laughed. "Well, Calvin, you might have to."

She cranked it again while pumping the gas, and as if out of fear, the truck roared back to life. "All right, Calvin," was all she said and then drove off looking for second gear, grinding away and eventually finding it, leaving me in the middle of nowhere. The orange glow of the cigarette at my feet faded and died as I stood there listening to the truck disappear into the night trying to figure out what the hell just happened.

"Christ, Dave. You would have loved this one," I murmured. "You would have loved this one."

THE RATTLE AND RUMBLE of the truck diminished with a slow analog fade into the encroaching silence of the summer night. Breathing in the cool night air I reached for some clarity. Sometimes looking up at the stars could help to get my bearings within the universe. Placing myself within the immensity of it all and the subsequent realization of my insignificance was always sobering, in the existential sense, but tonight the stars looked a little blurry and were of no help. So I walked. I figured to be in the woods between Quissett and West Falmouth, a good five miles from home. In the distance gray tree frogs chattered and the fluttering call of a screech owl settled upon the trees. The wind was as still as the stars. A mockingbird's song drifted down from the upland hills. Slowly the release of solitude overcame me as the night opened its arms, and the more I walked, the better I felt. I talked to Dave, and I talked to myself, trying to figure out where in hell I was going, and not just in the mundane sense of navigation but where my life was going. It seemed I'd been moving in circles for a long time, always ending up at the same place, alone.

Earlier in the week I heard a story on the radio about a guy in a similar situation. He was drunk and left by the side of the road in the middle of nowhere just like me, and not knowing better, he started to run. He ended up running miles and miles, found out that he liked running, and soon became a marathon runner. With that thought in mind, five miles didn't sound so bad, and so I started to run, heading north at a slow pace. Being drunk can make decisions like this sound utterly valid, but after the first mile of pounding, my brain had enough and I needed to pee. Standing on the side of the road relieving myself I looked up at the stars and wondered how this poor soul of mine had arrived at this place, what had brought me here, and where would I end up. There was no answer from the stars, again no answer from the darkness.

While gazing at the heavens above, I could make out the faint roar of a vehicle coming from Woods Hole. It sounded like a truck climbing the Quissett hills. I listened and tuned it in. It was definitely a truck, a beater with the telltale rattle and rough slow acceleration. It had to be Georgette, and figured that this could be good or this could be bad. Either she was coming back to give me a ride home or she had decided to skin me alive after having her way with me. Maybe she had one of her drunken fishing buddies with her and he was ready to kick some ass. The flair of headlights crowned the hilltop. Should I take my chances or hide? Before I could make up my mind, the truck topped the hill and I froze like a deer and stepped to the driver's side of the road. The truck flashed its high beams, slowed, and then stopped beside me. It wasn't Georgette, and it wasn't her truck but looked like a close relation.

"You need a ride?" A rough voice called out above the truck's stumbling idle.

"I need a ride," I answered, trying to sound cheerful, and not threatening.

"Okay."

It was difficult to see the driver. A man with a beard was all I could tell, driving an old beat-up Chevy panel truck, a moving relic. I walked around and opened the rusty passenger door, which creaked loudly.

"You have to slam it closed," he said.

I gave the door a good slam and was immediately startled by the strong smell of fish. The driver shifted into first, and off we went bouncing down the back road when it struck me then just how one's life can sometimes take a strange turn.

The man said nothing as we rumbled along until we hit the big pothole at Woodneck Beach and the truck made so much racket it sounded like we hit a land mine.

"I hate that damn hole," he said.

"You a fisherman?"

"Biologist at the oceanographic," he said without looking at me. "Do you like squid?"

"Excuse me?"

"Do you like squid?"

I had never been asked such a thing before.

"I have some in the back. You're welcome to take some if you like."

"Never had squid, but thank you."

There was a silence.

"I live in West Falmouth. That's where I'm going."

"I'm heading to the eastern part of town."

Now he looked at me. "Good luck. I can leave you at the crossroad, but you'll have a hell of a time finding a ride."

He was right; it was going to be a long night. We rolled past the quiet summer homes of Sippiwissett. The seasonal occupants would soon arrive to open the shutters, draw out the linen from the winter chests, wipe the counters clean of mouse droppings, and hoist the windows open for the pleasant evenings of June. But now there wasn't a house with a light on, and we soon came to the crossroads. The truck rolled to a stop.

"Well, thank you for the ride."

The man paused for a moment, and then he turned to me. "I have a number of people staying at my place, but there is a couch free if you like. You're never going to find a ride to East Falmouth this time of night."

He was right and we knew it. It was difficult to see him clearly, but from what I could see, the man looked familiar, or at least felt familiar. Having no better option, I took the offer, and after a couple more miles, we pulled into the dirt driveway of a large old cape house. Huge maples loomed overhead, blocking the stars, and a warm yellow light shone from the kitchen. We got out, the man grabbed a five gallon bucket from the back of the truck and asked me to bring in a couple milk crates loaded with metal objects.

"The dog's name is Sam," he said.

We entered through the back door, and were immediately greeted by a big black lab full of enthusiasm.

"Hey Sam, old boy." He gave the dog a hearty pat, and the beast moaned pitifully, banging his tail against the kitchen cabinets. Then they both stood there looking at me in anticipation.

"Sam, this here is…"

"I'm Calvin," I said apologetically.

The man extended his hand and held mine firmly as he

looked me in the eye and smiled.

"I'm Frank. Welcome."

I didn't know what else to say.

"Make yourself at home, Calvin. The couch is in the living room. Sorry if it smells a little of dog. Sam, you bad dog you."

The kitchen had a fair amount of clutter and a good assortment of cooking pans, the fridge displayed a healthy layer of kids' drawings and a number of photos of people with fish. The place smelled of garlic, wine, good music and many dinners. Frank crashed around in the cabinets, pulled out some brown supermarket bags, and placed the squid into a basin in the sink. Still in an alcoholic haze, I watched as he moved the squid from the bucket to wash them in cold water, and then lay them out on a brown paper bag to dry. He turned and looked at me with tired but friendly eyes.

"You've never had squid before?"

"Nope."

"You should drink some water. It will make the morning easier."

He continued washing as I looked about. Sam followed me into the dining room, where a large table held a pile of what looked to be scientific documents and charts, and a bottle of wine with a note and a hawk's feather attached. Next to the bottle sat a wooden box of harpoon heads, some sort of electronic device, a woman's bathing suit top, and several hard bound books.

"There will be a lot of commotion in the morning," he said, entering the dining room. "Grad students."

Frank stood tall, lean, and sturdy, the picture of the seafaring life. The rough character in the lines of his face now well defined, his eyes sharp and expressive, hair and beard scraggly and a bit grey at the edge, and a deep but kind voice.

"I'm going to bed. I've been up for two days. The couch is over there. Good night Calvin." He pointed towards the couch as he headed for the stairs, and then he stopped.

"Tell me, Calvin. Have you ever been to sea before?"

"Ah, no I haven't."

"What do you do, if you don't mind me asking? You look familiar, but I can't place you."

"Well, right now I'm working on cars. I used to have a shop in town with a couple of guys on Main Street, foreign cars – and I'm an artist."

He pondered this, lost in fatigue. "Artist and mechanic. Good combination. Well, good night, Calvin."

And off he went with tired steps, softly up the stairs, the dog Sam close behind. The couch felt like heaven and the house felt like home. A bit odd, I thought. Not the man but the encounter: two souls meeting in the middle of the night, a twist of fate, and an act of kindness. Have you ever been to sea? An interesting question that touched upon a yearning that stoked my imagination in the closing void of sleep. Within the flickering descent into dreams, I drifted towards a misty horizon where the whispering of angels beckoned with the sweet promise that a new day would soon be upon me.

3

At first light I awoke, hung over and disoriented, to the crunching sound of tires in the drive and then remembered where I was and went back to sleep. Sometime later, lost in a dark dream, it became difficult to breathe, the air smelled rancid, fishlike with decay, warm and in my face. I opened my eyes and jumped back against the couch in a panic. The unfamiliar surroundings aside, what confronted me was the large head of a black Labrador retriever.

"Sam! Christ, Sam."

He sat by the couch, panting heavily, tail wagging, and seemed very excited with my waking.

"Sam, leave him alone," came a woman's voice from the kitchen. Then a head peered around the corner as Sam retreated.

"Just tell him to go away if he's bothering you."

I felt awkward and quickly got up, inspected myself, tied my sneakers, and tried to fix my hair. The woman appeared again.

"Say stranger, are you hungry? I've got some French toast here."

She yelled up the stairway. "French toast, you guys!"

Voices hollered in reply, and soon footsteps beat down the stairs as two guys in their early 20s walked by. Both said "Hey!" on their way to the kitchen. After a brief conversation with the woman, they took plates of food outside. She appeared again.

"French toast?"

"Oh, sure."

"Syrup or honey?"

"Honey, please."

In the kitchen, she dished out two slabs of cooked

bread on a plate and handed it to me with a glass of juice and a smile.

"Frank said he picked up a hitchhiker. Local color was his description."

"Accurate description," I mumbled.

She cleared an area at the end of the dining table and sat with a cup of coffee.

"Coffee?"

"Ah, no thank you."

She watched me as I considered the plate in front of me.

"I'm Ellie."

"I'm Calvin."

"I know, Frank told me."

She was a little odd, I thought. We exchanged polite conservation while I ate but she acted as if she knew some secret and I tried to figure out what it might be.

"Would you tell Frank I really appreciated the ride and him putting me up for the night."

"I will," she said, compulsively stirring her coffee. "He often has a number of people staying here: grad students, interns, friends who rent their home out to tourists for a month in the summer, and sometimes people he picks up on the side of the road in the middle of the night. I'll bet there's a good story there."

"Yeah, a good story." I reflected on the previous night with apprehension. "Do you live here?"

"I'm working with Frank for a month. I'm at Stanford. I got my PhD working with Frank." She slurped some coffee. "Going on a cruise in a couple days," she said happily as if it was a trip to Disneyland. There was a pause and I sensed she was working up to something.

"Going out to sea, probably Hudson Canyon, tracking fish. It's going to be great, Hudson Canyon in July. Lots of fish. Have you ever been out to sea?"

That question again. "Ah no, but it sounds interesting. I hear stories from friends, at the Oceanographic, friends in the geology department mostly."

She smiled. "Well, we're going on this cruise, you see. Actually, its three one-week trips, and well Frank needs a mechanic. You know, just in case anything goes wrong."

"Uh huh."

"He's desperate for someone with some mechanical knowledge, and he would probably even pay you." She said this as if it would close the deal.

"I've never been to sea before, Ellie. I mean, I have a boat, but it's just for banging around here. Three weeks?"

She took another sip and smiled. "We realize it is short notice, but Frank is desperate."

My head felt like it was full of cotton balls, and this conservation didn't really make much sense.

"He needs to know today that he has someone he can count on."

"Good luck."

"Frank thought you didn't have a regular job..."

"Well, I'm sort of freelance, work on cars when I like. I live in a barn, have a shop below and live in the loft above."

"Sounds cool. So you have some flexibility."

I felt myself getting in a little bit deeper.

"All right, Calvin. Here's the thing. Frank left early this morning. He went back to the lab, and he called a few friends, scientist friends who used to bring their cars to your shop, the shop you had on Main Street. This is from Frank. He filled me in on all this. Anyway, he wants you... Scratch that. He would really love to have you go on this trip."

I said nothing, trying to figure my way out of this encounter.

"He's been looking for someone like you for over a month, someone who can help out mechanically, he's shorthanded. He's short of cash, but that's always the case. Christ, Calvin. Last night was fate, maybe an act of God." She laughed. "Come on, Calvin. It'll be fun. I've worked with Frank over the years, and I've learned a lot from him."

Her enthusiasm was overwhelming, but I said nothing.

Then, as if on cue, Sam went over and sat next to her, panting and smiling. Now woman and behemoth dog were looking at me in anticipation of some answer. I liked Ellie. I liked her directness. She definitely had that scientific look, more academic than feminine, more concerned with research than style. She was obviously bright, and she was persuasive. I had done crazier things before, and she could probably tell she had a chance by my silence.

"Frank's got this cool boat, a yacht really, and it's in great shape. Some rich guy donated it to the institution."

"I don't know, Ellie. This is all kind of sudden, you realize."

"We leave the day after tomorrow. You've got plenty of time to get yourself together. You should talk to Frank."

Then Sam walked over and planted his big head on my lap. As I gave his bony brow a good rub, I thought, "What the hell? Maybe this was the answer I was looking for."

"You could at least go out the first week and see how you like it."

"I love being on the water, but have little experience with yachts or sailboats."

"It's a really nice boat, very comfortable. You should at least talk to Frank."

I had fished long enough to know that, if something dangling in front of you looks really good, there may be a hook hidden within. But the prospect did sound interesting. I took the bait.

"Okay, Ellie. I'll talk to Frank."

ELLIE GAVE ME A ride home, asking question upon question all the way. I had encountered this academic type before, someone with a strange sense of social etiquette and a rampant curiosity that often crossed personal boundaries. You become the momentary focus of the inquisitive mind.

"How long have you lived on the farm?"

"The past two years. Moved in for the summer and haven't left yet."

"You must like it then."

"I like it, but it's hard in the winter."

"How did you end up here?"

"On the farm?"

"On the Cape."

"Fate, fate, and a second cup of coffee."

She smiled. "Okay."

"Yeah, that's another story."

I wanted to get more information about this trip, this voyage, this expedition – whatever it might be called – and it seemed she kept asking me questions so I couldn't. There were stories floating around Woods Hole about a Woods Hole Oceanographic Institution (WHOI) scientist that pressed the unsuspecting local land lovers into service late at night after the bar closed. Too inebriated to say no, the local woke up onboard miles at sea with no choice but to pitch in. My intuition aroused, I tried to pin Ellie down on some of the details, but she dodged the bullet right up until she drove up the dirt drive to the farm.

"Wow, what a great place."

My dog Banner ran out of the barn with his nose up, paused, and then ran over to the car.

"Hey, buddy. How are you doing?"

I gave him a few pats and introduced him to Ellie. He stuck his nose right into her crotch.

"Well, aren't you a nosy boy," she said, unperturbed, and gave him a good scratch on the back. He sniffed her feet as he wagged his tail.

"See, a black lab, just like Frank. You two have a lot in common."

Ellie received the quick tour of the farm, leaving out the loft and the house. I didn't like strangers looking at my work or my living situation, and she understood.

"So you'll see Frank?" she said returning to her car.

"Sure, Ellie. You've aroused my curiosity. Is it just the three of us, and what are you actually doing?

"Oh no. There's a cast of characters, a great crew.

We're working with sharks, tracking sharks. You need to talk to Frank."

"Sharks!"

"Just talk to Frank."

"Okay, I promise."

Her last words were: "This is meant to be, Calvin!"

Then Banner and I watched as she rumbled down the drive. He looked up at me. "I don't know boy. What the hell just happened?" As I stood there wondering what to do, Chance emerged from the farmhouse, walking with his usual swagger, his beard long and feet bare.

"My man, Calvin. You leave the bar with one woman and come home with another."

"Yeah, well..." I shrugged.

"You actually spent the night with Georgette?"

"No, I did not."

He laughed. "Oh boy."

"I'm sure you'll get all the details," I assured him.

"This makes me smile. This is a good one. Who the hell was that?" he asked, pulling on his beard.

"Sharks."

"Sharks?"

"No, that was trouble. Trouble or fate, I'm not sure which."

"Calvin, this makes me smile."

CHANCE AND I SAT on the back porch of the farmhouse and talked it out over a cup of coffee. He was most interested in my encounter with Georgette until I laid out the events of what followed, which I had to spell out in detail.

"Georgette will get over it. Once she sobers up, she'll probably feel better about what you did. She's good people. I'll bet she'll even respect you for that. Your ride, well that had to be Frank Carrie who picked you up. Now, he's a fish guy, big fish – tuna, swordfish, and sharks." Chance said this with all seriousness while rolling his morning Bugler cigarette.

"What's he do with them?"

"Man, who knows. These guys, they catch fish, chop em up, look at what's inside, measure things, see what makes them tick. You gonna go?"

"I don't know."

"Where they going?"

"Hudson Canyon. Where the hell is that?"

"Continental Shelf off New York. My dad used to work out there on the *Atlantis*. How long?"

"Three weeks."

"There's a commitment for ya. What they doing?"

"Don't know. Ellie said it involves sharks."

"What are you supposed to do?"

"Fix things in case anything goes wrong."

Chance laughed at this. "Right. What the hell boat are you going on?"

"I don't know. Some rich guy left WHOI his boat."

Chance pondered this for a moment. "This boat could turn out to be one Tasmanian cluster fuck. You realize that?"

"I never said I was going. All I said was I'd go talk with the man."

Chance studied me, slowly pulling on his beard. "We'll take care of Banner, no worry there."

I said nothing.

"Blue water."

"What?"

"Blue water. Once you get off the shelf."

Chance would sometimes break into poetic musing. Sometimes he would rattle out phrases like a madman. "Blue water of the deep blue sea. You shall gaze upon the blue water if it is meant to be."

"Who said that? I haven't even talked with the guy, Chance!"

"The wheels and gears of destiny are turning. I can sense this."

"The gears may be turning but…"

"Why not go?" he asked flatly.

I didn't have an answer.

4

With promises to keep early in the day, it was later in the morning before I made for Woods Hole. Apprehension and anxiety accompanied me as I took the back road along Surf Drive and Nobska Beach. To the south lay Vineyard Sound and the Elizabeth Islands, simply the best places to be on a summer's day. I loved being on the water, near it, or just looking at it, loved the sound and the smell of it, and had spent the last six years cruising around these islands, but had gone no further. Now there was a chance to get more.

Banner sat in the backseat of the old 1952 Plymouth I had been driving for the past couple of years, his head out the window with not a care in the world but to be with me. It's just that way with dogs. He picked me while visiting a friend with a litter of black labs. As soon as I sat amongst the pups, he wiggled over and got onto my lap, and a couple weeks later, we were laying about on the garage floor pulling out a BMW transmission for a clutch job. He'd lie down next to me while I worked, and I would attempt to explain the basics of auto mechanics. He never got the hang of it but would rather gnaw on a screwdriver handle or nibble on my ear. We went everywhere together, and we both loved Woods Hole where he could walk freely since that was the custom in town. I left him at the entrance of the WHOI Redfield building with a simple command.

"You stay here, mister friendly. You stay!"

He sat there wagging his tail with a big panting smile. We both knew that as soon as I disappeared from sight, he'd be off, walking around town looking for handouts and checking out the local talent. It was a game we played, being best friends it was easy to overlook some of his shortcomings – as he did mine.

Frank's lab was located on the main street of the village in the back of the Redfield building, and on first encounter, it appeared to be taken from the set of Mr. Wizard. He was sitting at a lab bench with a magnifying visor propped up on his head, a soldering iron to one side as he examined an electronic device the size of a stick of butter. Around him lay an assortment of apparatus and instruments reminiscent of my college biology lab and science fiction movies. Close to the door were milk crates filled with an assortment of scrap metal: aluminum, copper, bronze, and stainless steel. A drill press stood on a wooden bench covered with metal filings. Four large lab tables with black Formica tops were stacked with cardboard boxes filled with an assortment of charts, manuals, electrical cables, gloves, and fishing tackle. Several large plastic tubs held an array of fishing hooks that glistened around the rim. The black Formica sinks trickled with overflowing beakers, monitored by thermometers connected to electronic boxes with flashing lights. There was the smell of cutting fluid and formaldehyde.

Close to Frank, two oscilloscopes displayed sine waves, their leads running to a pair of breadboards secured to a piece of ¾ inch plywood. The shelves next to me were stacked with numerous sample jars with God-knows-what floating about. One had an eye the size of a tennis ball that scrutinized me with the good nature of a father meeting his daughter's first date, while another jar held something that looked like a penis but wasn't human and hadn't walked on four legs. I stood in the doorway and waited for Frank to put down the device amid wisps of solder smoke.

"Hello, Calvin. Ellie said you'd come by. I hope she didn't come on too strong. She's headstrong but sincere." Frank looked refreshed, but I realized he had probably gotten just a few hours of sleep. He seemed happy to see me. "See this thing? This device here, this transmitter, will not only tell us where the fish is but also how deep it is swimming," he said with a sense of amazement. "That is if I get it to work." He looked at me, smiled, and put out his hand. "Thanks for coming by."

"I heard you were going on this cruise and may need some help." I couldn't believe what I just said, but kept going. "I've got some free time, and it sounds interesting." I didn't know how much he knew about what I didn't know and felt nervous.

"Yes, I could certainly use some help. You've never been to sea before, but no matter."

"I've never been to sea, but do spend a lot of time out on the Sound, and love to fish."

"Good. Well, I hope you don't mind, but I spoke with some of your old customers. Buddy Jordan, who works on the AII, used to bring his BMW to the shop on Main Street. He had nothing but good words. Dick Francis too, who loves his old Volvo, which he said you rebuilt a few years back. So, if you're interested, I'd love to have you come along."

We went into an adjacent office that had a long table running the length of the wall with windows facing out onto Eel Pond. This area too was cluttered with reports, manuals, marine journals, and lab data. Several yellow legal pads with scribbled notes were piled near the phone, which rang as soon as we sat down. Frank gave some quick instructions and hung up.

"This trip has three legs, about one week each, depending on the weather. We leave Monday morning."

"Do I need to bring anything special, any gear? Could I bring my camera?"

Frank was rummaging through some papers. I thought he was looking to give me something, maybe a list of things to bring or a summary of the trip.

"What I really need is someone onboard who has mechanical experience," he said, now going through a desk drawer, then looking at me. "In case anything goes wrong."

It wasn't long after that day that I made a solemn promise to never get involved with someone who may need assistance with that qualifier: in case anything goes wrong.

"The boat's a 50-foot motor-sailor with a diesel

engine that is in good shape but maybe has a problem with the electrical system. How are you with diesels?"

"Okay," I said with confidence, but thought, "What's a motor-sailor?"

"It also has a 110 generator on an auxiliary four cylinder."

Things were getting more complicated now. "In case anything goes wrong" began to sound ominous.

"We'll be tracking fish for maybe three days at a stretch, and if something breaks down, we'll lose the fish." He had a look of desperation when he said this, but he smiled to hide it.

The phone rang again, and while he talked, I walked back out into the lab. Laid out on one of the lab tables was a nautical chart with pencil lines drawn out from Woods Hole south of the Vineyard to the closely stacked lines of bathymetry of the Continental Shelf. The weight of a legal pad held down one edge of the chart, and on it were hastily scribbled names and tasks: Ollie – get bait, freezer, harpoon tips; Joni – fish-finder cable, boots, hydrophones; Ellie – contact pilot, food, check sail rigging; Beetle – ?; Calvin – ?

"Well, I'm on the list. Is that a good thing or a bad thing? What the hell am I doing here?" Anxiety began to take hold and my mind was racing. "Just in case anything goes wrong. What if I go wrong? Hydrophones, acoustics, transmitters? I'm getting way over my head. I could really screw this up." The garbled voices of the little angels dancing upon my shoulders whispered: "You could really screw this up. You are here for a reason. You are getting way over your head boy. You came here because you want to do this."

The battle between anxiety and courage waged this minor skirmish as I stood waiting. Frank was soon off the phone, and he stood in the doorway to his office, apparently trying to remember what he was supposed to be doing next.

"Don't worry about some of this stuff. You'll get a chance to get up to speed on the boat. You just need to keep the boat moving."

We talked about the boat, his observations, concerns with the craft and potential problems, like a refrigeration unit, and eccentricities with the electrical system. The phone rang again, and he excused himself. By the looks of things, there was a lot going on, and I had to wonder why a pack of grad students weren't scurrying around tending to details. He finished with this call, which sounded like someone was having problems at a boatyard. He motioned to me.

"Calvin, I want to show you something"

He dragged a long gray wooden box from under the lab bench, and motioned me over to sit. I pulled up a chair as we sat opposite each other looking down at the box, which had the word HARPOON stenciled in faded military block lettering. Frank unsnapped the latches, threw open the lid, and looked at me with an inquisitive smile.

"Do you know anything about firearms?"

"Yeah, I grew up with guns. I had my own .22 when I was 12, and did a lot of bird hunting with my 20 gauge."

"Good." He cut me short with a smile. "This is your responsibility."

Again the phone rang. Frank slid along the desk in his chair to grab it while gesturing that I should get acquainted with my new responsibility, giving my situation a serious turn.

"What the hell is this thing?"

My first impression after hauling out the black rifle was that it was big. What I held was a 12 gauge Mauser bolt-action, single-shot harpoon rifle. I gave it the once over. The action was smooth, the bore clean with no pits or rust, and the safety worked. I shouldered it several times, trying to imagine the circumstances in which it would be used.

"Green Peace is going to love this," I whispered.

The box had several compartments, one housing a large can that snapped under the barrel. This canister held a spool of ¼ inch braided nylon line with an adapter to coil the line onto a spare spool, which would also facilitate installation into the canister. There was a small handy manual tucked in the box. The book was written in a casual manner, as if everyone owned one of these firearms. The harpoon looked like it meant business. It was constructed of a ¼ inch black steel shaft with a sliding looped bail; the bottom end of the shaft sized to the diameter of the rifle bore and fitted with a rubber O-ring. The butt end of the shaft was concave to accept the rounded head of the bullet. The business end of this harpoon was a heavy steel dart with sharp collapsible barbs. Another compartment held the cartridges packed in a thin wooden box. Each cartridge consisted of a heavy black plastic casing with a brass butt-end and a round-headed hard plastic bullet.

"Wow." I imagined the kick of the thing, and immediately reflected upon dropping my father's favorite 12 gauge double-barreled shotgun after a failed attempt at bagging a chipmunk from 40 feet. Being only 13 years old at the time, skinny and unsure of myself, didn't help matters. I still harbored guilt for the dent in the barrel. This memory fed the onset of serious second thoughts about the whole adventure.

"My responsibility? I thought I was going to be checking the oil and adjusting fan belts."

With the rifle shouldered I worked the sliding sight as some guy walked into the lab. He looked like a techno-geek with flannel shirt, sandals, and an attitude that someday his kind would rule the world. He stopped short once he caught sight of the rifle. Then he approached cautiously. Recognizing his apprehension and realizing I had the upper hand on world domination for the moment, I returned the rifle to the box.

"Frank's on the phone."

He peered into the room, and then looked at me. "Frank's on the phone," he repeated, as if my words needed some kind of corroboration. I felt like picking up the rifle again. "Are you going out?" he asked.

"I don't know. I'm getting the low-down now."

"Do you have any electronics experience?"

I wanted to say, "Yeah, I listen to my stereo a lot." But I didn't know the guy and replied, "A little."

"What's that for?" he said, pointing at the rifle.

"That's in case the chief scientist gets out of hand."

"You might need that," he said, raising his eyebrows.

He probably thought I was some great white oceanographic hunter, the hired gun, contracted on special assignment with a classified mission. Frank hung up the phone.

"No more calls!" he yelled as he spun around in his chair.

"Norm! How are the hydrophones?" Frank looked wild, enthused and exhausted all at the same time, but not overwhelmed.

"I'm potting the electronics, the next two transmitters, but you need to look at the thermal one, the green one. It's jumpy. The blue one is good."

I'm thinking, "Hydro equals water and phones equal audio, so listening in the water. Good. That makes sense. Harpoon equals shoot, and so we listen for something, find it, and shoot it." I was putting the pieces together.

"All right, let's go take a look." Frank was halfway out of the lab and then came back.

"Thanks for coming along Calvin," he said as he shook my hand.

But I was thinking, "We just made some kind of deal," and something about the fuzzy end of the lollypop came to mind.

"The boat's on the main dock. You should check it out – good boat, *Bird of Passage*."

The name came back in an echo, *Bird of Passage*, as the thread of their voices mingled into the pool of ambient hallway sounds of oceanography.

"I should check it out? I should get the hell out of Dodge. Oh man, what have I gotten myself into now?"

Frank's way of doing things was apparently to be intentionally vague, or was he just being thrifty with his words? He was certainly busy and distracted, but short on details in most things, it seemed to me. It would have been nice to know where we were going, when we'd get back, who *we* consisted of, and what the hell *I* was supposed to be doing with a harpoon rifle. Maybe he was evasive for a reason. Chance's reference to stories of local lost souls, the drunk and innocent, being enlisted from the Lee Side late on a Saturday night for one of Frank's cruises came to mind. I figured they were probably embellished tales when Chance mentioned this mythology of the Cape. Now I wasn't so sure. On the lab door, someone pinned a note to a large black and white photo of a harpooner on a pulpit at the ready with a swordfish clearly visible just below the surface. The note read: "hard work, no pay, and embarrassing conditions." Somehow this felt like home.

WALKING DOWN WATER STREET on my way to the Woods Hole dock, I stopped at the Eel Pond drawbridge. It was a typical sunny day in June, warm with a light southwest wind; the sunlight sparkled off the watery path to the Elizabeth Islands. It had to be close to lunch time, since a few of the WHOI carpenters were seated on the Community Hall steps, chowing down sandwiches and checking out the girls. Banner sat at the foot of one of them and ran up happily when he caught sight of me.

"Making new friends, I see." He looked very pleased with himself.

The sound of a small outboard caught my ear, and so we waited to see who would pass below. A wooden flat-bottom skiff appeared, heading out into Great Harbor with one of the locals at the tiller, a yellow lab standing tall in the bow, nose up and happy to be alive, a spinning rod along the seat, and a bucket of what appeared to be herring by the fisherman's side. If the herring didn't work, there were plenty of menhaden in the harbor as well. With three weeks of uncertainty ahead of me, I felt the strong tug to call the whole thing off, maybe come up with some phony excuse. Somehow I knew that wouldn't work with Frank, and he probably really did need me.

"I never said I was going, did I? He assumed I was going and then ran off. Don't be so nervous, you'll be fine.

You can't back out – you shook his hand for Christ's sake." The angels on each shoulder were at it again.

I walked down Water Street and turned down the drive towards the docks. *Bird of Passage* sounded too prophetic; it had that mystical sound to it. Passage to what?

Out on the dock two old timers, Dr. Bobby Days and Dr. Ed Richards were inspecting a shipment of stainless steel stacked up on a flat-bed truck. I thought these guys lived on the dock because as long as I had been around town, that's the only place I'd ever seen them. And they weren't doctors. They were just so damn knowledgeable and experienced that to my mind they became thus distinguished.

They paid no mind to my passing as I approached the huge open doorway to the Big Bay with Banner close behind. It was cooler and darker inside. The tools of the trade, which normally breathed compressed air, sat dormant amidst the vapors of cutting fluid and hydraulic oil. The lathes and mills, and the big sheer lay like articulated mechanical dogs at rest on this lazy summer day awaiting the voices of their masters to return. All shapes and sizes of oceanographic gear sat in various stages of construction, lots of stainless steel and aluminum fashioned with bare hands and know-how, sweat, inspiration, and necessity. The Big Bay was the mother of many a marine contraption and wonder, home of the best laid plans where many inventions became real. This was also the womb of careers as well as of the instruments of knowledge, built by men with minds bred on the milk of childhood erector sets. And their children were Alvin, Jason, Angus, and all the other prototypes created over the decades. Some were lost on first deployment never to be found and thus the reason never to be known, lost children cast out to sea for glory and science, sacrifices to the gods Neptune, Poseidon, Atlantis, Newton, Edgerton, Cousteau, and Murphy. Although Newtonian Physics governed the wheels and gears of the physical sciences, Murphy's Law was also in play, especially in oceanography it seemed. There's many a story of the experiment that should have happened, the brilliant idea, the months and even years of planning, the money and manpower all gone to hell because someone wrapped something with too much electrical tape or forgot a tie wrap. Murphy didn't have to lie under an apple tree for his inspiration – he more than likely was out on a boat tying two ropes together when he discovered even the simplest of tasks can be one's undoing. Within these walls, Murphy roamed, awaiting an opportunity to apply his doctrine, to prove his theory again and again. They don't teach Murphy at MIT.

We walked out of the coolness of the bay and onto the west end of the dock, where the Atlantis II was tied up. Its navy blue hull rose up proud, its upper decking lifted brightly into the noonday sun. Following the line of the dock, the AII's bow cast its shadow over the *Bird of Passage*.

"Christ, that's small," I thought.

Compared to a 200 foot UNOLS Fleet Oceanographic vessel, it was small, but it was also charming, and not being much of a sailor, I tried to figure the craft out.

"Okay, so you motor or you sail."

A main mast sprouted forward amidships, and what I learned later to be called a mizzen mast was situated after the wheelhouse. The white fiberglass hull had a nice line to it, but it looked rounded in the middle, more like the shape of a bath tub. No one was about, and so I jumped onboard. A cockpit sat amidships with an entry way to the galley, living quarters and engine room. Aft of the cockpit stood the wheelhouse, a comfortable setup with a stainless steering wheel, plenty of gauges, and a cushioned seating area to accommodate four people. On the starboard side of the wheelhouse was a stairway to the after master suite, and from there also an entry to the engine room. The arrangement had a good feel to it, and the details gave one the impression that the folks who formerly sailed it had worked out some of the design problems and things were shipshape.

"Why would someone give this up?"

There appeared enough room to sleep eight, not including the two foldout cots in the galley area which had a two burner stove, dining table, and plenty of cabinet space. I entered the engine room, figuring it best to take a look. It was tight going, made so by a behemoth Gardner in-line eight cylinder diesel engine, painted patina green that lay at rest like some metallic sleeping beast. I ran my hand along the valve cover.

"Easy boy."

The engine looked clean and had the markings of a well-maintained piece of machinery. Like a toddler close to its mother, cramped into the portside, sat a 4-cylinder Westerbeke auxiliary diesel with a large 110 AC generator saddled on top. This engine looked a bit beat up, its fire-engine red paint chipping off, the wiring harness frayed, and oil leakage around the valve cover. It was in a tough spot to get to, and my immediate thought was that it was probably used only in emergencies. A small work bench held a vise and toolbox, next to that ran the electrical utility panel, followed by a battery box housing two 24-volt marine batteries, all crammed into the small room which smelled of diesel fuel and old gear oil. The space would make one claustrophobic if you gave it a chance. I tried to imagine myself down there while at sea with the engine roaring louder than a cage of banshees on fire. The visuals gave me a very uneasy feeling.

"Three weeks down here? I'd rather pull my finger nails out."

I wouldn't have to spend all my time down there, but the thought of working in such a cramped space gave me pause. Diesel engines are loud, and a beast this big in a confined area would be deafening. The anxiety, fueled by ambivalence, embraced me. One moment I felt excited to be off on this adventure, and the next moment stricken with dread at the thought of three weeks of servitude on the high seas.

"Christ, you're not sailing off for three years of whaling in the South Pacific for crying out loud," proclaimed one of my warring angels. The scale of events lost meaning amongst my personal baggage.

"This is an adventure. You need to do this. You want

to do this. . . This scientist is nuts, he'll probably shoot me with that harpoon rifle." The inner dialogue continued as I departed the engine room, but once up in the wheelhouse, standing behind the wheel, I began to picture a rolling sea, the sunlight flashing along the jeweled road into the wild blue yonder, raging storms, and denizens from the depths with knurly teeth running on the end of a line. There was the scent of danger.

"Man, you need to get out of the studio and see some action." I could hear his voice. "You need to travel and see the world." I could hear my lost friend, his voice calling out from the past, or was it the present. "You need to grab a piece of this."

"I'm going to do this." I said aloud, startling myself. "I'm going to do this, damn it." And with that, I crossed a threshold and fell into something, something that had been there in the background all along – a story, a story that had now caught up to me, and as this realization fell upon me I wondered what part I might play.

5

The morning air felt cool and clear. During the night the wind had turned from the northwest to the south. The AII had left port, departed to distant shores for a months-long journey without so much as a note to indicate that it had been there the day before. The *Bird of Passage* looked smaller still nestled along the dock at low tide.

There was a lot of activity with cars coming and going. Boxes of gear were being stacked along the side of the dock while the crane-car loaded a horizontal freezer onto the port side of the bow, a couple of dock hands with tag lines signaled to Richards, who deftly lowered the freezer which appeared to be half the size of the boat. Frank wasn't around, so I watched until an older fellow approached me.

"Are you Calvin?"

"Hi. Yes, I'm Calvin. Is Frank here?"

"I'm Ollie. Frank will be along. You going fishing?"

I had my eight-foot Penn spinning rod as well as a duffle bag of gear.

"Well, I hope to. I've never been out there before."

"Oh, you'll have plenty of time for that. Endless sun-filled days." He laughed. "Here give me a hand."

Stacked along the dock were pallets of frozen fish that looked to be mackerel and menhaden. We loaded the bait onto the boat and then stacked the cardboard boxes into the two freezers on the bow, pouring ice as we packed. There were a number of people coming and going on the dock as usual, none of them familiar. I had my head in one of the coolers when someone called down to me.

"Calvin!" It was Ellie. She stood by a car that looked to be loaded with more cardboard boxes, when another woman appeared. "Calvin, this is Joni," she pointed. I waved. "Give us a hand with these groceries."

We began the process of loading the boat with groceries, passing them down from dock to boat, and then over the cockpit and down the steps into the galley, where the girls scurried about stowing the food under seats, in cupboards, and in the drawers of the rooms.

Joni had caught my eye from the get-go, but she paid me no mind. She moved with confidence and grace, with what appeared a good sense of herself. I figured it best to focus on the job at hand as Ellie approached me.

"Thanks, Calvin. Thanks for coming. We all appreciate it. It's taken some pressure off Frank, which takes the pressure off us." She smiled. "I knew you'd come on this trip. Something just told me."

"Well, here I am. I don't know what to do, so just give me orders. It's going to take me a while to figure things out."

"No problem. We're good at giving orders. Right now there's too much bait and not enough freezer. Frank wants bait on the stern to thaw anyway, so let's stack it there."

We were loading more bait pallets on the stern when Joni approached me. She addressed me with a simple matter-of-fact message. "Frank wants you to work with the NOAA pilot and check out the engine." She gazed off into the harbor with a faraway look in her eyes. "Oh yeah, and get a list of spares." She turned back to make sure I got the message.

"Sure, no problem."

The guy in the wheelhouse was nice enough to introduce himself, and from the patch on the sleeve of his khaki shirt, I realized that NOAA was the National Oceanographic Atmospheric Administration. His name was Tom and he smoked a pipe. He moved with ease and patience, more like a history professor than a seasoned ship's master. He also repeated everything you said.

"Frank suggested we check out the main engine."

"Check out the main engine." He nodded but didn't

make a move.

So I went below and did the basic once over. Checked the belts, oil level, maintenance records, searched for oil leaks and hose cracks, eyed the gear box oil, noted the corrosion on the battery terminals, checked the hydrometer levels and realized that this should have been done days before. I had assumed that at the prestigious Woods Hole Oceanographic no expense would be spared for one of the senior scientists, that the great holy oceanographic magic wand had been passed over the vessel and that all systems had been inspected, doubled checked, and certified for operation. Little did I know how projects were funded, or rather under-funded, and how little money was available for shop time. Another lesson learned: make no assumptions.

The boat had been donated as a tax write-off, and the Institution would work it for a couple years, then sell it. At the time I could barely afford the gas for my Johnson 10 horse, and so none of this registered all that darkly, as it certainly could have. Money was a mystery in my life at that point, something necessary but not a goal in itself.

Not finding anything that needed immediate attention, I leaned out of the engine room and yelled up to Tom. "Hey Tom, let's fire it up."

"Fire it up," came the reply.

This was going to be big, and I was thoroughly excited to hear this beast in action. First the warning buzzer sounded, a short pause for the glow plugs, and then she cranked. *Oomph,* she started, and then she banged like a diesel should, loud, pounding, and full of muscle. We let her run for a good half hour as we watched the gauges. Unlike a car engine, however, you can not listen for problems – this monster was just too damn loud. I donned some head phones to protect my ears and poked around looking for trouble, and then joined Tom in the wheelhouse.

"Well, everything looks okay."

"You want to shut her down?" he asked.

"Oh Christ, he's asking me what to do," I thought.

"Yeah, let's shut her down. She looks good. I'll be working on getting that list of spares."

"Sounds good."

The after-cabin was set up with a double bed and lots of storage. A bank of drawers surrounded the room, and here I found all types of extra gear and supplies. One drawer had nothing but gaskets, for thermostats, valve cover, timing cover, and rolls of various thickness gasket papers. The next drawer was loaded with hoses and stainless hose clamps, the good kind. There was sailing hardware too, blocks and pins and things that I had no idea how to use. Other drawers held mooring hardware, shackles, pear links, and chain hooks, manuals for everything in the engine room from the refrigerator, to radios, radar, and more electronics than one would ever want to operate.

"We got spares!" No one seemed to be listening.

After making a general list of the items that would be essential in an emergency, it became apparent that the former owners knew how to travel and were prepared. I guessed you need to do that if you are heading offshore, a thought that had not occurred to me before.

"Calvin, you down there? Frank's here and he's got more gear to unload."

When I got back on deck, everyone was unloading the rusty old red Chevy panel truck. All types of gear were being brought onboard: harpoon poles, plastic garbage cans, electronic devices, milk crates with provisions, milk crates with lead weights and grappling hooks, a case of beer, steel tubs filled with coils of a coarse brown line, plastic barrels lined with hooks, their steel leaders hanging into the barrels, coiled and new – and that was only half of it. The next several hours were spent stowing gear on deck and stocking more provisions in the galley. I tried to fit in where I could. Frank and Ollie were setting up the electronic equipment in the wheelhouse, Tom watched attentively as he pulled on his pipe.

Frank caught my eye and motioned me over. "How we looking down below?"

"Okay. We let her run for a while, and everything looks good."

He was half listening to me and half to Ollie, who had his head under the console snaking some wires up to the navigation table. He was talking to Frank while he worked.

"Check everything on deck. Make sure everything is fastened down. Work with the girls."

Ellie and Joni had been at this task since they finished stowing the groceries in the galley. This would be a good opportunity to get acquainted, but the girls were discussing some research project on bluefin tuna so I pulled some line from a spool hanging on the back of the house and started tying stuff down. The simplest of tasks until I noticed they were inspecting my work, and after a brief conversation, they approached me. Ellie was all smiles.

"Calvin, we're going to save you a thrashing from Frank."

I looked on in innocence.

"Okay, now imagine it's three o'clock in the morning and the weather has picked up over night. The boat is really banging around and you're lying in bed thinking: what's that banging around. Is it the chum bucket? Is it the echo sounder? Is it the boom flapping around? Is something about to break off and fall overboard?"

"You don't want to have to get up in the middle of the night to find that someone hasn't tied the gear down. We can't afford to lose anything," Joni said with a voice filled with overtones that suggested experience.

"And you don't want to lose any of Frank's gear," they said almost in unison.

I'm thinking, "God we haven't even left the dock yet and I'm screwing up."

So they took me around the stern and gave me a quick course in tie down. Each of them had their own technique.

"Look, if you use the knot to hold the object, the knot has all the force on it, but if you do a couple wraps and then tie it off, the rope itself does the work with the knot securing the wraps – this is much stronger." Joni demonstrated by tying a bowline with one hand around a rail. "And no granny knots," she said.

"Of course not." At least I knew that and hoped for a smile, but she was all business.

While working closely with the duo, trying to pick up their methods, Frank came out and conversed with Joni for several minutes, and then he waved to Tom. Abruptly the main engine fired up. No one looked at me as if expecting me to do something, so I kept to the job at hand. While the engine was warming up, Richards appeared on the dock. Forever dressed in blue denim coveralls, hands on his hips at the ready, he scanned the boat for anything askew. His eyes settled on me.

"How long, Frank?" he yelled down.

"One week at a time," Frank yelled back.

"Good fishing," he replied, and he stood back.

Then, without ceremony, Frank gave him a wave and Richards cast off the stern line to Ollie. He then slowly walked to the bow with the gait of a man who has cast many a line, and slipped the loop of the bow line over the bollard, we were free. The *Bird of Passage* slowly moved along the dock as I hauled in the line, coiled the braided rope, and watched as we passed the edge of the dock to move out into Great Harbor. Richards stood at the bollard and lifted his hand. Bidding farewell to a crew heading out to sea in a 50-foot motor-sailor somehow seemed a little different than waving goodbye to Grandma back in the Berkshires. We were heading out into the wilderness, days away from land, to strike it rich in the fields of scientific endeavor.

The *Bird* steamed south, leaving Woods Hole Passage with a rising tide rushing to the east, passing the navigation buoys that were forced to their sides encumbered by the assault of the tide, and on into Vineyard Sound with the Elizabeth Islands off our starboard bow we strolled down the Sound like a walk in the English countryside. These waters I knew well, all the coves and inlets along Naushon Island, the fishing rips, and most of the rocks. It always felt like home, and the more time I spent around these islands, the more beautiful they became with a quiet and simple beauty that slowly revealed itself. In the distant haze rose the mound of Gay Head, and somewhere beyond that the world of blue water. It was good to be finally moving, to lose all my last-minute doubts, to be a part of this expedition, this story, and it felt good to be on the water – but not for long.

6

It begins slowly around the frontal lobes. The lobes become disturbed, which then communicate this distress to your stomach and that organ begins to garner your attention. Once utter distress has declared sovereignty over the stomach, it moves on to all the other senses. The first scent of this beast hit me just before Gay Head, just a half hour after we left the dock. It was now mid-afternoon, the sky was cloudless, the wind southwest around 10 knots, with one to three foot seas – you couldn't have asked for better cruising weather. The *Bird* acquired a gentle sway as she steamed along, rolling on her tubby bottom, pitching up, rolling back, her backside wagging in the wake.

Something was happening. My head started to send out these weak distress signals and my vision became restrained. I sat down in the cockpit in an attempt to collect myself, to assess the situation, to get my bearings, but my bearings were rolling all over the damn place.

"Stop this," I thought. "Stop it here and you can deal with it."

But it wouldn't stop. As I sat there waiting, my friend's words crept through the mental fog. "You ever been seasick?" Chance had asked with a smile. "Ever throw your guts out on deck? My brother went all the way to England on the *Chain*, bed-bound the whole damn trip, puking morning, noon and night. He couldn't eat and nearly died."

Chance had a way of exaggerating things, but now his words came back in a haunting echo: "Nearly died!"

I discounted what he said after spending so many days out on the waters of Vineyard Sound in my 16-foot skiff, bouncing about and never feeling anything like what was presently crawling under my skin. Events in my childhood should have been a clue, however, because I could never figure out how anyone could enjoy the swings. Swinging was fine for the first several minutes. Flying through the air, feet out, then kicking back, pushing higher, rocking for more height, the squeaking chains, sawing the rhythm in the air; but then came the pounding headache, dull at first, then growing stronger with every cycle until I couldn't take it anymore.

"I don't know how you can swing for so long," I remembered asking my sister. "Doesn't your head hurt?"

"No, I love to swing," she would cry out, smiling, reaching higher with her toes as if trying to touch the sky. I could never understand how other kids could endure so much pain. Now, as nausea was setting in, I sat in the open cockpit attempting to collect myself. Frank must have noticed the change in my skin color, because he approached with a handful of harpoon heads.

"Here, see if you can get a good edge on these."
To do that would mean working in the engine room, and the prospect of that slowed my determination to rise to my feet and move because everything seemed to be moving, but to the engine room I went. Below deck, it was hot as a furnace. The diesel was cranking out 3,000 RPMs, louder than the screaming banshees of hell. The assortment of fumes rising from the mechanical beast added to the assault on my senses, which were now overloaded and out of balance. I worked at the vise on the workbench, with the vent above cocked open which provided no relief from the heat. With the shaft of the bronze harpoon dart nestled between the tines, I went at the face of the dart with a medium flat file, trying to stay focused, but I wasn't going to make it.

"Just stay focused. Sharpen the damn things and get out of here." The world was becoming tighter and tighter, something like tunnel-vision, impossible to concentrate.

"My name is Calvin Landry." I needed something to hold on to. If I could focus on anything, like a mantra, I might hit bottom and bounce back. Slowly the file ran across the metal tip, bringing a bright clean line to the bronze.

"My name is Calvin Landry."

By the time I finished the first dart, my physical situation was becoming intolerable. The noise and fumes accompanied by the boat's rocking and rolling, the cramped space with all sense of proportion lost combined to send me over the edge and into the abyss – I rushed past Ollie in the galley, said nothing, and kept on moving. Back on deck, the blue sky and openness provided relief from my descent into the belly of this abysmal beast, but just momentarily. The systemic turmoil that started off as a slow chugging in the freight yard of my inner constitution rapidly turned into chain of boxcars trailing behind a steaming, heaving locomotive hauling ass across the track of my insides. Ollie came on deck and sat next to me. He studied me for a moment, leaning towards me with concern on his face and a look of recognition.

"You know, you'd probably feel better if you could throw up," he said gently.

This was the signal I'd been waiting for and everything began to come together. It was like my insides were sitting on the taxi-way waiting for the tower to give me the go ahead – cleared for takeoff. The next moment my head was hanging over the port-side and I was letting loose, feeding the fish. My life flashed before my eyes, or at least the more memorable meals, which still seemed to be down there stewing: last year's Christmas dinner, sausage from the party pig roast, my brother's wedding cake, an old white American cheese sandwich from high school flat and pressed between outer layers of white bread, pot roast, stale beer, my grandmother's butter and sugar sandwiches, something that resembled pickles, chunky and green, my father's homemade brew, my mother's milk, and more. It all came out with a vengeance, in a cathartic purge that should have brought some sort of epiphany but fell far short. I turned, leaning on the rail, looking like Charles Bukowski on a bad day.

Of course, everyone witnessed this. We weren't even past Nomans Land and I was heaving over the side, not a good sign, but no one said anything and went about their business until Ellie finally came over and suggested I try eating some crackers.

"It may settle your stomach."

Tom poked his head out of the wheelhouse. "Eat some crackers."

Frank paid no heed. I couldn't tell what he was thinking. The boat moved with no sign of sympathy, rolled on to the south, taking me further away from solid ground. I stood there looking at my mess while holding onto the jacketed wire cables that run the perimeter of the boat, and thought I should never have come. Ollie approached and very politely tied a line to the topmost cable and the other end to the handle of a five gallon bucket, which he immediately tossed directly into the water below. He quickly hauled up a half bucket of seawater, dumping the contents along the side to wash away my shame.

In the distance, the contour of the Vineyard receded into the afternoon haze, and I started to do some calculations. First, if I was going to make a run for it, I had better start. Not being a strong swimmer, it might be possible to make the desolate island of Nomans Land, live in a hole in the ground and survive on goose droppings. Anything sounded better than the prospect of three weeks of seasickness and vomiting. I gravitated towards the stern, inching closer to land, and leaned over the side to let go of whatever was left. No one seemed to notice this time, or else they became too embarrassed for me, and so I attempted to clean up my own mess, and grabbed a line from the railing and brought the bucket to the stern.

"Okay, you take the bucket, throw it face down, grab some water, and haul it up," I told myself. Now it doesn't take a genius to figure out that throwing a five gallon bucket off a boat traveling six knots provides a pull in the opposite direction of motion. You could do the math. Just hauling up a bucket with 30 lbs of seawater is difficult enough, but when doing this while underway, the bucket becomes a sea anchor. The trick, I later learned, is to toss the bucket and haul up immediately, not allowing the bucket to get a pull.

This produced the second Law of the Sea discovered that day: never, ever wrap a line around your hand.

So I tossed in the bucket, and once the water got a hold, I was immediately dragged back along the port side to the stern, now desperately trying to haul the bucket back onboard. But the bucket was winning, and either my arms were going to pop out of their sockets or I was going in the drink. Ready to cry for help when two big hands reached out to grab the line and Frank, with a look of determination, pulled the line in enough to get me back on the right side of the boat and gave a hard jerk to the bucket, causing it to jump up and skid across the surface, dropping some of its contents. Then he got it back onboard. He unwrapped the line from my hand and inspected it. My fingers moved – surprisingly they still functioned.

"I'm okay."

He studied me for a moment, and his eyes told me he knew that he didn't have to say a thing. "You should maybe eat something. They're putting lunch together now. It may settle your stomach."

Food was the last thing on my mind. "I'm all right for now."

Frank nodded and stood there with me, looking back towards the line of land now vanishing in the summer ocean mist, and then he looked forward to where the boat was heading. "It's a fine day to be on the water. You'll be okay. It takes some time getting used to. Do what you can."

He went back to what he had been doing before saving me from an early demise, leaving me to imagine myself bobbing in the water with no life vest, wondering whether to swim back to land or call for help. Lost in a fuzzy contemplation with my thoughts of escape now abandoned and staring off into space, I realized that now, out of sight of land, for the first time in my life I was visually detached from solid ground. Now everything moved with fluidity, this new world, and I needed to adapt.

THE STERN DECK AREA of the *Bird* was clustered with

all kinds of gear. Several plastic garbage cans were lashed to the rail, and a number of frozen pallets of fish rested against the back of the wheelhouse along with some fish totes loaded with thawing bait. Ollie had secured a plywood cutting board to some milk crates and attached a pocket to hold four white handled fish knives.

"Well, it's either work or cut bait. I can do both."

Ellie appeared with a sandwich in hand. "Chips and sandwiches. I could get you one."

"I'm going to wait a bit." I must have looked poorly, but asked, waving my hand about, "What do you do with all this stuff?"

"Ah, the chum," she said and then went about the stern giving me a show and tell after dumping a pallet of frozen fish into an empty fish tote to thaw.

"When soft enough, the individual fish, in this case mackerel, will be brought to the cutting board and sliced into two inch sections, then tossed into the five gallon bucket temporarily, and finally deposited into one of the large 30 gallon garbage cans. There it will ferment for days mixed with a portion of sea water. This concoction transforms into an oily, foul smelling brew known as chum. Boy, after a few days, it is really nasty."

Ellie was being very methodical and compassionate with her demonstration. With the sandwich in hand and between bites, she pointed out the tools of the trade.

"Using a ladle, we scoop up the chum and lay it out as we drift along or steam at a low speed, usually drift. It leaves a nice oily slick. You don't just dump in the chum; you fling the chum."

"I need to do something," I interrupted. My head was still in a spin and needed to focus on some simple task.

"How about I cut some bait?"

"Well, sure. If you feel like it, go to it."

She set me up and demonstrated the way she did it and left me alone as I knelt at the cutting board staring at the body of a long, slender, bullet nosed fish. The mackerel has a silvery flank topped with deep blue markings as if someone had poured a heavy paint over its dorsal area and the drips quickly dried as it ran down the sides. At that moment the fish looked like one of the most remarkable creatures I'd ever seen. The sun reflected brightly off the tight array of tiny iridescent silver scales, the markings appeared so haphazard and abstract as to be an afterthought of the divine creator. I placed another mackerel alongside for comparison. The fish was nearly the exact size as the first, but the markings were quite different. A third resulted in the same finding, and I soon wondered if every mackerel that ever swam the sea had different markings. How could that be?

Kneeling at the cutting board, with the mackerel before me and the wake of the *Bird* trailing off beyond, it became a fitting altar for a sacrifice. With knife in hand, I severed the head and cut the body into sections. The fish was neatly separated into a chain of parts, the reddish-orange meat, the inner workings visible. Here the stomach; there the liver. The more I sliced and examined, I realized one could never find what makes a mackerel. This was what I needed to do. Cutting bait helped me focus and the seasickness leveled off to a stable point of misery.

My strange thoughts festered with my inner constitution as I worked out my method of cutting: first the head, then four or five sections, while holding the tail. Working like this, my body slowly rocked with the movement of the boat into a rhythm that provided some comfort, and for some reason, I began to chant. Actually it was some sort of moan that sounded like a chant, and although it made no sense, the chanting helped to ease the pain. Somewhere, there may be a religion where the unworthy must spend days at sea cutting fish, chanting ancient songs, praying for redemption. It seemed possible at the time. Slowly cutting the mackerel, comfortable with my new station in life, I thought, "I could do *this* for three weeks."

During this revelation, Frank had been standing behind me, casually watching. I'm sure he had heard me chanting, but at that point, it really didn't matter; now being beyond embarrassment.

He leaned over and spoke kindly. "You don't have to do that if you feel poorly."

"Thanks, but this seems to make me feel better," I replied stoically.

He said nothing, but he stood there, several feet behind me, holding onto a stay for at least a half hour watching me cut bait while I chanted. I couldn't figure out if he was worried I'd hurt myself or if he was interested in deciphering the strange dialect of my chanting. He eventually went back to more important tasks, leaving me with the bait cutting as the day lengthened into late afternoon, when Joni appeared.

"Christ, you've cut enough for the week," she declared sarcastically. I couldn't tell for certain if she was happy about this or not, but she seemed perturbed. "Dinner will be ready soon. You might want to clean up." She stood before me with her hands on her hips while surveying the stern.

"I'm not ready to eat yet, thanks."

"It might help," she said. "If you can look at fish guts all afternoon, you should be able to eat."

I wanted to ask her if she'd ever been seasick but somehow got the feeling she wouldn't admit to it if she had been. So there I remained, king of my domain, amidst the buckets of fish chunks and the severed heads watching blankly as the evening coolness fell upon us. Ollie came up to relieve Tom for dinner and suggested I join the others. So I left the stern and moved to the cockpit, but didn't dare go below to the galley. Maybe just being close to food would help. Plans were being made. Frank was listing times of the day and who needed to do what. It sounded like a schedule had been arranged.

"Calvin, poke your head down here a minute," Frank commanded.

The galley atmosphere was warm and bright. Plates lay on the table, and the crew was mopping up remnants of food with slices of bread while the gimbaled table swung with the roll of the boat. I couldn't take the pitching table, and so I sat in the stairway looking out at the sea.

"Okay, here's the watch. Six hours on, six off. Ellie, Joni, and Frank: 6-12. Tom, Ollie, and Calvin: 12-6. Tom you can sack-out in the night if we're on station. We'll make the Dumping Grounds soon and sit tight tonight, lay a slick at dawn, and see what we get. I have two transmitters ready and hope to get the rest operational tonight. Any questions?"

There were no questions. At this point, it seemed best to check the engine, and after a quick inspection of the vital signs, I returned topside while calculating the watch schedule, it started to add up like this. It was 8:30 in the evening. My watch started at midnight and went until dawn, which meant staying up all night. Feeling like death, with the prospect of remaining awake until dawn brought on a sudden depression. I understood the necessity for someone to be on watch at all times. Someone had to watch out for killer tankers plowing the seas with no concern for sleepy little motor-sailors out on a scientific journey.

The crew in the galley went on discussing the project details while the horizon faded into a solid mass, the joining of the water with the sky. With the horizon gone, I was left with the rolling of the sea and nothing to fix my gaze upon, but a pounding headache and the despair of my forthcoming hours on watch. What to do for the next nine hours? As the evening light faded, the night air grew clammy and uncomfortable. Darkness fell giving the wheelhouse an eerie glow from the red night-light that illuminated my fellow watch mates. Their conversations drifted out across the dark water. Sooner or later I would have to go in, and braced myself for the confinement. Frank was down below in the after cabin working on the electronics amid the sounds of beeping transmitters that drifted up the stairs. The big diesel idled smoothly as we lay abeam to the light southwesterly breeze, spewing out exhaust and hot water in an inconsistent babbling that broke the silence. My head was pounding from the hours of nausea and dehydration. I would try to get through the next few hours one step at a time.

Inside, the house seemed cozy and comforting at first. Ollie looked at bit green even in the red light, and it became apparent that not everyone was enjoying the trip. He stood on the port side holding onto one of the handrails, sometimes talking to Tom, sometimes staring off into the void. Tom paid no attention to me but studied the charts and smoked his pipe. It seemed evident he had seen plenty of rookies in my condition and knew there would be nothing I'd be interested in talking about this night. So I stationed myself on the starboard handrail, mirroring Ollie. We rolled back and forth for hours it seemed, listening to the staccato chatter on the radio, which made everything seem even more surreal. Parts of conversations floated into the damp air, disappearing into the black of night. I thought about home, my dog, and a soft bed. When Tom went down to the galley for another cup of coffee, he offered to check the engine, but I insisted on going myself. While in the engine room, Frank opened the after engine room door.

"How about we shut her down, run off the batteries for a while and give it a rest."

I nodded and relayed the message to Tom once he got back in the cabin.

"Shut her down," he said, coffee in hand as he stood at the wheel, probably also thinking about home.

It was quiet then except for the radio, and the clatter of the sail rigging against the metal mast. Frank continued to work in the stern cabin; the beeping of a transmitter bounced up the stairs. The night crawled on like watching your fingernails grow. It was a living hell.

"So this is what Sister Charles Frances meant about someday paying for my sins," I thought. The pounding in my head had grown louder. It felt like my brain was rattling in my skull every time we rolled and was getting harder, wedged like a lump of clay pounding all the air out of it.

"Anyone want a bologna sandwich?" Tom asked.

We declined and I silently cursed Tom for being such

a wise guy. Alone with Ollie, I joined him at the chart table. He had been marking our position on the hour, drawing an open circle, noting the time and date.

"You know, I don't think I've ever felt as bad as this."

Ollie nodded in agreement or in sympathy and said, "Just wait a little while."

This left me with a lot of speculating to do, but I didn't want to go there and tried to get a better grip on myself.

"Try to think positively and don't dwell on it, but what was that comment supposed to mean?"

More beeps echoed up from the after cabin, which drew me down the stairs hoping for a distraction.

"How's it going, Frank?"

"Good, I think. It will go better if this transmitter settles down. This one is a little funny and we'll save it for last." The room looked like a bomb factory. "And how are you faring?"

"I'll feel better tomorrow."

We sat quietly, he on the double-bed with all types of electronic gear and manuals spread out, and me, head in hands, too feebleminded to figure out what to do next. It seemed that the light in the room was getting dimmer, or it could have been my brain.

"Frank, I was wondering about those batteries. I'm not sure how much power we're drawing off them and how strong they are."

He thought for a moment. I expected he would prefer to run the main engine again for a while, but he didn't. "We should fire up the auxiliary generator and see how well they charge up with that."

After relaying the command to Tom, the little four-cylinder sprang to life.

"Starting auxiliary!"

The little diesel coughed and chugged, and after a short time settled into a smooth high idle.

"Switching on generator," Tom reported, causing the

idle to drop, but then he tweaked the throttle, boosting up the RPMs.

It was around 2:30 in the morning: three and a half hours to go. I prayed to the blessed virgin and all the saints that the next few hours would go quickly so I could crawl into a hole somewhere to sleep, and joined the others in the wheelhouse as they stood staring out into the blackness. Tom went down for another cup of coffee. Far off, the working lights of a fishing vessel twinkled. It felt like this fishing crew and we were the only inhabitants underneath the stars. As we drifted in this limbo, Ollie gestured with a particular twist of the head when one listens. What the hell else was there to do? It took a moment, but I too picked up on something and went to the controls to inspect the instruments. The voltage output of the generator gauge stuck at zero and the RPMs were slowly dropping.

"What's it doing?" Ollie asked.

"It's not doing anything."

The engine began to struggle and the vibration pulsated up through the decking. We both looked at each other; and turned to head for the stairs just as Frank let out a yell.

"Smoke! Smoke! Fire! Shut it down! Shut it down!"

Ollie killed the engine as I dashed down the stairs, following Frank into the engine room. He had the fire extinguisher in hand, as we were confronted by a cloud of heavy acrid smoke. Frank hit the engine with a blast of foam while Ollie came in from the forward entry with another can and also let loose.

"Open the hatches!" Frank yelled.

It was hard to see through the smoke. The girls were yelling down as they propped up the hatches and everyone was coughing. Tom was on the radio, ready to make the call for help.

"We got it, we got it, everyone's all right," Frank yelled up the stairs. The three of us hunkered down low and waited for the smoke to clear but checked to make sure that the fire, if there had been one, was out. The little diesel hissed like an angry cat and the room smelled of burnt rubber, and of serious electrical problems. The smoke burned my lungs and I started to gag.

"Let's let this clear out and cool down." Frank yelled with a look of despair in his eyes.

But I couldn't move and sat on the floor as the others stumbled out, my heart pounding hard in my ears. Now, under the effects of the smoke and stench, I finally hit bottom and just laid there, dizzy and gagging. Ollie turned and came back to sit with me. He was coughing and shaking his head, his eyes watering as the cool evening air raced in behind the smoke.

"You guys get out of there," Frank called down from the hatch.

"We're okay, Frank. There's cool air now," Ollie reassured him. "Son of a bitch, that was nasty." We sat there coughing, staring at the hissing engine. After a moment he put his hand on my shoulder. "What did you say earlier about feeling bad?" he asked with a grin.

Catching my breath and trying not to gag, I actually laughed. "Is every day like this?"

"Endless sun-filled days." He coughed. "You going to be all right?"

Looking up at the hatch with the faces of my fellow crew members peering down, I nodded. "I'm going to be all right."

WE SAT THERE AS the cool air filled the engine room, clearing out the smoke and heat. The diesel sat clicking and ticking as the metal slowly cooled and contracted. Ellie and Joni poked their heads in from the galley entrance. Both women had a serious look of concern.

"What the hell happened?" Ellie asked.

"We don't know yet. We're letting it cool down," Cilie replied.

We could hear Tom on the radio calling off the Coast Guard and trying to explain what had happened, reassuring whoever was on the other end that the situation was under control. Then he and Frank were having words. We told the girls that we would fill them in as soon as we figured out what went wrong, and they decided it was the perfect time for a late night snack for the crew. Ollie sat there, apparently going over things in his head.

"The engine would have seized up if it was a cooling problem," he finally said.

"It smells like a belt to me."

"Me too," he said with confidence.

We reviewed the possibilities, and after about ten minutes, we went in slowly like hunters stalking a wounded buffalo, crawling around the big diesel. Ollie approached from the rear as I came in from the front. It was easy to see what happened. The heavy drive belt that worked the generator had melted to a thin ribbon and finally broke after rubbing so hard. So much friction probably caused the belt to catch fire. With further inspection, we found the cause of all this to be the generator clutch drive, a magnetic type of drive coupling not unlike an air conditioning compressor clutch on automobiles – it was frozen solid from corrosion.

"Man, that's toast," I said.

"This smells like Akron, Ohio on fire. We're not going to fix this out here. We better tell Frank."

Ollie pondered a moment. "We're lucky it wasn't much of a fire."

Later on I thought about this possibility, a fire onboard. What if it caught a fuel line? The fiberglass would go up in no time. I imagined the boat engulfed in flames at night as we rushed to get out a distress signal before we all had to abandon ship, unable to get to the life raft on top of the wheelhouse, the hull a pillar of flames burning to the waterline. The boat finally sinking, hissing and steaming as it went down suddenly, gone in a heartbeat, the smoke drifting up to the stars as we bobbed in the dark water with a slimy substance around us. The brewing buckets of chum and pallets of fish thawing and now sinking slowly down through the pelagic layers, calling the creatures of the deep. Sharks and other creatures I feared but had little knowledge of, the killers. I had never seen a deep water shark, but like most humans, harbored an ancient fear. Real sharks, the tigers of the sea, the lone stalking predators constantly on the move, head swaying, searching for the scent, stirred an ancient fear of the man-eater.

The idea of fishing for sharks had been somewhere in the back of my mind since I signed on to the trip, the possibility of handling a shark up close exciting, but all I knew about the beast was that it is a large fish that could eat people if it wanted to.

A friend of mine, a captain in the Air Force, passed on several rules he learned in survival training: 1. bring a hat, 2. shoot the dog, 3. if the shark wants to eat you it will. Simple rules to live by, although sometimes I would tend to get them mixed up: bring a dog and shoot the hat. But I never got the last one confused. All the research into the species' habits, all the technology to delve deeper into the secrets of the sea, and all the fieldwork conducted in shark attacks and shark repellents yielded that one simple conclusion. I was glad we put out the fire.

The women were wide awake now, pumped up by all the excitement. They made a fresh pot of coffee, hot chocolate, and some kind of pastry from a frozen box. Frank, Ollie, and I went over the options and concluded that the generator could not be fixed without a new clutch. The only alternative would be to conserve on electrical power and to charge the batteries with the 30 amp alternator on the main engine. Frank was concerned. This was the first day out and we had already encountered a major setback. It became more apparent that my responsibility to keep things going would be crucial.

Our crew enjoyed the snacks, recapping the main event of the night, while waiting for the light of the eastern horizon. When it finally happened, it came on so suddenly and so brightly it felt like midmorning by the time I crawled down below to find a bunk. Exhausted, I could have slept standing, but it was a true comfort to lie down, to retreat from the world and find refuge under a blanket. Now I had to figure out how to survive the next week feeling the way I did. It didn't seem possible. Under the blanket, the smell of vomit, dead fish and burnt rubber encompassed my body like the fuzzy mold on an old peach from the bottom of the pile. I felt homeless and forgotten. Lulled by the sound of lapping water on the hull, I drifted off. The great blue mother of the sea rocked the *Bird* and cradled my weary body, bringing peace to my troubled soul, falling freely into the tender arms of sleep.

7

Later that morning, I awoke to brisk air and a bright shaft of sunlight dancing around the cabin. It felt almost chilly. No one was below, but voices filtered down from the deck as I took stock of my situation. Day 1: fragile mental condition, four hours of sleep, no food or drink for the last 24 hours – not good. I felt like crap and smelled worse. What to do? Surprisingly I needed to pee. Another learning experience: it's easier to just sit down. Smelling of fish and burned tires is acceptable, but not of urine. One does have standards. Sitting on the john, it became clear that I was going to feel crummy for the next week and had better get used to it, and not knowing if there would ever be a chance to do this again, I grabbed my camera gear.

"Screw it. Let's take some pictures."

The wind had turned to the northwest during the night, and the sky shone crisp and clear. Frank stood on the starboard side of the craft in his yellow foul weather gear working with a strange looking instrument, reading measurements off to Joni. This scene was a good place to start. He looked very photogenic with wind-blown hair and his scruffy beard, with a crisp blue sky and green water in the background. I started shooting with my A1 what would later become a series of many photographs. After exposing a half roll of film and bidding Tom good morning, I found Ellie on the stern mixing a barrel of chum.

"Care for some breakfast?" She smiled as she stirred the brew with a thin piece of wood which held a good sized soup can nailed at an odd angle attached to the bottom.

"I'll pass. Boy, that has a stink."

"Wait until tomorrow, then we'll have some really good chum. Usually the rookie gets an initiation with learning the steps to the chum dance, but we decided it best to wait until you get your sea legs."

"The chum dance?"

"Yes, a little ceremonial dance of sorts," she chuckled.

Behind the *Bird* trailed the chum slick. Little birds fluttered above the oily patches close to the boat, hovering and appearing to walk on the water. They pattered on top of the surface, scanning for a reachable piece of meat, maneuvering amidst the others, persistent but polite.

"Storm petrels," Ellie said.

"How do they live out here? I mean, where do they sleep? Don't they have to land sometime?"

"You'll see a lot of birds out here, especially when we have bait out."

"Do you mind?" I asked, poising the camera. She fit the picture frame well, standing with the bucket, the morning sun upon her shoulders, the blue sky behind her.

"Are you going to be doing a lot of that?" she asked with a timid smile.

"I shoot a lot of film, but you'll get used to it."

"It'll help Frank out if you can document the sharks."

"What about the sharks?"

"You're an artist, Frank said."

"Amongst other things, but I'm here in case anything breaks down. How am I doing?" We both laughed.

"The sharks... Well Frank wants to see how many show up here. We'll probably tag some and see what happens." She dipped the ladle into the chum, lifted it over the stern, letting it flow out of the can in a slow arch over the water. The large bits of meat settled down slowly, and some bits floated as the broth spread an oily sheen in our wake. Methodically the birds worked the slick.

"Did you have any breakfast?" she asked.

"I still feel crummy. I'll wait a bit."

"You have to eat. It really helps."

Frank finished with his present task and motioned for me to join him. He stood at the rail with a wicker basket full of coiled ¼ inch yellow ploy line, which was attached to a long cylindrical device the shape of a torpedo.

"Man, he's going to blow the suckers up," I thought.

He lifted the device and swung it over the side. The attached line ran up through a pulley that hung from the aluminum davit that was fixed to the roof of the wheelhouse. "Keep an eye on the line as it pays out," he said. He let the torpedo fall with a slow and steady pace, watching the line as it went. Black electrical tape marked the rope at regular intervals. "Meters," he said as he turned to look at me. "This is what's called a BT, a bathythermograph. I'm trying to get a look at the thermocline. I think it's down around 30 meters."

I didn't have a clue what he was talking about. He counted the marks as they passed the pulley, and after a specific count, he stopped and began hauling the line back in. I assisted with coiling the line into the basket and helped retrieve the BT, securing it to its wooden cradle on deck. From the side of the cylinder, he removed a glass slide similar to those used in a compound microscope, inspected it, and then handed it to me.

"There's a bimetallic spring that expands and contracts with temperature change, a crude device by today's standards, but I'm comfortable with it and you don't need power to run the thing. Here, give this to Dr. Kelley to log in."

Joni leaned over the navigation table with several laboratory record books spread out in front of her. She was very business-like, jotting data in a lab book and making notes in pencil on the chart. I studied her face, while standing there with the slide, waiting to catch her attention. Her Irish features were clearly defined, but there was another part of the mix in her lips and the slant of her eyes that I couldn't make out. She was a beauty, no doubt, and she knew it, but I couldn't tell how she dealt with it.

She finally looked up. "All right, Calvin. All the measurements are recorded into its own lab book, recorded by me, Ellie, or Frank, and initialed. You and Ollie will be recording data in the tracking books when we are on a fish and you need to initial who records the data. Ollie knows this. This slide data will be logged into the BT record book with today's date, time, location – that is lat and long – and weather conditions. As she held the glass slide up to the light, the rays filtered through the smoky lens, magnifying the intensity of her green eyes.

"Can you tell me what's going on here?" she asked.

No doubt with a dumb look on my face, she handed me the slide as if it were some kind of challenge. The slide consisted of parallel horizontal lines within a typical x/y axis. Across the face of the grid ran a jagged heavy curved line drawn by the fluctuations of the needle. The line was scribed as the BT changed its orientation in the water column. My mind scrambled through my long stale college physics lessons.

"Well it goes down and up, and Frank was deliberate in lowering and hauling the line back at a steady speed. So the left half would be the descent and the right half the retrieval. The y-axis would have to be temperature and the x-axis time. So the highest temperature is 23 degrees."

"Centigrade."

"Right."

"Good, Calvin. I thought you were a painter or something?" her voice softened.

"Minored in art, majored in science, I intended to teach, but the profession was too tight, too confining, so I ended up working on foreign cars to make a living."

She shook her head, puzzled. "Okay. Well, the temperature gradients are recorded in this book and interpreted as to where the thermocline is located."

"That thing looks as old as Jacques Cousteau."

"It works," she said.

"It works," Tom repeated and turned to face the stern. "I think Ellie has something."

"Shark! We have two sharks showing."

Ellie stood at the rail with the ladle in her hand looking like the grand mom of the soup kitchen. She pointed with the ladle as the crew rushed to the stern, anxious to see the first shark of the trip.

"Blue sharks," Joni said, sounding a bit disappointed.

About 100 feet from the stern, the rounded tip of a dorsal fin broke the surface. The shark was in the slick, slowly swimming behind the boat, following the scent, wandering off track, submerging and then reappearing again a bit closer.

"Two more." Ollie pointed further out.

"That's a good sign," Frank said. "Let's see if we can get them closer."

It was truly exciting to see a shark in the wild for the first time. The dark blue fin broke the surface again.

"Ollie, would you get the tagging pole and gear ready? I think we should tag today, and if we're lucky we'll put a transmitter on one tomorrow," Frank said as he surveyed the sharks and surrounding water.

The crew went about their business while I stood with Ellie, fascinated by the sharks. They looked fairly docile, not my expectation of a fierce predator on the prowl.

"Blue sharks?"

"You get a lot of blue sharks around here, mostly in the Dumping Ground. Once we get near the shelf, I hope we'll see more than blue sharks. Frank, they're coming closer!" she yelled.

Frank waved from the wheelhouse as Ollie arrived carrying a long wooden pole with a thin stainless shaft the size of a 16-penny nail protruding from one end. Joni returned with a folding log book and a plastic bag containing an assortment of tags. These were small metal darts attached to short lengths of heavy monofilament line with clear plastic capsules at the end. The capsule featured a detachable end-cap, which, when removed, revealed a tiny scroll of paper, a message in a bottle so-to-speak.

"I'll get four ready and see how we do." Joni spoke to Ollie as she removed the scrolls and recorded the date, location, and vessel. The return address was preprinted on the scroll.

A FEW YEARS EARLIER I acquired some familiarity with this type of tag after enjoying a brief summer romance with a marine biology grad student. One of her tasks consisted of redesigning fisheries tags for the National Marine Fisheries. It seemed like summer busy work, but we had fun tweaking the concept into something a bit more entertaining. We felt that most fishermen probably would throw the tag overboard and not spend the time to complete the task of recording the information and returning it to the proper authority. We had a better idea and thought fisherman Haiku would be more interesting, something that the guys on the deck would look forward to getting, something funny, or maybe even a fortune or famous quote.

We imagined being fishermen working a long line off Georges Bank, hauling in the last set on a cold, wet, rainy night, the rain streaking at an angle before the work lights, striking hard against your Grundens, the shapes of men staggering across the deck in the black of night. Cold and stooped with fatigue you haul in another blue shark tangled in the gear. Tired and angry, you unwind the shark, removing the knotted gangion to discover a fisheries tag at the dorsal fin.

"Hey Frankie, I got one," you yell. You and Frankie have a collection of these tags, always trying to one up each other.

"Let's hear it," he yells back from the rollers.

You are tired, and wet, mad because it hasn't been a great trip, because your wife has been telling you to get another profession, because the truck needs new tires, your kid's failing in school, and you just pulled in another blue shark. You need something to brighten your day. After you kick the shark overboard, you stand in the vastness of the world, in the middle of nowhere surrounded by a bunch of guys you sometimes hate and sometimes love, and you are about to read a message from another human, someone unknown. But it feels like someone made this just for you.

"Come on. Read the thing, will you?" Frankie hollers. You love to make him wait. With fingers numb and knurled, you unroll the scroll and read the script. Your buddy Manny, on hearing the commotion, stands by your shoulder.

You read, "This is all part of life's rich pageant!"

"What'd it say?" Frankie yells again.

And you yell back, "This is all part of life's rich pageant!"

"What the fuck is that supposed to mean?" He's pissed off, but you and Manny look at each other and laugh in the rain. Manny shakes his head.

"I like that. It's like what my grandfather used to say."

You like it too, and you carry on through the night, the bigger picture now the object of your focus because you were touched by a simple verse brought by a blue messenger.

I thought about that message, what was happening at the moment, about life's rich pageant while I followed the details of the tagging operation.

Joni removed several tags from the plastic bag to record their registration numbers in the log book, along with our position and date. After tightly rolling the scroll and returning it to the plastic cylinder, she rigged the dart end to the slot on the metal extension, securing the cylinder to the harpoon pole with a thin rubber-band. She turned to Ollie; she was ready.

Everyone seemed to have a specific task, and so I stepped back, grabbed my camera, and waited. Frank gave the order to throttle down to stop, and the wind caught the beam, turning the *Bird* into the trough of the waves. The seas were light, making the slick easy to see as Ellie continued to fling the chum. We waited. Intuitively, you could feel something was about to happen, everyone was focused and ready. Frank stepped up beside me to watch.

"You're looking a little better today. How's everything below?"

I couldn't tell if he was referring to my gastronomic affliction or the engine room, but reviewed the findings that Ollie and I came up with after discussing the events of the fire.

"Well, we know the generator clutch is toasted as we told you, and we don't know if the generator really works.

According to the techs on the beach, it did work for a while, but who knows when and how long. We need a clutch drive, which should be easy to get and install. This morning I found a hydrometer behind the tool box and checked all the batteries. We have a battery with some low cells. This could be from discharging last night or it could be an old battery."

Frank was gazing out across the water. "Okay, good. Keep an eye on that battery and let me know what happens. Look." He pointed. "Shearwater."

Above the boat, a bird the size of a hawk but with slender pointed wings flapped overhead, and then it swooped down stiff-winged to check on the slick. Frank smiled. "You should see them in a storm – they're really terrific."

I could wait for that part, the storm, but also wondered what would be so great about a bird in a storm. Furthermore, what were all these birds doing out here anyway? It didn't make sense to me, evolutionarily speaking, why they would choose to be out in the middle of nowhere, but I had much to learn about this part of the natural world.

The boat waddled in the sea with the mild afternoon breeze that had come around to the southwest, and the atmosphere remained brilliant, so bright it was hard to see.

"We have one up close," Ellie said. "He's coming up."

"Ellie, try some chum over here," Ollie suggested.

She brought a ladleful of chunky slop to the starboard side. "Come on, sharky," she sang.

Joni tossed a few freshly cut pieces of mackerel over the side into the slick. The shark, around six feet in length, slid right along the side snatching up the chunks.

"Boy, that's a blue shark," I said, and didn't care if it sounded stupid or not. That shark was as blue as a tube of Prussian blue oil paint, almost violet.

"That's why they call them blue sharks," Joni said, and they all chuckled. It seemed everyone acknowledged my lack of experience but appreciated my enthusiasm.

Joni had the tagging pole at the ready over the side, while Ellie strategically dropped chunks of bait. The shark reappeared once again, and with one clean swift jab, Joni planted the tag. Off went the shark with a thrash, but soon another appeared. Once more Ellie dropped the bait, Joni tagged, and Ollie recorded data into the log book while I took photographs. After a couple of hours, we had tagged nine blue sharks. All the while Frank was in the wheelhouse working intently on one of the transmitters, soldering, connecting wires from a DC power supply while following an electrical blueprint with one finger and tracing the leads on a matching printed circuit board with another. Tom smoked his pipe, watching the show from his position by the wheel.

More sharks appeared and we continued tagging, but at a certain point, the procedure changed. While we were tagging, Joni had placed several whole mackerel in a bucket as if waiting for something. She gave Ellie a look.

"I'm going to try a couple on this group."

"Do you want a harness?" Ellie asked.

"I'm good," she said as she grabbed a stay with one hand and leaned over the side on her stomach and reached down with her free hand, in which she held a whole mackerel. She placed the fish before an oncoming shark, and as she dropped it, the shark's mouth opened, the bait disappeared.

"Wow, Joni. That was easy. He just took it, Frank," said Ellie, obviously very excited. Before I could figure out what she had just done, she did it again with ease, paying attention to the details.

"We can do this as long as it's not too rough," Joni said, tossing back her hair.

"I want a rope on you next time, Miss Kelley," came the voice from the chief scientist.

"Roger that," she smiled.

Notes were recorded in the log book, while Joni and Frank conferred over an afternoon cup of coffee, and then Joni announced, "Okay, we're going to take one."

And with that, as if on cue everyone went about stowing the tagging gear and assembling various pieces of hardware. Ollie arrived with a 12' wooden pole tipped with a steel shaft, to which he fitted a bronze harpoon, one I had attempted to sharpen the day before. Ellie produced a galvanized tub full of hard rope coiled loosely inside. When everything was ready, Joni reported to Frank.

"Okay, give me ten minutes and I'll be done," he answered.

Ollie murmured, "Thirty minutes."

Ellie laughed.

"I heard that," came the voice from the wheelhouse.

"Just kidding, Frank."

"Boy, sounds like time for an ice cream sandwich break," suggested Ellie.

The three of them took stock of the situation. Everything was ready, and so off they went to the galley. Ice cream sure sounded good.

"Calvin, come and get an ice cream," Ellie called.

"I'm not hungry." I feared another vomit attack and figured if I didn't have anything in my stomach nothing could come out.

While they were below, Frank approached me. "Let's do a BT." He had a slide in his hand, and he showed me how to mount it. "What do you think? Want to give it a try?"

I rigged the device and thought it out before it went over the side. Frank stood in the wheelhouse ready to give instructions if needed.

"Go down 30 meters," he said.

The BT was heavier than expected, but I managed to get the line around the pulley and over the side, stopping the line to wait for the signal. Once Frank gave the word, I lowered the device with a steady descent to the 30 meter tape mark and retrieved it hand over hand to the surface, then got it back onboard without incident and removed the glass slide. Holding the slide up to the sun, the squiggly lines mirrored themselves along the length of the grid.

Frank inspected the slide against the afternoon light. "Looks like 23 degrees at 25 meters. Good cast." He showed me how to log the results and initialed the entry.

While retrieving the BT, the others returned on deck. Ellie kept the chum going as she munched on the remains of her ice cream sandwich. The fact that she could eat next to a bucket of rotting fish was impressive. More sharks were near the boat now, rising up to the surface magically, milling amidst the slick.

"Which one do you want?" asked Ollie.

"I'd like to get a female, but there's no way we'll be able to tell until it's onboard."

Frank appeared, donning some polarized sun-glasses. He looked very cool. "All right, Joni. This is your show."

"They're all about the same size."

And they were, all blue sharks about seven feet in length milling around like a herd of domestic animals.

"Here's a big one." Ellie pointed to a larger fin coming towards the boat.

"That one will be a good test." Frank nodded in agreement.

Then Ellie proceeded to throw large chunks of mackerel towards the shark, slowly enticing it closer, to tighten the circle. Ollie had readied the harpoon pole for Frank, running the line from the tub under the stays and rail cables up to the harpoon. The bronze dart flashed in the glow of the late afternoon sun.

"We're in for business now," I thought and climbed on top of the wheelhouse to afford a better angle to shoot photos.

We waited for the shark to come in. The sun was falling behind a layer of haze, turning the water into a deep slate color with bands of smooth-furrowed shallow swells. In the distance, patterns in the water broke the surface as baitfish rose from the sea into the air. There was a sense of life and a world unseen very close. Birds crowded along the slick astern and flew overhead. The earth rotated around the sun, instigating the cycles of day and night, moonrise, the swinging of the tide, the ebb and flow mingled with the rising and falling of wind. The breath of life cross-hatched the eddies and the river of currents that had no beginning. We were one little part of the big pageant. Looking down into this new world, I could see my reflection reaching out to touch it, attempting to break the surface of this great mystery. For a brief moment, I felt the scale of things and was filled with a sense of wonder.

Frank had the harpoon over the side as the blue shark swung around to the bow. The shark was now running along the starboard side, close, within range. With a swift and deliberate motion, he struck the fish close to the dorsal fin. The pole came up minus the harpoon, the fish disappeared in a snap and the line ran out like it was attached to a sinking ship, fast and steady. Then the line slowed, Ollie managed to run the lead across the waist of a cleat, giving it more drag. He leaned on it until he could get a wrap as the rest of the crew got ready for the next phase where Ellie and Joni were armed with four-foot long steel tee-handled gaffs, and Frank manned a long wooden pole fitted with an impressive hook at the end. I thought it best to just stay put and keep taking photos. Soon Ollie gathered a fair amount of line before there appeared much resistance. He pulled harder, looping the line into the tub bringing the shark back to the surface a good hundred feet off the beam as the line ripped out of the water. Ollie hauled the shark closer until Frank could get the long gaff in it, then holding it steady, Joni and Ellie worked with the deck gaffs. There was a lot of splashing as they managed to get him onboard. The shark thrashed tail and head, its mouth gnashing at the air, slapping the deck hard until Frank got its nose down, and after one hearty draw with a fish knife, he severed the spinal cord at the head. The blood ran out heavy and dark, making headway across the deck as the boat rolled, the rivulets searching their way back to the sea. Frank knelt there as we all stood in silence over the dead shark, witness to an ancient moment.

"Okay. Good job everyone," he said. He looked at his crew and smiled. "Good job."

We gathered the gear and made the deck ship-shape while the girls intently studied the shark. Ollie went off to start dinner; Tom decided to get some shuteye.

"Calvin, we'll need a flashlight soon," Frank requested.

The sun had disappeared behind a bank of cloud cover and the air was growing damp as the evening light began to fade. It seemed that the day had flown by, and another night of watch stretched until dawn. I did my routine check of the engine room, praying to the Blessed Virgin that there would be no more catastrophes, and by the time I returned to the stern, Joni and Ellie were in the middle of dissecting the shark. They measured the length of the fish from snout to the fork of the tail and the girth before the dorsal fin. They inspected its mouth, eyes and gills, noted its sex as male – because it had twin claspers – and that it had no unusual body marks or parasites. Then Frank bent over the fish, knife in hand, and sliced it open from vent to gills with the ease and swiftness of a customs agent opening a duffle bag, the viscera eased out onto the deck. Joni and Ellie went about examining the organs, the stomach and intestinal contents, removed the stomach and filled it with sea water to measure its volume.

"Look at these things," Ellie remarked as she carefully sifted through the stomach contents. She held up a reddish brown triangular object the size of a quarter.

"Squid beak," said Joni, "and a big one."

"Not much else besides the chum."

"Many of the sharks we find have empty stomachs."

"How do they function without eating?" I asked.

"That's why we're here, to answer those questions."

They poked through the remains, prospecting for telltale signs of fish behavior, one of our last sources of wild food. Who knows why they do what they do, these fish? Man-eaters, filter feeders, migratory schools, finned denizens at the bottom of the sea with flashing lights to lure their prey, fish that fly, fish that climb mountains, scaling the stepping stones of glacial melt in one final frenzy to spawn, fish that walked upon the mud flats of the primeval to smile a fishy smile, waiting for the apostles, swimming amongst the forest trees, laying still as death beneath the black winter ice, to still to die, one eating another, a world of fish to fry.

brook trout

8

My Uncle Bill taught me how to open a fish, typically the first keeper trout, to check the stomach contents for the "soup of the day" as he called it, to see what insects they were hitting on, which we'd then try to match with a fly from his tackle kit. I never did see an insect that resembled the Royal Coachman, a classic fly, three of which were nestled in my tackle box. Truth be told, most of my flies were, let's say, flamboyant, probably one of the first indicators of an artistic bent. Uncle Bill once asked to see my box of flies. We were sitting on a rock midstream trying to catch the early morning sun while admiring a couple of brook trout just caught. He wanted to see which fly had done the trick. I reluctantly handed him the thin Orvis tin box given to me by my father, the one which opened on both sides to display the green felt liner filled with a colorful menagerie of feathered critters.

He grunted upon first opening it. All he said was, "What the hell?" He knew I leaned toward the artistic path in life and didn't quite understand the beat of my drum, but we were fishing buddies and one needed to make allowances. He studied a number of them closely, admiring my nymphs, and settled on one of my Black Gnats. "Mind if I try this one?" he asked with a grin. I certainly owed him a number of flies and more.

Fly tying came early in my fishing career, during the long winters in the Berkshires. It seemed the natural evolution from building model cars and HO trains. My father had all the gear, which lay dormant in an old leather trunk in the attic for years. I would secretly steal away to the attic to survey this treasure. The animal hair smelled like old animal hair, dry and musty. There were peacock feathers, brightly colored tufts of fur, rooster hackles, an assortment of beads, spools of thread of all colors and styles, a table vise and an instruction manual published sometime after the war that looked like it had never been opened. It too smelled like old animal fur. My imagination got the best of me no matter how hard I tried not to diverge from the methods and styles in the book, but it seemed there were too many possibilities. I did manage to successfully tie a classic white wet fly which looks like a moth, although I doubted it could beat a good old wiggly night-crawler. It was, however, the first fly I landed a trout on, something one never forgets.

We had been working one of our regular trout streams in southern Vermont since sunup. My brother Dan was downstream fishing with worms and had landed a good sized rainbow trout. We hadn't seen my father all morning. He had started working upstream from the bridge when we first started off. It was the first week in May, when the trees explode in bloom, but there was still some snow and ice tucked away in the shadows. I signaled to my brother that I was heading back upstream to the bridge and fought my way along the bank, trying to avoid the brush and pine boughs from tangling my fly line. Our father made us stick together, but I relished any time alone by the water.

The bridge that crossed the stream connected the back road to a couple of farms farther up the mountain, and it was a rare occurrence to see anyone drive over it. Below the bridge, the stream opened into a wide pool, deep and pale green. The mist rose up from the cool water like ghosts, and the water rushed by several large boulders that bordered the pool as it flowed back into the stream. This was one of my favorite spots. It was open enough to afford a good swing of the rod and deep enough to convince you that a big fish was waiting there in the depths. The setting came from a *Field and Stream* cover, and I was the guy catching the monster trout that flashed out of the water, my fly in its mouth, a fish bigger than a cow. All that was needed was a pipe and fishing basket over my shoulder to be that cover image.

The sun was moving down the mountainside, and soon the pool would be in the spotlight, pushing the fish to the shadows. The water rushed under the bridge, forced on by the last of the snowmelt running clear and cold, the gurgling and splashing drowning out the sound of the wood. During the winter months, I would dream about this stream, how to work it, and about the trout that eluded me. After fishing these waters so many times I could walk them in my head, and at a young age discovered that you can take a place with you, inside you, and go there when you have no other place to find peace.

Sitting beside the pool alone was how I always pictured it, my box of flies in my lap, the rushing water, the cool air, the sense of solitude. This day, an actual day of fishing, I decided to go conservative with the Nurse Betty, a white wet fly the size and shape of a Black Gnat. I moved quietly up the side of the pool to within reach of the rippling white water that entered from beneath the bridge, and performed two hardy deliberate swings of the rod, dropping the fly into the wash. The fly slowly disappeared into the deeper water as the heavier line floated on the surface, and instinctively lowered my rod parallel to the flow. "Let the water do the work."

The line circled in the eddy-like current as it reached the center of the pool, and then began to disappear, but suddenly it straightened out in a snap with the tip of my rod fluttering. I had one on and couldn't believe it. My heart pounded as the fish ran and circled and then made a dash upstream, but it couldn't get past the rapids. Fortunately, there were few snags along the bank. I took my time bringing it in, excited and proud even before it was landed. Exhausted after a good fight, the Brook Trout finally lay in the shallow bed of gravel at my feet, the Nurse Betty in its lip. I removed the fly, took the fish in both hands, and with a snap, broke its neck. The fish struggled no more.

The speckled trout lay in a bed of young green ferns as the bright white sun rose over the mountain ridge, its rays shining off the silvery flanks of this beautiful creature.

"Thank you fish," I said, as was my custom with any

fish caught for the table. It might have been part of my good Catholic upbringing or part of a family custom. We always thanked the fish for its sacrifice, although some species of fish were just second class.

My buddy Dave loved to fish as much as I did, and we both got caught up with the fly tying thing. If anything, he nurtured my artistic pursuits in this area, encouraging me to push the envelope to the extent that most of our flies probably scared the daylights out of the fish that were unfortunate enough to encounter them. Our inventory of creations covered various institutions. There was the Sisters of Saint Joseph series that were exclusively colored in black and white. Among them, the Sister Charles Frances, a wet fly with a large broad black wing. The Sister Marian Leo, a woolly design with silver thread along the shank, and the Sister Superior, a large streamer fly with flowing black feathers and a large beaded head. We thought this fly would be a good Muskie lure and hoped to lose it down the gullet of such a wretched fish. Like some strange voodoo, whatever fate the flies encountered, we wished upon the flies' namesake.

We also had the confessional series: the Original Sin, the Venial Sin, and best of all, the Mortal Sin. Dave and I spent classroom hours drawing sketches for the Mortal Sin, and the fly went through a number of transformations from spider-like to wiggly serpentine with wings of the dark angel and a forked tail. We laughed until it hurt, and finally ended up with a sleek multi-colored streamer with large plumes of red and yellow wrapped with a peacock feather and gold thread. The fly was magnificent, but we decided not to use it. Somehow it seemed better to share it between us and keep in a conspicuous place in case anyone looked into our tackle box. We sacrificed some of our HO train figures and glued them to the body of the fly to depict the poor souls going off to hell, and even made a tiny cross out of the shank, but it ended up looking more like an anchor.

We made giant woolly worms, nymphs that resembled Benedictine Monk and cork-headed poppers that would have scared a snapping turtle. We had flies named after the streets in the neighborhood too: the Briggs Street, the Charles Street, and the Pontussic Avenue, which looked like an Indian headdress. The C.W. Parslow was named after the neighborhood bully, and the Dick's Variety was named after the corner grocery. We realized our efforts broke the bounds of tradition, but we relished fly tying all the more for that fact. The idea of even catching a decent fish on one of these things seemed doubtful. Christ, we had enough trouble catching fish with good live bait, but to catch a trout like you're supposed to with this kind of tackle would elevate us to heights yet imagined.

The trout became our holy grail. We spent days in the spring and summer catching all types of finned creatures in the two lakes on the outskirts of town. These lakes were clean and deep and hosted a variety of species of pickerel and pike, large and small mouth bass, yellow perch, bullhead, and of course bluegill. If we revered the trout, we despised the bluegill, a stupid fish in our eyes. One could plop a worm in front of it in broad daylight two feet from the bank, and the fish would take it without hesitation. They were scaly, flat, and brainless, the scum of the lake. When we fished the Onota Lake causeway, the best practice after hooking one was to haul it up in the air, slap it down on the roadway, and wait for a passing car to squish it to death on the simmering tarmac. Why we held such malevolent attitudes against this poor animal I don't know.

The trout, on the other hand, seemed a noble fish. The ethereal image of a beautiful trout lunging out of the mountain stream, leaping from all the men's magazine covers across the stepping stones of one's childhood, stayed with a fisherman for a lifetime. *Field and Stream*, *Sports Afield*, and *Outdoorsman* feed the dreams of the duty bound office warriors, the GE Plastics Plant men, the wire winders, postal carriers, Chevy mechanics, supermarket produce managers, the laborers of the blue and white collar, and all the rest of the two-week a year vacation, six kids to feed, go to church on Sunday fishermen of my town. The idea that, maybe someday, you would be on that mountain stream, trusty rod in hand, working the water when you stumble upon the trout pool of dreams, and then after tossing out your most treasured fly you meet your destiny as a true outdoorsman, consummated by a hit that feels like you tied into your old man's Oldsmobile. The mythic creature rising up clear out of the water would be that moment fixed in your head, the last image you see before your soul travels down the long white tunnel at your end of days.

Back at the stream by the bridge I remembered looking upon my reflection holding the trout with the white clouds passing overhead, and thought maybe a fish too had a soul, and the clouds were the spirits of all the fish that have passed on, and from these clouds the rains that fall on the gardens of this earth could wash away the sins of man and fill our eyes with the tears of regret for the wretched things we have done to the land.

As I STOOD ON the stern of a 50 foot yacht somewhere near the Continental Shelf with the evening light fading on my second day at sea, watching as two marine biologists inspected the lifeless body of a blue shark, my destiny as an outdoorsman seemed as breathless as the dead fish at my feet. In the scheme of things, something was out of whack, something was wrong with the picture. Instead of the image of the great outdoorsman, I stood weak and nauseous, holding the flashlight as the girls butchered the shark into two-inch steaks for the table. This wasn't how it was meant to be, not in my life movie.

After a while, Ellie went below to help with dinner, leaving Joni and me alone to clean up. She knelt over the carcass intently inspecting the shark's snout.

"Can you really eat blue shark?"

"You can," she answered softly as she studied the head of the shark by flashlight. "See these little holes in the snout. These are tiny receptors for electrical signals."

She studied the head intently while we knelt by the carcass wrapping steaks in plastic wrap. She worked methodically, with no wasted movements, helping to cut the fillets, laying each flat on the wrapping, folding it, moving it to a pile to her left. I felt funny and out of place, but at ease at the same time, happy to be there.

"The meat is acidic, but if you marinate it and cook it fresh, it's not too bad."

"What to do with this?" I asked, pointing at the butchered shark.

She looked at me with a blank expression. "Over the side."

"Dinner!" Ellie called from the galley.

"You go and I'll clean up."

"You haven't eaten yet, have you?"

"I will soon."

"You're no good to anyone sick."

"Exactly."

"That's not what I mean. If you don't take care of yourself out here, you or someone else can get hurt. We all depend on each other."

"Okay, but I'll catch a bite later."

"Just don't fall overboard," she said, and I couldn't tell if she was being funny or if that was a real warning.

She stood up and surveyed the surrounding water. It was almost dark. With her hands on her hips and the breeze throwing back her hair, she looked strong and beautiful. She studied the water, following the horizon with her eyes, and fixed her gaze on the twinkling lights to the west. "Long-liners," she declared and walked away.

"Man, what a hard-ass," I thought, untying the hold-down lines from the carcass. The shark had dark lifeless eyes that were barely visible and its mouth was open. There wasn't much left to it really, but enough to start me thinking about this new world around me. Growing up with dogs and familiar with their nature, you could understand the behavior of a wolf perhaps, but how can you ever imagine how a deep ocean fish like a shark operates, an apex predator? How can we understand cruising alone in the depths, the cold, the pressure, sensing tiny electrical pulses, constantly searching, depending far more on instinct than on learned behavior? And what the hell was instinct? If the shark wants to eat you, it will. I contemplated the lifeless body of the shark. "When you are dead, you're dead. And you're dead for a long time."

Grabbing one of the steel meat hooks, I wrestled the remains over the side and went about washing down the deck. As the edge of night drifted upon us, the wind lightened to a soft breeze. Below in the galley, the intimate voices of the crew struck a stark contrast to the vast sphere of water and havens that surrounded us. Under the twinkling of stars I wrestled with the size of things, and our place in it.

AFTER THREE HOURS OF sleep, around 11:30, Ollie gave me a shake for the night watch. He sounded apologetic. Sitting on the edge of the bunk, wrestling to get my shoes on, it felt like dawn was a long ways off, but actually, the night went smoothly. Frank gave Tom a pass to skip the watch since we weren't going anywhere, and he planned on being up part of the night working on the electronics anyway. Ollie and I held the bridge, trying to assist Frank whenever possible. We talked of sharks and fish generally, of fishing and boats, outboard motors and cars. I checked the engine room every two hours and became more comfortable as the night progressed.

"No fires?" Ollie asked.

"No fires." We laughed. "Something will probably happen when we are asleep. Those two batteries are not coming up like they should and we need to keep an eye on them."

"*Two* eyes," he said.

Ollie had this quiet sense about him. You could tell he was experienced and intelligent, not just academically but intelligent in a wise sense, the type of person whose look betrayed what he carried.

"How'd you get involved with foreign cars?" he asked.

"If you're in college and you drive a TR3, it's mandatory."

I went on to explain how I needed an occupation after

college that would afford a loose enough lifestyle to spend time with my artistic pursuits. By chance or fate, I fell into a position as a foreign car mechanic at a Falmouth shop where I used to buy parts for the Triumph. Having a trade worked out well. The three of us in the shop worked on anything that came in: Saab 95 two-strokes, the V4s, Volvos, Peugeots, Fiats, MGs, a few BMWs, Morris Minors and Minis, Triumphs, Jags and Mercedes. This was at the beginning of the Japanese invasion and the installation of emission controls. We even had a client with an old Bugatti racer and one with an Austin Martin. When working on this assortment of vehicles, you come to appreciate the engineering achievements of certain nationalities and the lack of sound engineering from others. If you could only combine the strong elements of each country's automobiles, you'd really have a winner. It would be great to design a car with the integrity of a Mercedes, the flair of an Alfa, the charm of British Leyland, the performance of a BMW, the efficiency of a Toyota, the sex appeal of an old Jag, and the exhaust note of an Austin Healey 3000.

Ollie was into trucks, old trucks. So we told car stories, tales of adventures in blizzards and break-downs in the middle of nowhere, stories of miraculous acts of ingenuity and phantom do-gooders who appeared out of nowhere with the correct radiator hose. Frank seemed to enjoy some of the stories while he played with a new echo sounder, or fish finder, which looked high-tech but didn't seem to do much. We drifted through the night, each taking turns checking the radar scope and casting an eye around the horizon. My head had settled into a low, dull, constant ache. Almost light headed, like I had been listening to heavy industrial noise for days, like strong electrical ozone could float from me and light up the night sky. I had to eat or drink something soon.

"It'll be light in an hour or so. Frank, how about some coffee?" Ollie asked.

"Coffee sounds good, but a late night snack sounds even better." They both looked at me.

"Yeah, I know. I need to eat something."

"I would recommend soup and crackers for starters."

"Soup and crackers it is." Ollie complimented Frank's choice like a wine steward at a fine restaurant. I didn't have time to protest the food or the offer before he was gone.

"There's nothing like a cup of soup after not drinking for two days," Frank said as if to the echo sounder. "I need you to stay on your feet."

"All right, Frank."

He told a few stories of past cruises and the hazards of dehydration, all the while the VHF radio squawked in the background with reassurance that we were not alone. Fishermen were calling up on channel 16, making connections and checking the weather.

"Sarah Jean. Sarah Jean, this is the Carl Rice."

"This is Sarah Jean. How is it up there, Bobby? Go to 81."

We would listen to see if we could pick up fishing information, but it was difficult to figure where they were stationed. Frank knew some of the boats and had fished with them in the past. Money for marine biology was historically hard to come by and forced him into hiring any boat that was cheap enough and seaworthy, leaving little money to pay a crew.

"Carl Rice is a sword fisherman. I wonder why he's working so far south. Tuna. He might be after bluefin."

I knew nothing about commercial fishing except that some of the guys who fished out of Woods Hole made a lot of money. I liked the fishermen I knew. They were the blue collar, rough, no bullshit kind of people I grew up with. They were distrustful of regulations and the academics, worked hard and played harder, and some drank huge amounts of alcohol and snorted coke by the pile. Some of the local fishermen brought their cars to our shop and always showed an appreciation for sound work and never complained about a bill.

"Switch over to channel 81, Calvin."

We listened to the fish talk and tried to read between the lines. The conversation was somewhat evasive about location and the amount of fish they were getting.

"How's your day going, Bobby?"

"Donny, we hit a few this morning. We got into some good water, but now it seems a little mixed. We're heading further north to run a set at dawn."

"Yup, yup. We're on the lower edge of this eddy, and it's gotten quiet down here now. You get the hydraulics worked out?"

"We scavenged a hose off a something – it'll go this trip. Like a walk in the park the past couple days. Looks like it might pick up a bit."

"Yeah, something coming in."

"You going to the fireworks for the 4th?"

"The Mrs. says we are to celebrate with the family. You know what that means."

"Donny, my kids have some boxing gloves." Laughter in the background.

"Bobby, I might take you up on that. Better yet, how's about your son going instead and I'll come over to your place."

"That's okay, Donny. Thanks, but I love my kid." More laughter.

"Well, I'll just have to live with it. We'll be on station soon. I'll give you a ring later on."

"Roger that, Bobby. Sarah Jean, out."

Then it was quiet again in the wheelhouse. The shadows of the voices lingered as I tried to picture these guys in baseball caps hunched over the wheels of their respective boats, a cup of coffee close by and a pack of Marlboros on the console. Men who have been fishing since high school, who have worked their way up to get their own boat and live off the sea, who live life somewhere between the freedom of movement afforded by fishing and government regulation. It seemed nothing was simple anymore. As we discussed the broader aspects of the fishing profession, Ollie arrived with a milk crate containing various goodies. He pulled out a large white porcelain cup, steaming with what appeared to be chicken noodle soup.

"Here. Eat some crackers first, then try the soup."

It smelled like heaven. I retreated to the cushions and sat crossed legged. My body had gotten the scent of sustenance, and my world now consisted solely of the cup of soup before me. The crackers only intensified the need to drink something, but the warmth and taste and the need for nourishment brought the moment to something you would want to tell your grandchildren about, one of those experiences you know they probably would never understand because you could never tell it right. Boy the soup was good! It went down easy and fired up something that hadn't been working for the past couple of days, an act of regeneration to make me feel like a functioning human again. The broth lifted the gate and a free man stood outside the prison door. It took a good half hour to get the soup down, with me quiet as a mouse in the corner. Ollie and Frank were amused at my intent consumption and finally had to ask.

"So, how's that soup?" They both chuckled.

"I saw a straw in the galley. You might use that to get what's left," Ollie offered.

"That's good soup."

"Well there's more when you're ready,"

The banging in my head slowly softened and I actually felt a bit of optimism come over me. Maybe there really was a light at the end of the tunnel.

The night lingered on. Frank turned in before sunup. I wasn't sure if he had slept since we left the dock.

"Frank doesn't sleep much, does he?"

"He'll be up for days, especially when we're on a fish. We were out here last summer. Frank got a call about a dead fin whale south of Montauk, so we hired a sport fisherman for a week and found the whale. God, what a sight. Sharks were everywhere, big sharks. Other sport fishermen were there trying to hook up. These sharks would come straight up on the whale, their heads out of the water, to grab a big chunk of blubber. They'd thrash back and forth, leaving these gaping holes in the side. It was amazing. Someone had left a red balloon float tied to the whale, and this great white came up and grabbed it, punctured it but couldn't get it down or get rid of it. It swam around with that float all day in its mouth. We baited up and tagged a 15-foot white shark with a transmitter, but it went back in for more. That evening, it left and we followed it for three and a half days."

All I could say was "Wow."

"It was the first great white tagged with a transmitter. What a ride. The weather turned bad and the captain of the boat wanted to turn back. Frank almost went at him with a knife. He hadn't slept in days and so he was a bit off, but when would he ever get a chance to track a great white? So it turned into a battle of bravery, or rather stubbornness. Frank called the captain a pussy, and the captain called him a raving lunatic. I think the phrase "Fuck science!" was heard several times on deck. We followed that fish until the signal weakened and it was clear on all accounts it was time to head in. By the time we neared Montauk, the weather let up a bit and we had the seas to our back. The sun came out and the two of them were suddenly best of friends, sitting out on the stern trading fish stories. The captain had a good yarn to tell, and Frank had his data, but it got a little hairy out there for a bit."

"What kind of data?"

"Well, it was the first white shark ever tracked, and having had a full meal, it was interesting to monitor its movement and body temperature. We measured the lag time between water temperature and body temperature."

"Body temperature?

"Rete mirable."

"Huh?"

"Muscle temperature versus water temperature. These sharks are warm bodied not cold blooded as we used to think. They keep their brain warm with this network of blood vessels. That's how they can dive deep. Frank is working out a correlation of metabolic rate of blubber and calories burned. Talk to Frank or Joni they can give a better account than I."

"Warm bodied. There's a lot more going on here than I thought. Are we going to see any white sharks?"

"Not likely. Mostly blue sharks, but hopefully a mako, and possibly a tiger."

"So we put the transmitter on the shark and follow it."

He looked at me blankly but smiled. "They didn't tell you much, did they?"

"What was Joni doing hand-feeding the shark?"

"She's studying the digestive rate in sharks, how often they need to feed, and their rate of metabolism. The way I heard it, we feed the shark whole mackerel, get a transmitter on it, track it for a determined time, then get it back and open it up."

"Get it back?"

"Harpoon it, which means we need to get close enough for the harpoon pole or the harpoon rifle."

Well that answered the question about the rifle.

"It's going to be tricky getting up on a shark."

It sounded more than tricky, and we would deal with that when the time came. Gradually the night sky softened to the unmistakable point when the horizon is visible but the world still feels void of light. This lasts a few moments, and then the sky turns to blue as the east brightens with the coming dawn. The stars dim and the blue gets stronger. It's like there is a panel of cosmic dials, and either something is getting turned up or turned down, and then, boom. There it is, the glow, and then the brightness as the brilliant yellow star rises. We stood in the open cockpit gazing off at the eastern horizon, mute and still as a pair of pilgrims as the sun rose, casting a golden radiance across the sea. All we could do was stand in quiet reverence.

9

The morning watch took over with eager enthusiasm while Ollie and I stumbled below deck to hit the sack. I slept better this time around, managing to get in almost four hours. By the time we got back on deck, there was a problem. Ellie and Joni had been chumming since 7 a.m., and although sharks had been sighted, none would surface near the boat. A visible slick trailed behind the *Bird* as it steamed along at a slow easy speed, but no sharks approached. Everyone but Tom was stationed on the stern, perplexed, trying to figure out what was wrong and what to do.

"Okay, let's sit still for a while, keep chumming, and see what happens," Frank decided. More chum went over the side, and an hour passed with still no sign of the sharks. Ollie gathered more frozen boxes of mackerel to thaw in the fish totes and I made ready to cut bait.

"We can see them way off in the slick, but they will not come close." Ollie shook his head. "What's different from yesterday? Joni was practically petting them yesterday."

"I know they're down there," Joni said as she gazed over the side.

It was time for some creative thinking. We were sure the sharks were below the slick feeding. The question was: how to get them to the surface? "I have an idea," I announced and retreated to the engine room.

Under the work bench were several large drawers of spare parts: fan belts, gaskets, filters, and all types of miscellaneous hardware stored in a large plastic boxes with a snap lid. I emptied the contents into the drawer and then drilled a number of 1/4 inch holes in the bottom and sides, attached 50 yards of 100 lb. test monofilament line from the tackle supplies, cut a slab of Styrofoam for the inside, and then filled the container with chum before securing the lid with duct tape.

Ollie only nodded and chuckled. "Frank will love this. Are we allowed to take pictures of this thing, or is this a top secret prototype?"

"This, my friend, is the Chum Float–Mach I, civilian issue," I answered with pride. The women just gave us both a look of feminine exasperation.

"Ellie, if you could stop chumming for the time being, we'll see if this thing works."

She gave me a "Who is this guy?" kind of stare, but at this point she and Joni were willing to try just about anything.

"Hey, let's see what happens," she smiled.

I lowered the Chum Float over the side and let it trail off into the slick as we drifted. The breeze from the southwest pushed us along with the short chop of waves. As my invention was easing away from the boat, Frank came to investigate.

"What the hell is that?"

"Chum Float-Mach I," Ollie replied authoritatively. Frank looked around at everyone as they all pointed towards me. I smiled sheepishly. Intrigued, he watched the plastic container bobbing in our wake as a plume of oily substance began to generate from the package. He laughed. "Good idea. Let's see what happens."

So we waited. Ollie figured it would take a while for the fish to realize that the chunks of bait weren't coming anymore, that they would pick up the stronger scent from the chum float and presumably come up to investigate. About 15 minutes later, we had our first shark, fin first, nosing around the float. Ollie was the first to congratulate me.

"I never doubted you for a moment," he said as we shook hands. Soon we had four blue sharks circling the float.

"Frank, we've got sharks," Joni called out to the wheelhouse. He and Tom came back to check it out.

"What is that thing?" Tom remarked.

Ellie was quick to respond, "Don't ask, top secret."

"I've got a transmitter ready to go. Let's see if we can get them closer." Frank seemed encouraged.

Close to 150 feet of line ran out to the float, and we hoped that, as we hauled it in, the sharks would follow. They did, but only to a point.

"When they get close enough, throw more chum in the water," Frank instructed. The sharks then got to within ten feet of the stern.

"Try to get them alongside. Joni pick one out. You have the bait ready?"

We made way for the feeding, Frank had the transmitter mounted to a harpoon pole, Joni donned a rigging harness, Ellie chummed, and Ollie gathered three smiling mackerel while I pulled the float to the stern trying to maneuver it to the side – but the sharks went down. We all stood there in disbelief. No sharks.

We refilled the chum float and went through the whole maneuver again, and like before, as soon as they got to within 10 feet of the boat, they disappeared. This went on all afternoon, and we couldn't get one close enough to get the transmitter in. We tried all manners and methods to persuade the fish: we drifted, motored at slow speed, turned the power off, and dispensed more chum. Nothing worked. I even offered to vomit into the slick, but everyone felt I already did my part and they probably had seen enough of that display for one trip. By late afternoon, we had expended so much chum with no results that Frank called it a day, a very frustrating day.

After stowing the gear everyone retired to the galley for cheeseburgers and shark steaks while enthusiastically discussing the day's events, offering ideas for tomorrow's approach. Being uncomfortable still with the close quarters and food, the rocking gimbaled table, and aromatic overtones all combined, I settled down in the cockpit area with a bowl of Cheerios. As was the case with the soup, this was the most memorable bowl of cereal.

THIS RESPONSE TO nurturing my body, feeding fuel

to my fire was something I always expected to feel after receiving Holy Communion, which invariably became such a disappointment. Growing up and educated within the parochial school system, that bastion of Roman Catholicism, my friends and I would ask questions, as irreverent as they were and express our disappointment with the church as we waited out the clock. We believed in the foundations of Christianity, to do unto others and to love thy neighbor, which Dave took literally with Betty Jean Hayes. Often on a Friday night after the weekly armory dance, we would be hunkered down in one our dad's cars outside the only sub shop in town. Heavy snow would be falling faster than the wipers could clear it, and we would wait outside in the car until midnight so we could then get our cold-cut sandwiches. We were good Catholic boys who couldn't eat meat on Fridays, and in fact it was because of this silly law that we eventually fell from grace and left the church. We were frustrated with the confines of the religion we were all born into and raised with, frustrated with the hypocrisy, the cruelty, the hubris, and the big new white Cadillac in the rectory garage.

So, my friends and I started asking poignant questions. We were only 16 and 17 at the time, but the more we thought about it the more questions we had. Why did we have to wait until midnight to eat meat? Why couldn't we eat our subs on Fridays? Tony said they could eat meat in Connecticut on Fridays, and Bob calculated that Connecticut, being only 40 minutes away, was worth the drive, but Dave reasoned that there surely wasn't a sub shop on the border and it definitely wouldn't be an Angelina's sub shop. Denny opted to wait as did I. This is how the wheels started turning, how the cart ultimately fell apart. Every Friday night we waited, discussing the ins and outs of theology, offering our adolescent insights into the structure of guilt and the gift of absolution.

"They lay it on; they take it off. It's a good system," said Denny.

"We could buy them and then drive to Connecticut and eat them there," Bob suggested.

Dave said crossing the state line, even if it wasn't to commit a crime, somehow broke the law and got the Feds involved. We all laughed, but by the end of that winter, we all dropped out of the church. All of us except Tony, that is, who held on to his faith no matter how we poked at his reasoning. He never let go.

Now, with the bowl of cereal in my lap and the feeling of rebirth rising in my non-Catholic soul, I listened as the conversations and the plans for tomorrow rose up from the galley.

"Calvin, sure you don't want one of these burgers?" Ellie yelled up.

"I'm very happy right now."

"Ellie's even happier, now that she can eat the last one," Ollie added.

The evening water mixed with the sky as the clouds blocked the western horizon. Off to our starboard side, upwind as we drifted, floated the scattered pile of cardboard bait boxes we had thrown over the side; the pile of boxes and the black triangular dorsal fin of a very large shark. The head came out, the mouth opened to smash and grab one of the boxes, thrashing wildly.

"Hey, come see this shark, a big shark."

"How big?" someone asked casually.

"Where is it?" asked Joni.

"It's hitting the bait boxes we threw over."

No one seemed in much of a hurry, maybe because I was the rookie who would probably get excited by almost anything with a fin on it.

"It's big and black."

The shark thrashed again at the pile of debris.

"I'll go," I heard Ollie say.

When he came up, the shark went down. Ollie waited as I described it to him. He took me seriously and was ready to return to the galley when the shark hit again, its head rising out of the water as it smashed the floating cardboard.

"Whoa! That's a big fish." He studied it for a moment

as the dorsal fin appeared and then the tail. "White shark! Frank, we've got a white shark up here."

In a wink, the crew was on the deck, but the fin disappeared just as quickly, not to be seen again.

"Well, that's a good sign," mused Frank. "A big fish?"

"It was a big fish, Frank," Ollie replied. "We couldn't handle a fish that big."

Frank surveyed the water for a good ten minutes. We waited. The dampness of night was creeping quickly across the darkening sea. "We'll keep with the plan. Chum at dawn."

During the night watch, Ollie and I talked of trucks, travels, and great white sharks.

THE NEXT DAY, the sharks appeared in the chum slick as before, repeating the same frustrating behavior of shying away from the boat, but around noon something in the scheme of the underworld shifted. Different sharks arrived, behaving aggressively and approaching the boat with no apprehension.

This contrast in behavior puzzled everyone. Why these fish were acting so differently from the others had the crew scratching their heads. But now we were in business: Joni sized up the new arrivals and decided to go for the biggest of the bunch. The chumming became very specific as Ellie ladled small amounts along the starboard side, drawing the fish closer to the hull. When a large blue shark came within range, we hit it with a Fisheries tag to help identify it for the next step, as well as for future data collection. Joni laid out five whole mackerel each with a light monofilament line attached to its tail. She knelt looking over the side, with her hair tied up, the harness secured around her waist and shoulders with a length of rope attached to the back.

"Calvin, man that line for Joni when she needs it," Frank instructed.

I positioned myself behind her with the line wrapped around a fixed brace on the side of the cabin. If she fell, she couldn't fall far, but I had no intention of letting that happen.

"All right, that tag didn't seem to bother him too much. Let's see how long it takes for him to come back," Joni said with restrained excitement.

"He's right here," said Ellie, pointing to a shark right off the stern. "He's coming on – here he comes."

Joni had the bait ready, and without looking back, she leaned down with the mackerel trailing by the line as our shark came up, rolling a bit, to grab the bait. Joni gave a slight pull on the mono, which popped off with ease and the shark swam off in a tight circle towards the stern.

"He's a hungry boy," Ollie said as he logged the time in the record book. "What are we to call this fellow?" he asked.

"Blue shark #80-1," answered Frank.

"He's here again," said Ellie.

Joni trolled the second mackerel. If another bluedog tried to get it, she could easily snag it away, and without mishap we were able to feed five mackerel to the shark. Frank waited patiently with the harpoon pole that was now fixed with an adaptor that held a brightly painted red transmitter. After the shark took the last bait, he planted the small dart with the transmitter at the base of the dorsal fin. The fish bolted away in an instant, and right on cue, a loud beep emitted from the wheelhouse. We all cheered.

"Good job, Joni."

Frank and Ollie dropped everything to get back into the wheelhouse to man the hydrophone and verify they were getting a good signal.

"All right," said Ellie, all smiles. "We're on a fish."

She and Joni stood beside me looking out across the sea; we listened to the beeps from the transmitter. The tether was still attached to Joni's back, and I wanted to give a little tug, say something like "down girl," but figured I'd end up in the chum bucket. She turned to remove the harness, surprised by my seriousness as I stood holding the line in earnest. She looked me in the eye and said, "Thanks." We were standing close, and it wasn't the way she said it but more the way she looked at me when she said it that indicated she recognized my determination.

She went off to work with Frank while Ellie and I tagged as many fish as we could with the Fisheries tags. Ellie gave me some pointers on the procedure, and we swapped tasks, logging to tagging and back to logging. The trick is to wait for your shot and to jab without hesitation. I mistakenly placed a tag in the gut of one shark, too low, as it rolled. With the boat moving, trying to hold the long pole steady and hit a mark smaller than your hand is harder than it might sound. But Ellie reassured me the fish would be okay.

"Sharks are hardy creatures. You should see the females sometimes. They get all bit up by the males during courtship, and their backsides can be all scarred."

"So how long do we follow this one?"

"That's up to Joni and Frank. It also depends on how often it surfaces, and we can't get it back during the night or bad weather, so this will be interesting."

"It's already interesting; I guess it will just get more interesting."

She laughed. "Frank's trips are always beyond the norm. Just hang on and enjoy the ride."

We stowed the gear, then joined the rest in the wheelhouse. By the look on their faces, it appeared everything was going fine.

"He's heading more to the southwest, Tom. Let's get closer," Frank instructed. He and Ollie were as serious as a couple of World War II sub chasers.

"Heading to the southwest," responded Tom with his pipe puffing smoke like his head had been connected to the engine below.

The *Bird of Passage* swung to the west and the chase was on. Somewhere ahead, the shark swam, in pursuit of a meal or escaping from us or just wandering. We were electronically connected to this fish now, and our lives would be centered on its activities until we got it back or until it got away.

The tracking operation was simple. The fish carried the transmitter, an electronic sending device powered by a battery with a lifespan of approximately three days that emitted a given frequency signal in relation to the depth of the instrument. The faster the intervals between the beeps, the closer the fish was to the surface, and the intensity of the signal equaled the proximity of the shark to the boat. The transmitter had been calibrated in a pressure chamber on shore and tested in Vineyard Sound. Beeps per minute were counted every five minutes using a stopwatch, and that number was then recorded into the log book.

The beeping sounds were similar to the sonar signals you hear in war movies but without the echo. Ollie manned a clothesline reel that was mounted near the ceiling of the house on the starboard side. This reel controlled a rope that traveled forward to a stainless shaft, which traveled straight down, through the cabin and through the hull to the housing for the hydrophone, the receiving device. This receiving unit, in turn, was mounted in a hydrodynamic housing that could rotate to pick up the strongest signal.

Ollie rotated the pulley wheel trying to get a fix, honing in on the clearest beep. The wheel had a large red arrow mounted across its face to help orientate the operator to the position of the fish. The setup was rudimentary, but it worked. The hydrophone had a hardwire connection to a black box mounted on the navigation table, which had switches for volume and gain, the speaker, and a plug for headphones. All of these devices had been designed and built by Frank. The gear had a makeshift appearance, but that appearance bestowed confidence: the device was obviously well thought out and heavy duty in construction.

We steamed along slowly in a southwesterly direction for approximately 15 minutes until the signal became clear and strong in all directions.

"Hold her here, Tom," Frank said before he took another count. The boat shifted in the breeze, which had gradually picked up from the south, causing us to move away from the shark.

"He's moving slowly, and I think he's down in the

thermocline."

We all stood there listening, looking out at the open water.

"We pick up a lot of wash from the prop once we get past him," Ollie noted.

"That hydrophone should be deeper," replied Frank.

"Maybe next trip."

Everyone seemed pleased. We had seen a lot of sharks since we arrived, the weather was cooperating, and the gear was working. From a personal perspective, each day became easier, although I was becoming aware of an ever increasing dilemma. Since that first day out, I had promised myself that, once this trip was over, I wouldn't be stepping on another boat for a long time. Now after getting more involved, I could see myself fitting in with the crew, becoming one of them, part of the team. The question was: would this sense of involvement overpower the call for self preservation, the need for dry land, stable footing, a clear head? There was no way I wanted to feel seasick for another three weeks. I would just have to wait until the end of the first leg and see how things went.

Frank finished a count. "OK, looks good. Let's get some data. Ollie, you work with Calvin. We plan on tracking this shark for 24 hours, and then we'll see if we can get him back. He may surface towards sunset. We'll see if we can get up on him then. Ellie, Joni, and I will work out the plan for that."

As we listened to Frank's instructions, the interval between beeps became longer. "He's going down," Joni said. Frank did another count, pumping his hand, holding the stopwatch as he counted.

"He's down around 10 meters. All right we're looking good."

"We're looking good," Tom confirmed. Frank smiled, patting him on the shoulder.

Holding the afternoon watch meant that Ollie and I were on tracking detail. Tom drove, Ollie counted the beeps and recorded the data while I manned the hydrophone pulley, turning it this way and that in search of the strongest signal, working with Tom to keep the boat close to the shark. After several hours, we got into a rhythm, working the boat with the shark's movement and the wind, and it soon became intuitive how to track this fish. As the boat moved closer on a track, we positioned ourselves upwind as we got abeam of the fish, with the wheel in neutral, and then drifted over the shark, marking the Loran coordinate position in the log book. Our method and teamwork seemed effortless, but our conversations became staccato-like, with breaks every five minutes. Often you would forget what you had been talking about before the count started, and then a new conversation would erupt only to fall back onto something you had talked about earlier. Someone would start telling a story, then we'd break to do the count and get all consumed in locating and tracking, and then there would be a moment of silence only to have someone launch a new story that somehow–or not–related to what we had previously talked about. I ended the watch with a pile of half-told stories about expeditions in Patagonia, research at the Bermuda biological station, instructions for barbecued shark steaks, and resources in locating hard to find International truck parts.

As for the shark, we followed its progress in a southeasterly direction all afternoon, with it swimming in an undulating pattern between six and ten meters at about three miles per hour.

"The sharks tend to move in a saw-tooth pattern through the boundary layer, surfacing at times, especially at sunset. It's going to be interesting trying to get up on this fish," Ollie offered.

"What's this boundary layer?" I had to ask.

"If we were on a WHOI ship, I could show you. They have an instrument like an echo sounder."

"A PDR sub-bottom profiler," Tom interjected.

"This device has a constant printout as the ship travels profiling the bottom. It prints out on a roll of paper and you can see the thermocline."

"It's full of critters," Tom added.

"Copepods and small fish that hang around this temperature gradient in the water column. It's thick with them."

"You can see them come to the surface on the chart at sundown, see them rise right up," said Tom. It was like a tag team conversation. Now Ollie was doing a count, and so Tom kept talking.

"The water gradually changes to, I don't know, let's say anywhere from 20 to 30 meters, and then boom, it's cold, cold all the way to the bottom. The water is a different density too."

"Someone told me…" Ollie was back in. "That when the sub *Alvin* is descending it will hit that boundary of cold water and slow right down because there's such a density difference. Okay, we should move again."

Tom engaged the prop and we eased on to the southeast, shadowing our shark.

I knew a little about the water world, having spent my childhood messing around the lakes and streams in the Berkshires, studying wave dynamics in college physics, and living by the ocean. But it wasn't until I took the proverbial plunge and bought my first boat that I got a full measure of the ebb and flow, the standing wave, the following sea, the phases of the moon, and the gravitational forces between two bodies.

10

My first boat didn't cost much and was less to look at. Molly and I bought it for $250 from a "friend." Actually, I think we paid $250 for the 10-horse Johnson outboard and the boat came with it. We made the deal one evening after our friend Lori took us for a quiet ride around Great Harbor in Woods Hole. It was a warm, calm, beautiful mid-summer outing, and after we scooted under the Eel Pond Bridge, it seemed a whole new world opened up before us. We poked around the glassy harbor, visiting indigents in their houseboats, admired the yachts at anchor, drank wine, and walked about Devil's Foot Island. The romance and the sense of freedom were intoxicating. This new world lacked all the congestion and clutter that riddled the Cape during the summer, and gone were the strip malls, the traffic, and the crowds. We bought the boat that evening.

Our new skiff had to be decades old. The layers of paint told part of the story, but the various repairs to the hull gave a more detailed picture of how many owners the thing had accumulated over the years. The 14 foot lap-strake skiff had heavy planked sides that sat on a flat bottom, and the present color of chipping dark green barely hid the bright orange underneath, or the gloss black under that, or the fire-engine red further down. There was so much paint on the boat that even if it wasn't seaworthy the paint would keep it together. The stern appeared substantial enough for the 10-horse, but not much more. Various types of hardware held the planks together, perhaps depending on who owned the boat at the time and what method of engineering they believed in. Part of the lower planking showed bronze nails that had been clinched over, where in other areas, stainless #8 flathead screws were nicely set. At one time, a conscientious owner installed oak knees at the stern seat, whereas the seat forward consisted of a ¾ inch plywood board that had been wet for too long and was bulging with delamination. The boat was quaint, within our budget, and it came with the outhaul in Eel Pond. To say it leaked would be stating the obvious. Optional equipment included two oars, not matching and of different sizes and colors, plus a cut-up gallon bleach bottle to assist in bailing. We were young and in love, devil-may-care, summertime happy, and life was good. Molly christened the floating disaster Lilly, after her grandmother, who I had never met and could only hope was in better condition.

We couldn't wait to get away to one of the islands off Woods Hole and find a quiet spot in some hidden cove all to ourselves, far and away from the rest of the world. So the next weekend we packed a picnic lunch, blanket, towels and my new eight foot spinning rod. The world was our oyster.

We loaded up, and after giving the 10-horse a mandatory dozen pulls it coughed, belched, and roared to life. The motor sounded strong but was finicky as hell to get going. It had a two-hose fuel system that required you to pump a button on the tank with your thumb and after pumping long enough to make it hurt, the thing would eventually start, bellowing blue smoke. I popped it into gear only to turn and see the look of concern in Molly's face.

"Is that thing all right?" she asked as if looking at a dead animal on the side of the road.

"It's just old and needs a good running to clean it out," I said with confidence, and it's more the way you say things at times like that than what you actually say. But I was thinking, "This piece of crap is going to get us out there and die." As I messed with the low speed knob, I waited and listened, hoping it would smooth out. The midmorning sun held the promise that this would be one of those glorious summer days, and figured, "What the hell." We pushed off into the quiet Sunday morning waters of Eel Pond and slid under the bridge past the Fishmonger Café where the clank and clatter of the restaurant dish washing could be heard above the ever present call of the gulls. We eased into Great Harbor after passing the Oceanographic ship *Atlantis II* with its dock lines bowed at its tranquil berth, and in the distance, the head of Martha's Vineyard could be seen and the grassy knolls of Naushon stretched out like the Promised Land.

We decided to pass through Great Harbor and the boats at anchor for the inner harbor route was now familiar territory after our first excursion. Molly looked lovely seated on a blanket in the bow, the sunlight reflecting the water across her face as she turned and smiled.

"It's lovely," she yelled back.

It was indeed lovely. The southwest wind that typically rises in the afternoon had yet to arrive, leaving the waters glassy smooth, but as we cut our way along the harbor, I became a bit apprehensive about the next leg of our trip. We had been warned of the Hole, or Woods Hole Passage as it's properly called. Stories circulated about the Hole with its notorious strong currents and standing waves that swamped boats and ran ships aground in broad daylight. I expected that these stories were partly true, that these conditions and negative outcomes most likely occurred during storms or unusual tides, and after our pleasant little picnic on Devil's Foot, the island that sits next to the Hole, there appeared to be little to worry about, especially on such a beautiful day.

The evening Molly and I strolled around the little island, the sea was calm and the current had been next to nothing. We watched an old wooden sloop approach from Buzzards Bay, sailing by in the channel not 50 yards from where we stood, the main sail catching the last of the southerly breeze as an elderly couple waved to us. The boat passed silently like a dream. We waved back, and I think we both wished we were on that sloop, heading out into the Sound; but now we had our own vessel to dream upon.

Woods Hole Passage is a break between the chain of islands that run to the southwest off the mainland of Cape Cod. The islands separate the waters of Vineyard Sound and Buzzards Bay. Several passages cut through this chain, Robinson's Hole, Quick's Hole, Canapitsit Channel at Cuttyhunk, and Woods Hole Passage. Quick's Hole is the widest passage, and Robinson's Hole the narrowest, running a scant 200 yards at Naushon Point. Channels for navigating these passages are marked with the standard red and green marker buoys, allowing safe passage for sail and power boats alike. Larger vessels up to 100 feet, including fishing boats and the ferries from New Bedford, are only able to pass through the channels of Woods Hole and Quick's Hole. The islands form a kind of wall, holding back the water in Buzzards Bay as the tide ebbs east through Nantucket Sound, and as it floods west from Vineyard Sound back into the Bay. Depending on the phase of the moon, the tide, and the wind, the currents in these channels can move at impressive speeds and great force. When the current is cooking in Robinson's Hole, a channel buoy can actually submerge from the force of the rushing water, and suddenly pop up on an unexpected boatman, which happened to a friend one fine spring day while passing through the Hole in a fog. With a couple of fishing buddies onboard his 16 foot skiff, they were moving with the current and looking for the markers when the red can shot out of the water right under the boat, caving in the side. My friend lost the boat, the motor, and a few years of his life. Groundings are a regular occurrence in Woods Hole Passage, and even seasoned sailors fall prey to the rushing waters, as witnessed by the locals when three large sailboats from the New York Yacht Club left Hadley Harbor and soon piled themselves side by side on the reef at the east end of the channel.

The islands hold the water back as the tide goes through its cycle every six hours, and Vineyard Sound flushes out quicker than Buzzards Bay because of the island barrier, resulting in the rush of water through the passages. It's not just the speed of the current that presents the major hazard, but the resulting waves and turbulence that make weary travelers' hair stand on end when they encounter this phenomenon. The terrain under the water channels the energy, creating powerful eddies and vortices, and when big sport-fishing boats plow through the passage, it all gets worse, concocting formidable standing waves that will chew you up. It's the wrong place to be at the wrong time in a small 14-foot lap-strake skiff.

There are two ways out of Great Harbor. The main entrance is a wide expanse big enough for the ferries from the Steamship Authority, the Oceanographic vessels, the Fisheries ships and any of the commercial fishing boats that tie up on the outer town dock. There's another route out of the harbor that is much more picturesque and tranquil as it cuts between the peninsula of Penzance Point and the small islands that dot the edge of the harbor. This narrow gut runs shallow at low tide, and shore birds congregate there while families play and picnic on the sands of the inner shore of Devil's Foot. But when the harbor tide is running out, the surge picks up tremendous force as it passes between the island and the point, and the water is forced into a bottleneck that flows with purpose into Woods Hole Passage.

We chugged along that morning trailing smoke amongst the anchored boats, waving now and then to mariners seated with a cup of coffee or a morning paper. Molly's long black hair looked vibrant tied up in a bow, her face lifted up to the sun, her hippie blouse open to her bikini top – every man's dream.

It was exciting to be there, to be with her in our little boat on such a beautiful day. As I turned the boat into the back channel, the water was deceptively calm and shore birds waded in the shallows of Ram Island. Close by a school of young fish broke the surface as if rain had suddenly fallen, and crabs scuttled upon the sand bar as we passed over. The water was shallow here, just three or four feet at this stage of the tide, and I was wondering how larger boats managed to navigate this channel when I realized we were moving fairly fast over the bottom. I lowered the throttle down to idle, but if anything, we were speeding up.

"What are those white birds called?" Molly asked pointing to the shore.

"Egrets. Snowy egrets," I said distractedly, while trying to process what was going on.

Somewhere deep in the recesses of my chromosomes, my ancestors were reaching out to warn me, sending a message, causing the hair on the back of my neck to bristle. Looking past Molly and out beyond where the gut funnels into the Hole, the water looked like the Dead Sea after the Egyptians got what was coming to them. I knew then what my ancestors were yelling: "Get the hell out of there!"

Molly caught the look on my face. "What?" she said. Then she turned and we were into it.

The current sucked us out into a river of no return. The torrent picked the boat up as if on a conveyor belt and plopped us into the maelstrom. Molly screamed. I tried to keep the bow into the waves that were coming upon us, but the motor was useless. We had no control and headed broadside into a cascade of huge standing waves, when we hit the first wave the boat nearly capsized causing a good amount of water to spill into the boat.

"Grab the boat cushion," I yelled to Molly, who had been hit with the brunt of the wave and was holding on with both hands, wet as a Labrador retriever in heaven.

"Do something," she cried out.

I was trying to do something, but with all the water in the boat, it couldn't get around. I abandoned the motor and started to bail, scooping water like our lives depended on it. Then Molly screamed again. "Oh my God, look out!"

We were headed straight for one of the huge red nun marker buoys, that was heaved over at a 45 degree angle from the force of the current. We were going to hit it. I grabbed my boat cushion to hold over the side to help deflect the blow and we hit with a crack but not hard enough to cause serious damage. The boat took on more water.

"Bail, damn it!"

I tried desperately to get the motor to push the boat to safer water, all pretenses of romance and protocol now gone over the side. The 10-horse cranked as high as it could go.

Molly was down on her knees, bailing in a fury, too afraid to look up.

After we passed the red nun, the standing waves abated a bit, but we were still moving really fast. Just when I managed to point the boat out of the channel to calmer water a huge sport-fisherman passed within 30 feet of us. The boat pushed a big wake behind it that curled towards us and dropped our skiff into its trough, knocking Molly on her ass, allowing more water to crash over the side. I stood up, waved my fist in the air, and yelled obscenities as loud as I could.

"You asshole!"

Molly crawled about with her hair all wet, dangling and twisted in front of her face. She was spouting in a fury. "Stop yelling at me! You're just like my father."

"I'm not yelling at you!"

"You're the asshole. I thought you knew what you were doing."

By the time we stopped cursing each other, we had drifted through the rest of it and the 10-horse managed to push us back towards the mainland shore and calmer water.

"Look at this mess," Molly cried as she continued to bail. "Everything is wet, the towels and the blanket – and the food is gone. Where's the food? Where are the damn sandwiches? I want to go back."

Gone was the hippie love princess: she now looked more like one of the wretched witches of Macbeth. All attempts to pacify her came to no avail, we collected ourselves the best we could and got things ship-shape.

"Man, we could have bought it back there – someone could have gotten hurt. Now how the hell do we get back? The current will be rushing for another three hours and there is no way we're going back the way we came."

I explained this to Molly and pointed out a route we could take around the outer reach of the Hole, close to Naushon Island, to try to beat the current on the far side to get into Vineyard Sound. We would then go back to Great Harbor through the main entrance. She just looked at me blankly.

Gone was the sweetness of the new romance. The comment about her father should have given me a warning.

It took us more than two hours to get back to Great Harbor, during that time I tried to gather navigational information about the current characteristics of the Hole as we fought our way against the tide; making a note to remember the locations of fast water, where large boulders hide just beneath the surface outside the channel, surprised at how they raised a boil, the quieter water off Nonamesset, the rush at Grassy island. This was better than a picnic. Every part of the Hole reacted differently, depending on the bottom. I watched the magic of water and how it worked, how the current built standing waves at the end of the channel, how a large wake would break over the shallow ledge. All of this could be seen as we inched our way back up the far side of the passage.

Molly sat in the bow totally pissed, and uninterested in the world around her. The current was still too much for the motor to beat, but the water was flat running. It gave the impression of movement as it rushed by with the motor cranked up to full throttle and the afternoon breeze blowing in our ears, but we were standing as still as a fence post. I watched Molly and realized she thought we were actually making progress, deceived by the activity around her. She failed to look further than what was in front of her nose.

"We're not moving," I yelled.

She turned slowly, first looking at the water, and finally at the shore.

Startled, she concurred. "We're not moving." She looked surprised and confused. "What do we do now?"

When you look around and you're doing everything possible under the circumstances while still trying to figure how to make things right, you can only answer, "We keep going! Things are bound to get better!" But they didn't with us.

TOWARDS THE END OF our watch, the shark slowly but steadily swam closer to the surface.

"He's coming up. Better get Frank," Ollie said with anticipation.

Frank had actually been resting, but he was halfway up the stairs by the time I went to get him. He knew where the fish was.

"Give the girls a shake and tell them he's coming up."

The girls roused with much excitement and raced to the bow to join Frank. They had it all worked out. Ellie scooted up the mainmast to stand watch in the spreaders, while Joni stood by, navigating outside the wheelhouse. As Ollie and I tracked the shark, Joni would pass the information to Frank on the bow, and Ellie would try to spot the fish once it was close to the surface. The conditions were a little rough due to the late afternoon breeze, raising apprehension if we'd be able to spot the shark.

"He's at two meters a little off the starboard side," Joni yelled.

Frank stood at the bow with the harpoon pole, but without a harpoon tip or a transmitter attached, so I surmised that this would be a practice run. One look at Ollie confirmed this.

"Practice," he said.

"Practice," said Tom not looking at either one of us.

"Man, you guys are reading my head now."

The beeps were very close together, coming crisp and clean. "He's up. He's on the surface, almost dead ahead," Ollie reported.

Joni gave the call. "Ellie, it should be dead ahead."

Tom inched the *Bird* slowly forward into the waves, a good approach, with the sun to our right. The signal was very strong, and everyone had their eyes on the water until Ellie called out.

"I see him. I see him. He's about 50 meters a little to port. You got him, Frank?"

"Not yet," he answered.

Moments passed.

"Okay. He's dead ahead. He's in the trough; he's out

on top now."

"I have him." Frank raised his arm and pointed a little to the starboard.

Joni spoke softly to Tom. "Slow ahead, five degrees to starboard."

Soon Frank's arm moved to the path we were traveling. Then I could see the shark, the dorsal fin slicing the silvery water dead ahead. Frank held his arm out parallel to the horizon.

"Slow now," Joni cautioned.

Then Frank raised his hand up in a fist.

"All stop," she said.

Frank positioned the pole over the side, and with the tip, he followed the shark as we drifted past within range. Then the shark disappeared. We all rushed to the side to see the shark, but it was gone. No one said a thing.

"We can do this," Frank said with confidence.

Joni smiled as she hollered up to Ellie, "We can do this."

"No problem," came the reply.

"No problem," commented Tom while relighting his pipe.

WE FOLLOWED THE SHARK all evening into the night and next morning. The transmission signal remained strong, and we continued to get good numbers. The shark spent more time on the surface during the night, swimming in a "sine wave" pattern from the surface and down through the thermocline and back up again. He headed down as the sky lightened and remained there, moving towards the southeast slowly. By morning the sky had clouded over gray and dark with the promise of rain. Everyone gathered in the house during the watch change with a look of pessimism, all of us except Frank, who couldn't be fazed by the prospect of poor weather. But as the day progressed, the weather deteriorated further, the wind picked up from the southeast and spread whitecaps across the seascape by the time Ollie and I were back on watch.

The plan had been to track the shark for 24 hours, and if all went well, we would attempt to get it back before evening; however, with the weather getting worse, we could not see the shark even if it surfaced, which was unlikely in such conditions. So it was decided to forgo the hopes of harpooning the shark that day and continue tracking through the night. We hoped for better conditions, but according to Tom, that wasn't in the forecast.

We slogged on through the rain and windy night, taking a beating as we tracked the fish. Under kinder conditions, the tracking operations worked without a hitch, but now the sea presented a number of new challenges. As the seas grew, our direction of travel presented particular obstacles that had to do with the structure of a wave and how the shape of a boat responds to it. In all cases, because of the gradual slope at the back of a wave, it is better to have the seas coming at you from the stern, and thus the saying: "A fair wind and a following sea." Going into a wave presents a far greater conflict, with the forces meeting head-on the steeper slope on the face of the wave produces the dramatic rise and slam as these forces meet. Moving broadside in the trough of the wave produces an obvious problem. Whether you call it wallowing or rock and roll, being broadside to the waves stinks.

With the wind and the seas coming at us from the southwest and the shark traveling to the southeast, our line of pursuit was right in the trough of the seas. For the crew, this made everything difficult and uncomfortable, if not dangerous. You had to hold on to something at all times, and for me and Ollie, this also meant holding on to our cookies.

We tried to predict the shark's heading and hoped to go downwind or at least keep the seas on our stern quarter, to get in a position where the shark would eventually end up. The plan was to wait there with our nose into the wind. But every time we got broadside to the waves, the wash and resultant bubbles under the hull distorted the signal, sometimes we would loose it entirely for a minute or longer. Then Ollie and I would really get uptight and Tom would start puffing on his pipe as we'd hunch over the box, headphones pressed to our ears in an attempt to filter out all the sonic clutter. Around three in the morning, we were in the middle of one of these hunts, Tom puffing so hard we had to air out the house for all the smoke, when a strange noise came over the receiver. At first it sounded like static, very regular, but it was structured, too consistent for static. It sounded more like clicking, and then squawking and squeaking. Puzzled, I looked at Ollie. He mouthed something. I removed the headphones.

"Dolphins. It's a school of dolphins."

"Wow! Dolphins! I've never seen a school of dolphins."

For some reason, the idea exited me, the idea that a group of intelligent mammals were so close, cruising around in this water world with no boundaries to impede them, no 40-hour workweek, junk mail, telephone calls, credit cards, religion, or war. What were they doing? Were they attracted to the frequency of the transmitter? Could they sense the presence of the boat? I wanted to see them, get some photos, and follow them for a few days.

After we got back to the shark, Ollie predicted that we'd see dolphins before the end of the trip – if we survived tracking this fish. The wind had to be blowing 20 to 25 knots by then, and we felt the shark was onto us. It kept traveling to the southeast, keeping us in the trough on our drift. With the high seas and a hull shaped like a bathtub, we were taking a pounding.

"We need some carnival music and some cotton candy," I said.

By daybreak, it wasn't funny anymore. The three of us looked like we'd been busting broncos all night, and when the morning watch appeared, they looked almost as bad. Both Joni and Ellie had bed-heads, and although Frank looked refreshed, he looked concerned.

"This weather sucks," moaned Ellie.

"What's the forecast, Tom?

"It sounds like more of this with rain until Saturday."

We stood in the house looking out at the day as the world around us lightened into a gray rolling sky with a troubled green sea.

"We will never get this fish in this weather," said Frank, confirming all our thoughts.

He and Ollie bent over the navigation table, reviewing the night's track.

"He do anything exciting?" Ellie asked.

"He went deep once," I said.

"Almost lost him then," Tom added.

"How deep?" asked Joni.

"400 meters."

"That's a good dive," muttered Frank.

The sky was beginning to darken rather than give us hope of some sunshine. Joni had a look of concern on her face, and I caught myself watching her more often with the realization that this trip meant a lot to her, that getting this fish back had more importance than I could measure.

Frank studied the data for several minutes while the rest of us stood around waiting for the other shoe to drop, for we had a distinct feeling that a decision was about to be made. In the distance came a rolling bowling ball of thunder, deep and muffled. As I stood there half comatose from lack of sleep, seasickness, and data fatigue, hanging on to the door-rail and looking out at a world of wet, the sky opened with a torrent of rain.

"Peachy," exclaimed Ellie in a low voice.

"Endless sun-filled days," Joni added.

We all managed a chuckle before Frank announced his decision. "It looks like today is a bust as far as getting this fish back, and if this weather is going into tomorrow, there's little likelihood of our chances getting any better. I'm thinking we'll track until sundown and then head in. We could be at Gay Head by... What you figure, Tom?"

"With this tail wind, approximately 7 a.m.," Tom replied with the concerned detachment of a funeral parlor usher.

"I figure, if we get in before noon, get the batteries checked out, rebuild the generator, change the crew, we could turnaround within 24 hours and leave again before noon on Sunday." Frank looked thoughtful as he spoke.

We all agreed, and the plan to head in was the best news I had heard in days. Later, in my bunk, I had visions of hostages returning home, falling to their knees and kissing the tarmac on their fateful return. Those images, mixed with the oath I made never to set foot on a boat again began a torment. The internal dialogue, the conflict between the battle of the weak and the proud, the pitiful and the duty bound, was sheer torture.

We tracked the shark until sundown as planned, and then Frank gave the word to Tom who, without ceremony, turned the *Bird of Passage* to the northwest. "Head for the barn."

We had tracked the shark for over two days, recorded some good data and felt confident that, if we had better weather, we would have gotten the shark back onboard. Now, with the wind on our backside, the following seas gave us a gentle rocking as we headed home, and enjoyed a warm pleasant dinner in the galley. Ollie and I prepared the best meal we could: an entrée of hot turkey sandwiches made of week-old wheat bread and sliced deli turkey, mashed potatoes, and canned gravy. We ate with relish while discussing the agenda for the next trip out. I was disappointed to find out that Ollie would be off to an International Truck convention in North Carolina and Tom had other commitments on a NOAA vessel headed out to Georges Bank. Ollie's leaving left me feeling more vulnerable, indeed more valuable: if I quit, half the crew on the second voyage would be new.

Our crew talked of trucks, Cape traffic, the upcoming 4th of July celebration, and the canyons. When discussion of the canyons crossed the table, the tone grew serious.

"It's a haul to get there, but we'd have deep water," said Frank.

"You get those eddies coming off the stream."

"Good fishing this time of year, but it's a ways to get back, especially on this boat, and you've got those tugs hauling out to the 106 Mile Site, big barges dumping New York's finest sewage," said Tom.

"We'd be up near the Hudson Canyon, away from the dump site."

"A fishing boat bought it near the site last year," said Ollie with a tone of respect. "Four men lost in a fog ran between the tug and the barge, the cable snagged the wheelhouse, and no one knew what was happening until it was upon them. The mate was the only one to survive. He jumped for the cable as the barge came on and was able to hold on. All he saw were the lights fade into the fog and then the crushing of the hull and the screams of his shipmates."

"How'd he survive?"

The barge crew winched the cable in with him on it, and he still had enough piss and vinegar to haul off and slug the first guy he saw."

"Horrible."

"Fishing is a tough, dangerous business," Ollie said and we all waited for Tom's reply.

"A tough, dangerous business."

11

The *Bird of Passage* cruised through the night with a short watch for the crew. By dawn, the clouds had thinned to a layer of smoky mist, and as the sun rose the atmosphere intensified with a glow of radiant diffused light. It was strikingly beautiful; I had never seen anything like it. As the sun climbed higher, the intensity grew, rendering a deep contrast to the shadow of the waves with the highlights splashing the light back up to the low ceiling of cloud cover. In the distance, the profile of Gay Head appeared like a haunted land. I had hoped for a special phenomenon of light on this trip, and here it was. The illumination grew yet more dramatic as we neared the island, stretching the range of grey tones, giving the contrast more weight. The moisture in the clouds dissipated the light, and then there were moments when a rent would open to reveal the heavens above, causing the brilliant rays to fan out across the water as if the prophet himself would appear and walk upon the waves. I loaded the Canon A1 with some Illford low-speed black and white film and shot the water and the island in the distance with the crew moving about the deck in deep contrast amongst the dark lines of rigging against the bright sky. As we neared the tip of Gay Head, the clouds began to thin, diffusing the light to a radiant glow.

"Did ya get enough pickchas?" Ellie asked with a smile.

"Photographs really," I replied. "Photographs, not pictures. I shot two rolls!"

She didn't say anything.

"It's about light. It's about the light"

"Okay," she said a little defensively.

"Sorry, but I've never seen light like this. You don't get light like this on land. From land you don't get this reflection off the water, that vibration bouncing off the waves."

"I never thought of that," she said.

"Did you see the glow above the water, the glow in that mist rising off the waves, the diffusion giving the water that metallic shine?"

"Molten like."

"Yes."

"And when the sun broke through the clouds and the reflection lit up the underside brighter than the sky, revealing a ghost of the island?"

"Okay," she said smiling. "How about people, Mr. Ansel Adams? How about taking our picture in this beautiful light?" she asked as she gestured towards Joni who was working on the stern. I was happy to set them up with their backs to the west. The cloud cover was thinning but remained diffused enough to give a soft shadow to their faces. After capturing six shots of them smiling and kidding around, Ollie called for some assistance on the bow.

"I'll go," volunteered Ellie rather quickly, leaving me alone with Joni.

"Go ahead and shoot," she said boldly, standing with her arms crossed and legs spread in a look of defiance.

"Take that bow out of your hair please," I suggested while changing the wide angle lens to my standard 50 mm, not wanting any distortion.

"Hurry up and just take the picture."

"This is important." I knew she would need some coaxing. "I want you to think about years from now, sitting with your children, then years later, your children sitting with your grandchildren and looking at this picture of you." I needed her to relax and maybe realize that someday this trip would only be a memory captured on a piece of photographic paper. She dropped her arms, pulled back her hair, and actually smiled.

"Don't smile. Don't force yourself." I spoke calmly, shooting, moving closer towards her.

"Grandchildren. Good lord, who thinks of children let

alone grandchildren."

"All women think of having children – you're hard wired for that. I thought you were a scientist. Remember instinct?"

"Someday maybe," she said, trying to skirt the subject.

"Me? Just two. Girls or boys. I don't care which."

"Maybe someday," she said with a funny laugh, but now she was taking me a bit more seriously, you can always tell by the expression in the eyes. After several more shots she ended with the comment, "So now you have my soul, as the primitives believe."

We were standing close to each other, and without thinking, I replied casually, "I want your heart and your soul."

There was a pause and then she looked at me, into my eyes, deeply into something, and I let her in.

"Okay, well good luck with that." She smiled and walked away.

I was startled by this sudden intimate moment. "You idiot!" I thought. "You stupid idiot! What the hell did you say that for? Where did that come from?"

I couldn't believe I crossed this delicate boundary in a working relationship with a woman I hardly knew and would be working with for the next two weeks. "There, I said it – the next two weeks."

"Am I really going to do this? Damn!" The bird was in my hand, as my grandfather would say, and a decision needed to be made. We passed Gay Head on our way up Vineyard Sound, ahead lay Nobska Light, and home. Then, as if on cue, Frank appeared on deck. He said nothing, but smiled at the open water as we stood there and I think he knew what I had been thinking. Finally, he turned, put his arm around my shoulder, and asked with an inquisitive smile, "So how about that generator?"

"We can get that turned around in a day," my mouth said involuntarily.

"Thank you." He smiled and gave me a pat on the back.

We stood and watched the rising of the mainland from the mist. Flashes from car windshields gave signs of human activity on the shoreline of the Vineyard, cars driven by people going to the beach, on the morning shopping trip, the weekly pilgrimage to the dump, people with normal lives oblivious to the plight of this hapless sailor who had just sealed his fate to journey back out into the great blue wilderness.

Shortly after, Tom brought the *Bird* up to the WHOI dock and delivered us into the caring arms of Richards, who probably had better things to do on a Saturday morning but knew we were due sometime before noon according to the Port Office.

The vessel *Oceanus* had returned while we were away, so we tied up close to her bow at the head of the pier. Tom said his good-byes quickly after the boat was secured. He stood above us looking down from the dock, bag over his shoulder, pipe in hand.

"I'm off. Best of luck and fair winds."

Frank had Richards' ear, hoping to get some mechanical help. He wanted to do a quick turnaround so we could get out on Sunday as planned, but that sounded like a challenge on a sunny summer weekend. While they discussed the options, Ollie waited around to make sure we were okay. I could tell he felt funny leaving us, perhaps mostly leaving Frank in the middle of a cruise.

"Don't you need a copilot on your trip to this convention?" I asked.

He laughed. "You know, come to think of it, you never know when a generator is going to freeze up on you and catch on fire." He looked like he needed a good night's sleep. "I think Frank is relieved you're going back out. He needs you. He's got so many other things to think about. I should be back in a week or so. Take care, eat some soup, I'll be looking for your return." We shook hands before he climbed the pier ladder and waved goodbye.

The girls left about the same time to go food shopping. Joni asked if I wanted anything special and I requested some Dramamine and more chicken soup.

With everyone gone, it was a perfect time to get a real cup of coffee and a footing on dry land. The dock area of the Oceanographic is isolated from the rest of the town by the buildings that line Water Street. You have to pass through a narrow drive between Bigelow and Smith to get to the outside world, which I did, venturing like a jungle boy out of the woods where the world suddenly seemed very complicated, busy, and rushed. The summer crowd of Cape Cod mingled along the walkways, and everyone appeared in a hurry. The contrast of living conditions and tempo between the boat and land were striking and uncomfortable. I ventured to the Food Buoy and purchased a dark chocolate bar, some peanuts, and a Coke, instead of coffee. In spite of my discomfort at the speed of things on land, it was good to be back, but there was little time to slack off.

Back on the boat, I made a list of mechanical tasks that needed to be attended to. Frank returned with the not-so-good news that we were pretty much on our own until Monday, and getting anything accomplished was questionable because the 4th of July holiday was on the horizon.

"Do the best you can with the generator. If we can't get it going, maybe we'll try without it and bring extra batteries. I'll be in the lab all day but hope to spend the night with my kids. The girls are off to get more bait and supplies, and I've got another NOAA pilot showing up before noon."

We surveyed the boat for other things that may need attending to before he left.

"You sure you don't want to go with Ollie to his truck convention?" he asked, testing me.

"No," I said simply but with appreciation.

"All right then. Don't kill yourself getting the repairs done, and get some sleep. I'll see you in the morning."

He left me with the boat all to myself, as I reflected on how far I had come in the past week. Standing on the stern, however, I had that uneasy feeling of being watched.

"I'll be in the shop until four, if you need anything." It was Richards looking down from the dock.

"You got an AC Tecumseh magnetic clutch drive?" I yelled up to him.

He laughed as he walked away. "Good luck."

The afternoon consisted of tracking down the parts needed to fix the generator which required a trip to Hyannis and then to CW Douglas in Buzzards Bay. It was five o'clock before I got back to the boat, and it looked like a long night ahead. There was a note taped to the wheel.

"See guard at front desk if you need shop - Richards."

I attacked the generator with determination and optimism, knowing there would be the ever present road-block or surprise mechanical dead-end. This turned out to be two seized 3/8 inch attachment bolts, forcing me to remove the complete generator carriage, the works weighing in easily over 70 pounds. The generator and its base had to be wrestled over the main engine, out of the engine room, up the stairs, up the ladder, across the pier and into the shop where I could get some heat from the acetylene torch to free things up. Getting it up the ladder turned out to be the hardest part and I played with the idea of just letting it drop over the side and solve all my problems. It was going on nine o'clock by the time I got everything back into the engine room, but the components still needed to be assembled and tested. While in the shop, the girls must have returned because we now had more food, snacks and plenty of bait in the freezers.

It was Saturday night in Woods Hole, and the one thing I would rather be doing than bilge wrestling with a generator was sitting at a bar, any one of them. The sounds of the nightlife echoed down into the engine room – drunks whooping it up, cars peeling out, laughter at the water's edge by the MBL Club – but I remained duty bound.

By midnight, everything had come together, and the whole assemblage looked like it might actually work. Not only was the clutch replaced but now the adjustment mechanism worked freely with the wire terminations cleaned and soldered. There was a new belt, the brushes and commutator were lightly sanded, and the bearings greased. The generator looked good and I felt good about it. My sphere of maintenance broadened gradually to the rest of the diesel engine, checking for leaky gaskets, frozen bolts, bad connections, cracked hoses, anything that would cause trouble during the next couple of weeks. From the auxiliary diesel, I got distracted by the refrigeration system mounted aft of the small diesel. While in the middle of following the refrigerant lines, footsteps approached overhead, soft footsteps, then the familiar clinking of bottles, then humming, and a moment later Joni was leaning in the engine room doorway.

"Hey deck-monkey, want a beer?"

After wrestling with rusty steel parts, grease, acetylene torches and bilge goop, any member of the opposite sex would have looked good. But Joni looked more like a vision from above. Her auburn hair was now silky after losing the frizz of a week at sea. She was dressed in a loose fitting white summer blouse and looked fresh and radiant, a little wild and a little lit up. She totally caught me off guard.

"You've been working here all day. We thought we'd see you at the bar. You weren't here to help us unload, were you?"

"I was in the shop with that thing."

"Sure, in the shop with all the big tools. Here, silly."

She sat down at the doorway and just watched me with a stupid look on her face. "Well, you gonna drink it or you gonna talk to it. You a Mormon or something?"

"Hardly," I said, raising the cold bottle to my lips. The first gulp felt like heaven.

"Boy, that's a good beer. Sometimes, the harder you work, the better it tastes."

"Like a lot of things."

"What's that supposed to mean?" I asked.

She said nothing but looked around, taking another slug of beer. "Calvin, you're a mess. I think you'll need to stay in here for the next trip. You really going back out with us?"

"I'm here for the duration," I said, gathering some of the tools.

"Boy, it's crowded in town. Everyone's in the bars."

"A small town with a big thirst – the locals like to party."

"I think we met a few on the street."

"I can show you more."

"I'll bet you can," she said, drifting off. She had a buzz and was almost at the slurring stage.

"Where's Ellie?"

She looked at me blankly. "You think we're attached at the hip or something?"

I watched her with amusement, and then she said reflectively, "She's with some 'colleagues' talking shop. Some guy was hitting on me. I got bored."

"Thanks for the beer."

She nodded and said nothing but smiled.

"What?"

"Nothing."

"What?"

"Christ, Calvin. If you're not covered in vomit or knee deep in fish gurry, you've got grease up to your eyeballs."

"Some women like that kind of thing."

She gave me that don't-play-coy-with-me look.

"Is that thing working now?"

"I need to road test it."

"Road test. Well, it's a great night for that. Let's go. Come on. Let's take her around the harbor." Then she got up and came right at me.

"Look out, silly."

She passed by me, brushing against my greasy body, and exited out the aft door. She scooted up the stairway to the wheelhouse as her muffled voice cascaded down the stairs.

"Come on, Calvin. Fire it up," she yelled.

I could tell she was at the wheel. She was having a good time. "Man, she's a fire cracker," I thought.

I poked my head up the stairs. "I think, with a couple more beers, I'd do it. And you're going to drive, I suppose?"

"Full speed ahead, Captain. Ready about." Then she spilled her beer on the control console. "Oh shit! You dumb bunny! Calvin, look what you made me do." She rummaged around the room for something to clean up the mess while I got some clean rags from below, and soon we were beside each other on the dark wheelhouse floor.

"This place is going to smell like a brewery. Frank will have a fit."

"He won't even smell it with me around," I said.

"Boy, you do smell – like burnt toast or something."

"It's the torch."

"Torch, is that some kind of cologne?" She fell back on her ass and we both started laughing.

"No, it's not. And neither is seasickness scent."

"Boy, you had enough of that."

"Couldn't help it. I'm the sensitive type."

There was silence and then she extended her hand.

"Yeah. Well, you know what I think?" she said somewhat defensively but somewhat openly at the same time. I waited, but she stopped. There were voices. It was Ellie and others from the bar.

"So, what do you think?"

"I think, you better finish your beer and check out that there generator."

Then she went off to welcome the newcomers to show them around the boat while I attended to mechanics, briefly starting the auxiliary and engaging the generator to get some juice. By now, my brain was fried, and any problems would have to wait until morning anyway. I shared a beer cordially with the others, took a shower, and crashed in the forward cabin. Dead tired, too tired to think about tomorrow – which was already today – I lay there wondering about Joni's comment "you know what I think" when there was a soft knock on the door. Joni poked her head in enough to see me get up on an elbow. There was a moment's pause.

"Good night Calvin," she said almost with a giggle and closed the door.

"Good night Joni," I whispered to the darkness.

blue shark

LEG II

Bob's Your Uncle

12

The next morning, the sounds of the shoreline played a gentle awakening. The cry of the gulls, a distant outboard motor, and voices sliding across the water announced the new day while the *Bird of Passage* lay in the shade of the dock buildings and the hull of the vessel *Oceanus*. It was sleepy quiet except for some delicate tinkling coming from the galley as if someone was brewing a pot of tea, which in fact it turned out to be.

"Howard Ashley Pitt. Pleased to make your acquaintance," said the gentleman seated comfortably behind the galley table with a cup of tea and a plate of burnt toast. I introduced myself. "People call me Ashley. Care for some tea?" he asked politely.

I declined and couldn't help but wonder who in the hell this guy was.

"Lovely morning. How's the generator?" he inquired.

"I think we're okay."

"Need any assistance?"

"I need to do one more test run, put a load on it."

"Right, then. Let's get started."

The guy appeared to be as old as my grandfather, with white hair, a hawk nose, a ruddy face, and a ratty old sweater that looked like he had slept in it for the past decade; but he was as spry as a boy scout.

"Uh?"

"Ashley Pitt."

"Right, Ashley. I'm sorry, but are you going on this next leg?"

"At your service. Couldn't wait for you folks to get in. Sorry I missed Ollie. Where are the girls? Up all night partying, I suppose. Better let them sleep – hard workers those two. Frank said he'd be here by nine. He's having breakfast with his children." Then he looked expectantly at me.

"Okay, Ashley. Let me get some caffeine in me and we'll have at it."

With a fresh cup of joe in hand we did a recap of the technical problems encountered on the last leg. He nodded his head, sucking it all in, pondering the probabilities, asking the right questions. It wasn't long before I realized Ashley knew his stuff. He took in information like oxygen, wanting more and all the while exhaling possibilities along with technical options.

"So we still don't know if the batteries are up to snuff?"

"Right, but now we have a dependable generator for back-up."

"If she checks out properly, which I'm sure she will," he said with an apologetic smile.

We proceeded with the testing, and the commotion roused the girls, who went through all kinds of "Hellos" in between catching up on Ashley's recent projects, his trip to the Bermuda Biological Station, some sort of whale expedition to Patagonia, and his two month stay in the Antarctic. While this was going on, the new NOAA pilot arrived looking like Bob Marley at the tail end of a concert tour.

"You the chief?" he asked.

"Hardly. He'll be here shortly," I replied.

"How is the boat? Heard you had problems, some kind of fire."

"I think we're all set."

"My name is Jim. People call me Jimbo."

Actually, he looked more like Bob Marley if he had acted in the *Cane Mutiny*, with a sour expression, shifty eyes tucked under his black curly hair and khaki cap. He seemed uneasy and overly cautious. He followed Ashley and me around as we finished our testing, looking at times grave but then detached. Ashley paid no heed to Jimbo's disposition but included him in all of his questions about the boat: the sail rigging, sails, the deck layout, our chum station, and the tracking arrangement.

We were in the engine room going over the charging voltage for the generator when Frank arrived. Ashley had already calculated the load in amps and what the expected charge should be. Frank listened while he eye-balled the generator, which did look a whole lot better than before.

"Well, I think these numbers look good," Ashley concluded.

Frank looked very pleased. He put his hand on my shoulder. "You're wonderful," he said with a smile.

We assembled on deck to review the checklist of things to do. With crew on board, food stored, bait loaded, repairs made, and our NOAA pilot present and accounted for, we were ahead of schedule. Frank thanked Jimbo for showing up early on a Sunday morning, but Jimbo had other things on his mind.

"The glass is dropping. A front is moving in from Canada and it is going to get sloppy." This brought a measured silence to the group.

"How powerful is this frontal system?" Ashley inquired.

"You want to lash those coolers down proper. They look secure, but we can't have those tops flying open. If one of those things breaks free, it'll come right through the wheelhouse."

While Jimbo went on about the weather, I imagined a freezer loaded with bait breaking loose, snapping the lines and crashing through the wheelhouse windows. I didn't need to hear about bad weather. The world had been stable and comfortable for the past 24 hours, but now a gray depression began to fall over me with the prospect of nausea, pounding headaches, and vomiting on the horizon. Joni was seated across from me. She looked like she had slept in her clothes, which is customary, but appeared a little more disheveled than usual. Nevertheless, she was still bright and chipper. Ellie had a big bed-head of hair and looked a bit tired and hung-over, but otherwise, she looked quite happy. I don't know how late they stayed up partying. It seemed "work hard, play hard" was the creed with this crew.

As we made ready, Jimbo cornered me with a list of questions. "When was the last fuel filter change on the main engine? Was there any water in the filter canister? Where did we get the fuel? Did we run the auxiliary in heavy seas? Did it pull to starboard? Did the mizzen sail help steady the boat?" The questions went on until there were no answers. He seemed overly cautious compared to Frank's approach: "We'll do the best we can, and if it breaks we'll fix it and make it work anyway." And his dire predictions of foul weather dampened my spirits. During my Q&A session, a WHOI pickup truck pulled up to the dock, and shortly after, Frank was giving Richards an update of our itinerary, which ended with both of them staring off to the western horizon as if attempting to catch a glimpse of this impending weather.

Shortly thereafter, without ceremony, we were steaming down Vineyard Sound, which was sunlit and calm, as we double-checked the gear above and below and took appropriate measures just in case the roof did fall. I hoped to get some time alone with Joni to try to get back to where we had left off the previous night, but she was as business-like as usual. I did manage to catch a moment with her on the stern while she checked the chumming gear.

"Another batch of bad weather is really going to hurt. We've been waiting a year and a half to get a boat so we could get out here. This guy Jimbo is pissing me off."

"It's not his fault the weather will turn."

"Some people bring bad weather." She was fuming.

"At least he's got us ready for it."

"Sure, he brings the latest government weather report, but does he bring the latest Gulf Stream charts like he's supposed to?"

"He told Frank they weren't available. Anyway, he did note that the wheelhouse smelled like his old college dorm."

She laughed. "Yeah, well, no need to tell that story."

"Did I thank you for that beer?"

"You can repay me when we get in," she said. "Better yet, if we get a fish back, I'll buy you a whole bunch of beers."

"A whole bunch? Okay and you'll tell me what you think?"

She looked at me blankly. "About what?"

I had to think fast and smiled. "All about life's rich pageant."

She pondered this for a moment. "I'll need a few beers for that one."

"So we have a date?"

"Don't get cocky, deck monkey," she said seriously but obviously a bit flattered. "Here, help me with these fish totes. We'd better double check everything. The way Jimbo's talking, we'd better expect the worst."

The worst hit us right before sundown.

As we left the sight of land, the sky to the northwest darkened with a long black band of clouds stretching across the horizon. Jimbo had his head close to the radio monitoring the weather reports all afternoon. It seemed the Connecticut River Valley had been hit hard with violent thunderstorms earlier in the day, knocking down trees and power lines. That was apparently the storm heading our way. Jimbo said he had hoped it would skirt the coast or peter-out by the time it hit the Cape, but as the afternoon waned, the band of darkness rose slowly higher behind us, gathering everyone's attention.

The girls and Ashley went below to prepare dinner while Frank and I hung with Jimbo to watch the northwestern horizon.

"It hit Springfield hard. Usually these storms lose energy by now, but there were reports of gusts up to 70 knots."

Frank stood at the door watching the storm's slow but steady progress. "I expected this to move to the east but it keeps coming on."

It looked bad, a dark black mass looming higher in the sky that, to my mind, contained a hint of evil. Jimbo gave me the wheel in order to join Frank at the doorway.

"Frank, I do not like the way the glass is falling. I am going to have to make a call on this, sir."

"No, you're right, chief. Let's head in. Let's see if we can make Block Island before it hits."

Jimbo swung us around to the northwest while Frank informed the crew below. Soon Joni, Ellie, and Ashley joined us on deck, surprised at how quickly the system was moving and how ominous it appeared.

"That's ugly," exclaimed Ellie.

"How long to Block Island?" Joni asked.

"Several hours, but hopefully this storm will skirt the coast. We need a good southwesterly breeze right about now," said Ashley, but there was little breeze and no sign of ship or sail.

Frank and Jimbo worked out the calculations. They figured it would take a good three hours to make Block Island with the tide in our favor.

"If that thing hits us at the Race, we will never make it in." Jimbo never ceased to bring us happy moments.

Ashley had already thought of that, however. "That's right. The tide's flooding to the west, running into Long Island Sound. With high winds out of the northwest, the Race would be quite nasty, and it will be dark in a few hours." He laughed. "Well, dinner's ready." He turned and went below. Eventually everyone else followed except Frank and me.

"It seems to be moving more easterly than to the south." He tried to sound hopeful.

"Man, it's black."

"You look at weather differently out here. You better double check things down below."

"I'll do that now, and pass on dinner."

Frank patted me on the shoulder and went down to join the others. The scene really was amazing: three-quarters of the sky was clear and blue abruptly contrasted with a black and gray wall of cloud looming up like a blanket to be drawn over the sea, the color of which had turned pea green under the oncoming shroud. Jimbo gave me the wheel so he could join the others for a sociable dinner.

"Just hold her steady on course 3-5-0. Nothing like a big dinner before a storm."

"Great. Another comedian onboard. I wonder if he'll say that after I toss lunch all over his shoes. But he's probably seen all that before."

After dinner, everyone did a double check on the deck gear and secured the galley below. Around seven, the cloud line reached overhead. We stood on deck watching and waiting. Ashley played with his binoculars scanning the area for birds, excitedly making identifications. I helped Frank and Jimbo assemble a bundle of chain on the stern for a sea anchor.

"Okay. We want approximately a boat's length and a half of line, and we'll tie it off both stern cleats, like this. Frank, I'll need two people on watch through the night if we can't make it in."

"That'll be me and Ashley."

"I want the engine room checked on the hour and a report to me."

"That's me," I said. "I'll be up all night – probably wouldn't be able to sleep anyway." I had been praying to make it to safe harbor, but that wasn't going to happen.

"Block Island on the horizon," shouted Ashley. The news gave me hope. Ashley piped up again. "What?" He panned the horizon with the glasses, and then Jimbo joined him with his binoculars.

"We've got a white line of weather coming on fast."

The distant water was in a state, changing dramatically, as a covering of dark slate-colored surface water approached us from the northwest trailing a herd of white-capped waves galloping hard to keep up. The wind came upon us like a passing tractor-trailer rig hauling ass for Hades. The Lord had put the hammer down.

We all witnessed this in awe, and then the rain hit us at a horizontal as we ran for cover. The next moment we were in the wheelhouse looking out at nothing but the splatters on the windows. There was a lot of whooping and hollering at first, but we all sobered up quickly as Jimbo wrestled the wheel, trying to keep the nose into the wind, which kept getting stronger. It didn't take long for the girls and Ashley to clear out, leaving Frank and me to watch Jimbo dance with the wheel. The wind kept picking up as the rain fell harder.

Frank and Jimbo settled in, getting the feel of the boat as the seas built. They talked about wind speed, wave height and period, and something called "fetch."

"We're not going to make it into Block Island in the dark with this weather. It's best to try to get into the lee of the island or we'll turn it around and head out with it. This can't last that long. It's got be blowing at least 50 out there."

"Let's try to make the lee side."

Frank and Jimbo had to shout over the pounding of the rain. By now the hull had acquired four legs and a tail and was a bucking and kicking. I figured it would be best to do an engine check before the weather got any worse. Already in a cold sweat and slowly receding into tunnel vision, I knew the worst part of the coming night would be that I was *not* going to die.

After an hour of banging into the storm, Jimbo decided he'd had enough and turned the *Bird* around to head downwind. We surfed through most of the night as the wind gradually fell to a steady 25 knots out of the northwest.

All night we wallowed at a slow steady pace just

trying to stay comfortable, and it was during the night that we confirmed we had a battery problem. After running the generator, which worked perfectly, thank God, and checking the hydrometer levels, the two batteries in question never passed the fair condition level even after charging them all night. This became a concern. If the battery voltage fell too low and couldn't regain a charge, we would be left with one reliable battery, and if the condition that was draining these batteries began to affect the good battery, we could be in trouble. If we ran into mechanical problems and needed to continually crank the engine to get it going, we would need a good solid power supply. If worse came to worst, we could sail home. However, word was that the *Bird* sailed like a dead cow. The cruise would be a bust, a year's worth of planning and preparation down the tubes.

In the morning, there weren't many happy faces around the breakfast table. Frank and Joni were losing valuable cruise time, the weather didn't look promising, and we needed to figure out this battery problem before we went further. We had been caught by surprise because we thought the charge levels were low because of the drain during the first leg when the generator was out of commission, and we expected the levels to rise after receiving a good charge like the one we had given the previous night. That didn't happen, so we needed to determine if there was a voltage short that caused a continuous drain or if the batteries themselves were bad. Frank decided to have the girls chum while we tackled the electrical problem. Outside, the seas were pushing four to six feet, making it difficult to maneuver. It was possible to function as long as you were holding on to something, but it was nasty on deck. I helped the girls set up the chumming station as the rain came sporadically and hard, whipping against our foul-weather gear. With the conditions as they were, I couldn't see how we would manage tagging a shark. Ellie said Frank wanted to keep people working regardless.

For the rest of the morning, Ashley and I did a thorough investigation of the electrical problem. We isolated each battery and charged them independently, scurried through the wiring diagrams that we laid out on the navigation table, following lead after lead, looking for newly installed equipment connections or anything that seemed suspect. Ashley worked like a hound hot on the trail, talking to himself as he went, answering his own questions, presenting hypothetical situations, deducing his own conclusions. I tried to fill in the gaps, and he would respond with "Good man." This is how it went until noon, when we finally decided what the outcome had to be.

"Frank, I'm afraid we have two bad batteries. Bob's your uncle." Ashley smiled apologetically, happy to find an answer but uneasy with the options it left us.

Frank didn't want to hear this. He didn't need problems with the boat on top of the bad weather. We were into our second day, and the girls couldn't get a fish to the surface all morning. The question was now: Should we chance it and head out into deeper water for the remainder of the leg or head in for a battery refit and lose a day?

The crew assembled in the wheelhouse for another decision session. It was cramped and damp, and the girls looked like a couple of wet rats, but thankful rats that they were now inside. According to Jimbo, the weather report predicted diminishing southwest winds and fog for the next 24 hours. Joni, Frank, and Ashley tried to work it out, taking into account the weather, the possible problems, and the prospect of voyaging out to deeper water with two undependable batteries. It was a tough call, and the more they went over it, the more the word Montauk drifted around the cabin until the discussion distilled into that one word. So turn around we did to run back against the seas, heading for the tip of Long Island and Montauk Harbor.

During the transit, everyone had a chance to catch up on lost sleep and to straighten things up after getting hammered by the storm. Ashley manned the wheel while I read some of Frank's research reports, which chronicled his expeditions tracking sharks in the Mediterranean, off Baja, Bermuda, and Hawaii, as well as along the east coast. The reports were heavy on the technical jargon, but each had diagrams that depicted the patterns of travel in course and depth for blue sharks, makos, the great white, big eye threshers, and swordfish. Ashley nodded several times while I leafed through the pages, encouraging me to read more. Finally he commented, "A lot of time at sea; many days away from home."

"And a lot of work."

"Yes, hard on a family with kids."

"He was talking about tracking tuna."

"Frank would love to track a bluefin, but that would require one hell of a snapping boat."

"We couldn't do it in this thing, could we?"

He laughed. "We might be able to track a swordfish with this craft, but a tuna? Never. We would need one of those big cruisers out of Montauk, twin screws and lots of horses. Giant bluefin are wonderful fish, with a magnificent design like a bullet, built for speed. They have a recess along their sides to receive their pectoral fins to cut down on drag, and they are voracious eaters. Years ago, folks in Maine called them Horse Bunker and nobody wanted them except for cat food. Now, of course, they are bringing in the big money, flash frozen and shipped to Japan. We may see some in Montauk."

Ashley stopped short when he heard Frank's voice rising up from the after-cabin announcing the vessel's name. "Bird of Passage, papa, alpha, sierra, sierra, alpha, golf, echo," he called out slowly and distinctively.

"*Bird of Paradise?*" came the voice from the other end, somewhere in the electronic world, the voice known as the marine operator.

"No, Passage. Bird of Passage."

Frank was below attempting to make contact with a marina in Montauk through the marine operator but she couldn't get the name of the boat right.

"Bird of Passage, Passage".

There was a pause and then her crackling voice asked, "*Bird of Sausage?*"

Frank was obviously getting exasperated. "No,

PASSAGE: papa, alpha, sierra, sierra, alpha, golf, echo."

"*I'm sorry, but your transmission is intermittent. I have vessel MS 842700, Bird of Paradise.*"

"Passage! Passage, you idiot!" he yelled into the handset.

Silence.

"*Yes sir, Bird of Paradise calling Montauk Marine.*" Then there was dial tone and Frank got through.

We had to muffle our laughter. "*Bird of Sausage.* That's a good one. Can't wait to tell the ladies that one." Ashley grinned.

All afternoon we wiggled our way north, managing to pick up speed as the wind diminished and turned to the southwest. As it did so, the air grew heavier and moist, the horizon began to fade, and the sky and the sea slowly turned to gray. Then we moved into a cloud of thick soupy fog and the world disappeared. This was totally different than cruising at night. Now everything seemed equal, in fact utterly the same, and as the waves decreased it became harder to figure our direction. We were totally dependent on the compass and the radar.

We roused Jimbo as the weather set in because we were near the shipping lanes and no one wanted to take any chances. I manned the radar, looking for the wolf packs. On several occasions, we heard the echoing of fog horns, the sound waves wrapping around the moisture particles in the air and refracting their direction and distorting their tone. So, at times the horns seemed as menacing as the call of our ancestral predators. Jimbo had me tag each blip on the radar screen, keeping track as we edged on. The southwest wind flattened the sea, the boat seemed in a cloud, rocked by gentle turbulence and a mischievous invisible force, almost floating above the water as the prop tried to gather purchase in the thin soupy mix. The atmosphere surrounding us became so cloud-like I expected to catch sight of the earth far below. In the distance, another howl of a great iron beast fell upon us, lingered for a moment, reverberated and then faded. One could imagine the faint hush of a huge bow wake coming on fast as a gigantic wall of steel bears down upon you, with little time to even bless yourself good-bye.

"What have you got?" Jimbo asked.

"I've got two out beyond 20 miles, both past us, and two within a ten-mile radius, one coming behind us but veering to the northeast and one coming at us on the port side a good two miles away."

"That's the one we heard." Jimbo slid over as he had done a hundred times that afternoon and buried his head in the radar shield.

"Okay, looks good. Sailboats are hard to see even with the reflector hanging up there, but this guy's got us. Montauk on the screen."

Sure enough, as I looked at the screen again, the contour line of a land form crept into the ten-mile radius of the scope.

"Montauk on the Fourth of July. They won't be seeing any fireworks tonight." Jimbo smiled.

As we got closer, we began to pick up a lot more chatter on the radio, and the sound of other fog horns popped up too, smaller blasts than the blaring tanker, some like party horns, and some talking back to one another. As we merged towards the harbor entrance, it really did sound like a party. We had a number of radar blips around us, and we could hear the deep throaty exhaust note of a formula and the heavy diesel rumble of a sport fisherman. The commotion drew our crew on deck. I guess we wanted to be part of the celebration too.

Ellie and Joni were all smiles as though they had a secret plan, and Ashley looked a bit odd dressed in a blue cardigan sweater, his white hair frizzled out clown-like as he listened to all the commotion, picking up on the party energy.

"The sport fishermen are coming in, a day out with a crew of drunken business men no doubt. I don't know how I should feel about this holiday," he said, hoping to elicit some comment.

"Bloody Englishman, back to the brig," Ellie

commanded.

"Colonial suppressor! The brig is too good for him. Make him walk the plank," cried Joni as she and Ellie grabbed him by both arms and forced him to the rail.

"Mercy please," he cried. "I am but a poor Scotsman, a wayward scientist trying to reach the New World."

"What should we do with him?"

"If you really want to punish him, let him stay onboard," I said, and they all laughed, including Frank.

"Oh, come on. It's not that bad is it?" Frank smiled. "We'll only be here a couple of hours, so don't travel far. It sounds like folks are fixing for a celebration tonight – too bad about this fog. We could see some big fish coming in with these sports now."

"The great white monsters," said Joni.

"Wait," said Ellie. "We're getting close."

"What is it?"

"I smell fried clams."

Now I know why the girls were getting excited. They were talking food, and the thought of French fries and clams sounded pretty good to me too.

We slowed as we passed a harbor buoy on the starboard side; Jimbo fell in behind a beamy sport-fishing charter with a dozen poles holstered on the bridge and four beefy guys staggering on the stern. As we crept further up the harbor, the sounds of civilization seemed to ooze from the gray atmosphere around us. The vague outlines of boats on moorings were just barely visible. A piling would suddenly appear to reveal a line of boats on a marina slip. Sometimes, the fog would open enough to see a house in the distance, and then it would close in again and there would be nothing but sound. Jimbo worked his magic up the channel as we stood guard on deck watching and listening. It was like a scene from *The Heart of Darkness*, except we hoped to end up with a basket of French fries and a couple marine batteries instead of meeting a mad man, but crazy it was.

We made fast the lines on a transient dock that

Montauk Marine made available to us. Joni and I secured the bow, and after getting the okay from Frank, who was on the stern, we surveyed our surroundings. On the pier above stood a crowd staring down at us like we were a band of boat people from Cuba arriving in the free world. The *Bird* did look a little different than the beautiful yachts next to us, with our buckets, fish totes of bait, and chum barrel, freezers tied on the bow, harpoon poles, and the clothes line running above the deck to the pulley with the big red arrow. We must have looked a site ourselves, bedraggled as we were. The crowd was full of vacationers of all ages carrying ice cream cones and balloons and American flags and wearing funny hats. It seemed every one of them had a camera, and almost on cue, flashes started filling the air.

"Christ, I should have a picture of this," I said.

"Just smile and wave," Joni said, waving. "Maybe they'll go away."

And they did, aimlessly wandering off to the next venue of entertainment, searching to fill the void of holiday excitement. It was as if we had stumbled upon a land of lost souls awaiting some magical ship to land that would fulfill their expectations only to be disappointed to find the new arrivals were just like them, happy to get fried clams. We soon joined the wandering masses, climbing the ramp to the pier of lost souls where the crowd had that weird energy that exists before something is supposed to happen. In this case, the fireworks display over the water was supposed to happen, but with the fog thickening, the mood seemed to be of disappointment. On our way to the marina, we passed an excited crowd at the weigh-in of a large mako shark hanging by its tail, mouth agape and teeth protruding, with four happy campers standing beside it like book-ends, smiling. One sport wore a tee-shirt emblazoned with "Maui" in bright red letters, that hung over his huge protruding gut. He had a can of beer in one hand and the other hand held on to his buddy for stability. I wondered what Frank would do. Would he engage these guys to see where they caught the fish and what else they may have seen during the day? Would he ask them how deep they hooked up, did he jump, did he dive, what was the water temperature where they found him, what time of day, what was in his stomach?

All he said was, "Looks like they had a good day fishing. Let's get the batteries."

The girls disappeared on their secret mission, while Frank, Ashley and I meandered our way to the marina. As we walked along the pier, I felt torn between two worlds, the one before me and that of my new tribe. Some part of me felt akin to the guys in the fishing party who were happy to capture the big monster and share bravado, just having a good time while blowing a couple hundred bucks, happy to end the day with a picture of them all standing proud beside the limp carcass of an incredible fish. Somewhere deep down though, the image stirred uneasy; unsure if it was the display of pride over capturing the prize or the deeper need to destroy those things that we fear. Working with sharks was a unique experience, and maybe after a while our monsters lose their mystique. Maybe after spending so much time thinking about them, pursuing, handling, writing, photographing, and talking about them, they are no longer monsters. I wondered about these creatures of our nightmares, why we needed to track them down and put them down, the lions and tigers and bears, oh my, with their heads mounted on the wall and their genitals ground up to fuel the fires of our passion. When we've finally destroyed all these creatures, will we only be left with ourselves to hunt and capture?

Montauk Marine was busy with people buying fishing tackle, clothes, spare parts, and holiday sovereigns. Carl sat in his office behind a glass door and seemed to be expecting us. He was a big guy with a deep voice, a slow manner, and a kind way of handling people. He looked like a fisherman, talked like a fisherman, and walked like a fisherman – kinda slow and easy. He gave Frank a warm greeting like they knew each other, and Frank made introductions.

"From your call, it sounds like you fellas need some gear. Come with me," he said.

We passed through some swinging doors into the inner sanctum of the marine supply, past wooden bins loaded with shackles, pear-links, swivels and chain of all gauges, sail rigging and floats. In one bay all kinds of line hung from the rafters, from fine yacht braid to coarse manila, the spools running up to the ceiling and the fair-leads hanging down like colorful vines. We passed harpoon poles and fishing tackle of all types. Between two bins hung an old faded sepia-tone photo of a young man beside a huge swordfish. Ashley picked up on it before I did.

"Carl got a big one," he said softly over my shoulder.

In one vacant bay, a sheet of plywood lay on a couple of sawhorses loaded with the remnants of the 4th of July shop party: an open bottle of gin, smoked fish, barbecued chicken, limes and lemons, barbecued ribs, and bowls of potato salad all neatly arranged but half battered.

"There's a charter crew coming in soon, but they'd better hurry. Help yourselves." Carl gestured to the table. Then he plunged his arm deep into a fish barrel full of ice, caught a 6-pack of Bud and peeled one off for each of us. We popped the cans all at once. "Happy Fourth," he said, and smiled. It felt like home. He took a big gulp of Bud and wiped his mouth. "So what you catching out there this time, Frank?"

"Sharks again. We've only seen blue sharks so far," Frank replied seriously, "and bad weather. What's been coming in on the boats?"

Carl worked the table, sized up a slice of smoked bonito and went for it. "A couple guys got some good-sized makos last week. Big, Frank – 600 pounders. And you heard about the big white those guys got last May."

"Yes, Casey came down to get a look at it, and he sent me some photos. I was out in Baja at the time. They just stumbled upon it?"

"They were out getting squid and saw the fin. Got him on a hand line, 18 feet. Barely did in the davit getting him on board. Damnedest thing. So what can we do for you today besides fixin' the weather? You need some batteries."

"A couple of charged 24 volt marine batteries would do us fine, Carl."

"Follow me," he said, pointing his can of Bud towards our new direction.

We worked through another bay of electronic gear while I nursed my can of beer, feeling that cozy way I get in places like junk yards and libraries. Bobby, one of the mechanics, had the battery cabinet open, the lights on, and a cart ready. Carl had it all worked out. We discussed the specs of the boat's electrical system, our need to run the scientific equipment, and the size of the battery box; and soon we settled on the batteries we needed. You had to figure that these two guys had better places to be on this holiday than setting up some wayward sailors like us, but you also knew that they understood our position, carried empathy for the desperate soul, and expected nothing extra in return but a recognition that as fishermen we belonged to this fraternity of the sea.

Bobby tossed the batteries onto the cart and Carl added a case of Bud as we passed the picnic table. Outside, the fog seemed to be getting thicker, or maybe it was the darkness setting in. The marina lights set a yellow glow on the inhabitants as we meandered through the crowd of vacationers wandering about like dazed Christmas shoppers. I now had a purpose and a destiny: the *Bird of Passage* waited our return. We would set it right, go back out to do this thing, and come out the other side. I could feel it now, and wondered where Joni was.

Carl kept bumping into people he knew along the way, and by the time we got back to the *Bird,* we had seven guys down in the engine room, passing batteries, drinking beer and telling stories. There were tales of big fish and bad weather, cheating clients, big money from the city, and one guy who always showed up with a new girlfriend every charter and all he wanted the skipper to do was drive around the Sound all day while he romped with his girl down below. We laughed and drank, and the stories got better.

At one point, Ashley toasted the gang with, "We

colonial suppressors knew when to quit; you're all a bunch of scoundrels."

I managed to tell the story about the burning generator, minus the part about vomiting in the bilge. The fact that we all fit into the engine room seemed impossible, but the tight fit made it all the more fun, and by the time we finished the girls arrived with a load of fries and fried clams. The presence of women seemed to perk up the conversation as we sat on deck drinking and eating. Carl's laughter echoed up the gangway and attracted some other locals, and then more people kept arriving with more beer. One guy had a small cooler with oysters and cherrystones, and someone else produced fresh loaves of round home-baked bread. The boat next to us turned on its radio, and now we had a party with music – gravity began to set in. With the cancellation of the fireworks likely, this impromptu party started to gather steam, and I caught the look of concern on Frank's face. He corralled Jimbo into the wheelhouse, and I picked up the cue to join them. Meanwhile the girls were surrounded with admirers, like the proverbial flame surrounded by moths. Joni knew some of these guys, had fished with them tagging tuna a year back, and she loved talking fish.

"I hate to break up the party, but we need to move on. Let's check down below and make sure we got everyone off. I'll settle up with Carl. Jimbo get her warmed up."

Moments later, the loud beep of the diesel pre-start sounded, with the roar of the Gardner soon to follow. The signal caught everyone off guard, and there were a lot of surprised looks and disappointment, but then it seemed everyone got the message and they became all the more jovial. There were vows of devotion to the girls as we slipped off the dock, and calls of "Don't forget to write." The girls yelled back "Send me flowers" amidst the final farewell of "Good fishing" as we shoved off into the fog. Like the closing of a book, we were back together again, our happy crew heading out to sea with warm hearts and full bellies, a little tipsy, with the hopes and best wishes from our new comrades still fresh in our ears.

As we ghosted out of the shelter of the harbor, a southerly breeze rattled the halyards of the gilded yachts at anchor, some with barbecues ablaze and others with a lone couple snuggled under a blanket caressing a drink. The harbor was as crowded as a local bar on New Year's Eve. We passed the slips of the commercial fishermen, boats with the names *American Beauty*, *Alice Marie*, *Miss Julie*, and *4 Kids*. The crews were undoubtedly off celebrating with family, partying with friends, bitching about the fog, or shooting fireworks in the gravel parking lots, their kids running through the yards with sparklers among the floats, traps, and high-fliers. We stood on deck quietly listening, thinking about past Fourth of Julys, what our families were doing, what we did as kids, the parades and the picnics as the sounds of celebration receded behind us. Then the breeze stiffened, pushing the fog along as we passed the last inner harbor marker to round the bend into the Sound and the night, heading for deep water.

"This breeze may lift the fog," said Frank still holding a can of beer.

"We may see fireworks after all," said Ashley. "What a fine bunch of chaps. You had the feeling they'd take you home like a long lost brother. A great common denominator, the sea."

"You should consider yourself lucky they didn't string you up, Ashley," I said.

"Yes, right alongside the shark. What a prize."

"Where did you guys get the beer?" asked Ellie, somewhat puzzled. "I thought this was a dry cruise, Frank." She and Joni were seated on the forward deck finishing off the last of the oysters.

"It came with the batteries – today's special."

"We've got more oysters if anyone wants one," said Joni, holding up an oyster knife.

We joined them as they hunched over the basket, each of us taking a shot at an oyster, demonstrating a special technique or theory as to the best way to open the shell and with what tool.

I watched Joni as she worked the knife firmly but delicately into the hinge, talking to it gently like scolding a stubborn child, happy to free it open as she lifted it to her mouth, the slippery slab sliding across her tongue. She knew I was watching her and didn't care. Her eyes widened as she handed me the knife. "It's good," she said with a warm happy smile.

"You should use a towel in your left hand just in case."

"In case of what?" she challenged.

"In case you slobber on your face, then you have something to wipe it up with."

"Good recovery there, Calvin," added Ellie.

Frank muffled a laugh.

Then we sat quietly, looking at nothing but the late evening shroud of damp dark air, content with the settling of food and drink and the comforting feeling of the boat now being right and ready, knowing the next several days would be filled with hard work and little rest. The crew gradually drifted off to read, or sleep, leaving me and Joni alone in the dark. I didn't know what to say, so I didn't say anything; it just felt fine being there. Directly above, the air opened to reveal a half moon in a deep dark sky. The atmosphere around us looked impenetrable, but overhead the soup was thinning.

"Hey maybe they will be able to have the fireworks," she said hopefully.

"I couldn't get enough when I was a kid."

"Me neither, and I still like them, but you just don't get excited like when you were a kid. Why is that?"

"I think you live in the moment more when you're young. When you're older, it seems there's too much going on, too much to do. Life's gotten too complicated. It's like most people are either tied up in the past or else worrying about the future, making plans, wanting to be anywhere other than where they are." It was quiet for a moment, and then we looked at each other and laughed.

"Calvin, how is it lately that every time I have a couple

of beers we end up together."

"I like hanging out with drunks."

She gave me a big shove in the shoulder. "Thanks. You sure know how to make a girl feel better."

"You been feeling bad?"

She didn't say anything. We sat looking at the moon as wisps of low clouds scooted by and the moonlight cascaded down along the banks of the clouds to light up a path ahead. Behind us came the low deep rumbling of cannon fire in a slow melodic rhythm. We turned to see flashes in the clouds, muffled colors of red and yellow out of sync with the low rolling booms that followed.

"I'll bet the kids are happy," she said, her face lit up in the moon glow. "My dad and I used to watch together. Mom didn't like the crowds. We'd always have a family party on one of the Finger Lakes. My uncles played bocce and drank all day. We'd fish or go sailing."

"Sounds familiar."

"Every Fourth, we'd take a family picture, and my dad would always get one of me and my brother alone, wherever we wanted but usually at the same place each year. It's strange looking at those photographs now. One year when I was quite young, I told him that the natives believed the camera could capture a person's soul. He told me he wanted my heart and my soul. I can still remember that day; he was always patient and made it feel the moment carried some importance, that he really cared about the picture. You startled me when you said that the other day."

"Sorry," I said and kept quiet, sensing she was back there with her dad.

We watched the display until the big battering finale, when all we could discern were the low frequency booms, when the flashes became faint flickers like a battle in some distant land. You could imagine all the faces looking up into the night sky, the faces of young and old alike with the smiles of Independence Day.

13

That night I held watch with Jimbo and Ashley, discussing family picnics and barbecue recipes until morning. The day rose fair and warm, and by the time I stumbled out of the bunk to get some breakfast, Frank, Ellie, and Joni had already tagged a shark and we were in pursuit. Ashley and I jumped into our watch eager to "do what we came to do," as Jimbo put it.

"We chummed for about an hour after dawn and had plenty of sharks, all blues," explained Ellie, giving us the lowdown. "Joni fed a big blue four mackerel, and Frank stuck him, but he hung around for an hour waiting for more food.

"All blues?" asked Ashley.

"All blues and they acted hungry. They couldn't care less about getting close to the boat."

"Well then, maybe we'll get this one." He sighed.

Jimbo nodded. It looked like we were in the zone.

We tracked the fish all afternoon without a problem. The equipment worked well, and best of all, the batteries stayed fully charged. Ashley concluded that the batteries we replaced had weak or failing cells that would never allow them to accept a full charge. When a battery gets in that state, it can outright fail, go dead. We had made the right decision to do the refit in Montauk. Now we needed a little luck to stay with this fish and get it onboard. We thought things were looking good until Frank joined us in the house with a cup of soup in hand and a look of frustration.

"Not a favorable forecast, is it Frank?" said Jimbo, standing at the wheel looking out the window.

"There's another front coming our way tomorrow. It looks like we get beat up for a couple days, but after this one moves on, the Bermuda high sets up and we should have good weather for the last leg at least."

"Has Joni heard the forecast?" asked Ashley. "She's worried we won't get this one."

"We may have a good shot at it before the weather turns," said Frank.

We all agreed. "Hope for the best," Ashley said, setting the tone.

The afternoon sun lit up the surface of the water to a light cerulean blue-green with silver flashes. The seas were moderate and from the southwest, the air warm and finally feeling like summer. We tracked blue shark #80-2 along a line to the southwest through the afternoon. Frank relieved Jimbo for a spell, and we spent the time talking about boats, cooking, gardening, fish, and fishing. Some of these subjects I had little experience with and less interest – cooking for instance – but when Ashley and Frank went into detail about some of their favorite recipes for grilled striped bass or roast turkey, even stuffed flounder, I wanted to take notes.

We would pursue, stop, listen, count, drift, listen, count, write, listen, count, and pursue again, all as naturally as walking the dog around the neighborhood. At times, when there was no conversation, everyone seemed to drift off into their own world. After a count, I would dwell on some of my favorite sexual fantasies, only to get snapped back into reality for the next count. When you are tracking, it is like leading two lives. One is immersed in a technical world of electronics and calculation, recording the data, but the other life is allowed to roam around an open landscape of casual conversation and daydreaming. I found myself spending more time daydreaming about the woman who hand-fed sharks and felt something was happening but didn't know how much stock to place in my intuition. Joni was way out of my league; I wasn't even in the same franchise. She was playing for the majors and I was in the backyard with the wiffle ball bat. But I also knew that, when it came to women, one shouldn't even bother to try to figure out the situation. All I knew was that, whenever she was near, it felt electric, and needed to keep this to myself. Frank was sharper than the sharpest hook on deck, there would be no room for romance.

AT 18:00, ASHLEY and I relinquished our watch. Frank lowered the boom of the bad weather news on the girls, which changed their mood considerably. So I retreated to the stern with a Klondike Bar to rummage through my fishing tackle, which needed some attention, with the hope of constructing some newfangled big-game lures. Ashley soon joined me with a cup of tea and a handful of stoned wheat crackers.

"A bit late for tea." He sighed. "My god, it's lovely out here. I love this time of day, the break between late afternoon and evening." Even now, with the days getting warmer, he wore his cardigan sweater. He sat on an overturned five-gallon bucket, looking a proper gentleman, sipping his tea, beaming as he admired the world around us.

I liked Ashley. You could tell that he was probably the smartest guy in the room most of his life, but that intelligence was disguised by his boundless curiosity and childlike manner in observation. He was a quintessential man of books and research, of treks into the wilderness and lands of strange inhabitants, a far cry from the men I grew up around: all the hardworking scrapers-to-get-by with a beer in one hand and a butt in the other. People trapped by circumstance that seldom read a book and never lived anywhere else, never thought to do so. Men who fought the war and came home.

"My Lord, what is that?" said Ashley looking at my array of lures.

"Well, this is my custom tuna lure, although I've never caught or even seen a tuna. I whipped this up after doing some comprehensive reading."

"I think the fish might rather want to mate with that than eat it." He laughed.

"I have some custom trout flies also, but I didn't bring those."

"I miss trout fishing. I used to do quite a lot in Ireland with a college chum. We stayed with his mom, a fantastic cook. Good fishing there."

We talked of fishing as I tried to figure out how to set up my new tuna lure.

"So what makes Calvin so interested in science?" he asked with some curiosity in his tone. "Frank tells me you're an artist."

"I've been painting most of my life. My mother said it started with what I found in my diapers. A bit abstract at first but very expressionistic."

He laughed. "For some reason I get the feeling you are not dabbling in the typical Cape Cod venue."

"Inner landscapes, abstractions," I said, flattered that he would be interested. "They are like journeys to interesting places, and the paintings are historical documents of the journey. Some have more to do with philosophy, questions, and a line of inquiry that can only be answered visually, not with words or calculations."

"Line of inquiry?" he asked.

"Okay. Just to go a little deeper, I have a question for you, something I don't really have a solid answer to." He raised his eyebrows. "You walk into a museum and approach a painting. You witness this object, and then you walk away. What happens?"

He said nothing.

"Why do people do this, stare at paintings? Obviously there is a need to do this activity. After all, we build grand museums to house these works of art. Why? How do we change after witnessing these objects? Is it just culturally important to see them or is something else going on? If we change in some way after experiencing these works, how do we change? I mean music will transport me, inspire me, and it's just my damn eardrum vibrating. It vibrates all the time. Why does a certain vibration inspire me?"

"Hold on, Calvin." Ashley laughed. "My, you have been watching paint dry. But that is an interesting question."

"I feel that all artists drink from the same well. We just express the energy in different ways. This energy is a human expression, a human experience that can be transmitted to the viewer; it's not an intellectual transaction."

"Hmm, yes. Have you ever seen Van Gogh's self portraits?" he asked very solemnly.

"I have, at the MFA, and they blew me away."

"Me also. I knew they were supposed to be wonderful, but seeing them in person..."

"Yes. I always thought he was an important painter but smaller than his myth, and I felt that most of his work existed at a certain level. But his self portraits are beyond anything created by another human that I've ever witnessed. They were electric, and I became electrically charged while viewing them. I left the room and came back at least five times to see if what I was experiencing still held. Christ, he painted a couple of them on cardboard. He drank deep from the well."

"Unbelievable, indeed. I had to hold back the tears when I first saw them. I feel the same when listening to Beethoven's *9th Symphony*. I always make it a special occasion when I listen: no interruptions, late in the evening, alone. As you say, he too drank deep from the well."

Joni strolled out to check on us. "What are you two so intent on?" she asked with an inquisitive smile that indicated she had been watching us.

"Electricity, young lady!" Ashley spouted. "Now go track your shark."

After he shooed Joni away, he smiled. "Electricity, indeed," he repeated after Joni retreated to the wheelhouse. "A remarkable woman, that Joni."

"Yes, I've noticed."

"Artists have an eye for beauty."

"The eye yes, of the be-hold-her..."

"The beholder?" he suggested.

"Something like that."

"Well, where were we Calvin? Right, I think maybe everyone walks away with something different, but I always feel inspired and even hopeful after viewing an artist's work, in just knowing that people will pursue doing what they do as artists. God knows some of us do such dreadful things. And what greater feat can be done than to inspire another?"

"We drink the sweet water of inspiration. It falls like rain. From where, we are uncertain. By whose hands that wring the clouds, we know not. And when it will rain again, one can never tell. At times we walk the barren plain in search of the magic, and at other times it will descend upon us like locusts. It's a strange land to explore, but we love the strangeness."

Ashley smiled and nodded. "Ah Calvin, it's a life, a wonderful life. Lovely description, that. Even scientists travel that road, wandering into the unknown. Long lonely nights in the lab, searching, often stumbling upon things as you said."

We had a lot to talk about, but the world all of a sudden seemed so big that to talk anymore felt pointless. It was enough to just sit there and think about the great pool of inspiration and the many that came to drink from the well. So we sat quietly and shared the big wide world together. I wanted to ask him more because it wasn't often I had a chance to engage in a discussion with such a man, but didn't. He seemed content sitting there, watching the water, drinking his tea, when suddenly he stood up and slowly walked to the stern.

"What? Calvin, come see."

At the rail he pointed past the line of water running from the wake of the boat. A good-sized fish was swimming alongside, then we spotted another, and as our eyes focused to just below the surface, we could see a school of bluefish swimming in the same direction.

"Bluefish!" Ashley yelled.

Frank poked his head out of the house. "Ashley, dinner!" he yelled back.

I rushed for my pole, rigged up an 8 oz. popper and cast out ahead on the port side. Wham! At least three fish hit it at once as others swirled. I set the hook, the fish jumped – off he went. Now the trick was to land him while under way, to get him in before he got behind us, but that wasn't going to happen. My next option was to hold on to him until we got to the next station when the boat would stop. But that wasn't going to happen either. The line kept creeping out even with the drag set tighter. It was a good sized blue but it got way behind us, and we couldn't ask Frank to stop for a fish while in pursuit

"You're losing all your line Calvin," said Ashley.

It was a lost cause. I grabbed some slack, wrapped it around the stern cleat, and snap, off it went.

"Shit! Lost the fish and the line."

"This is maddening," said Ashley, staring out at the school. "They won't be here long."

We searched for another alternative, a net, anything. Hanging on the back of the house was a large coil of heavy green monofilament line, which was strong but I wouldn't be able to haul that in by hand – it would slice me up. The winch, I could do a couple wraps around it and crank the fish in. With a steal leader looped in the mono, I snapped on another popper, told Ashley to stand back, and swung the thing over my head like Roy Rogers. Ashley laughed as the plug hit the water 20 feet out. I let it trail a little, snapping it along the surface, and wham, another blue was on. The line ran out through my hands hot and fast before getting two wraps around the mizzen winch, where I cranked with my right hand, slowly bringing the fish in, trying not to horse the hook out, and got the fish alongside where Ashley was ready with the gaff. With one hearty jab he hit the fish and in a wink we had a ten-pound blue flopping on the deck. In no time we caught two more and ended the excitement with a hardy handshake and applause from the crew.

"Fresh fish tonight, Calvin. Good job," he said, all smiles. "Good job, son. You dress them out and I'll go prepare the galley."

The blues lay gasping on the deck until I dispatched each one with a hearty blow on the head and a cut across the spinal cord. I then scaled and cleaned each one and wondered why the school was this far offshore. Were they following bait, were they migrating? They move off to deeper water during the heavy heat of summer, but then again we weren't near Cape Cod when the fishing gets stale in July. I cut the fillets, examined the stomach contents like a good sharktracker and found remnants of what appeared to be Menhaden, along with one squid beak. The reddish purple fillets would become our dinner, the carcasses went to the chum bucket where the large heads bobbed on the surface of the foul smelling brew, their vacant black eyes watched from a distant afterlife, with resentment or understanding, it was hard to tell. I closed the lid and wished them well.

bluefish

14

Bluefish are one of the marvels of the sea. I relish eating them and love pursuing them because they are one of the most exciting of the smaller game fish to catch. A blue will fight aggressively, jump and tail-walk across the water, run and run again. It is strong, aggressive, and its teeth can chomp a herring in half, leaving as clean a cut as a butcher's knife.

My first encounter with this fish was, by its nature, memorable. This happened in the days when WHOI celebrated every Friday evening with an open TGIF party at the old Fenno Estate, before the lawyers took all the fun out of partying, when you could drink and drive and not fear imprisonment if you got caught, back when life was simpler. On this particular evening, by the time I arrived, TGIF was in full swing. My friend Brody stood behind the bar as usual, dispensing beers drawn from a couple of kegs in the kitchen area. All types of characters attended these events, but there was never any type of class distinction, the senior scientists laughed it up with the welders and dock crew, the administration mucky-mucks could be found in heated discussion with the copy people. And the topics would be work-related or not: raising chickens, what causes rolling thunder, raising children, some new submersible, raising hell in South Africa, or why the beer tasted so good. It was a tightly knit family of scientists and support staff that appeared to understand the importance of each other's role in making their world turn. Brody had two beers in hand, one for me, and his "half full" as he would say, as he fended off women and took orders for more beers before things closed down at 7 p.m. At that time he would holler out above the din of conversation, "Drink up, you slobs," to the moans and protests of the gathering.

"What's shaking brother?"

"Could you spare a farthing for a widow's son?"

"How about one of these frosty ones? Hey, there's a party over at Wuthering Heights, but I've got a better plan." Brody always had something cooking, and if the big plan didn't work out, we would end up at the Port-O-Call playing pool until closing.

"Logan's been hitting the blues out in the Hole, and he's got some pogies. We are to meet him at 7:30 by the bridge."

"Sounds like a plan," I said, wondering what a pogie was. Although I'd been living on the Cape for two years, I had yet to do any saltwater fishing, and now my chance had arrived.

"We should get some beer," I said, thinking of priorities.

"Logan's got it covered."

Later, as we drove into Woods Hole, the air piled up into a blanket of gray fog. I had envisioned an evening's boat ride with the sun setting across the blue horizon, the wind in our hair as we hissed across the twilight laughing at the moon. Now it looked more like a scene from the Hound of the Baskervilles.

"This blows. I'll need a jacket."

"Logan's got something."

By the time we got to the WHOI parking lot, the fog had condensed into a layer so thick you almost had to wave your arms to get through it. I lost Brody before we crossed the bridge. The only way we found Logan was by honing in on the loud laughter coming from the general direction we were heading. He and his pal Looney sat in a whaler tied up at the Eel Pond Bridge, each with a beer in hand, immersed in some story about some cruise in some godforsaken sea. They were laughing about some guy the ship forgot in some port and had to go back and rescue. They were pissed, as the English say, and didn't acknowledge our arrival for the first couple minutes, after which they realized – with much fanfare – that we'd finally arrived. Logan and I had met before, but not Looney, who greeted me like a long-lost brother and acted like he knew a lot about me.

"Calvin, we finally meet. Where's your camera, 'cause hey, ain't this a pretty picture?"

"It's a little thick, isn't it?"

"Here. Have one of these. The alcohol thins the blood and helps you see through it."

He handed me a cold Foster's Lager, a big blue and gold can from one of the large coolers on the bow. One cooler had beer and the other had what appeared to be some big fish fillets. In the stern sat a barrel half full with seawater, a hose draining over the side, and the dark shapes of a good dozen herring huddled in the bottom. Before I could get the beer open, Logan had the outboard fired up and off we went into the soup.

Now, normally, the idea of running out into open water in a small boat in dense fog as night approaches would trouble me, especially given my past experiences in Woods Hole Passage, plus the fact this channel runs right next to the Steamship Authority where huge ferryboats regularly come and go. But somehow I felt this umbrella of security being in the company of oceanographers, world travelers, seasoned journeymen of the seven seas with salt in their veins – or maybe it was just the beer.

You couldn't see a damn thing. My three companions were immersed in a story about some fateful cruise in the Indian Ocean, laughing and drinking. Logan was at the wheel and didn't seem to be paying much attention to anything outside of the story and the can of beer nuts Brody had placed before him on the console. It was cold and damp, but soon the Fosters applied a layer of sensory neoprene around me, calming any remaining concerns about self preservation until the loud blast of a fog horn called out from beyond. This was no toot of a fishing boat horn. Something big was headed our way with the mother of all fog horns, and whoever it was could see our little radar blip and called out again to get out of the way.

"He's comin' up on ya, Logan," commented Looney,

as if it was some kind of challenge.

"We're out far enough."

"Yeah, well he's coming," repeated Looney.

Now I could hear the heavy repeated beat of the ferry's engine coming closer, the hollow thumping noise that transmits through water. The ferry seemed very close, and then the blast of the horn came almost right over us.

"Punch it, Logan!" yelled Looney.

Logan's right hand casually removed itself from the can of beer to bury the throttle. The Whaler leaped out of the water as if it was as scared as I, when on the port side a huge dark gray shape passed as big as a city block, horn blasting.

"Holy shit, that looks big," squeaked Brody as if he'd never seen a ferry before. "Gee, Logan, have another one."

"He was out too far. The tide's running east so he can get right up to the channel. I heard him coming. See? Here's the marker."

Out of nowhere the first red nun of the channel appeared. It was leaning a good 10 degrees towards us, quietly standing vigil for the mariners foolhardy enough to venture out on an evening such as this. The goose bumps that ran up my spine were beginning to ease, and I thought maybe another beer might calm me down. By the time I got one open, Looney had the poles rigged and ready.

"It's getting low over the ledge. Let's try Grassy Island."

Looney grunted in agreement as the Whaler took a hard turn to the left, although I couldn't see a thing through the mist on my eyelashes. After our lives had been spared from a collision with the ferryboat, my companions' business-as-usual attitude now gave me a sense of relief. We finally reached the spot, and as Logan throttled down, Loony passed out the poles. Then he netted a herring for each of us, passing out the wiggling fish like he did the cans of beer, each with a belch. That's when the realization hit me that I didn't have a clue what to do. Most of the freshwater fish I caught in the past would be the size of the bait I was about to attach to my line, which now had two hooks dangling from it. Brody stood next to me, and so I followed his lead. First he passed a hook through the forward dorsal part, and the second hook went through the tail, leaving the fish to hang in the proper manner, mouth open and gasping, its tail waving but getting nowhere.

"Go get' em," he said as he dropped the herring in close to the boat, peeling out a good 20 feet of line.

Following the same procedure my herring acted pretty feisty once it got back into the water, it had the pull of a good sized pickerel. This is when I started to think about what we were trying to catch. I had heard about big blues and bass, but up to this point, the biggest fish I'd ever been attached to was a 22-inch pickerel up at Uncle Bill's camp.

Logan killed the engine, and all was quiet except for the sound of Loony peeing off the side and the rush of water through the outcropping of rocks that we now drifted past.

"Christ, where the hell are we?" I thought.

We all had a line in and everyone became very serious. There was no more conversation, no more drinking.

"If they're here, they're here," said Logan softly.

Looney began humming some ancient chant to call forth the finned creatures, while Brody stared off into the fog, mentally connected to his herring swimming amongst the rocks below.

I reviewed my strategy: "Keep the drag light, let it run, tighten the drag, set the hook." This sounded like the right plan.

We stood there like commuters waiting for a train. These guys knew it was coming; their heads cocked listening for the fish to strike. "Fish!" Looney got a hit first. Then my pole took a lunge downward and stopped. I thought Brody had grabbed it, but he had moved to the other side of the boat. As I slowly lifted the pole back up parallel to the surface, it throbbed with two big heavy tugs, and then the line screamed out a good 30 feet and stopped.

"Whoa!"

"Calvin's got one on," said Brody. And then, "Oh,

yeah!" He'd hooked up too.

Looney also had one on fighting off the stern. Things were get a little too crazy so Logan pulled his line out to man the boat and avoid entanglement. I slowly reeled in, wondering what happened to this train that just took off with my line and found the herring in two pieces, a little part of the head and a little part of the tail, both parts hanging from their hooks. The middle section was cleanly chomped off like it was cut with a knife.

"Whoa, Calvin got a tweener." Brody laughed.

He had moved to the bow still fighting his fish, which looked like it had no intention of getting into the boat. Loony, in the stern, just hoisted his in, this whapping fish with heavy lips and triangular teeth and big slate blue eyes. The fish was strong and flopped aggressively on the deck until Loony bent over to whack it on the head with a tiny baseball bat. Brody landed his after a good five minute fight, a smaller fish but with a big attitude, leaving me surprised that such a fish could give a grown man such a battle.

"Calvin, ya get one?" called Loony from the stern as he bent over the fish with a fillet knife, cutting its head to let the blood run out. I held up my pole with the two pieces dangling. "Hah, he got ya." He laughed. "Put that back in – ya might catch two."

All I could think was, "Man this isn't trout fishing."

"Nun coming up!" called Loony, as out of the darkening world a tall coned shaped figure approached close to the boat. We all stood there watching it pass, we were out of the channel now and would be drifting into the sound. Then, as if on cue, Brody's head went down into the opened cooler.

"Who needs one?" he yelled as if someone lived in that little box down two floors in a lower apartment, and without a reply from anyone, four more beers came out to waiting hands. "Let's go get some more," he said, and off we went, back up the channel, feeling our way through the dark, the fog, and the alcohol.

I was thinking, "Hell, I could get into this."

We fished until it was too dark to see, the glow of lights from Woods Hole completely obscured. Logan caught one more, and Brody hooked up but lost the fish at the boat. Loony dressed his fish and said he had enough for the weekend and his smoker. I fished seriously after seeing what could be pulling at the other end of the line and came away skunked but impressed with the magnitude of the fight these fish gave, and also by the enthusiastic pursuit of my companions. After another drift, we crept back to Woods Hole as wet as rats. I was shivering and fantasizing about a glass of sherry and a big bowl of chili nestled between two slabs of warm bread. That's what I wished for, but instead ended up with my inebriated friend insisting the night was still a pup and we needed to seize the moment. We said our goodbyes at the stone wall by the bridge, each of us with a wrapped fillet in hand, watching the two oceanographers disappear into the night to haul the boat down at the town landing.

"Do you think they'll make it?"

"If Logan has his way, they'll head to Robinsons Hole and keep fishing."

"Those two are nuts. You know that."

"Yeah, yeah. Me too. Me too."

Unsure as to the amount of beer he had consumed, I could usually get a reading by Brody's navigational abilities once on dry land. In the parking lot, he walked as if one leg was six inches shorter than the other, making it easy to walk in circles but difficult to get back to the Land Cruiser. It didn't seem to faze him though – at least he wasn't crawling – but as he said, the night was still a pup.

"Let's play some pool and get a pizza," he murmured, lighting a cigarette.

"I could go for a big bowl of chili right about now."

"Where the hell you gonna get that?"

"Right there, at the Fishmongers."

"Never been in the place."

"You've lived here for years, work in town, and never been in there?"

He didn't answer. He acted like it was a dumb question.

"Well, I'm shivering my nuggies off. Let's go, but turn on the heat."

We climbed into the Land Cruiser to head off to our next adventure, but first he had to remember where he hid the keys. He finally realized they were in his shirt pocket but not until after he rummaged through the stash box between the seats, pulling out a flashlight, shackles, nylon twine, an old birthday card with writing on the back, bottle caps, hose clamps, coins from distant lands with holes in the center, and a postcard from Panama.

"I forgot how much cool stuff I had in here," he mused.

"Can we go? Can you cut the crap and quit this archaeological dig? You got the keys, so let's go."

"Right. Where we going?"

"Pizza and pool. Pizza first!"

"Roger that, good buddy."

And off we went, tearing up the road back to Falmouth. We smelled of fish and beer, wet, chilled and driving to endanger. Young, stupid, and happy to have gotten out on the water, I remembered thinking yet one more time, "Hell, I could get into this."

15

By evening, the wind picked up as predicted by Captain Jimbo, blowing up steady from the southwest and whipping the seas to white caps, snappy waves building four to six feet. The waves ruined our dinner and promised a rough night to follow. We assembled in the wheelhouse as night fell, and I could feel the nausea coming on strong.

"A couple days of this, and then summer is going to slide right in." Jimbo tried to pick up our spirits. It was obvious that Frank and Joni were getting frustrated with the weather, and if conditions continued as forecast, there would be no way we could get our shark.

"Joni and I have talked it over and we think it best to track this shark until midnight and then head in. We can turn around the stores and crew and be back out for the weather window, maybe stay out ten days or longer."

No one protested. As darkness fell it seemed that the night watch lay huge and insurmountable and the idea of quitting the fish at midnight seemed like a blessing. I could wallow in my seasickness on the cushions, helping Jimbo when needed, check the engine every couple hours, and maybe get a few nods. Joni didn't say anything the whole time. She and Ellie were in pursuit mode, tracking in earnest. When she was on a shark, her mannerisms changed. She became more carnivorous, cat-like, listening, sensing and calculating. She moved differently too, slowly, with purpose. She and Ellie made a tight team and didn't even have to speak when in pursuit. Ellie would point with her hand, first directly forward then in the direction of the hydrophone. She would do this twice. Joni would listen, and then she'd direct Jimbo on the course heading: "Ten degrees to port." That simple.

Jimbo would make the turn and reply, "Ten degrees to

port."

Between counts, Joni would often be recording data or adding notes to her journal. This night she seemed far away, maybe swimming with that shark, trying to figure out why these creatures do what they do. I couldn't tell exactly where her mind was at, but she was writing a lot.

Ashley and I decided to get a couple hours shuteye before our watch at midnight, and we retreated to the foldout bunks in the galley. The bunk situation evolved in a strange way. There were plenty of bunks onboard, but as it turned out, our watch shared the bunks with the 6-12 team; or in ship terms, we were hot-bunking. The situation worked out this way for a number of reasons. First, attempting to sleep forward in the bow cabin was extremely difficult in bad weather. The bow would lift up and smash down into a trough, causing the would-be sleeper to get airborne, and so we stowed a fair amount of the gear forward. The next cabin was given to the pilot, a courtesy, to have a little privacy from the scientific crew. Frank had the after suite in the stern, which was also loaded with gear, leaving the two foldout bunks in the galley area usable for the trackers. As it turned out, Ashley swapped with Ellie and I swapped with Joni.

At first the procedure was formal and polite, but as the cruise progressed and we got to know each other a little better, it became more casual, at least with Joni. In the beginning the bunk would be totally stripped of everything but the mattress. Even the life vest she used to prop up the outside of the bedding would be put away. Gradually though, more and more stuff would be left behind: a comb, a flannel shirt, her flashlight. This evening, as I fell into bed hoping to read a bit before sleep, I noticed she had left a tee shirt, a used one, right up by the headboard. If a guy had done this I would have been offended. Who wants to crawl into bed with a smelly tee shirt? But this was different. If anything, it smelled pleasant, sweet, and distinct, and it left me wondering if this had been planted on purpose or if I was reading too much into it. Joni was no dummy. If anything, she was complicated, focused and intelligent, and she knew how animals worked. The aroma trickled in – her scent and I couldn't help but get the feeling she had left it there as a sign of intimacy or as a tease. Unsure, I neatly folded it and left it on the pillow when it was time to change the watch.

Ashley, Jimbo, and I made the shift change at midnight, after Frank swung her around to the northwest. The girls listened until the signal faded and finally disappeared. Joni made some recordings and said good night. Frank stayed up until after two and then he turned in. Around four a.m. it started to rain with a bright array of lightening flashes on our path to the north.

"Hey mon, someone's getting a poundin'," said Jimbo, leaning towards the cabin window looking up at the ceiling of clouds.

Ashley mused, "Jamaican born, eh Captain?"

"Yes, sir. Jamaican born. Sorry, I let it slip, my native tongue, sometimes." There was a long pause. "Yes, sir.'" Jimbo laughed.

"You miss your home?" Ashley asked.

"Yes and no. Everyone is gone. Everything has changed." And he left it at that.

In the dark of night, alone with men I hardly knew, the moment felt very personal. The man next to me, born into a different culture so distant from my own, sounded sad when he said, "Everything has changed."

Ashley read in the corner of the wheelhouse with his flashlight as he sipped tea, immersed in a scientific journal on fish farming in China. I slumped on the bench and tried to keep the watch happy with coffee, tea, late night treats of warm muffins or bread. Jimbo appreciated the gesture and his morale lifted, probably with the prospect of going home.

"You would make a fine steward, young man."

"Thanks Jimbo, but I'm good for frying eggs and that's about it."

"You care. You show caring."

"Just doing my part."

"A good steward can make a happy ship. It's the little things that touch people."

It was difficult to see his expression in the dimly lit wheelhouse, but you could tell by the tone of his voice that he wanted to talk. This was a bit odd because up to this point during the cruise he had been either brooding over the weather or stoically manning the wheel. A flash of lightning lit up the cabin with an impressive thunderclap close on its heels.

"Close, close, close," Jimbo sang. Far off a deep rumble echoed towards us. The boat felt very small.

"This will pass. This will pass and you will have pleasant skies. You will see."

"I sure hope so, Jimbo."

"You will see. If there is one thing I know, it is weather."

Another rumble of thunder rolled towards us followed by an impressive boom.

"Rolling, rolling – he is rolling the big balls tonight."

"It sounds angry out there."

"I know weather. In Jamaica the weather can come, can blow you away, these storms with the names of women." He took a slug of coffee and continued. "One such woman took my grandfather away when I was just a boy. He was a fisherman, he disappeared. I waited by the sea day after day, rode my bike to the shore waiting for his little boat to return. *Poinciana,* his boat, his pretty red boat. He never came back, never came back. Her name was Hazel."

We were quiet for a time after hearing the story of the lost grandfather. The three of us weathered the rest of the night with little conversation as we made our headway north, harassed by the electrical discharges of supernatural bolts and diffused blankets of light. The dawn came on gray and depressing, raining like the days after Noah got the call from the Almighty. This would be my second time coming home, and it surprised me how the sense of time became distorted after only two weeks at sea because it felt I had been doing this seafaring thing for a long time. Events and people on land seemed distant and very far away.

As the morning light prevailed, I reviewed the previous night's records. The shark had been traveling to the south-southeast for most of the track, moving in the typical up and down pattern we had seen with the previous shark. The notes in the log book were scribed in the perfect handwriting of a hand strictly instructed in penmanship at a parochial school and initialed JK – Joni Kelley. She sure got the hook in me. The more I tried to stop thinking about her, the less I could. It was becoming a bother; she was in my head most of the time. It was best not to dwell on it, to stay focused on the project and get the job done. She would return to Monterey after the trip anyway and I could go back to playing wiffle ball in the backyard.

Next to the logbook rested one of her hair bands. I picked it up, stretching the elastic over my fingers, studying it, smelling it. Ashley chuckled. I shrugged my shoulders, threw my hands up, and sat next to him.

"They sure are fascinating creatures."

"Are you referring to sharks or women?" He smiled.

"Both," I replied diplomatically.

"Ah Calvin, there are forces at work that are out of our control, or so say the bushmen. Our meeting and passing has changed both of our lives. Maybe this entire expedition has been arranged just so you and I would meet, arranged so that, upon this meeting, the track of your life or mine leads now down a new road. Or we could get struck by lightning right now and all meet our demise."

Jimbo caught some of this and slowly turned his head towards us and scowled as a deep rumble of thunder rolled above.

Ashley spoke the words of the shaman, the seer, and the prophet offering stories of the African tribe that lives by the river and throws their spears into the water blindly, per chance to stab a fish – if the gods so decide. They have survived this way for centuries. He spoke of the polar bear hunters that can foretell the approach of a great storm and get dug in before it hits, and of homing pigeons' innate ability to return home despite all attempts to foil their navigation, and of dogs who anticipate their master's return, and of the way a school of fish moves in unison with no apparent communication.

"There are things afoot, forces we have yet to understand," he mused.

Jimbo turned to us, "And Bob's your uncle!"

Ashley gave a hearty laugh. "And Bob's your uncle!"

WE HIT WOODS HOLE by early Sunday afternoon. The rain came down in sheets as the wind pushed us across Vineyard Sound, which looked desolate and forlorn for early July. A lone figure stood on the pier beside his red pickup, dressed in yellow foul weather gear as still as a figurehead. Jimbo brought the *Bird* up along the dock as I threw the line to the trusted hands of Richards.

"Good trip, Frank?" he yelled down, barely audible above the battering rain.

"Yes and no," Frank answered with a smile from under his hood. "Could you throw down a little sunshine?"

"You'll have to wait until tomorrow. You headed back out?"

Frank nodded. "We'll turn around for tomorrow noon, but we have to round up a new pilot and crew."

Richards waved, got back into his truck and drove off. You got the feeling by the words not said that he understood how things can go wrong and it's better to ask questions later. We made the boat secure, and then it was time to say our goodbyes to Jimbo and Ashley, which went quickly because of the rain. I realized the possibility of ever seeing either one of these guys again would be remote, which saddened me because I had grown fond of Ashley. Just watching him and hearing him talk became an amusement on the trip – I'd never met anyone like him. Up on the pier, we said so long to Jimbo, who wished us plenty of sunshine, fair winds and a cold beer if ever we met on the streets of Woods Hole or Montauk. Ashley struggled up the wet ladder and waved goodbye to the crew as

I helped with his bag. We shook hands.

"You're a good sod, Calvin. You've the soul of an artist. That's why I love Frank. He's an artist at heart, a renaissance man. You will learn a lot from him."

I didn't know what to say. "Ashley I never met anyone like you. I hope we get to do this again."

"That would be rather nice. It has been pleasant." Holding my hand, he cocked his head to the side and smiled. "She's a special bird, Calvin. Take good care of her."

He smiled, turned and walked towards the gate, his shape transparent in the rain as he wandered out into the streets of the world like some wizard of old spreading the words of the wise. I stood on the dock at the end of another chapter in this story I couldn't put down, wondering what he meant about the special bird.

Back onboard, Frank watched the rain fall across Great Harbor. "I love Ashley. He's just like a little kid."

"He couldn't come on the next leg?"

"He's off to Africa for a month to visit his brother, an anthropologist. What a team."

"He didn't see much action."

"He knows what to expect. Sometimes there is lots of action and sometime none at all."

The girls emerged from below deck carrying several milk crates and a couple bags of garbage. "We're off, Frank. We'll load up. See you in the morning?"

"I'll be here early. If Beetle shows up tonight, set him up or tell him to call me and I'll pick him up. I've got to round up our pilot at the fisheries in the morning."

"I'll toss that stuff up to you, Ellie," I volunteered.

Joni brought up some bags that looked like laundry. "You want to come shopping with us?" she asked.

"I'll stick with Frank and check things out." The rain came down harder.

"This is supposed to stop and clear," she said.

"You guys staying onboard tonight?" We were both hollering to be heard.

"We'll bring you back some cookies."

"I like sweet things."

She gave me a look.

"And I like sour things."

She climbed the ladder.

"I like hot things too."

At the top of the ladder, she turned. "Good bye, Calvin. I'll bring you back something special."

Frank gathered some of his belongings and waited on deck. "I've got to go home and see my kids. There's more to do here, but I have to go."

"I'll get everything checked out below and clean up the deck."

In the distance, thunder rumbled across the bay. Frank turned his head to the heavens and the rain splattered off his forehead and ran into his eyes and dripped in rivulets from his beard. I thought he would swear, but he sighed. "Maybe Beetle will bring us some luck." He smiled at me. "This wind will die down. Next trip, good weather," he said hopefully. "You should go home and get off this boat."

"My dog is staying at a friend's house up the Cape, and I'll just get tied up with nonsense. I could stay in town with someone, but I'll stick with the boat, fend off any pirates."

"My brother is due to arrive, sometime today or tomorrow. He's delivering a yacht to the Vineyard. I hope he makes it. He's good with everything. Put him to work."

"Roger that, Frank."

He looked about the boat one more time. "Okay, I'm off." And he climbed the ladder and walked away.

OVER THE NEXT COUPLE of hours, I worked diligently sorting things out in each room, organizing gear, making sure everything was in the right box and secure. I thoroughly inspected each system in the engine room, the belts, hoses, cables, fluid levels, the stuffing box, the controls under the console, running lights – anything that could cause trouble on the next leg. The most crucial item consisted of corrosion on some of the fuses in the buss under the console and some rusty adjustment screws on the Gardner's alternator bracket. By the time I emerged from the engine room after making things right, the rain had stopped and the clouds had thinned enough to see the ball of the sun. Above the western horizon, a clear band of blue sky stretched from north to south, the air felt warm and heavy, like summer had finally arrived.

With a cold-cut sandwich in hand, I sat on deck watching the colorful evening rise with the sunset. It seemed the change in weather drew people out of their holes as tourists could be seen walking the streets of Woods Hole, mariners were coming in on their inflatable from the sailboats anchored in Great Harbor, locals were rowing out in their dories to catch the end of day, and heading out in skiffs to fish the passage. Gradually the sun emerged from the clouds with a blazing vengeance casting an orange radiance across the landscape.

A car door slammed, and I turned to see Joni standing on the pier gazing out at the spectacle, her auburn hair glowed in the evening sunlight like a vision. She waved and smiled and seemed happy to see me. We quickly unloaded the supplies and spent the next half hour putting things away. The girls were excited, especially Joni.

"Gee, Calvin. You're really living it up eating a sandwich after a week at sea," she said joking with me.

"We're hitting the town, dinner at the Kidd."

"Dinner and dancing." Joni motioned with a twist of her body.

"Where you going dancing in Woods Hole?" I asked.

"We'll find a party."

"We'll make a party," Ellie corrected. "I get the shower first."

They were all fired up for a night on the town, and that sounded like a pretty good idea. As a young man, I wasted so much time sitting in bars, hanging out staring into space waiting for something to happen, that it harbored some personal guilt. But now a night on the town sounded exciting, that and the chance of spending some time with Joni. The prospect of a romance developing seemed slim, but to be alone with her, to walk the quiet streets of town would be enough. While Ellie showered, Joni was in the forward cabin making a lot of noise with some shopping bags. Then she jumped into the shower, Ellie dressed and then joined me at the galley table.

"So, you're coming with us to dinner?" she asked with an amused look on her face. I couldn't tell if it was a question or a demand.

"I didn't know I was invited."

"Calvin, you're part of the team. We stick together. We're shipmates. You have to come."

"You don't have to twist my arm."

"I kind of figured that." She laughed.

It felt like I was missing something, and for the first time, we spoke as individuals rather than workmates. The work persona lifted, it felt a bit awkward at first, we both felt it, and then it was okay. I gave her a questioning look.

"Joni's been really down for quite a while. I mean depression. We talk a lot on the phone. She's had a bad couple months, well a bad six months really. I was worried. She was hoping this trip would turn things around."

"Well, we got two sharks and we're bound to get some more next trip. I bet we'll get one back for sure," I said reassuringly.

"I'm not talking about fish, Calvin," she scolded. "Joni is one of my best friends, and this is the best spirits she's been in for some time. So let's have fun tonight."

"Best friends?"

"Yes, best friends." She could see something in my expression. "What?"

"I just lost mine."

"To what?"

"Heart failure."

"What?"

"Yeah. Dead at 31 years old."

"Jesus, Calvin. When did this happen?"

"Weeks ago."

She said nothing.

"He's been with me. I'm glad I'm here."

She reached out and took my hand. "Let's have fun tonight."

Joni was out of the shower now and getting dressed.

"Are you ready yet, Miss Kelley?" Ellie yelled. "Calvin, as strange as this may seem to you, Joni really wants you to join us tonight. Who knows? Look, I'm really happy we're all together. Just, you know, be engaging."

"Engaging? Okay, that should be easy," I thought.

Ellie gave me the raised eyebrows look just as Joni came out, and she caught us both by surprise. She looked stunning, her hair pulled back and face a little done up, wearing a new summer dress as vibrant as a bouquet of flowers. We both said it together.

"Wow!"

"You like it?" she asked coyly, her smile suggesting she did not feel self conscious in the least.

The first words that came to me were, "Sweet Jesus." But I kept them to myself. "Well, Joni. We'll have to beat off the men of Woods Hole with sticks and clubs."

"I'm not overdressed, am I?"

Ellie and I both shook our heads and smiled. She really was a beauty.

DINNER WAS A BUST. We had to wait at the bar in the Kidd for a half hour before getting a table, and while there, some pals of Ellie's joined us, visiting scientists at MBL who were very polite and very intelligent but very boring. These were academic types utterly immersed in their profession, the kind who enjoy hearing themselves speak. The loud one, Andre, paid no interest to me once he realized that my role on the team was as deckhand, and he put the moves on Joni. She behaved politely, drank too much, and in no time the situation became irritating and was not what we had planned. Andre couldn't hold his wine, and the situation started to get messy. Even his companion had enough after several loud outbursts.

The girls kept eyeing each other, obviously wanting out. Joni leaned over and whispered in my ear.

"Let's get out of here." Her voice felt intimate and arousing despite the circumstances.

We paid up, and once outside, we ditched Andre and friend, making some excuse about other plans, and decided to try the Lee Side. The locals would be much more entertaining.

On the crowded streets of the village, tourists roamed about in shorts and tee shirts, some dressed for the nicer restaurants. It was getting late, and soon the streets would clear and the bars would be full. The wind had pushed in some warm moist summer air that felt refreshing. I could have easily walked around town, gone to the quiet places like Stony Beach or Penzance Point, but felt it would have been presumptuous and we couldn't just ditch Ellie.

The Lee Side came on like a carnival. Everyone seemed in high spirits, and several people actually appeared happy to see me. The place was packed so we took a position close to the bar where a couple of friends came over to get a status report on the "expedition" and to check out the new talent. In fact, walking in with two new women caught some attention, and suddenly I was Mr. Popular.

"Heard there was a fire at sea or something? You don't look burned to me," Harry said right off, exaggerating with his eyes bugging out, his long beard hanging down to his chest and his baseball cap pulled down tight. "No, really. Nobody got hurt, did they?"

"No one got hurt."

Otto had been talking to me also, he had just returned from Penikese Island, but the place was so loud I couldn't hear a thing he was saying. I did note however the whole time he spoke to me he was checking out the girls. Then Tripper came over with an open potato chip bag and made an offer with his spacey grin. Being familiar with the routine, I looked in to see the bag half full with psychedelic mushrooms.

"No thanks, Tripper. I am on the job."

"I can see that," he said as he eyed the girls.

He offered the bag to Ellie, who declined, and I'm sure she had no idea what the contents were. She had Nick on her ear unfolding his life story, and the more I got acclimated, the more the bar seemed electric. Half the place appeared to be tripping, and someone had the music cranked up higher than I've ever heard before. Pete the roofer sat at the bar talking to himself, which wasn't unusual, except tonight he seemed happy about it. Turk had his dog Bell lying at his feet, a dog as big as a polar bear, its tongue hanging out and lapping up the beer his master would occasionally spill on the floor for him. Some of the commercial fishermen had a couple of tables pulled together, piled with more beer bottles than a redemption center. Irene and Natalie came over to meet my new friends.

After downing two beers between stories, I corralled Joni, who looked distracted and overwhelmed. Ellie appeared to be getting a buzz on with Nick. She rolled her eyes and I nodded in acknowledgement: "You got that right. Watch out. Big-time mover." It's funny how you can say so much with a wink and a nod. Avoiding further entanglement, I motioned to Joni in hopes of making a break for it. She had been talking with Irene, laughing; I had to yell into her ear. She smelled like the first day in May.

"Let's go for a walk."

By the look in her eyes, she was more than ready to leave, but when we got to the door, I remembered Ellie.

"She's a big girl," Joni said and kept me moving.

Outside, the contrast startled us. The quiet of the night stood warm and heavy as the world suddenly slowed down. Across the street, the steamship ferries gently creaked in their berths like giant breathing buildings slowly rising up then sighing down and the further we walked from the bar, the better the night felt.

"Wow that was crazy in there. Everyone was really cranked up," she said, surprised.

"Everyone was really cranked up," I repeated and laughed.

She stopped, and rubbed her forehead. "I drank too much, or drank too fast. I need to sit down for a minute, Calvin."

"Let's go over here." I took her hand by instinct and she gave it a squeeze as she stumbled onto the road.

We walked down Luscomb Street and crossed to the Naushon ferry parking lot and stepped over the chain, our footsteps crunching across the gravel parking lot behind the house as we approached the short pier for the little island ferry. The place was abandoned and quiet. We sat on the bench under the pier's roof in the lee of the huge steamship ferry pier, where the harbor water lay still and black.

"I come here sometimes when I need to get away from the maddening crowd."

"I drank too much wine at dinner."

"We can sit here until you feel better."

"Christ. Do people here always party like that?"

"It's worse in the winter. Did Nick hit on you?"

"He hadn't been talking to me for two minutes before he told me he wanted to get into my pants."

"What did you say?"

"I told him there was one asshole in there already and he went back to hit on Ellie."

I laughed out loud. "Welcome to Woods Hole."

The crazy energy of the bar melted away as the magic of still water surrounded us. In the darkness, a black-crowned night heron croaked overhead, the water lapped against the dock pilings, and the tide slid slowly towards Vineyard Sound.

"It's nice here, Calvin," she said in a strangely distant voice. Then she turned to me and whispered into my ear. "Is this where you put the moves on me?" She laughed.

I looked at her, half aroused but surprised by her taunt.

She moved closer. "Is this where you bring your girls after a few drinks – it's so romantic." Something nasty was unfolding. "Come on, Calvin. Put the moves on me." It was more of a challenge than a tease, and I didn't know what to do. Caught off guard, with this dark side, she continued. She whispered again into my ear. "Kiss me, Calvin."

I started to move, but she quickly swung around, sat on my lap, and started kissing me wildly. "Come on, Calvin, my artist lover. Come on, kiss me."

Her mouth was warm and wet with the smell of wine and heaven. Her tongue searched and found mine. I tried to keep up.

"Come on. Touch me. Feel me." Her mouth ran over my face.

Buried in the fragrance of her hair, I reached for her breasts, and she stopped suddenly and got up.

My heart raced, trying to catch my breath. She walked slowly across the dock with her arms outstretched, spinning in a slow uneasy pirouette. She was humming, "Calvin, come and get me. Don't you want me?"

She twirled there tauntingly. I wanted to smack her and rip her dress off, fuck her like she was some drunken tramp dog bitch right there on the dock. Fuck her until her knees bled while my hands twisted her long beautiful summer hair. I could feel my anger coming on and had to hold it back. It always felt like some 18 wheel tractor trailer rig barreling down the road with a cargo load of rage I'd been carrying my whole life and all I had to do was to put out my thumb to catch a ride and make a delivery to some poor asshole who was in the wrong place at the wrong time. I was timid about a number of things but it was my anger that I feared most, what I might do some day. It wasn't meant for this woman, not Joni, if anything I needed to get closer to her, but this wasn't right. She meandered about humming before me as she turned. I let out a slow measured breath.

"Don't play with me," I said firmly. "Just because I don't know my way around a boat doesn't mean I don't know my way around a woman."

"Is that so?" she sang in her taunting voice.

I waited and said nothing, letting her play this game

a bit longer, allowing my pulse to drop and my aggression to settle.

"Yes, that is so, Doctor Kelley."

She stopped cold, and the two of us faced each other. She reflected for a moment and returned to sit next to me. Neither one of us spoke for a long time, but in the quiet we seemed to find common ground as we sat there listening to the sounds of the town and the harbor. In the distance, the laughter from the bar would find us, but we listened for other things.

After a while, she said in a sincere voice, "My dad would take me out at night when I was a kid and teach me to listen. He would ask me all the things I could hear. We would sit in the dark together, listening."

"Where is he now?"

"Can you hear the mockingbird? It's way off."

The drone of a distant fishing vessel faded in with the sounds of traffic on Water Street. Somewhere, rigging slapped against a metal mast like the frantic ringing of a bell. The water lapped along the seawall, and I could hear her breathing as I struggled to filter out the extraneous noise. Through it all, the chatter of the mockingbird reached out.

"Yeah, I can hear it, in waves. It fades but comes back."

She looked at me. "I'm sorry I did that. I get a little crazy sometimes."

"I like crazy, but I don't like playing games."

"I don't like games either, not those kinds of games. It's been a while since I've been with someone... I... I've been busy, working."

"Christ, Joni. You could have any man you want."

She said nothing but looked away.

"Hey, look at me."

She turned but said nothing. She took my hand and caressed it like she held a newly found stone and was deciding whether or not to bring it home. I waited.

"Do you want to head back?"

She said nothing but held my hand. We sat like that for a long time, listening, and it felt like I had always been there by her side, like I had been walking in some kind of dream before this and finally awakened. She was working out something in her head, trying to hold it back, not wanting to let it come to the surface.

She spoke very softly. "Put your other arm around me. Hold me."

She moved her back against me with both my arms around her, my chin at the back of her head. I could feel her body become stiff as the tears fell across my arm, a sprinkle at first, and then she began to tremble and cry. It passed quickly. She moaned a bit, and then she started to laugh, wiping away the tears. She turned to face me, laughing and crying, her cheeks wet, totally vulnerable, her arms around me, I held her like I'd never let go.

"Boy, I didn't expect that to happen," she said in my ear, sounding embarrassed.

"Do you want to talk about it?"

She pulled back to look at me, arresting her sighs, collecting herself, the strong Joni returning between the self-conscious laughs. She kept looking at me, wondering, wrestling with doubt.

"No, I don't want to talk about it."

"Being a little drunk doesn't help the wounds of the psyche."

"I feel a little better now, just sitting here."

"We could walk."

"Okay, let's walk."

We meandered through the quiet streets of town with the gravity of the evening pulling us along the road to Nobska Beach. We talked about growing up, schools, travel and music. She liked jazz and folk, watched a lot of Hitchcock, read fiction, believed in a higher power and loved dogs. While majoring in marine science at the University of Miami, she experienced her first shark encounter while on a vacation dive off the Bahamas. A couple of years later, she started working with Frank. He was hesitant at first and said he couldn't offer to pay her, and accommodations were primitive at best, but she stayed on while doing her thesis. They tracked fish in Hawaii, off Baja, Nova Scotia, and along the east coast, sometimes sleeping in the fish hold, sometimes not sleeping for days. She loved working with Frank and considered him her mentor.

Between conversations, we would fall into a long silence. It just seemed she needed time to be with someone who could listen. On the shore road under the canopy of trees, we approached the beach where the sky opened up suddenly to reveal a summer celestial spectacle, the stars shining almost as brightly as the lighthouse on the far end of the road. We were captivated by the scene and stopped to gaze at the heavens. I couldn't tell what Joni was thinking but I began to feel this was some kind of pilgrimage of love. We stepped off the road onto the soft warm sand as a white line of waves washed the edge of the beach with a seductive hiss. The only other sound came from a channel bell-buoy rolling in the night sea.

"This is beautiful, Calvin," she said, kicking off her sandals. "Look at the stars." We gazed upon the waters of light. She stepped out into the waves. "It's warm!" she shouted, slowly wading up to her knees.

I stood watching her dress become part of the waves, her hair flowing, her arms reaching out to touch the water. It was one of those moments when everything else seems to drop away. I felt terribly alive.

She turned from the water, ran up to me laughing and began to strip. "Come on, Calvin," she said, pulling her dress over her head. "Come on, let's swim." She tossed the dress on the sand and stepped out of her panties to suddenly stand naked before me like an apparition. In the starlight, with the faint flash of the lighthouse beam traveling across the landscape of her body, she was the loveliest woman I'd ever seen.

"Come on," she said, imploring softly.

My clothes came off without thinking. I could tell she was smiling, giggling while I stumbled to remove my clothing, and then we were both standing there naked before the world. She reached out, took my hand and together we walked into the sea.

The rush of the cool water, the taste, and smell, the stark darkness of the water and the beautiful white body close to mine overwhelmed me so I couldn't stop laughing. We both laughed uncontrollably as we went deeper and began to swim.

"Oh Calvin, isn't this wonderful!"

It was truly full of wonder. Her naked proximity overshadowed the other natural wonders, and to be swimming at night under the stars in this continuous unfolding adventure approached an epiphany. I swam to her and grabbed her around the waist, barely able to touch bottom.

"I can't touch," she said.

"Sure you can. I'll let you."

She laughed. "That's not what I meant."

We both laughed. I hugged her closer.

"Hmm, you're warm," she said softly.

She lifted her legs around my waist. Her breasts were firm, her nipples hard against my chest. Our mouths met in a long wet kiss.

"Take a deep breath," she whispered. "Take a deep breath and let go."

Our mouths met again as my legs lifted off solid ground. Holding on to each other, we twirled in the darkness, our tongues wrapped and played like creatures of the sea, finding each other in a dance as old as life itself while flashes of phosphorescence swirled about as we tumbled weightless and numb with passion. My heart was pounding and my lungs running out of oxygen. Feeling disoriented in the darkness and lack of air, Joni calmly pressed on my stomach, expelling bubbles, and then took my head in both hands and breathed into my mouth, into my lungs, and she kissed me more. I couldn't tell up from down and floated weightless in the throes of ecstasy, my blood raced with electricity but my wind was giving out when she gently let go and pulled me back to the surface. Gasping for air, swallowing a little water, I tried to get my bearings but couldn't hold her and tread water at the same time.

"Joni, Christ."

"What?"

"My God, Joni… I think I feel like…"

"What?"

"A fish."

"Really!"

"Oh yeah, like I'm swimming upstream and need to spawn."

She laughed and kissed me once more. "Sorry, wrong season for spawning," she said, and gently pulled away.

"Not for me."

Swimming off, she laughed again. "You'd better watch out. Some fish might bite that thing off."

With a twinkle, she dove and disappeared leaving me alone in the dark sea, treading water, somewhat timid after seeing so many fins, I gave chase as the night quickly swallowed my body heat and began to shiver. The water sobered us both, and by the time I caught up with her, the burden of our responsibilities beckoned as we headed to shore.

"We need to get back, Calvin."

"I know, but it's too hard to leave."

"It doesn't look hard anymore." She laughed. "You're shivering, Calvin."

We stopped at the water's edge. Caressing in the breaking waves, we kissed again.

"We need to get back. Ellie will stay up worrying about me."

I wanted to remember the shape of her body, the curve of her hips, and smell and taste of her skin. My hands ran down her neck, across the V of her chest and over the curve of her breasts. She watched as I touched her, feeling my hands searching and returning.

"Can I trust you, Calvin?"

"No one will know what happened this night?"

She pulled me closer. "But can I trust you?"

"You can trust me."

We hugged once more, not a lovers' hug but more that

of friends, the caress of finding a lost loved one.

Heading back to the boat along deserted Water Street, I think we were both wondering how this evening would change things. I now harbored a deep grounded feeling of hope, for what I couldn't say. My life had taken a sudden turn and the world now felt full of possibility, but I could only see as far as the next trip and then she would be gone.

Back at the boat, Ellie looked frazzled and relieved. She could tell that Joni had been through something that something had happened. They hugged, and then Ellie went into the series of crazy events that ensued after we left the bar. First, she ended up at a dance party on Park Street where half the crowd went off to the beach for some nude swimming. She swam with her clothes on, and on their way back, she and some others took a detour to come back to the boat, but one of the girls, the beautiful Laura, as she was called, decided to go for a swim with the seals in the tank at MBL. None of the guys would go in, afraid the seals might bite off something important, but the beautiful Laura had a grand time and didn't want to leave. Finally, after much coaxing, and convincing her that it was a crime to kidnap a marine mammal, they all ended up back at the boat for a last drink, where Ellie nearly had to beat Nick off with a harpoon pole. She finally got rid of him by tossing a cup of chum juice on him and threatened more if he didn't remove himself from the vessel. He went away quickly and in disgust, swearing and cursing, calling her the foulest names.

"That chum is really bad. He'll have to burn those clothes. Man, people in this town strip naked in a wink of an eye," she said, astounded. "Before we left the Lee Side, there was a guy crawling naked down the bar. Naked!"

"I love Woods Hole," I laughed.

We ended the night with a cup of tea and lemon, and then Joni and Ellie retired to the forward cabin, talking and laughing. It was good to hear them laugh. Tomorrow we would head out on our last leg, and as I listened to their voices in the dark of night, I wondered how this would turn out, and couldn't see a happy ending. The hands that twisted the fairleads of our fate, tying this lovers' knot, would they get it right?

The *Bird of Passage* rocked gently at its berth. Tomorrow we would head out to the bitter end of this line on the chart, beyond the horizon to the blue water of the canyons.

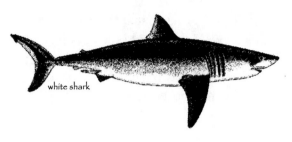

white shark

LEG III

Pursuit and Passage

16

The wind blew steady and hard from the southwest all morning, giving the Sound a silvery metallic look. It promised to be a rough ride out.

"Looks like a good blow all day."

"Christ, not another one," Frank muttered as we made ready.

"But after this lies down, it should be like a day at the beach."

Our new pilot arrived, and he seemed straight from Malibu. The Fisheries couldn't spare a NOAA pilot but found this guy, who was licensed and had good recommendations. His main line of work dealt with piloting one of the SEA schooners on their education forays to the Caribbean. He certainly looked the part – tall, handsome, well-tanned, a solid build, beard, stylish sun-glasses, Teva sandals – he was full of bravado and full of himself. I disliked him from the start.

Before we even left the dock, he had acquired a nickname: California Joe. Frank appeared just as irritated with him. He behaved as if we were lucky to have him onboard; now that Joe had arrived everything would be alright.

Frank and I reviewed the checklist before departure. He crossed things off the list, speaking aloud as he went. "Bar stock, stainless hardware, duct tape, quarter-inch nylon line, gulf stream charts, food supplies. You guys brought enough food to last a month."

He was reviewing the food list when Ellie poked her head down from above. "Frank, where did we get this guy?"

"He's from California. He can't help it," I replied.

"You want to get some more bait going?" she asked.

"Pull out a couple pallets to thaw."

"I can cut bait on the way out," I offered.

With this wind, I'd be battling seasickness, and cutting bait somehow seemed to help. Each morning I prayed for good weather. If there was a patron saint for fair winds his plastic figurine would hang from my neck.

Frank left the list for a moment. "No sign of Beetle? He was probably up all night and then had to catch the ferry from the Vineyard." He looked at his watch. "We'll wait until noon."

We made the boat shipshape, double checking everything. While in the engine room, giving it one last check, Joe graced me with his presence.

"So, how's this baby running?" he asked, patting the big diesel.

"We had a few problems with the generator and batteries, but we've got things ironed out."

"I've never seen a Gardner before. It sure is big. Is this English?"

"It's a good mill, has a solid feel to it, like it wants to work for you."

"Jabsco pumps," he said flatly.

"Excuse me?"

"Jabsco pumps. Does she have Jabsco pumps?"

"I have no idea."

"You have to watch out for those Jabsco pumps."

"Okay." I replied and wondered why they needed to be watched when he leaned over the big diesel.

"Man you've got a four-cylinder auxiliary?"

"It's a 110 generator with a prop."

"No way. Holy shit, this is quite the rig."

When he leaned over he managed to get some grease on his hand from the throttle linkage. He looked at his hand as if this was an insult to his mother.

"Okay. Just keep her running." He hurriedly walked out carrying his hand before him.

"I doubt we'll ever see him down here again," I thought. "All the better."

Frank looked in from the aft doorway. "How we looking?"

"Good, Frank. Everything's buttoned down."

"Check with Joni and Ellie to see if anything else is outstanding."

I doubted that would be the case with those two. They were working on a couple chocolate Klondike bars while discussing the bait situation on the stern.

"They're all boxy like," Ellie pointed out. "Like a fish bar."

Some of the bait had been squished into the corner of the box and their thin bodies frozen into a hard right angle.

"Would make a good frozen fish sandwich," I suggested.

As we considered this, our new pilot seemed to feel left out. "Hey, any more of those Klondike bars?" he asked in a tone that insinuated that one of us, preferably one of the girls, should rush right down to the galley to get him one.

We all looked at each other, thinking again, "Who is this guy?"

"Ellie, give me your wrapper," I said in a hushed voice.

I broke apart one of the boxy mackerel from a clump in the fish tote, knelt at the cutting board, and prepared a nicely sliced, squared-off piece of frozen fish, and wrapped it in the foil wrapper. It looked perfect.

"I'll go get some more," Ellie yelled back.

We were laughing. "Maybe it wouldn't be such a long trip with this guy after all." Then a voice came from above.

"Ahoy, down there. Is Frank onboard?" A bearded fellow with duffle bag and baseball cap waved to Frank.

"Late, as usual. We were just about ready to leave," Frank yelled back.

"You mean, if I stopped for an ice cream, I could have saved myself from a week of abuse with my brother. I'm going back for some ice cream." He laughed.

"We'll come too," said Joni.

"Sounds like a mutiny is brewing, Frank."

"Just get down here." Frank smiled.

"Aye, aye, Captain." He tossed his bag over his shoulder and down the ladder he came.

"Are you yachting or did you come to work?" asked Frank as they shook hands.

"Glad to see you still have a crew. I expected it would only be the two of us heading out by now. How much are you paying these people?"

They went at each other like this a little longer before embracing, and then introductions went around. From the cabin came a loud scream of disgust as new pilot walked out carrying his foil wrapped treat and threw it over the side.

"That's not right," he said, revolted.

"I hope that's not the cook," said Beetle in a hushed voice.

"That's our new pilot."

"He can't help it. He's from California," whispered Ellie.

This seemed an adequate explanation for Beetle, who didn't wait for further details but went below to stow his gear.

Minutes later, the *Bird* came to life, spewing diesel exhaust from her portside, pumping water out, chugging and belching as we made our final preparations. The lines were made free from the dock as Joe leaned the *Bird* into the wind and out toward the mouth of Great Harbor. The WHOI dock was alive with loading activity with the crew of the *Oceanus* making ready for a long cruise due to depart the next morning.

As we crept along the dock a forklift truck loaded with a large spool of acoustic wire scooted along beside us, then stopped with the typical squeaking of dusty brakes. Richards waved from his seat for a brief moment, then popped the clutch to steer the truck in the direction of a loading gang on the other end of the pier. We all waved back, the *Bird of Passage* was off again.

The crew hung out in the wheelhouse until we passed Gay Head, and then everyone slowly filtered out to settle in for the long ride. Ellie and Joni went below to read, Frank and Beetle retired to the stern suite to catch up on things. The wind was still blowing about 20 knots, so by the time we left Vineyard Sound the waves had a good pitch to them. It was either the onset of nausea or Joe's continual humming of *Hotel California* that made me realize I needed to stay close to fresh air. With a half stack of saltines, I situated myself on a milk crate behind the wall of the wheelhouse and prepared for another rodeo ride. The day was brilliant, with puffy clouds and a steady breeze – a perfect day for sailing. Buzzards Bay showed stacks of white triangles as far as the eye could see. The air had finally gathered that warm, dense summer feeling, and it was obvious that the next couple of weeks could be scorchers.

I sat there all afternoon, sometimes leaning against the wall wallowing in discomfort as the boat heaved up and down, heading into the wind while we crawled our way south. The spray covered the deck and the wake streamed out from the hull to slap the waves throwing water into the air. The wind would whisper and hiss as the sea foam passed, with the voices of angels barely audible speaking the words of the ancient mariners. I listened with my new sense of the sea as the land line grew fainter and eventually vanished.

SEVERAL YEARS EARLIER I found myself in the galley cabin of one of the local Fisheries boats, drunk and disorderly with the ship's cook. He came from the Bahamas, loved his job, missed his country, missed his family, and talked of the sea. He spoke of angels and the voices of his forefathers, voices from the land and sea and wind. "The voices speak of the ones who traveled before and sing the song of the sea," he said. "The song that begins somewhere in your head and slowly brings you, if you allow it, to a place deeper. You sing the song of the sea because that is from where you came, the sea in your mother's belly, floating, listening to the voices muffled but familiar, not knowing what they mean but knowing the meaning by the way they sound." We sat in the dimly lit galley smoking a joint, each with a coffee mug half full of rum before us. "We have gills in the womb, swimming in that internal sea, breathing underwater, yet we have evolved into this creature that looks upon the world as something other than ourselves. The sea runs in our veins, the water from the sea falls from the heavens upon the fields of life, turning the rivers into torrents, the veins twisting across the body of the earth. We draw the water to our lips, cool and sacred, the gift of life. The voices of the sea will speak to you if you listen. You must go to sea, my friend."

His story recalled the notion I had as a child – having a guardian angel – and I wondered if he still watched over me. I would talk to this angel as a child, and ask why he chose me. Was he still there after all these years?

THE WAVES PASSED in our wake like the wheels of our endeavors fashioned so by forces beyond our comprehension.

"I thought you may have made a run for it. I didn't see you below," Beetle said, now standing next to me. "Not that Frank wouldn't turn the boat around and go after you."

"I feel better sitting back here."

"Well, it looks like Captain California knows what he's doing. At least he can read a compass and he hasn't hit anything."

He walked over to inspect the chum bucket, removed the lid, quickly closed it again and laughed. "Good God, that's really some chum you got there."

"It's been brewing for a few days."

"We're going to get all kinds of nasty critters with that stuff. Can you imagine if that spilled on deck?"

"You'd have to burn the decking."

"It would probably peal the paint."

"Ellie had a romantic encounter the other night and had to throw some on the guy to get him to leave," I said.

He just stared at me. "She threw some of that on someone? Remind me not to piss her off." He untied a milk crate from the bundle and sat next to me. "This is nice back here."

The wind dropped slowly during the afternoon but the seas took a while to follow. Beetle sat with me while I brought him up to date on the previous legs. He had a comfortable familiar feel to him, maybe because he was Frank's brother. He resembled Frank in some respects, a bit shorter but broader with a big chest, with a heavy beard and a warm smile.

"Frank worked out the watch schedule. You, me, and Joe are on the 12 to 6 watch. That's what you ran before."

"I imagine you've counted beeps previously."

He laughed. "I have beeps going off in my head for days after some of these trips. Frank says the gear is working out well."

"We had some problems with the boat, but the tracking gear is working fine."

"Well we won't have to listen to beeps tonight, nothing but *Hotel California.*"

"I think I'd rather listen to the beeps."

At 6 o'clock we made the shift change. Frank and the girls shared dinner, while we relieved Joe from his duties. He seemed a little miffed that he had to share his watch with us rather than with the girls. I decided to leave what happened the previous night with Joni back on the beach, and managed to get a little sleep. By eleven, I was up again, checking on the engine room and putting down enough coffee to help withstand an all-nighter with nothing to do but keep Joe company and stay on course.

As the night progressed, Beetle and I seemed to

have the same outlook on how to get through it. First we got into playing with the light sticks and made some glow stick sculptures with wire and duct tape. Then we shot a roll of film holding the shutter open and performed all kinds of antics with the sticks, drawing in the dark, spinning them in tight circles, causing the green light to form a fluorescent doughnut in the dark cabin. Eventually Beetle cut one open and spread the liquid over his hands, holding them up illuminated in the night, ghoulish looking. I couldn't imagine what the pictures might look like.

We studied the navigation chart for over a hour, speculating where the sharks would be, as if I had any idea. But we worked off our imagination and the Gulf Stream charts, calculating the location of warm core eddies that spun off of the northern edge of the Stream. We compared older charts to see how the eddies traveled to the southwest to be later sucked back into the Stream, the edge of the eddy forming a radical temperature gradient with the surrounding water. Our destination was Hudson Canyon, one of the many indentations along the line of the continental shelf. It was the largest geological feature on the chart, deeply carved into the landscape, a remnant from the ice ages when the shelf was once dry land and the Hudson River flowed out another 100 miles from its present shore. The features on the map looked like something taken from the Grand Canyon, it looked mysterious and dark, if there were truly monsters from the deep, this is where we would find them.

Beetle told stories of former trips with Frank, of working off the Carolinas, Georges Bank, and Nova Scotia, and of a place called the Tuna Ranch where large bluefin tuna were held in pens. He pointed to locations along the chart where they had worked years earlier and talked about what had happened there.

Joe would attempt to change the conversation whenever there was a long enough pause, hoping to start a new exchange that would eventually involve him. At first we were polite and would listen to his stories about surfing at

Mavericks, partying with movie people, or cruising for chicks at Venice Beach – everything centered on California and of course Joe. Around three in the morning, Beetle went below to make some coffee.

"I like mine dark, no sugar," Joe clearly specified to Beetle. "You know, if you go into Dunkin Doughnuts and ask for coffee with a little cream, or a tiny bit of cream, or not too light they always put in two pumps of cream. What you have to do is tell them 'coffee dark,' and then they get it right."

This seemed like one of Joe's life lessons, and he was letting me in on it. All I could muster was a good "Really!"

"So what's the story with the girls?" he asked.

"What do you mean?"

"Joni's nice to look at. She with anybody?"

"She's with Ellie."

There was a long pause.

"Christ, they're not gay are they?"

"Not gay," I said, amused.

"Sometimes you get lucky. What you do is work things out on the trip so by the time you get in you've laid all the ground work. It's hard being discreet on a small boat. But you can do it."

"I'm sure you can, Joe."

"Gives you something to think about on these long trips."

It remained quiet for a bit, and I could tell Joe was thinking about his strategy with the girls when Beetle returned with the coffee.

After a while we just ignored him, allowing him to go on about his former west coast lifestyle, and we would stay on course with whatever we talked about. Eventually, he got the hint. By morning we had established our boundaries. We would remain civil but uninterested and restrained. Joe was okay, it was just that he was Joe and it couldn't be helped.

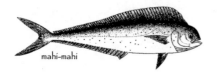

mahi-mahi

17

The morning burst open with a clear soft blue sky. The wind had dropped to a gentle breeze, and a feeling of grandness to the day made me want to stay on deck and not turn in at the end of the watch. Joni and Ellie caught that same fever as soon as they got on deck, and we sat together in the cockpit watching the day unfold. The sea had turned from the drab green of the shelf water to a tropical cerulean blue, clear and lovely. Joni looked excited. We were in a new land and could sense a great notion that things were about to happen, and we were there to see that they did. She gave me a warm smile.

"I love this water," she said.

"I've never seen anything like it."

"It's clear all the way to the Caribbean."

"It's magic. Now I know why Sergeant went down there."

"And Homer, his watercolors, and the guy on the shipwreck with the sharks circling the boat – what a story," she said.

"*The Gulf Stream*. I have a photo of that painting on the wall in my studio."

"People got so upset about that painting he had to paint one where the guy got rescued," added Beetle. "There was a watercolor show of his work at the Met a couple years back."

"Sergeant did those murals with the mythic figures, too graphic, too decorative," added Ellie.

"He was a portrait painter. That's how he made his living. It got so he hated portraits."

"I'd like to see Homer paint a picture of this morning."

"How about *Breezing Up*, the kids in the beetle cat?"

"We had a print of that in our dining room when I was growing up. That's how I got my name," said Beetle.

"I thought it had to do with bugs," I said, kidding.

"My parents had a bassinet built like a little cat boat. All the kids went through it. My cousins, the neighbors, hung it from the rafters in our house. Give it a push and you rocked away, and my grandfather built me a fort out of an old cat boat a friend was trying to get rid of. He set it up in our backyard and we played on that for years. It had sails and a rudder."

"That is so cool," said Ellie.

"By the time I turned 11, he figured I was ready for the real thing and gave me his old twelve and a half. It leaked, but I sailed that thing for years. My parents couldn't keep me out of it."

Frank had joined us while Beetle told his story. "It kept him out of jail, Father used to say."

"Yeah, I was the black sheep of the family. I was into boats and motorcycles, while Frank hung around the science club."

Frank laughed. "I think you worked on motorcycles more than you drove them."

"I had this old Indian…" Beetle stopped short, stood and pointed. "Look, a fin!"

He pointed off the port bow about 70 yards. The dark shape broke the shine of the surface, a large triangular fin rounded at the top. Ellie made for the mast, scooting up like a monkey on a palm tree, while we stood silently watching. It went down momentarily but surfaced again. Frank motioned to Joe and pointed with his finger to the port side. The *Bird* slowly turned, and as we lined up to pass ahead of the shark Frank aligned his hand forward. Joe stopped the turn to continue on course.

"Hammerhead! A big one!" Ellie called down from her perch. She stood on the yardarm, holding onto the mast and the outer stay. "He's a beauty."

We passed within 30 feet of the shark, its body clearly visible in the crystal water. It turned upon our approach and went down slowly.

Frank turned to me. "You could have hit that from this distance." He said it more like a question. Joni and Beetle waited for my answer.

"Yeah, it looked like a clean shot," I replied, but wanted to add that I had never shot a harpoon rifle before while standing on a moving object at something underwater with all that weird refraction to deal with.

"If it stays like this, we'll get one," Joni smiled.

"We'll get twelve," Beetle added.

THAT MORNING I managed to sleep for a couple of hours, but the excitement got the better of me. It was difficult to sleep with the morning sun bouncing around the cabin like a searching spotlight, invariably finding my eyes. The day was hotter and summer was now bearing down upon us full throttle. The heavy summer air cushioned my short interval of sleep that morning while a strange and distinct dream came upon me. A line or path rose up into the sky like the high arch of a roller-coaster falling somewhere unseen. The line drew itself up and up and finally leveled off, then descended in a graceful curve beyond. The line was a rope and I was attached to it, not so much literally but it meant something, possessed a heaviness to its meaning.

Troubled with the strangeness of dreams and the inability to sleep I joined the others on deck to find we were still a couple of hours off station. The girls looked happy working with the hand line tackle on the stern, making leaders and attaching them to gangion lines. Frank was at the wheel.

"We've seen fish all morning, tuna and several sharks," Ellie said with excitement.

"Schools of bait, a lot of fish working the surface," noted Joni in her scientific mode.

She sat crossed legged on the deck with a pile of 3/16th stainless steel cable on her lap. Behind her, the water had flattened out to a plain of gentle low rolling swells. The brightness of the sun gave the day the overexposed look of an old Kodachrome slide. If anything broke the surface you could spot it a mile away. The color of our wake looked like we had traveled to the Bahamas; the water looked so clear, and blue, like what dreams are made of.

"Calvin, take over for me, will you?" Frank asked from the wheelhouse. "I need to call Casey."

"Don't crash into anything," cautioned Joni.

In the house, Frank gave up the wheel. "You know what you're doing. Keep her at 1-7-0." He went below to connect to the mainland through the marine operator.

Ahead of me lay the vast expanse of horizon, the sky, and the metallic shine on an ocean we had all to ourselves. The *Bird* chugged along with a slight pull to starboard, I corrected, feeling the weight of the hull respond with the turn of the wheel back to 1-7-0. It felt good standing there, like being the master of my own vessel and I could easily imagine cruising across the Atlantic, island hopping in the Caribbean, a solo crossing alone in a storm at night so far away from normal living it seemed forgotten, sailing with Joni on this boat heading for Bermuda, jumping from port to port, passing our days in the sun, catching the rain for water, eating fish just taken, making love under the stars in the middle of nowhere. My imagination would always get the better of me.

The line of the horizon stretched so far you sensed the curvature of the earth, the tectonic plates of liquid and atmosphere merged. No longer did the sea leap up, reaching to become the other, the sky, nor did the winds whip and churn the surface in a torment. The gods of the sea and wind smiled upon us. The prophet of the fish-tracker bid us, "Go now and cast thy nets and the sea shall be bountiful." On a day like today, anything seemed possible. "And God saw that it was good." I smiled, "Thanks my friend."

The girls finished working on the stern. Ellie took her position up the mast to watch for fish, and Joni came in the wheelhouse to sit with me. "You look good behind the wheel."

"I feel like this thing needs a stick shift. You know, to

pop it into a higher gear."

We could hear Frank on the radio with his colleague Casey. He was giving details about the weather and the fish sightings, he sounded positive and upbeat. Joni checked the chart after getting the 11 o'clock Loran readings. We had another hour before we'd be on station north of Hudson Canyon west of the rim of the closest eddy.

"What's up with these eddies?" I asked.

Beetle appeared on deck with Joe soon to follow. At first they both walked around like they'd been blinded by a nuclear blast, shielding their eyes, almost stumbling into things the sun was so bright.

"Wow, Frank wasn't kidding when he said endless sun-filled days." Beetle laughed.

"Oh no, the ship's mechanic is at the wheel – prepare to abandon ship," said Joe as he sat next to Joni. "We're not there yet? You should bump it up a notch, Calvin. I calculated we'd be on station by noon."

"Aye, aye, Captain," I replied, trying to sound humorous and pushed the throttle up to 3,000 RPMs.

"Calvin, just floor it. Let's get this thing up on a plane," yelled Beetle, countering Joe's authority.

We waited for Joe's next jab when Ellie shouted from her perch. "Whales! Two whales about a mile off the port side."

Joni got out there first, followed by Beetle and Joe.

"Two whales, Frank," I hollered down to his cabin.

He came up casually and went out on deck. Joe seemed the most excited about the whales, which appeared as two dark shapes blowing spray off to the east, the spray sparkling as it shot into the air.

"Oh, we have to go see them," said Joe. "What kind?" he yelled to Ellie.

"Big ones," she yelled back. "They look like humpbacks."

"Oh, wow. Humpbacks."

He looked at Frank, who said nothing but watched as

the whales disappeared again. Then Joe realized that Frank had no intention of going whale watching, and he drifted to the stern with his binoculars, gazing at the dark shapes that broke the glassy surface.

Frank and Joni came back into the house. "How's she handling?" he asked.

"She steers like an Oldsmobile with a flat tire."

"Good. Stay on course. I'm going to work with Beetle on some things."

"Joni's giving me an education," I said.

"You're in good hands."

After Frank and Beetle went below, Joni came over and stood next to me. "Frank likes you," she said. "He doesn't take too many people. I've worked with him long enough to appreciate that. He'll be civil to people, but he likes you."

I tried to make light of the fact that this meant a great deal. "How about you?"

"You have to get me drunk first." She laughed.

"Okay, then. When we get in, I'm running off for a bottle of champagne."

She gave me a good jab in the ribs as Joe walked in from the stern.

"I'm not intruding, am I?" he said with a smart tone. "It's noon, Calvin. I'll take over."

Relinquishing the wheel to Joe, who had to comment once again about the fact that we were not on station and insinuated that somehow my piloting had something to do with that. Then he began a monologue about his past life in Maui. Joni stuck around for the oration. I couldn't tell if she was being polite or whether she was really interested. Needing some air, I joined Ellie in her perch.

This was the first time I ventured up the mast, and once there, realized why she liked it so much. You were away from the boat but still connected, and the view was phenomenal. With the sway of the boat exaggerated tenfold, I would be able to stand it only on a day like today.

"I saw a pod of dolphins way off a couple of minutes

ago." She pointed toward the starboard horizon. "You'll see all kinds of things. I stopped calling down unless it's something important."

She stood on the spreader holding on to a line tied around the mast and the outer spreader cable, and once situated and comfortable in my position on the opposite spreader, I began to look around. "Wow!"

Ellie smiled. The breeze held her hair back revealing a face full of pleasure. I felt I may be intruding, but she seemed to enjoy sharing the moment with me. It was quiet except for the low murmur of the engine and the hiss of the hull breaking the water. The sun bounced up at us from millions of miles away, and below the sun, the clear blue water lay thin as a veil a mile and a half deep.

"I saw some Sargassum weed a few miles back – that's a good sign."

"Is that the yellowish floating weed?"

"That's it. It comes up on the Gulf Stream and brings all kinds of fish, the Stream that is."

"I don't get it. How can the ocean have a river running through it? It doesn't make sense."

"It doesn't, but it's there. It's been there for a long time. Where's your camera?"

"The light's too flat, and we're swaying too much."

"You should come up in the evening, then."

"Too much sway."

"Sway, sway," she mocked me.

We surveyed the horizon for ships, and Ellie pointed out an eerie mirage of a ship that looked more like skyscrapers on the open sea.

"You and Joni went for a little swim last night."

"I guess that was obvious. We both looked a bit wet."

"She said she had a good time."

"Well, I did. I know I won't get a straight answer, but she's a little screwy."

"Screwy?"

"Well, not screwy. Troubled."

She waited a long time to answer. "Last year, having gotten sick from some bad food, she arrived home early from a research trip in the Channel Islands. She and one of her assistants drove all night to get her home only to find her best friend at the breakfast table while her fiancé William was in the shower. She said she couldn't comprehend what it all meant, except that it was all bad. She said she stood there in the kitchen staring at her friend, listening to the running water in the shower. All she could do was to walk out."

I said nothing but felt poorly for Joni.

"The worst part came after she got back on her feet after lying low with some colleagues. Good old William barely tried to make amends. By the time she got in touch with him, he explained that what they had would have never worked, but he was sorry that she had to find out the way she did."

"Christ, I guess that would mess you up."

"She was head over heels for William."

"What did he do?"

"A lawyer. Smart, on the move, and full of himself. I met him several times. I think it's the best thing to happen to her. He was an ass."

"She'll get over it – she's strong."

She looked at me.

"What?"

She smiled. "You're smitten, Calvin."

"What?"

"You've got it bad for her, boy."

"It's that obvious?"

"Hah! It happens everywhere she goes, and every time I've shipped with her. Watch that Joe. He'll be after her next."

"You think she likes that type?"

"Not Joni."

"Man, I can hardly sleep."

"I'm not one to give advice. *C'est La Vie*, say the old folks. Sometimes you never can tell." She smiled then her gaze focused on the water ahead. We remained there not speaking, just watching the water pass below. The *Bird* swayed in a gentle metronomic rhythm of the day. You couldn't help but smile. After a while she asked, "Are you watching the weed?" She pointed.

"See that large patch of Sargassum? Keep an eye on that as we pass."

Ahead lay a mat of weed the size of your average living room rug, an ochre colored, frilly weed, something I'd never seen in the water around the Cape. As the boat drew near, three dark, bullet-shaped fish darted from underneath the weed as the boat approached.

"Mahi mahi," she said.

"What?"

"Dolphin fish, fun to catch and good to eat. I think Frank might even stop if you hooked one of those. Joni loves fresh mahi mahi." When she saw the look on my face, she laughed. "Go get 'em, cowboy."

I didn't need any prodding. She backed off and added, "We could grill one up for dinner. It's a real treat, Calvin."

"Okay, okay. I'll bag a fish for you, but I need your help. I'll get my gear ready, and you spot for me."

We worked out some hand signals, and when I passed the house, Joe was still rambling on to Joni. I couldn't tell if she had taken to the guy or not, but now his presence really started to irritate me.

On the stern, the chum bucket let off whiffs of incredibly bad odors, even with the lid on tight, but it was the best place to fish. My pole was tied behind the mizzen mast with some new 30 lb. test monofilament that had yet to get wet, along with a new 18 inch steel leader to which I attached a 10 oz. Atom popper. I knew nothing about dolphin fish, but remembered seeing illustrations in magazines of these fish madly in pursuit of flying fish and figured a good smashing surface plug would do the job. Beetle showed up intrigued.

"Are we sporting for giant bluefin, or do you think you can bag one of those finbacks. We don't do mammals here, Calvin."

"I'm hoping to land some fresh dinner."

Beetle caught my line of sight.

"Ah, so you have a spotter working for you." He cupped his mouth with his hand like a radio operator. "Bandits, bandits, 9 o'clock high!"

"Shush. Don't blow my cover."

We waited and watched. After five minutes, Ellie circled her right hand, meaning we had a patch coming up within casting range. Then she pointed to the port side, her arm slowly moving as we approached. Beetle and I spotted the patch and signaled back. Then as we neared, she held up two fingers.

"Two fingers looks like," said Beetle, but it was hard to see with the sun. Then she waved her hand showing five fingers.

"Holy crap, Calvin. There's an orgy going on under those weeds. Go get 'em."

The bed of weeds lay a good 80 feet away, and it started to resemble a scene from the magazines. In position for a good cast I snapped the pole, sending the popper beyond the weeds, and before the plug moved a couple of feet the water broke in an explosion of spray as if someone had taken a shot at the lure with a shotgun. Beetle and Ellie both yelled at the same time as the fish broke the surface, tail walking and dancing in a frenzy, the spray sparkling in the sun. With all the yelling, Joe instinctively slowed down, and then he saw the fish and stopped the boat. He must have gotten the okay from Frank because he and everyone else were now on deck watching the action.

The fish ran the line out fast and hard like a bluefish, but kept on going. I tried bearing down on the drag, feeling confident with the 30 lb. test and managed to slow him down. Then the line went dead, I cranked hard retrieving the slack when the line became taut again and he jumped clear out of the water, his odd looking round head waving, shaking the thing in its mouth, his body an iridescent green and yellow. He eventually tired, and when he came close to the boat, he looked a magnificent purple. I had never seen a fish with such color and brilliance. Beetle stood by with a gaff, waiting for the word, and after a good amount of thrashing, the fish lay on deck. We stood over it as the colors along its flanks faded quickly to a dull green gray. I gave it a good whack and slit it back of the head. The cool red blood flowed out onto my hands, "Thank you fish."

"That's a good sized dolphin," Beetle commented, congratulating me.

"Here, look," said Frank as he pointed to the water close to where we hauled out the fish. Swimming along were three dolphin fish. "For some reason, they sometimes tend to stick with the one that's caught. It's like they're looking for him."

"We could catch more, Frank," Beetle suggested.

"That's a good-sized fish and will feed us all tonight." He waved to Joe, who engaged the engine and on we went.

"We'll be on station soon. Calvin, these fish need to be prepared a certain way. Joni can show you how."

Joni had been watching this sporting event. "Nice, Calvin. I haven't had a fresh one of these in months and months," she said happily.

After rummaging through the deck box, she came over and knelt next to the fish with a fillet knife and a couple pair of pliers.

She smiled. "Here, I'll show you something. This is one of those things you see once and never forget."

"What are you going to do with the pliers, pull its teeth?"

"Just watch, silly."

Beetle joined us, saying nothing, but I guessed he had probably seen this many times before. First she gutted the fish, and then she cut the skin at the head and tail. Holding the body flat on the deck with one hand, she then ran the knife along the dorsal and underside of the fish, cutting the skin as casually and precisely as a surgeon. She returned to the tail section, cutting the meat below the skin enough to lift a piece up about two inches. She turned the head of the fish toward me and handed me the pliers.

"Here, grab that skin." I got a good hold as she took the tail with the other pliers. "Now pull straight back."

With a fair amount of effort at first, the skin began to come off like stripping bark off a tree or contact paper off of an old shelf, and then it stripped easily, revealing the orange colored flesh underneath. What now lay before us was a perfect fillet of fish over two feet long.

"Now if we had a grill, we could barbecue this for something else you will never forget," said Beetle.

"We have a grill," I said.

"We have a grill?" Joni said excited.

"I found one in the cabinet below the seat in Frank's room, and there's charcoal."

Then we all said it together, "We have a grill!"

This is when Frank came out to check on our progress. "We have a grill below," he said.

We laughed. "Okay. If there's one thing we're sure of it's this, we have a grill." Beetle stood and shouted up to Ellie, "We have a grill."

We heard a faint "What?" coming from the forward part of the boat.

Frank shook his head, and laughed. "Let's get this cleaned up because we're about to begin."

18

We fixed our position northwest of an eddy that recently passed the eastern reach of Hudson Canyon, in the deep water off the Continental Shelf. The water didn't look any different to me than where we had been for the past six hours, but it was.

Ellie and Joni manned the chumming station like a pair of matrons in a soup kitchen heaping out large portions of the foul gruel, eager to get rid off it and get a new batch brewing. The chum was so rank it seemed it could conjure up the dead fishes of the deep. They held their noses and ladled it out as we drifted broadside with the southerly breeze. In no time, the birds began to appear, a couple at first, and then more, seemingly out of nowhere. The worse the chum, the better the slick, and we had a good oily path trailing off.

After about half an hour we had our first shark. A medium-sized blue shark appeared within a boat's length of the stern, but Frank had his eyes on something else. He had been monitoring the slick with his binoculars, patient as a breeder waiting for his pigeon to come home. Joni and Ellie were discussing the merits of the blue shark when Frank broke in.

"We have a big fish coming in fast up the slick. Could be a mako or a small white."

This stopped the conversation cold as we all searched the water along the slick, until, one by one, we caught sight of the dark fin wandering, then moving closer, wavering, looking for the scent, then coming on fast.

"Big fish," Frank said.

We watched as the shark got a strong hold of the slick and came directly to the boat, but it spooked when it saw the hull and disappeared.

"Mako," said Joni. "That's a big fish. I don't think we can land a fish like that." They waited for it to appear again. "Do you want to track it anyway and try the mackerel on another one later?" asked Joni.

"Let's see what else appears," Frank said.

It didn't take long. We soon had at least eight blue sharks meandering close to the boat. The mako remained distant and wouldn't come closer.

"We have what we came for. Let's pick one, Miss Kelley," Frank instructed. "And dump the rest of that chum, please."

We geared up for the next procedure, this time Joni donned a harness and with a tether that I led through a cleat hole on the mizzen mast.

"I got you now, Miss Kelley," I said softly snapping the steel buckle to the harness.

"You think so, deck monkey? It's going to take more than your little rope to hold me." She smirked.

"Hook, line and sinker, I'm going to land you like that fish."

"Aren't we feeling confident today?"

"Something's in the air – I can feel it."

She smiled as the rest of the crew was making ready.

"I think it's the chum. Look, I leave the day we get back, unless we get back early. I've got tickets. I'm going home." She looked at me with those big green eyes.

"I want you to meet my dog."

She laughed again. "Calvin!"

"What?"

She watched the sharks take the chum.

"Hold that line mister."

"I'll never let you go."

She said nothing but looked at me, serious but trying not to be. She started to move to the rail when I stopped her with the rope. She didn't like that, but I knew it would change what she was thinking.

"I don't like that," she said.

"You be a good doggie and I'll give you a treat."

"Calvin!" She squinted her eyes.

I smiled and gave her all the slack she needed. We were ready.

Ellie had four mackerel rigged for the feeding procedure and Frank had the heavy harpoon pole loaded with a bright red transmitter. Beetle manned the smaller tagging pole. He tagged a large blue shark with a yellow Fisheries tag, and over the next twenty minutes, Joni managed to get the four whole mackerel to the shark by hanging over the side, trailing the bait with the thin mono line, and waiting patiently for the shark to return. The operation went like clockwork. We were in the zone. As soon as the shark took the last mackerel, Frank planted the transmitter into it just behind the dorsal fin. The fish disappeared in a flash, and moments later, the telltale beep of the acoustic signal echoed out of the wheelhouse and we were in pursuit.

Frank and the girls took charge of the tracking, even though their watch wouldn't start for another couple hours. He wanted to personally get Joe up to speed on the tracking procedure. I think Frank expected some complaints on Joe's part, and he was right. After a half hour of tracking Joe came to the realization that conceivably we could be listening to nothing but electronic beeping noises for the next week. Beetle and I stood on the sidelines listening to the signal, getting a fix on the shark: how it behaved, how deep it settled, and which direction it was headed while Frank gave instructions like a stern parent.

"All right, we're coming up on him. He's heading east and we want to get a little ahead of him. Take it out of gear and drift until he moves on. Watch your drift. At night with a wind it gets tricky."

Joe said nothing, but it was obvious he didn't like being told what to do as far as his piloting was concerned, and pursuing beeping signals did not seem very glamorous.

"This will be a fun night," I said to Beetle.

He smiled. "We can drive this guy crazy. How about

you get that grill and we make some chow."

Beetle turned out to be a first-rate chef. Delivering yachts was only a side interest for him, mainly because it got him out on the water. He lived in New York City and worked as an architect. After a deal he had to design a Soho restaurant fell through, he ended up part owner of the place. For fun he spent a good deal of time in the kitchen, learning secrets of the trade, secrets he enjoyed sharing. He laid out the portions and instructed me how to prepare certain parts of the meal, the roasted potatoes, and the salad, how to mix a simple dressing. We worked on the stern while he prepared the mahi mahi, and spread the fish fillets across the grill in four sections, completely covering the grate, but instead of the distinctive orange meat color, the fish now had a layer of bright green goop covering it.

"It's pesto. I got it from my sister on Nantucket. Pesto and olive oil: two of the greater things in life."

"Do you always carry stuff like this with you?"

"I try to. It all helps, especially at the end of a long day on the water. You can work all day in bad weather on a crappy ship, but a good cook onboard makes all the difference. We were out on the *Gosnold* once, and they had a new cook, Simon. We called him simple Simon. He was short, unkempt, and looked more like a homeless person. He lived in Maine. We worked all morning the first day out on a light breakfast, and when it was lunchtime, I went below first. Simon had our first meal ready. I sat down and he put a bowl of soup in front of me, and like Simon, it didn't look like much, but after a taste, the first words that came out of my mouth were, 'Wow, that's good soup.' Then George came in and sat down, and he said the same. The next five guys came in and did the same thing. Then Simon served us dinner. Man, he could cook. We fell deeply in love with the guy and wanted to take him home. We couldn't wait for the next meal. A good cook makes a happy crew."

"Looks like we'll be happy tonight," I smiled.

The fish tasted like nothing I'd eaten before. Maybe

it was the setting, or maybe it was the pesto, but the meal was certainly remarkable. The girls were also impressed with Beetle and his pesto, and loved the fish as well. Frank just moaned and nodded his head with pleasure.

During dinner, we took turns tracking so everyone had a chance to eat and relax, watching the afternoon linger into evening. The barometer remained steady and it looked like the weather could only get better. Now that we were on the fish, its presence was always in the back of our minds. You could tell by the interval between beeps if it was deep or not, and you would check the arrow on top of the hydrophone pulley, and instinctively look off in the direction of the signal. The whole process became second nature: the pattern of steaming ahead, drifting, getting a fix, recording the beeps, logging the numbers, working as a team. The rhythm set in for Beetle, who had worked this task many times before with Frank, and even with Joe. After a couple of hours of tracking, he got the hang of it, caught the rhythm of the dance.

WE TRACKED BLUE SHARK #80-3 through the night without incident. Beetle, Joe, and I worked our 12 to 6 shift, plugging along after the shark like porkpie-wearing detectives on a stakeout. The fish surfaced a number of times during the night, and we managed to get fairly close but kept a safe distance away so as not to spook it. We didn't know when Frank and Joni planned to go for this shark, but it sounded like they expected to wait at least 24 hours.

The morning sky came on quickly, and as soon as the sun jumped off the horizon, it seemed as bright and as hot as midday. I'd been falling behind in sleep and was determined to try to get at least four hours in, and with one of Joni's smelly tee shirts tucked under my pillow like a toddler with his special blanket, I went out like a light. The days would surely go by quickly tracking day and night, one of us always on watch with no time to cultivate this thing between us. It would be nice to spend a few days together, just another night.

"I leave the day we get back, unless we get back

early. I've got tickets. I'm going home, Calvin." The words repeated in my head. We lived worlds apart. She had a career with prospects, as they say, I had a studio filled with paintings, and no money, no credentials, not even a checking account. But for some reason, at the bottom of everything, none of that mattered. All I knew was that it felt right, that something had brought us together, maybe something bigger than ourselves, and this part of our story had yet to be written.

About ten in the morning, I awoke to the sound of voices yelling. It was Ellie. It sounded like she was up in her perch, a distant voice yelling, I rushed up on deck, closely followed by Beetle and Joe, all of us looking around like blind men as we tried to figure out what all the commotion was about.

"Can you see it?" she called down. "Frank, as far as I can see."

She was pointing ahead of the boat, out toward the vast flat plain of silvery water. Frank came out to join us, with a puzzled look on his face.

"She says there's some strange water ahead." He had his glasses up and was scanning the surface. "There's something out there." He advanced to the mast and climbed to get a better look.

In the distance we could see a line in the water that appeared to extend in both directions. And as we drew closer, the line extended as far as you could see. Frank came down quickly and gave some instructions to Joe, who turned the boat to run perpendicular to the line. When we got close, Joe throttled down to idle but Frank motioned him to kill the engine. We slowly drifted up to this band of water trying to figure what strange phenomenon we had fallen upon.

Frank let out an ironic laugh. "No one's going to believe this."

Just ahead of our bow lay a river of water as wide as a four lane highway, all ripples and tiny standing waves, the water babbled like a brook, water upon water, a convergence of forces driven by planetary sorcery, a wonder seldom seen.

"Would you listen to that," said Beetle.

"It's the Stream!" Frank yelled up to Ellie.

"What?"

"It's the edge of the Stream," he answered.

Joni stood next to me. "I've never heard of this."

Joe stood behind us. "Looks like Route 66 across the Texas Panhandle, straight as an arrow. Man, no one's going to believe this."

"Frank, I can hear it," Ellie called down. "Unbelievable!"

Joe seemed most amazed. He looked south for a minute, then north with his head cocked to the side. Then he'd do a 180 and look south again, hands on his hips, looking as if someone had played a trick on him. I tried to get some pictures but knew there was no way a photo could do it justice, especially in such bright light.

Frank figured what we encountered was either the edge of a Gulf Stream eddy or the Stream itself, the rip of current that snakes across the Atlantic affecting the climate, lives, and habitat of the continents on both ends of the compass. The Stream was no longer a vague boundary line on a map. This current possessed a planetary energy, its origins far south beyond the curvature of the earth, a force of nature hidden within itself, invisible in some respects like the wind, its counter part, both possessing enormous power, gods to themselves.

Beetle just shrugged his shoulders. "Well, now we know where the Gulf Stream is. She woke us up for that, a once in a lifetime look at one of the most incredible features in the Atlantic Ocean. Man, I need some coffee before I encounter such strange phenomenon in the morning."

"I'll join you," I said shaking my head.

At noon we were back on watch, in pursuit of blue shark #80-3, with the plan to try to get the shark that afternoon. This would provide data on the digestion rate for a 24 hour period, but it would depend on whether or not the shark surfaced and if we could manage to get close enough for a shot. The early afternoon sun spread an overexposed glare across the sea, turning the sky and water a silvery white. The wind died and the temperature rose. We were on the trail, moving slowly to the southwest, ghosting through a molten landscape. The air became more humid as the afternoon passed, and we moved slowly through the dense atmosphere, tracking the fish that lay in deep cool water, down in the 30 meter range as it headed to the southwest.

Around four in the afternoon, Frank and Joni joined us in the wheelhouse, monitoring the fish's movement, checking the data, hoping it would make some movement toward the surface. After they got a feel for what the shark was doing, Frank approached me.

"Let's get ready. He could come up anytime now. We'll take a shot at him if we can. I'll man the harpoon pole. Let's see how we can work the rifle."

Joni and Beetle listened intently. Joni looked serious and excited as Beetle and I carried the box up to the cockpit area where I opened the case and began to prepare the rifle. Behind the glass of the wheelhouse, Joe's comment said it all.

"Holy crap! What's that for?"

Beetle just smiled. "That's a serious looking piece of scientific hardware. My friends at Green Peace are going to love this, Calvin."

Joe stood behind Beetle, staring as I worked the rifle.

"Not loaded," I demonstrated. "It has a safety. I'll keep it pointed down at the water." Then I loaded the harpoon, sliding it down into the barrel, and extended the barbs.

"Jesus. Look at that thing. You're going to shoot that?" asked Joe.

"That's my job." Holding the spool of line, I snapped it under the barrel. "If I get a shot off, I'll need some help tending the line: 150 feet, or 3 boat lengths."

"I'll provide backup," said Beetle.

Joe watched as I opened the box of cartridges.

"We only have six of these: 12 gauge, plastic casing,

rubber bullet." I could tell by the look on Joe's face that my ranking in his world had just bumped up a peg.

I HAD SEEN THAT look before, in Boy Scouts, with the jock types at Camp Eagle. My ranking was low in the food chain because of my poor hitting skills at bat, but on the firing range I made my mark. With the troop watching, while in a prone shooting position, with a single-shot bolt-action .22, I moved up the firing line while the others with a lower score got bumped. My shots repeatedly hit the black center circle, the spotter behind me with binoculars calling out the shots, after each rotation I moved up the ranks to the top alley. Then the spotter called out my shots with excitement, "center bulls-eye!" I would reload, breathing slowly, in the zone, sighting a little high to the left to offset the wind and squeezed off to hear "center bulls-eye" again. The range master standing by me instructing the controller to give me five more cartridges. After ten hits it grew quiet and I turned to see the others just staring at me, the shy skinny kid, the look on their faces surprised and embarrassed me. Soon after I acquired the name Hawkeye. I liked that. I had been called worse.

If I could see a target, I could hit it, but now there were the effects of the water, the motion of the boat, a moving object. Joni stood to the side with a serious look, the look of someone who dislikes and is fearful of firearms. In her mind, this wasn't cool; she just wanted the shark onboard.

We followed along a southerly track for another couple of hours, past the six o'clock shift change and on to dinner time. The shark had been moving in a long lazy undulating pattern, swimming between 10 and 20 meters below the surface, producing a monotonous trail of beeps. I took a break to check on Beetle, who was in the galley making dinner, and to do the routine engine room check. The diesel had been running continually for days now, mostly at low RPMs. The big engine had some sluggishness, a logy tone to it. I knew that most engines will load up with a continuous running at a low speed, but didn't know if it affected a diesel as much.

It was hotter than blazes in the engine room. Suddenly the engine idled and shut down. When I removed the headphones someone was yelling from above, the vent hatch flew open. It was Joni.

"Calvin, quick. He's up. He's on the surface."

There's was shouting and all kinds of banging above on deck. By the time I got up there, everyone was standing at the starboard rail looking down at the water where a taught white line in Frank's hands ran out to the sea. Beetle held the harpoon pole while Ellie worked the rope out of the tub, letting it feed to Frank, paying it out as the shark pulled.

"He surfaced on the other side and swam under the boat. Frank got the harpoon and stuck him when he passed by."

Joni looked elated. Frank held the line steady, and then slowly and methodically retrieved the line hand over hand, to Ellie who coiled the slack carefully back into the tub. The line became heavier, Beetle pitched in to help, and then the shark broke the surface, rolling on it's side, its white belly trailing blood.

"Okay, let's get him onboard," said Frank.

Like before using the fish hooks, we landed the shark which appeared dead by the time it got onboard. Frank made a cut at the head to make sure.

"We got him, Joni," said Ellie thoroughly excited.

"What a stroke of luck."

Beetle put his arm on my shoulder. "Yeah, Calvin. Where were you? Hiding in the engine room?" They laughed. Everyone felt happy and relieved. We didn't know if it could be done but we did it.

Frank looked most pleased. "Let's analyze the contents, get the measurements, save the meat, add some to the chum bucket, have dinner, sit tight tonight, and go for another one in the morning."

The crew responded in unison, "Sounds like a plan," and we got to work.

19

Ellie and Joni went about dissecting the shark, logging the data, paying close attention to the stomach contents. Ellie removed the viscera, cut the stomach free of its attachments, and dumped the sack into a bucket. The chunks of mackerel splashed and floated, the pieces were removed and laid out on a patch of old sail canvas. There were markings where each mackerel had been bitten around the mid section before being swallowed, some of the halves fit back together like a simple puzzle. The skin of the fish shined with a colorful iridescence and became something other than fish, the dark corrugated dorsal colors melded into reds, yellow, and silver, a fish never seen, an inspiration, and I saw how I could paint them.

After shooting many photos of the investigation the light was fading, so I switched to the flash with some concern about the light reflecting off the silvery scales. I shot photos of Joni and Ellie working, with their hands tending the body parts, cutting with the knife, measuring and logging the data, and imagined one of these pictures one day posted on someone's refrigerator door, framed in an office amongst a stack of books or found in a notebook years later, the viewer holding the photo with a faraway look, transported to a time long ago. There was one photo I would keep: Joni looking up at me and smiling, a smile she could share when she knew no one was watching. Holding the camera at my chest, I shot blindly as she cocked her head and smiled, more with her eyes than her mouth.

"Let's stay focused on the task at hand, children. Recess is after lunch," Ellie suggested.

We finished up in the dark and retired to a late dinner. Frank and Joe decided to just heave to for the night and drift for most of the evening, keeping the same watch schedule, and follow the plan to chum at dawn and get on another fish as soon as possible.

Beetle and I passed the night getting the boat shipshape, preparing the mackerel, cleaning up the stern deck, thawing more bait, and telling stories. Every couple of hours we'd make a snack for ourselves and Joe, who spent most of the night reading and checking the radar.

Frank rose before dawn and the three of us started chumming blindly in the dark, attracting several blue sharks before the sun rose. By the time the girls appeared with the sun, we had more sharks, all blues and all about the same size. Frank wanted to wait. "Let's give it another hour to see what shows."

We congregated at the stern rail taking stock of the number of sharks to choose from when Ellie spotted a large dark fin way up the slick. This fin got everyone's attention. It belonged to something other than a blue dog, which were now commonplace and familiar. This shark behaved differently, it advanced cautiously but with bold intent, working the slick with a steady pace. It would stop and hold for a moment, then swim closer, moving effortlessly compared to the blue sharks. This shark appeared to barely move its tail.

"It looks like a mako," said Frank with the glasses up.

He passed the binoculars to Joni who made a quick study and gave them back. "I can't tell Frank, but he looks manageable in size."

"Let's see if we can get him in close."

We chummed for another half hour and managed to get the shark within a 20 foot radius of the stern but no closer. This wouldn't work. We needed the shark close enough to pass the bait and to plant the transmitter. Frank calmly watched the shark with patient eyes.

"Mako," he said confirming his suspicion. "He doesn't look overly aggressive, and he's had a fair amount to eat. He's not bullying the blues. Calvin, let's see if we can use your fishing pole and toss the bait to it."

This task happily fell within my area of expertise.

Just like casting a pogie at a bass hole. With a mackerel tied by the tail with a 10 lb. test leader, Frank gave me the word, and I managed a good cast five feet in front of the mako. The bait sank right off and the shark took it. This was met with controlled jubilation. Beetle had three more mackerel ready to go, which he gave to Joni to hold for me while he, Frank, and Joe wrestled the inflatable off the wheelhouse roof.

"What the hell is he going to do now?" I had an idea and hoped not to be part of this risky strategy.

They launched the zodiac off the port side, and without a word Frank and Beetle got in. Joe passed a length of rope back to the stern and made it fast. Then he gave Beetle the tagging pole. I made another successfully cast to the mako, and with Joni's help we got two more whole mackerel ahead of the shark and he took both. That was enough for Frank. He didn't want to miss this opportunity and gave the order to shove off, and they slid along the hull and cleared the stern as Beetle paid out line. The inflatable looked incredibly small and precarious amongst the sharks. I couldn't imagine how Beetle felt, but he calmly let out more line as Frank directed until they were about a boat's length off, and then Frank stood with the long transmitter pole at the ready. We waited and watched, hoping this would soon be over. After several minutes, Beetle tied the line off and grabbed an oar and immediately made a jab at something.

"Jesus, he's hitting the damn things," said Joe. "I don't like this. I don't want to lose anyone on my watch."

"Frank knows what he's doing. Calm down," said Joni in a quiet voice. "Ellie, keep chumming."

The mako surfaced on our starboard side and swam toward the stern. The shark looked big and dark. He looked like an athlete, like a linebacker, the kind of shark you wouldn't want to pick a fight with. He disappeared for a moment but surfaced again heading straight for the zodiac. As he neared, he spooked and veered off, but he was close enough for Frank to take a poke at it. The pole hit home, vibrating as he planted the transmitter dart, and a huge splash followed. Beetle immediately started hauling in the inflatable, I pulled from the secured end and in no time, they were back on deck, Beetle huffing, out of breath and glad to be onboard.

"Wow that was fun. Thanks, Frank."

But Frank and everyone else were already in the wheelhouse listening for a signal. Immediately the high pitched beep of the transmitter signal echoed out of the wheelhouse. We had the shark on.

"This is not going to be like the blue dogs," said Beetle as he removed the life vest. "We're going to have to stay frosty with this fish."

He was right on that account. It became immediately apparent we were not tracking a blue shark. This fish could swim. The *Bird* swung around to the southwest and off we went on a wild, hard chase for the first half hour. Then the mako slowed to a reasonable pace and hung in the 20 meter depth area for the next three hours, swimming around four knots. We soon realized that because this fish could move so fast, if we ventured too far away, lost power for too long, got sloppy, or ran into bad weather, we could easily lose the signal and never catch up again. Its pattern of cruising differed from the blue sharks also, by moving in a broad arc while threading through the thermocline.

"You're going to have to stay focused for this here shark," cautioned Joe.

We all knew it, but now that Joe alerted us that "we" had to stay on top of our game, I once again had the feeling that he really didn't give a damn about what we were up against.

The day passed quickly, magically, as we pursued the mako. Dinner was eaten without ceremony, and by nightfall Frank, Joni, and Ellie had gotten totally absorbed in the shark's behavior. When it came time for the midnight watch, we had to pry them off the headphones, but they wouldn't leave. Beetle rolled his eyes. "Crazy scientists." However, right away we clicked in, impressed with this incredible fish that moved in a spiraling sawtooth pattern, our connection to this creature nothing but a thin thread of electronic pulses, a common bond for us all to share for the next couple of days. We had to lean on Joe to get into it – the nights of the cross-country stories were over.

"He surfaced twice before midnight but dove quickly to 80 meters. We would get up to his position when he was deep but tried to stay off when he surfaced." Frank showed us his track on the chart. Tick marks in pencil at every navigation reading on the hour. "This is one active fish. If we can get this shark back and see how it metabolizes that bait…" He stopped for a moment. "Well that would make for some good information. That would make some people very happy."

"How long are we tracking this shark, Frank?" asked Joe in a casual but concerned tone.

"We decided to shoot for three days. Meaning, we need to track until noon two days from now, and then we'll see if we can get up on him."

No one said anything but I knew what we were all thinking: "It'll be a long three days."

20

The next morning the sun rose hot with a summer vengeance. The girls were up before dawn and ready to go. Frank worked with us all night and looked like he had no intention of sleeping until this fish was on board. Joni looked excited to be back with the fish and gave me a "happy to be alive" smile, she even put her hand on my shoulder as we bent over the navigation chart. No one seemed to notice and no one cared. This would be the last shark of this trip, and we had a good one, that's what mattered. We had good weather, and everyone onboard appeared confident that we could make it happen.

The next 24 hours went by in a haze of heat and humidity with the stop and go pattern of the track, the monotony of the pursuit, and the ever present beeping interrupted only by fragmented conservation and chatter on the VHF radio, which gave us a favorable forecast for the next 48 hours along with a navigational warning of a dead whale in the vicinity of Atlantis Canyon. We listened to the weather update of a tropical storm building in the Caribbean, and the blips of fishing gab from the boys from Barnegat Bay. After a while, it felt more like we were a team of federal agents following a notorious mob boss every move, listening, shadowing, eating fast food and making smart conversation on a stakeout.

Before our noon shift began, we sat in the sun on the forward deck taking in the scenery as Beetle developed his vendetta against the shark.

"You're going to nail this bastard right off. I think this shark is trying to kill us by keeping us up all night, luring us out here in the sun to get baked. I know it has some evil plan. It's just waiting for one of us to go for a quick swim, and then good bye sharktracker."

"I'm just hoping to get a shot at the thing."

"It's big enough. We got a mako on the *Cape Hatteras* two years ago. Got it on deck to suture a transmitter on it. Lifted it with the crane, a seven footer. That thing was like a Texas chain saw massacre once it got on board. It was incredibly powerful and took two men to hold the head down before we got the saltwater hose in its mouth. We followed it for two days and then lost it with bad weather. The crew hated us. We would stop to drift once on the shark, and the ship would turn into the trough and roll. God, stuff in the galley crashed about, the ship's crew cursing at the fish the whole time. It got on people's nerves. Frank just told them to do their jobs. That really pissed them off. He's got a knack for doing that."

"He's certainly intense," I said.

"How'd you get chosen for the job of the white hunter?"

"I'm not really sure. He pulled the thing out from under a table and asked me if I knew anything about firearms."

"Calvin, that's when you say no. You never saw one before?"

"Well, that's the problem; guns have always been there in my life. My Uncle Bill collected guns, I mean he had a cellar full of guns. He collected stamps and coins, but mostly guns. A real horse trader. He had every kind of weapon you could imagine. I remember going into his collection when I was a kid. It was like being in a room full of naked women. You wanted to touch them, knew you couldn't and didn't know what would happen if you did."

"Good analogy."

"When I got older, around twelve, I would spend summers with him up at his cabin in southern Vermont. He'd let me take a rifle out into the woods, I was allowed to kill only snakes, mostly with small caliber rifles. We had a firing range set up behind the old sugar shack: tin cans, bottle caps, playing cards. We had a game shooting at the playing cards. After dinner we'd go out into the field to shoot. At fifty yards, hitting a card that small while standing isn't that easy.

Sometimes he'd bring out a .30-06 lever-action carbine or an old muzzle loader. Seldom would he let me shoot a handgun. My hands were too small. But boy, he had some beautiful rifles. My dad taught me to respect firearms, the responsibility of it all, but my uncle taught me how to shoot. Very technical about it. He didn't really hunt, at least when I knew him. He loved to fish though."

"With the firearms! Jacking bass, now there's a sport. Where's he now?"

"He died a few years ago, actually. I lost touch with him after college. Never had a chance to thank him."

Beetle said nothing but shook his head in understanding. Then asked with amusement, "So what's the deal with Joni?"

"I don't know what the deal is. What do you mean?"

"When's the wedding?"

I laughed. "What are you talking about?"

He smiled. "I don't know. I overheard the two of them talking in the galley. Ellie said something about not going back right away. You have some kind of romance going on here that we should all know about?" He looked at me with an expectant look.

"Wow. I haven't heard anything about that."

"Joni is one of Frank's favorite people. He'd be happy to have her around for a while after this is over. She did her undergrad work with him." He paused for a moment and became serious. "Frank said she saved his life once. Neither of them will talk about it, but it was during a trip off Nova Scotia."

"What happened?"

He shrugged his shoulders and I quietly contemplated the array of ways one could meet their demise doing this work.

"They sure work well together. I don't know, Beetle. Something's going on but I'm not sure what. I'm not really in control; it's more like I'm waiting to see what happens next. You know I'll never be able to figure women out."

"Can't be done. Many have tried."

WE DID THE NOON shift change, and for an hour the entire crew participated in the tracking. It was obvious that Frank and the girls had become so engaged in the shark's behavior that it was difficult for them to detach. We now had two days of data collected, and the weather remained promising. The big question remaining was whether we would ever have the opportunity to get the shark onboard, and how difficult that might be. A Texas chainsaw massacre on deck – I could picture the mayhem.

The shark remained deep for most of the afternoon, swimming in long sine waves through the thermocline then taking a dive down to 400 meters. As he dove further, the interval between beeps grew wider and wider. We listened and watched each other wondering how deep it would go. Beep, beep, beep – one beep every five seconds, Frank did the math.

"550 meters. Let's see how long he stays there."

"It's pretty cold down there," piped up Joe, who had been unusually quiet all afternoon. "You'd think for a cold blooded animal, it wouldn't want to stay down there."

Frank smiled. "Good observation."

He and Beetle nodded to each other, like they acknowledged a little secret. Then the beeps quickened as the shark climbed back up the water column from the darkness, the cold and pressure, passing through the boundary layer, lingering for 15 minutes, and then it came right up to the surface. Frank turned up the volume, the beeps echoed out of the cabin, and threaded down to the lower deck, rousing Joni and Ellie who rushed on deck to see where the fish had risen to swim in the sun.

They first looked at the arrow on the hydrophone pole, and then out 100 yards off the bow on the starboard side as the large black dorsal fin broke the shimmer on the water. We all watched patiently like we were stalking a deer, intuitively not moving too quickly so as not to spook it, almost whispering. We drifted at a safe distance as the shark spent the next 10 minutes basking in the warmth of the surface water, swimming slowly in a meandering curve to the south. There was a moment when both Frank and Joni considered going for the shark then and there, realizing any number of things could happen within the next 24 hours that might jeopardize an opportunity to capture the shark.

"We'll stay with the plan. The weather looks good."

Joni nodded, they knew it was a gamble either way, but she looked worried. After the shark submerged everyone went back to their posts, Ellie climbed up the mast for a better look, and I managed to get a few minutes alone with Joni.

"That's a good sign, isn't it? That it'll surface during the light of day."

"I wonder if we should have tried to get up on it?" she asked herself. "How far can you shoot that thing, Calvin?"

"As far as it will go."

"How far is that?"

"I have no idea. I'm just hoping to get close enough for a shot. Anything over 30 feet will be sketchy."

"Sketchy?"

"Yeah. You've got drag from the line paying out, the weight of the harpoon, the boat moving, the refraction of the water, and the water itself. What happens when that thing goes through the water?"

"I hadn't thought about all that."

"I have. Sketchy."

She gave me the smile. "You can do it."

"Oh thanks. Nothing like a little pressure."

"You'll do it for me. Won't you?" she said, not coyly but matter-of-factly.

"No. I'll do it for science."

She laughed. "Right, the big fan of science. Do it for art then."

She had something there. Technically, I felt doubtful about this whole harpooning operation, but looking at it from my artistic side, from the right hemisphere, it felt doable. Everything felt possible with these people, but there was more to it than that. Since becoming part of the crew, I had felt in the right place, becoming part of this story, like I was supposed to be there doing this.

"Yeah, I'll do it for you, and for Frank."

She uttered a sigh of surrender. "Okay, Calvin."

Then Beetle called for me to get back on station.

"Okay, and if I get this shark, we have a dinner date, alone at a restaurant of my choice, even if it's at the damned airport."

"What happens if you don't get it?"

"You take me out to dinner for all the aggravation."

"I can't make any promises, and forget about the other night. I was drunk and not myself."

"I can't forget about the other night. I will never forget the other night."

She said nothing.

"We'll get this shark. Don't worry."

"Calvin, I'm going back to California. No sense getting something started."

"Nothing lasts forever."

Her face looked hard and distant as she got up and left me there.

"Christ, now you've done it. Just do what you came to do. She's right. Am I really going to shoot that thing?" I had no idea what would happen with the harpoon rifle. It would have been practical to at least take a practice shot at a float to check the margin of error, to see how it kicked, to find out if the thing even worked, but the ammunition was limited and I knew Frank wouldn't go for it. There was no practice with Frank. You just do it.

THE SHARK SURFACED four more times that afternoon, giving us confidence that we could make the catch the next day. After a couple hours of sleep following dinner, we were back on shift at midnight. Beetle stayed in good spirits, but Joe seemed to be sinking into a depression. He was beginning to tire of the whole thing and just wanted to go home.

We bumped along through the night under the stars

and a near full moon. After our second cup of coffee, we picked up on a school of dolphins that seemed to be meddling with the shark. As the pod acoustically appeared in the mako's vicinity, the shark began to swim erratically for several minutes and then went deeper and settled down. Around 3:30, two whales arrived off our port side announced by a series of strange clicking sounds. We could hear their spouts, and see them as they crossed the moon's reflection with their black shapes rolling above the water – their presence turned the night into magic. The whales would rise with a roll and blow, the spray catching the moonlight, which turned it into a puff of shimmering light as big as a maple tree. They stayed with us for over an hour even as we steamed along after the shark. Frank had been lying down but sensed something and joined us as we watched and listened. They would disappear for five minutes or more, then come up within a short distance, sometimes a little too close for Joe. Their presence gave me a sense of connection to a world beyond my grasp and this I shared with Joni later that morning.

"That's special. Not many people get to see something like that. If I had to do it over again, I'd be tracking whales, before they're all gone."

"Before they're gone?"

"Sometimes it feels like everything will be gone. Even the blue sharks have diminished in the past ten years. I've seen the changes just in the little time I've been out here; Frank has seen it too. Look at striped bass. Ashley once showed me fishing logs of striped bass from the turn of the century. The catches were huge. It wasn't uncommon to land six-foot stripers in the nets, that's a 100 lb bass. Imagine what it was like before we arrived."

"We're pretty good at messing things up, I guess."

"I wish I had seen the whales."

"Joe said they were finbacks."

"He wouldn't know a finback from a flounder."

I laughed. "Can I quote you on that?"

She smiled and looked beautiful in the early morning

light, her hair tied up, her eyes a little puffy from sleep. She looked past me across the water like she could see the future.

"It's going to be hot today. You better get some sleep. You're going to have to be on target today, if you know what I mean."

"If we get this shark today, we could be home in a day or so."

She kept looking out upon the water. "Your dog misses you, I'll bet."

"I miss him. Christ, Joni," I said in frustration, but then I too became captivated by the beauty of the early morning sparkling sea. It lay flat and molten smooth, with a gentle roll of swell cascading in from the south. "Yeah, I'll bet he does. I haven't thought of him much, or of anything else for that matter, since I've been out here."

"That happens," she said, as if to give me a hint. She looked at me and smiled, then went to join the others.

A short time later in my bunk, I tossed about to get comfortable after searching for Joni's tee shirt unsuccessfully. I lay there thinking about the whales rising up in the moonlight, spouting their magnificent silvery breath and knew it was a sight I would never forget. It wasn't long before Joni's voice was in my ear like a dream, soft and close.

"Calvin, Frank wants you on deck. The shark's up. He's near the surface. He wants you ready."

It took a minute, but then the adrenaline hit. On deck, Frank had the harpoon rifle case open and ready.

"He's very close. We spotted his fin once. He's still near the surface."

We had worked out a plan earlier, which found the best shooting location to be on the bow, and there I positioned myself, but soon realized we had a problem. The main stay ran directly to the very foremost point of the bow, if I positioned myself behind this cable I would lose the ability to pan the rifle the full radius across the bow, making it necessary to step back to clear the barrel past the cable. The only solution would be for me to stand in front of the stay on the very point of the bow, a precarious position especially if I had to lean forward to get a close shot. Frank arrived with a solution and set me up with a ship's harness to strap me to the forward stay. This worked well. With the harness tethered to the cable I could lean back on my work vest as a cushion while we pursued the shark.

Ellie held her position up the mast standing in the spreaders. She would be my spotter, the first to locate the fish, and guide the pilot, giving the heading and distance as we closed in. We loitered about for an hour with the shark not showing any sign of surfacing until it dove to 30 meters and remained there past the noon shift change. By then, the sun had gotten unbearable, with Ellie and I taking the brunt of it. Beetle gave me a canvas hat with a wide brim and brought drinks for us with words of encouragement. He became our guardian, helping us get through the afternoon heat while Frank and Joni continued to track with Joe. Patiently we followed and waited but the shark wouldn't surface.

Around two o'clock something changed. The mako slowed its movement and circled. The beeps became faster, then faster still.

"He's coming up," Joni yelled.

"We can hear," Ellie yelled back.

After about five minutes came the call. "He's up! He should be a little to starboard."

We steamed ahead slowly. With the rifle across my arms, I reviewed in my head what to do for the hundredth time.

"Hold it tightly forward, expect the kick, wait for your shot, breathe ease, squeeze off, and don't drop the damn thing. Wait for your shot."

One might think this procedure rudimentary however my new perspective afforded an interesting and distracting outlook: something I had been close to but missed, something that had been there all the while but overlooked. Once positioned on the bow I could see nothing but water and sky. At first it felt a little unnerving, a bit like vertigo, but once I got used to it, the sensation was phenomenal, like floating. Nothing but sea and sky and space, the experience was something no photograph could capture. The sun bounced up from millions of miles away over this chasm of blue tranquility where the haze of dense air met with the sea and all became one massive veil. It was like flying and floating all at the same time, a special effect you might never imagine experiencing except in a dream. This enchanting sensation, drifting through this glare of light allowed my mind to gather the momentum of the clouds and I unwound the coils of expectations of those behind me. Before me lay an expanse of luminance, a vision uncluttered, the volume of space so enormous that my flesh and bone seemed to dissolve, to become vapor, leaving my spirit alone to hover there.

Pulling myself back, I realized that somewhere out there in this universe of shining light, a fin would soon appear, the only living creature in this vast world before me, our destinies bound by a thin line of electronic frequency, and I was ready to kill it.

"I see him! I see him," Ellie shouted. "He's out about 60 meters, a little to port and just breaking the surface."

At first I could see nothing, but soon the fin appeared at a distance, broadside to the bow and moving to my left side. The boat turned, Frank would be guiding Joe, telling him how to move. From my position, I could barely hear the motor and wondered how well the shark could hear. Would it sense an electrical disturbance? My throat tightened as I lowered the rifle, opened the chamber and loaded the cartridge, closed the bolt and flicked on the safety. The barbs of the harpoon were collapsed down to lessen the resistance as it passed through the water. The shark was within 40 yards and Ellie was yelling as if everyone were blind. I made ready and put the rifle to my shoulder.

"He's dead ahead. He's going down! He's going down!"

He was indeed going down, and fast. By the time we got close enough, the only part visible was the red fluorescent transmitter. I kept a bead on him, then lost him, but when I saw the red instrument again, I figured, "What the hell."

Kaboom! The gun nearly dislocated my shoulder, and the line disappeared into the blue, and then everybody was on the bow looking while Frank hauled in the line.

I missed and knew it. My right cheek throbbed and my shoulder felt out of place.

"He went down really fast as we got close," said Ellie excitedly. "He spooked."

Frank seemed okay with it. "Not surprising with this big thing coming up on him. Did you get a good look at him?"

"All I saw was the fin and then the red transmitter. I think I shot over him.

He patted me on the shoulder. "We'll have another go.

"We need to come up on him from the south. There's too much reflection from this direction. Now I've got a better feeling what this thing can do."

"We'll get him next time. You look like you're getting baked. You better take a break, he'll be down for a while," he said, looking out across the water.

But he wasn't down for long. No sooner did I go below for a rest than the beeping quickened to a rapid interval. He was close to the surface again. So back to the bow I returned, and remained all afternoon on into the night, until it became too dark to see. The shark became unpredictable; it would stay close to the surface, go down five or ten meters, and then come up again. We attempted two more approaches, and each time he spooked and disappeared before we could get close enough for a shot. Ellie could see the shark just under the surface from her perch, but as soon as we neared, the shark would dive. With so much exposure to the sun I was speaking in tongues, my legs had gotten rubbery and my vision distorted. By the time we called it a day, I couldn't have shot straight and didn't care. Later, during dinner the chills hit me and I crashed in the forward bunk while the rest of the crew ate. Joni checked in on me to see if I was okay.

"Where did all the junk go?" I asked in my groggy state.

"I cleaned it up this morning. A lot of the stuff fit in the empty bait freezer." She looked at me funny, or maybe it was my condition. "You got a lot of sun today."

"I feel like I've been tied to a rotisserie."

"We'll get him tomorrow," she said softly. She sat on the bed beside me with her hand on my leg. "We'll get him tomorrow." I closed my eyes and fell into a hard sleep.

SOME TIME LATER, a voice tore open my semi-consciousness. "Get up. The engine's seized." It sounded funny, the voice, the words, it was Joe.

"Get up, the diesel's seized up. It overheated, it just stopped, those damn Jabsco pumps!"

For a moment it was difficult to determine whether this was a nightmare or for real, but when I stumbled into the engine room the look on Frank's face said it all. The big diesel was hotter than hell. Fumes rose from its belly and all the smells of the industrial revolution lingered alongside. The auxiliary diesel cranked away in the corner, so I figured the rest of the crew was on the shark trying to keep up. We had to yell to communicate.

"We'll have to let it cool," I said while motioning for us to get out of there, knowing this could be serious. The little diesel had a fraction of the power needed to keep up with the shark, and worse, it would take days to get back home if we couldn't get the Gardner fixed. We retreated to the galley.

"Those damn Jabsco pumps always burn out. Those rubber impellers," Joe ranted. "She started to get sluggish, then it stumbled a bit, and by the time I realized it, it overheated and came to an abrupt halt."

"The pistons expand and seize in the cylinders."

"It'll take days to get back with that damn Westerbeke," cursed Joe with contempt.

The more we went over what had happened, the more I surmised it was a sudden lack of coolant, like a clogged intake, but Joe insisted on a bad pump impeller.

"There's some bad weather down south, which I didn't

worry about because it's days away, but now we could be in for it," whined Joe. I could tell he was really getting on Frank's nerves.

"Okay. After it cools, we'll pull the impeller and see what we find."

We went at it after an hour of waiting and praying, and after disassembling the pump, I pulled out a slightly worn but perfectly fine Jabsco impeller.

"Jabsco pumps," I said, thrusting it in Joe's face. "We've got a clogged intake and we're not getting any water. That's the problem!"

"Shit," he said apologetically. "But hell, I'm not going out there in the dark."

After refitting the water pump, I checked out the big diesel. It had cooled to the touch, and with a breaker-bar on the front pulley, the crankshaft turned over freely, followed by many thanks to all the saints in heaven and hell. While performing this diagnosis the Westerbeke shut down, there was some commotion on deck, and then a splash, someone must have gone in to take a look, and I wondered who. Once finished with the Gardner, I soon found Beetle on deck dripping wet with a coat hanger in hand kicking a large lump of Sargassum weed. "There's your culprit," he said flatly. In the background, the beeping transmitter signal faded in and out.

Frank stood beside me with an expectant look. "We should be okay. It's freed up. I got it to turn several times. I'll pour some water down the intake of the pump to make sure it's primed and we'll give it a go."

Moments later, I gave the signal; she cranked over just three times and fired up. The big diesel sounded a little unsure of itself at first but then it cleared its voice and smoothed out, bringing a number of happy faces to the crew as we continued our pursuit.

It was past midnight by now, but Joni and Ellie stayed on watch until two in the morning. The adrenaline dried up shortly after that and they called it quits. My watch slogged on through the dog hours of the night with little conversation, trying to remain focused through the fatigue and tedium of the night. The radio occupied our thoughts as we listened to the weather forecast, navigational warnings, and fishing fleet chatter. It sounded like the swordfishing season looked promising, and the forecast expected the storm off Bermuda to push east. The sighting and location of the dead whale was reported by a crew from Barnegat Bay.

The mako continued to swim in a pattern similar to the previous evening until just before dawn, when it again sounded as if the transmitter had fallen off. The interval between beeps grew longer and longer, and the beeps themselves grew fainter. This grabbed our attention, pulling us away from our mundane, scrambled, sleepless thoughts. We listened as the beeping grew slower and slower: 585 meters came the count, and then 600 meters.

"Christ, he's dead," said Joe.

Frank kept counting until the depth hit 620 meters and leveled off. Slowly at first and gradually, the beeping increased as the shark rose from the depths.

"How in hell can it do that?" asked Joe.

Frank waited for a moment. "It's not a cold-blooded animal – it's warm bodied."

"What?" was all Joe could muster. It was either too late or too early to get into it. Needless to say, we had just witnessed something probably never before recorded, and Frank seemed very pleased.

For the rest of the night, coffee kept me going, but by morning the gathering fatigue flattened my spirits. Slowly the horizon lightened to reveal a cloudless sky as our crew stood on deck facing the golden star, greeting the new day as the sun rose. Witnessing the miracle of dawn always transcends all immediate preoccupations. If there is a sacred moment, it is when the star rises above the horizon, the burning sphere blazing across 90 million miles and more. Someone once said that we are a manifestation of the life force power of the universe. At first light, it all seems very possible and very humbling.

21

Beetle and I decided to remain on deck for a while to see if the mako would surface at sunrise. Joni joined us on the bow as we shared our morning coffee, and I recounted how during the night we thought either the transmitter had fallen off or the shark had died when it took its slow, dramatic dive to a depth of 600 meters. How Frank patiently stood by, listening, counting the beeps, his hand holding the stopwatch, his arm pumping slowly with the count. I had a cup of coffee in one hand and the Mauser on my lap. She watched and smiled as I told the story.

"Why are you smiling?"

"You're a real shark tracker now, Calvin. Look at you sitting there all salty, half covered in diesel grease and chum, with a damned harpoon rifle in your lap. Christ, you're a picture."

We laughed and looked at each other but said nothing, because nothing needed to be said. We had gotten to a point where we recognized how good it felt being together. She spoke after a while.

"Frank has tired of tracking blue sharks. I'm glad we got onto this mako."

"I've got a better feel for this thing now that I've shot it. If we can get close enough, we'll have him."

"The transmitter batteries are getting weaker. Frank thinks they'll last the day, but that's it," she said with concern. "We really want to get this fish back. How far will that thing shoot?"

"As far as the line in that spool and as far as Calvin can hold on," said Beetle, who joined us.

Whenever I had the firearm ready Beetle wouldn't leave my side. He said he was my Tanzanian tracker *M'Cola* just back from the Green Hills of Africa, and he started calling me *B'wana*.

"Well, if we're lucky, we may find out... *B'wana*," Joni said and returned to work with Frank.

Ellie had been up in her spotting position in the spreaders since breakfast. She knew there wasn't much time left, it would have to happen today if it was going to happen. Beetle and I sat patiently waiting for the fish to come.

"You're going to nail this bastard, right?"

"I thought you were a big Greenpeace fan?"

"I am, but this shark is evil. He put those weeds in the engine intake, and he'll do it again. He was just poking at our defenses."

"I just want to get him and go home."

"Now you sound like Joe. All he's been talking about is some Grateful Dead concert he's hoping to get to. Shoot him too, will you?"

WE SAT THERE patiently for a couple hours listening to the faint beeps of the transmitter that trailed out of the wheelhouse. The mako had been down in the boundary layer for most of the morning, but now it was ever so slowly rising toward the surface. Beetle spoke of Frank's work and his theory of a warm-blooded system operating within the shark, how the interior arrangement of blood vessels keeps the brain warm and functional at great depths and pressures. Frank had measured the interior temperatures of shark's cranial cavities, placed thermistors in their bodies while they were alive and swimming, and used infrared telemetry to record temperature gradients of muscle tissue after dissection. He designed and built his transmitters, managed the expeditions on a shoestring budget, and rustled as many volunteers as he could while he pioneered the art of fish tracking. Beetle told stories of prior trips to Baja and the Mediterranean, he spoke in zoological terms I knew nothing of, and by noon my head began to get fuzzy.

The sun overhead had become unbearable, and the

fatigue of three weeks at sea seeped deep into my bones. We could tell by the sound of the transmission that the batteries had weakened too. The beeps sounded more like squeaks, barely audible on the bow. We tracked and waited, meandering across the molten silver sea. The sun reached its zenith, making the world around us flat with a voluminous haze. The temperature rose with the sun, and with the light bouncing off the water, there was no place to hide. The wind remained nothing but a whisper, and the swells from the south gradually heightened to resemble gentle furrows as far as the eye could see. We squinted against the glare to where the shark ought to be, waiting for a sign. Beetle had one of the rifle cartridges in hand, and he began scratching into the plastic casing with his pocket knife. When we got the call to get ready, he handed me the cartridge. "Here, that'll get him."

It took a moment for my eyes to catch the engraving in the light. "Bob?"

"Yeah. The bullet has his name on it. I named the shark Bob. You got a problem with that?"

"Bob!"

"What's so funny?" Ellie yelled down.

"The shark's name is Bob."

"Bob?"

And then the mako rose to the surface. I scrambled to get into position, placing myself before the forward stay; Beetle buckled my harness to the cable. There was a lot of yelling back and forth, from above and from Joni in the wheelhouse. Ellie disappeared in the glare of the sun, I could just barely see her arm pointing out to starboard.

"He just broke the surface out about 150 yards. Calvin, you got him?"

"Take it easy. We need to get closer." I loaded the cartridge with the shark's name on it into the chamber, bolted it down, set the safety, and made sure the harpoon shaft sat firmly in the barrel. Gradually, the boat turned to line up with the fin, which looked larger than before and black against the silvery white sea. The *Bird* slowly moved into range.

"*Hapana B'wana*," Beetle said from behind.

"What the hell does that mean?"

"*Hapana simba*."

"*Simba* is lion – I at least know that."

"Look *B'wana*, if you wound this monster you'll have to go into the bush after it. We can't have a rogue shark roaming the countryside, now can we?"

"Yeah, well I'll need my trusty guide to go with me."

Then everyone stopped talking and stood quiet. The fin disappeared for a moment, and then surfaced again only 50 yards ahead. I raised the rifle keeping the sight on him; he went down again and didn't come up. The motor stopped and we slid across the spot where moments earlier the shark had been swimming. From the wheelhouse the interval between beeps got slightly longer, he went down but not deep. We waited.

And we waited. The sun wouldn't let up, it just bore down harder, the swells rolled in from the south with a pitch and beat like a lazy metronome, slowly rocking away another hour, and then another. We kept our distance and devised plans on how to get near enough for a shot. I, on the other hand, like the *Bird*, started to drift. Lost within the world of dazzling light before me, my mind began to let go, to travel back to Vermont with my Uncle Bill, to the day we ventured onto the floating island, a place he warned me never to go alone but would one day take me.

northern pike

22

The island covered more than 40 acres and was noted as being one of only two floating islands in the world, the other being in Africa. I had no idea if that was true or not and didn't care. The place gave me the creeps. Its terrain consisted of a dense layer of brush and vines, tamarack trees, mosses and strange plants.

We spent the morning fishing the southern tip of the island and had caught plenty of yellow perch and one smallmouth bass for dinner. The day had clouded over, making it cool and comfortable with a light breeze. Along the way, Uncle Bill would often point out particular details on these excursions that he knew I might overlook and thought important, like the type of clouds and the kinds of weather to expect, or a pool of flat water where the groundwater up-welled into the pond, the call of birds and sightings of animals along the shore. He had a wealth of knowledge and felt compelled to pass it on to me. As we rounded the far side of the island, he turned the canoe into one of the many tight channels that creased its perimeter. We were going in.

The canoe pushed into the dense brush, which appeared to be impenetrable, as if it grew upon the water itself, but after scraping 50 feet in, the brush opened into a little lagoon, the brackish water below dark and deep. We landed on what appeared to be a mound of moss with a walkway of old planks at the footing. The planks looked as if they had been there since the dawn of man, older than the wheel, soggy, punky and shaped with the outline of the tree from which they came.

"Locust wood, wears like iron and is good for fence posts. We put these in after I built the cabin," said Uncle Bill.

He led the way along this boardwalk into the primeval swamp. The ground moved where we walked as if the planks lay upon some great floating mattress. His bulk made an impression, the planks giving way in the soft spots as we followed the meandering path through the knurly vegetation. A stand of old tamarack trees leaned towards the sky, red-winged black birds hung on the reeds, and a strange cacophony of amphibian noises surrounded us as we went deeper into this prehistoric land. After some maneuvering of planks to continue our journey we came upon an opening in the brush that formed a pool about half the size of a basketball court. The water was so black it looked unnatural.

"We used to come out here at night with lanterns and fish for the big ones. Andy was convinced a pike so big it could eat a canoe lived here, but he said it would only come out at night and was hiding under the island during the day." It wouldn't take much to convince me that such an animal could live there. "Here, look at this." He bent over and pointed to a plant shaped like a cup with long bristly hairs inside. "Pitcher plant. There's a better one here if we can find it."

We backtracked a bit, walking slowly, feeling our way along the planks, the water squishing under the wood making a strange sound as my uncle surveyed the exotic vegetation. He squatted next to a clump of reddish purple plants. "Look at this one. It's like a Venus fly trap." The plant featured a clump of heavy-headed pod-like appendages. He touched an open pod the size of a spoon with a blade of marsh grass and the plant snapped shut. "Carnivorous. They eat bugs."

This was better than a movie. It was like being in a movie. In the same clump another pod contained a buzzing fly, its silhouette clearly defined through the transparent leafy skin. I could now imagine a larger species waiting for us to make a wrong turn, and stayed close to my uncle as we walked toward the middle of the island. In a small clearing, he stopped and stood quietly for a moment, then pointed at a clump of moss, "Here's where I fell in."

It took me a minute to say, "You fell in?"

"Around ten years ago. We used to come here in the early morning, me and Roonie, still hoping to get that big pike.

We walked through here I don't know how many times. We would walk on the bog back then. I walked over there to take a leak, and in mid-step it just opened up."

We stood there staring at the moss and plants as a pair of electric blue dragonflies joined at the torso hovered and darted in the air above the spot. "I went down and it closed right up over me, dark as night, roots and weeds hanging down. I could hang on to stuff but couldn't get through."

Looking up at him, his face serious and contorted, I had to ask, "What happened?"

"While I thrashed about, I could hear Roonie yelling. He had been lagging behind and never saw me go down, but he heard me shout when I fell through. When he got here, he saw the tip of my fly rod poking out of the bog and knew what happened. He grabbed a big plank and laid on it crossways and plunged his head, shoulders, and arms down until he got a hold of me and pulled me through. He later said it was like delivering a baby, my bald head and all covered with muck. It took a good half hour to get me out of that hole. Roonie saved my life."

He stood there thinking about that day and Roonie, his old friend who had recently left this earth. "Goddamn Roonie," he said softly.

As a twelve-year-old, this was the most intimate moment any adult had ever shared with me. My uncle would always look different from that day on, and by the time we got back to the canoe the island seemed less mysterious and hostile. Uncle Bill approached slowly, as was his manner upon engaging open water.

"If you're quiet enough, you'll see things you wouldn't have," he'd always say. He approached the canoe and suddenly put out his hand to halt, then waved me slowly forward. I stood behind him and peered to where he pointed. Close to the canoe, out about eight feet from the shelter of the island, just under the surface, floated the biggest fish I'd ever seen. It was long and narrow like a torpedo and looked to be the size of the family toboggan.

"Big pike," he said. I nodded. "Get your bow," he whispered.

The fishing poles were placed in the bottom of the canoe when we made our approach to avoid the lines from getting tangled. It would have been impossible to get them without spooking the fish, but my trusty Ben Pearson bow was within easy reach. I had a special fishing arrow with a length of line that would pay out from a clip that could attach to my belt. Many hours had been spent with this gear attempting to bag bluegills close to shore with disappointing results.

"You've got to aim low, under the fish," he whispered.

With a fish this size I felt sure I couldn't miss and would rely upon Bill to deal with the aftermath. We moved as slow as tree growth to get ready. The pike remained suspended in liquid, its pectoral fins waving slowly and its mouth slightly open, almost smiling. I drew back the arrow, aiming under the fish at a good offset, and let it go. The arrow appeared to pass right through him. The fish darted off in a flash and disappeared, taking the line with him. Bill had the loose end wrapped around his hand. The line came taught and then went limp.

"Whooo! Did you see that fish? The biggest damn pike I've ever seen. Andy was right. Goddamn, Calvin. You almost got him. You hit him in his fin. God what a fish. Don't know what I'd do if you did hit him. He'd probably pull me under the island. Wait 'til we tell Andy."

It turned out poor old Andy was in some nursing home somewhere suffering the effects of too many birthdays. Uncle Bill felt that this revelation would maybe bring him back to life, and somehow it seemed best the pike got away. It made for a better story. The creature would still haunt the island and the minds of those hunkered around the fire on the cold and snowy winter nights. The best thing though was that we would become part of the island mythology.

"You've got to aim low, under the fish," he said.

HIS VOICE A DISTANT memory, now everything consisted of white light and garbled sound as I had drifted into a strange land of overexposure. All the cosmic rays, ultraviolet light, and photons of the sun passed through me like wind through a screen door, whistling as it passed. My ears hummed with it, my eyes barely able to focus to see the crew trying to entice the shark, which remained close to the surface, by throwing chunks of bait in its direction. Ellie repeatedly spotted it but then lost it again. It dove once but came right back up. They took the gamble with the bait knowing it could attract more sharks, but they were desperate because the transmitter batteries had gotten so weak Frank feared losing the fish if it went deep again. Amongst the babble of voices someone was calling my name. It was Joe.

"Calvin, the shark. We must feed the children!"

Ellie would yell down excitedly when she spotted it, then get angry when it disappeared. My world became fuzzier and fuzzier. Someone was speaking into my ear.

"Calvin."

"Calvin!" It was Joni. "Are you all right?"

"Are you kidding?"

"If you get a shot now, take it. If he goes down again, we'll lose him."

"Feed the children," Joe shouted.

"Mako, B'wana, kufi, kufi."

"He's up! He's on the surface off to the port side," someone shouted.

But I had become distracted by the little black birds that fluttered above the white liquid before me, gently touching down and making ripples as they dipped for food. And then the petrels flew off and my dog Banner ran across the water in big bounding leaps in slow motion, his black sleek body prancing across the water as he ran where the birds once were. He passed before me several times, his feet splashing in the pools. I had to be laughing. Someone put a firm hand on my shoulder.

"Calvin! You got him?" Frank's voice brought me

back. "Calvin?"

I shook my head and collected myself, slowly drifting out of the strange hallucination I had fallen into. "I'm okay, Frank. Stay with the shark." It all seemed like a dream, like the threshold between a dream and being awake. Ellie's voice echoed in my head as she called down from the spreaders.

"He's up, dead ahead, a little to starboard!" The swells had grown in height so that, when the shark was in the trough, I couldn't see it, but she could. "Calvin, do you see him?"

My head was spinning and I tried to focus. Then he went down again.

"He's down," she hollered.

"We're losing him, and the power's going," Joni yelled from the wheelhouse. Several minutes passed, they killed the engine and no one said a word. "We lost the signal! We lost the signal," Joni shouted.

The last time we spotted the shark it was over 100 feet away. There would be only one chance for a shot. The sliding sight on the barrel had four tick marks engraved along the side with the numbers 20, 30, 40, and 50, I had to assume that meant meters and put the sight on the top, 150 feet, give or take, a big margin of error. Everyone was out on deck now watching and waiting. The sun was to my right side, surprisingly low on the horizon; I guess it had been a long day.

"He's up! He's up! A little to port and on top of the swell."

The fin stood out clear and dark. Everyone started to yell until I raised the rifle, and then there wasn't a sound but the blood pumping in my ears. The shark was moving to my left. He disappeared in the trough. Everything became weightless, the rifle, my body, my life. When the shark came up again, I sighted a tad forward, and fired.

Wham! The harpoon rose in an arch as my shoulder wrenched back with the concussion. Through the blur I could see the shark disappear in the trough again; the harpoon came down in a sloping curve into the swell where the fin had been, and the sea exploded as this huge silvery creature leaped clear out of the water, its mouth open, its teeth white in a strange smile as it crashed the glassy surface, the sparkles of light suspended into a brilliant flash.

"We got him!"

Beetle grabbed the rifle and worked the line around a cleat just before it went taught with a snap and nearly pulled the boat around. Joe was whooping and howling like a cowboy. The shark leapt one more time, and then everything went back into slow motion. Someone had their arms around me and was yelling into my right ear.

"You got him, Calvin! You got him." It was Ellie. She looked like a crazy person on fire, her face like a cooked lobster.

My head was spinning and the world became detached. As everyone tended to the shark, Ellie managed to get me back safely on deck where I stood dumbfounded. One minute she had her arm around me and the next minute I was laying face up to the sky with Ellie looking all panicky down at me. Something was poking me in the back, and I rolled to find I had fallen onto the pile of harpoon poles and boat hooks. Things got blurry real quick, and then I went away for a while.

Floating, floating, with voices in a tunnel calling out to me. Someone was calling my name from far away, pulling me back to consciousness. When I finally opened my eyes two heads were looking down at me with a brilliant blue sky above them perfectly framed. The figures spoke to each other and to me. It was all very strange, like being in a box, in a television looking out as these beautiful pink and white clouds passed above me. Someone with long hair spoke, asked me my name. It was becoming very uncomfortable. There was the strange sensation of wetness.

"Calvin? Calvin, who am I?" the voice said.

It was hard to tell. The figures looked dark against the bright background. One figure seemed to be stuffing something down my pants, and then everything started coming back very quickly. First I recognized Joni, who was holding my hand, and then Frank who was shoving ice under my clothes. I seemed to be a big box, with water because there was a lot of splashing. Lifting my head I could see the rest of my body floating in one of the bait freezers in a stew of sea water, frozen fish and ice. After answering some dumb questions, they let me sit up.

"What the hell happened?"

"Frank says you've suffered heatstroke, Calvin. You passed out on deck and nearly stabbed yourself. Good thing you had the work vest. Your temperature is coming down, it was way up there. You need to stay in longer."

Then Frank poured more ice down my clothing while Joni held my hand. There was a lot of shouting coming from the stern.

"They've got their hands full with that mako," she said, touching my forehead, brushing back my hair with her cool wet hand.

The mako seemed very far away now as a strange sense of relief overcame me. It was over. We would be going home. No more challenges, no more night watches, no more counting beeps, no more sea sickness. I had to be coming to my senses because the foul smell of fish was becoming overwhelming.

"I've got to get out of here."

When they finally got my body out of the ice, Joni kindly offered to hose me down. The warm sea water felt like it could cleanse all the worries of the world away. She smiled as she stood with the hose.

"You got him, Calvin! I'm so proud of you."

"I believe we have a date," I mumbled in a feeble voice.

"We'll discuss that later, silly."

Frank came back looking concerned, happy, and crazy like the rest. My bones had turned to rubber and I could barely stand. "We'll get you down below to rest, Calvin," he said.

Something was poking me in the groin. I stopped them, and after wrestling with my underwear, a half frozen mackerel fell out of my pant leg. They couldn't help but laugh.

"Christ, Calvin. I think you just gave birth to a fish."

They struggled to get me below and then set me up on

a bunk in the forward cabin, and Joni left to help the others. Frank persuaded me out of my wet clothing and got me settled. "Joni's going to get some fluids into you. You need to drink and rest. You were really burning up. Didn't you feel funny?"

"Frank, I've been feeling funny since the moment I stepped on this boat."

He gave me a long look and smiled. "Christ Calvin."

Joni soon returned with a container full of liquid, and sat on the bed beside me with a motherly look of concern.

"You're in good hands," Frank said and left.

It was quiet in the cabin, the commotion from the stern had ceased, leaving only the sound of water sliding along the hull and the glare of the evening sun bursting through the porthole. In the golden light, Joni looked like an angel, with her green smiling eyes, and chestnut hair radiant about her face. She took my hand. I think we both realized then that, somewhere within the proximity of unlikelihood and beyond our better judgment, we would find it difficult to walk away from each other. She looked out the porthole at the setting sun as I slowly slipped away into exhaustion.

Sometime during the night I came to with the sound of voices from the galley, and Ellie's haunting laughter. Someone had their hand on my shoulder, shaking me.

"Drink some more of this," Frank said. When I gave it back, thanking him, I could see Joni asleep on the other bunk. "Any headaches? Can you eat?" he asked.

"I'm just really tired, Frank."

"Then sleep."

With my fate in the hands of friends I fell into the sleep of the weary, gently rocking with the roll of the swell, my body spent and wrung out from the days of pursuit and overexposure, but my spirit buoyant and floating freely above the strange waters where dogs dance, islands float, and green eyes carry you across the sea back home.

23

Next morning the foul smell of fish greeted me while I lay in bed surveying my condition. For the first time in a long while there was a sense of inner peace, maybe it was the fatigue, maybe it was the journey, but there was the feeling of a new beginning that I had been tested and came through in one piece. Like some wandering saint walking out of the wood, I felt blessed by an unknown spiritual power that guided the way and would now bring me home. My body was spent, I felt like crap, smelled worse, and needed a shower badly, but dallied there in my bunk watching the late morning sun roll around the cabin as the *Bird* steamed along at a good clip. Joni had spent the night in the cabin, she stood by me just as I would stand by her had our fortunes been reversed. Tomorrow we would arrive in Woods Hole and this story would be over.

Today I would take it easy and get my strength back, but first a shower. The warm water felt like a cathartic revelation, it ran across my face and body, tingling my senses, quickening my pulse, bringing clarity. I lingered there not worrying about using too much for we would soon be home. The pattering sound beat against my head, the swirl at my feet gurgled in the drain; lost in the magic of water, I stood transfixed until the shower door suddenly swung open.

"Hey!" It was Joni in her bathing suit. She moved in beside me.

"I just need to rinse off this chum smell."

"What are you doing?"

"We were cleaning up the chum station. God, what a stink. You don't mind do you?"

There's barely room for one in a ship's shower. She spun around, whipping off her bathing suit and began rubbing her arms with soap, working the lather along her shoulders, over her breasts, across her tummy. The touch of her skin aroused me. She turned rinsing off and lifted her face to mine, our lips met in a slow, long, wet and ready kiss.

"Everyone's working on deck, don't worry." She smiled. "Glad to see you're up." Then she laughed. "Have to go now." And she jumped out of the shower stall just as suddenly as she appeared.

I stood there in suspended animation. A moment later, the door flew open again. She was wrapped in a towel now.

"Oh. By the way, we're not heading home."

"What?" She closed the door quickly and was gone, leaving me with the hunch that maybe this is why hurricanes were originally named after women.

After gathering some food, I went up on deck to see what was going on. Beetle sat in the open cockpit reading in the sun. The wind had picked up a little on our backside and the swells had gotten bigger, rolling in from the southeast onto our starboard beam. It looked like we were heading in a northeasterly direction. Beetle gave me the once over.

"Well, well, we thought you would be sleeping all day. You looked like you'd been dragged through hell yesterday."

"Feeling much better today, thank you, *M'Cola* or whatever your name is."

"Frank wants to talk to you when you have a minute. He had to report your condition to the port office."

"Where the hell are we going?"

"Oh that. I thought I'd wait and let Frank tell you." He smiled. "You didn't hear the row last night?"

"I didn't hear a thing."

"Things came to a head yesterday. Joe had been getting on Frank's nerves since the moment he set foot on the boat, as you can imagine. But yesterday he was yelling at you, "save the children," going on and on about losing the shark, he wouldn't shut up. We finally got the mako onboard, and man what a fish, had to wait until it was practically dead. We figure he was over 400 lbs. Well, Frank and Ellie dressed the shark after getting all the measurements while Joe watched and kept going on about getting back to the beach and that Grateful Dead concert. That's when Frank dropped the bomb. He told Joe that we had a couple days left and wanted to check out that dead whale they've been squawking about on the radio. Joe had a hissy fit and started pissing and moaning and wouldn't stop. Frank just lost his patience. He had a fish knife in one hand and a fistful of guts in the other. What a sight, he turned to Joe and said, 'If you don't shut up Joe, I'm going to cut you open like this fish."

"Holy cow."

"Joe just froze in his tracks with his mouth open. Frank looked like he was ready to do it too, and that was that."

"Christ, now what?"

"Well, we're heading for that whale – wherever that is."

I stood and waved good morning to Joe who manned the wheel, but he didn't acknowledge me.

"He's in a snit. He assumed we'd be heading in after that dramatic ending yesterday. By the way, how the hell did you do that?"

"I have no idea. It was like I was watching myself in a movie. My body felt disconnected. I can still see that damn harpoon shooting up to the sky."

"We were all very impressed, especially with the part where you were swimming in the bait freezer and gave birth to a mackerel. You don't see that everyday." We both laughed.

"Thank God. So what do we do with a dead whale?"

"Better ask the chief scientist." He nodded as Frank joined us. Frank looked rested and assumed more of a composed demeanor than he had in the past weeks. "Did you straighten things out with Joe?" Beetle asked.

"We are on speaking terms," Frank said with a serious but amused tone. He turned to me. "That was some shark you harpooned yesterday. I'm not even going to ask how you did it because no one would believe it. You sure look better." He studied my eyes for a moment.

"I'm feeling much better, just a little tired."

"Good. Look. I need to call into the port office and give them an update on your condition. I'd like to stay out another day or two if we can find this whale." They both gave me the hairy eyeball.

"I'm fine, really."

"There's a tropical storm to the south of us, off Bermuda, that's pushing these swells, but it's predicted to move east. If we can't find the whale today, we'll keep on heading home."

"And we can all go to the Grateful Dead concert," added Beetle.

Frank went back to reviewing the past weeks' data with the girls while Beetle and I sat in the sun. The sky wore a thin gray overcast that darkened toward the southeast, but it was a fine morning, the air had cooled from the previous day's humidity, and it felt pleasant to be sitting there, cruising along the continental shelf with the job done, still in one piece, heading home.

With my face to the sun, I sighed. "Ya know, this shark tracking ain't so bad.

"Endless sun-filled days."

"So Beetle, what *do* we do with a dead whale?"

24

We were steaming along a northeast track following the rim of the continental slope in search of a dead whale in the hopes that, if we found it, we would also encounter some extraordinary sharks. Beetle and I sat in the sun while the others poured over the previous three weeks of data. The *Bird of Passage* wallowed between the swells, her diesel engine sounding robust as ever. One more day and we would be home.

Joni came out of the wheelhouse to sit with to me. "So how's the patient," she asked with a tender smile and no fear of betraying a secret.

"Thanks for watching over me."

"Yes, I watched over you."

"I think that means something."

"It could mean I might want to change my profession and become a nurse."

"You might want to check my pulse right now because every time you're near me my heart goes pitter-patter."

"Calvin!" she said sternly.

"Just pretend I'm not here," said Beetle. "Just reading."

"You get rid of that chum smell?" I asked.

"All gone. Say Beetle, are there any good restaurants on the Cape?"

"I suggest you go to P-Town."

"I've never been to P-Town," she said, looking at me expectantly.

"We can fix that."

She smiled. "Well we'll have to make it quick. I'm due in San Diego by the end of the week."

"Yeah, we know," grumbled Beetle. "Dr. Kelley has a

class to teach."

I didn't know what to say, but wondered if she was really going to walk out of my life.

"Good. Well, let's see if we can find this whale," she said and went back to join the others.

Beetle and I sat there for a few quiet moments.

"Can I come?" he asked jokingly.

"Go back to New York City with your Bohemian friends."

"You're one lucky bastard."

"I don't see how this can play out in a good way."

"She'll be back next year," he said lightly. Then he turned to me with a look of sincerity, "You never know how things like this will turn out."

I wrestled with the prospect. "And to think at one time I would have bagged this trip. This whole thing has felt like it's been stage managed from the beginning, like fulfilling some destiny."

"Yeah, well, to hell with your destiny. You're a shark tracker now."

"Do you think Frank would have gone at him with the knife?"

"No, he's not crazy – he just acts crazy. He was a sight though."

"That would have been a great picture. I can see him standing there."

"I'll bet Joe will never forget it. I hope he doesn't do anything stupid and press charges."

"Be kind of embarrassing," I said.

"He's not a bad guy. He just needs a little mentoring. It's a good sign if they're on speaking terms."

We sat there for a couple of hours talking about the mako and other shark encounters, about Frank's research, and Beetle's life growing up with his older brother. It was clear they loved each other and enjoyed each other's company. Beetle's sense of humor could usually buffer Frank's intensity, and Frank trusted Beetle's judgment on most things, which came in handy with so many pans on the fire. Having someone around with sound judgment proved invaluable.

The overcast thickened during the early afternoon, off on the southeastern horizon, the gun-metal sky made me appreciate the fact we were heading away from what looked like nasty weather.

"It's got to be some storm that's pushing swells like this," said Beetle.

"As long as the storm stays put, I'm happy."

Ellie and Joni made lunch for everyone, and we all sat in the cockpit enjoying our last day together, all except Joe who manned the wheel and gave us the quiet treatment. I think he was embarrassed and needed to work things out.

Frank scanned the horizon for signs of fish while he ate; his windswept beard and hair gave him a wild look. He listened as we talked, enjoying a quiet moment with his crew until Beetle brought up the subject of our search.

"If we find this whale, I have no idea what condition it's in or what we'll find there." Frank now seemed to betray some excitement at the prospect. "There may be some big sharks – there usually are. If we can get our last transmitter on one, we'll give it a go. It could just end up staying in the vicinity of the whale for days."

"We have no idea if they'll be interested in the bait when there's a whale to feast on," Joni added.

"If we find it and everything looks good, we'll try several hand lines with a clump of mackerel per line. If we get a shark and it's too big, we'll at least try to pull it close enough to get a Fisheries tag on it. If you can't manage it, you cut it loose. Watch your lines. We work two on a team: Joni and Beetle, me and Ellie. Calvin, you work with Joe. Help him where he needs it."

WE FINISHED LUNCH, and then everyone got ready. We were back on a mission with the expectation that this whale could be something worth seeing. I gathered my camera gear in the wheelhouse and laid out my lenses and rolls of film on the navigation table. The day was turning into a slate-grey landscape, and hopefully a little light would break through the clouds to provide some contrast. Joe watched as I changed lenses.

"Nice camera?"

"I love this camera. It's never let me down." He seemed to be reaching out so I tried to keep the conservation going. I loaded some Ilford fine grain medium speed film into the Canon A1. "Do you mind if I shoot some photos of you while you're at the wheel?"

He didn't, so I began taking my time between shots, asking him to cooperate by looking this way and that. We talked about the magic of photography and the elusiveness of catching the magic. This interaction softened him a bit and for some strange reason he seemed to come to the realization that now, on this day, he would be immortalized on film, the day we found the whale, and *he* would be the one to find it.

"Fucking dead whale," he mumbled. "Damn whale. They've been yapping about that thing for the past three days, those guys on channel 81. I'll bet they're the guys who hit it, ran it over or something. Here, take the wheel."

While the rest of the crew assembled the gear on the stern, Joe went back to the log notes and did a second take on the radio sightings. He set me up on the wheel and began talking to himself, mulling over the chart, reviewing the last reported location and the sightings previous to that. After 20 minutes of this, he gave the command to turn 30 degrees to port. Then he started playing with the radar settings and buried his head in the radar scope. All the time talking out loud either to me or himself it was hard to tell.

"If you crank up the range, and turn the gain up all the way we might be able to see something. Come on birdies, I know you're out there."

An hour passed like this while the crew made ready, and he never wavered from his focus. He would make little corrections as we cruised along at our top speed of seven knots, and after another hour, he gave me a compass reading of 0-5-0.

"Keep it on that course. I'm going up to have a look. I'll find this goddamn whale." He flung the ship's binoculars around his neck and ventured out to climb the mast. In the beam swell, the ship rolled with these long rolling swings, making the mast pitch out over the water. I couldn't have lasted a minute up there, and don't know how he did it. After several minutes of hanging on for dear life, he yelled down to turn the stern to the swell, and this greatly diminished the sway. The wind had been picking up from the southwest. The waves slapped our sides as we rode with the swell, and the boat weaved around, getting a footing as I tried to keep her steady. Joe searched the sea to the northeast, his body in dark contrast against the gray sky. The others were startled by his sudden change of attitude and the fact that he would be so adventurous as to get up in the air under such conditions.

"What's gotten into Joe?" Frank asked.

I shrugged my shoulders and shook my head. "He says he's going to find this whale."

We watched the lone silhouette. "Well, whatever you're doing with him, keep doing it."

Another half hour passed with all hands scanning the gray sea for a sign. We were cruising along the shelf line close to Atlantis Canyon. Farther to the east, if we kept going, we would cross the Great South Channel, a geological feature of deeper bathymetry between Nantucket Shoals and Georges Bank, a feeding ground for whales. Perhaps that's where this whale had been going to or coming from, but I didn't know that much about whales and figured there was probably a lot more to the story. Joni told me that whales sometimes get hit by large ships and guessed that probably happened to this one.

We cruised along under the darkening skies as the heavy layer of clouds from the southeast reached over us. Joe flagged me when he needed my attention by giving me simple hand signals for course correction. Then I sensed he had something. He had the glasses up and started to yell. "Birds!

I've got birds." Then a moment later, "Something big!"

He fixed on a position a few degrees off the starboard bow for another minute before he climbed down. He approached Frank and they had words as he pointed. Frank climbed the mast, had a look, and came down, nodding with a smile to Joni as he planted his arm around Joe's shoulders. Joe beamed like it was his birthday. He became very animated, pointing out yonder, and they all laughed, and then he entered the cabin.

"Got the goddamn whale," he said as he took the wheel. "To hell with the Grateful Dead. I got this whale. Man, I can't wait to see them sharks."

Joe had good eyes. The whale appeared to be nearly two miles from our position, but it was the birds that gave it away. As we neared, we could see the large black shape of the body lift on the passing swells, floating perpendicular to them with a bright green veil trailing behind, the water breaking as it passed, covering the body as if it were still alive, the many dark triangular shapes appearing and disappearing in the vicinity as the birds rode shotgun in the sky.

We approached from the lee side of the swells, which allowed us to drift by. As we drew closer, the reality of the scene dampened the spirits of our crew. We could now see the large black bulk of the whale, a huge rounded hump floating, and halfway along its body the net twisted in a rat's nest of knots, the entanglement draping into the water and flowing behind like a colorful tail nearly 100 feet long. But it was the sharks that mesmerized me. As the swells passed, the trough of the wave would expose the sharks feeding, their heads straight up, perpendicular to the carcass as they thrashed and tore out great amounts of blubber leaving gaping holes of exposed flesh as the birds scrambled for remnants.

"Holy shit!" Beetle said it for all of us.

It looked like there were sharks everywhere. In comparison to the whale, they looked small, but when one passed nearby that had to be nearly 12 feet in length; and when that one mixed in with the others, and was obviously smaller than some in its midst, I knew we were into something extraordinary.

"You getting all this, Calvin?" Frank asked.

It took me a moment to snap out of my trance before I could use the camera.

"I don't like the looks of this," Frank said in a low tone. "There's too much going on."

But the girls were too fascinated with the spectacle, trying to identify the species, pointing out certain dorsal fins, tail fins, body color, and size.

"That's got to be a porbeagle. Frank that one by the clump in the net is a big porbeagle. Whites over there. Look, Joni. That could be a tiger. Frank, a big tiger."

We drifted slowly past, watching as the whale rose up on the swell, now seemingly back to life as the water broke over its body. But then it would lay still again, wretched as the wave moved on.

"I don't like the looks of this," Frank repeated, this time loud enough so Ellie and Joni could catch his tone.

We all stood in a cluster watching the whale as we drifted away. I was in a daze, as were Beetle and Joe. I had never seen anything like it.

"There's too much going on. The water's tricky with this swell, and the sharks are too big. The wind is picking up and I don't like that net."

"I don't like the net either," said Joe. "As a matter of fact, I hate nets."

"We can stick here for a few hours and observe," Frank said trying to appease the girls' enthusiasm.

They were quiet for a moment. Then Ellie spoke for them both. "Couldn't we try maybe two hand-lines away from the whale? Maybe we can get that last transmitter on one and track it at least until tomorrow. You've always talked about tracking a porbeagle, Frank."

He stood there looking back at the whale. "What do you think, Joe?"

"The whole thing gives me the creeps." He hemmed it

in after a moment. "I suppose we could try for a couple hours and head home after tagging a few.

I kept my mouth shut, as did Beetle. We both felt that this was a call for the professionals. I couldn't keep my eyes off the whale though and wondered how long it survived entangled in that net and how come the fishermen responsible couldn't notify some whale organization to attempt a rescue. When the sharks first hit it, was it still alive? Eaten alive – the slow horror of it troubled me. The size of the sharks, the oily slick in the water, and the stench, a heavy wet smell that could stick to your clothes, all condensed into an intense drama before us. The crew stood in frozen anticipation as I worked the camera.

"Alright, we'll try two hand-lines with floats, one off the bow and one off the windward beam. We stay away from the whale, set the drift upwind, and make a pass to see what we get. If it's too big, we cut it loose, and if it's a bluedog, we cut it loose. Anything else, white shark, porbeagle, or tiger, we tag with the transmitter. With the wind on our beam, we should be able to manage these swells. Two on a line. Calvin works with Joe like we planned. I want work vests on everyone."

It sounded easy enough, but I had an uneasy feeling, maybe because of Frank's reluctance or my lack of experience. It seemed, though, that everyone moved differently, with more caution but also with a certain amount of distraction as we all looked at the whale's body, underwater as the swell passed, then exposed, the net riding up on the wave like some exotic tail, the gray sky, and dark water. It wasn't a pretty picture.

We motored upwind and made ready. Frank and Ellie manned the bow line while Joni and Beetle had a line paying out from the starboard beam cleat. In this position, we would drift by facing the whale, our bow into the swells, and Joe could monitor things in case he had to back down. Both lines had an abundance of bait tied to several shark hooks on a 20 foot gangion under a red poly-float. Frank let his line out about a boat's length; Beetle let his out about twice as far. Then we waited.

Fins appeared and submerged. A variety of dorsal fins and tails would rise up in the waves, some moved fast while others meandered about. As we drifted closer, sharks would approach the boat, rubbing up next to it, and we realized that because there was so much of a slick in the water they probably mistook it for the whale. When a big white shark rose up, attempting to get a mouth full, we knew things weren't right. Frank saw this and gave the signal to call it off, waving both hands to Beetle shouting, "It's no good!"

Then the bow float took off, disappearing for a moment only to pop up again on the other side of the bow. Ellie and Frank tried to identify what they had on the line, but Frank was too distracted by what Joni and Beetle were doing because they also had a fish on. Joe was getting nervous, too much was happening on deck, and he couldn't keep track of what everyone was doing.

"Go help Beetle. If that fish is too big, cut the line. I'll keep an eye on Frank."

By the time I got to them, Joni looked electric with excitement. They had an immense white shark on the line that wallowed along the surface like some big old cow. It rolled to its side exposing a bloated white belly. They both had a hand on the line trying to haul it in, with the hopes of getting a Fisheries tag on it. The shark looked big enough to pull a freight train.

"That's a big shark. I don't think you can pull that fish in," I said, hoping to remind them of the plan, but they paid no attention.

"Let's try the winch," suggested Beetle eagerly.

Joni nodded in agreement as they wrestled to get enough slack to get to the mizzen winch near the stern. This took some doing, and seeing they now had their own agenda, I went to see if the others needed help. They had a Porbeagle on the hook that appeared to be about six feet long, a reasonable size to work with, but it was aggressively resisting any attempt to get near the boat. While they labored in this tug-of-war, Frank turned to me.

"What are those two doing now?"

"They've got a big white shark that they want to get a tag on."

"How big?"

"Too big Frank."

"Tell them to cut it off, damn it!" He looked back towards the stern with concern and told Ellie to stand by. She let the line down to look back, as did I to see Beetle and Joni bent over the stern.

"Christ, now what?" cried Frank.

When we got back there we discovered the white shark had passed under the stern and tangled the float line at the rudder. Joe came out cursing. The shark was still attached and thrashed wildly on the surface.

"We've got to cut that line and get this shark off."

He went to get a boat hook. Then Frank went forward to cut the Porbeagle free, and while all this was going down, it seemed we were drifting closer to the whale. As the swell lifted the boat, the wind pushed us a bit closer with each wave as the boat surfed down the side. Either the rudder's locked position or the white shark pulling to free itself brought the stern around.

Joe noticed this as soon as we rode up on the next wave. The *Bird,* now abeam to the swell, bobbed unsure of itself as the stern came around and we drifted closer to the whale and the net.

"We've got to get that fucking line off!"

Beetle ran for the harpoon pole to attach his folding knife. He grabbed two hose clamps from the junk drawer in the cabin and hurriedly screwed the knife handle to the pole while Joe leaned over the stern desperately trying to get at the line. Beetle worked the cutting pole, but the shark was down and pulling hard. We could see the float wedged in between the rudder and the line must have gotten tangled on some part of the running gear. The boat rose up on the wave and came down splashing the stern in the trough while Beetle made desperate jabs into the water, hoping to cut the line as the boat swung around further. We were almost to the whale now. The floating green polypropylene mesh lay along our path, splayed out like a web, waving in the sea like some synthetic carnivorous plant passively awaiting its next prey.

Joe jumped to his feet. "We've got to get out of here!" He ran for the wheelhouse and revved up the diesel. Frank came running from the bow.

"Hold it, Joe! Hold it!" he shouted.

But it was too late. Joe put her ahead and all kinds of mayhem happened below with the rope and float followed by a loud thud. He tried to back her down to free it up, but by then we had passed over the net, and as we came down with the next wave, the net rose up and the engine stalled. He started the engine again but the boat wouldn't move. The prop had entangled in the net not 70 feet from the whale. We all froze where we stood, looking out at the black body, the water turning green as it washed over it, the birds screeching above, crying and laughing at this ship of fools.

Joni stood next to me and moved closer, uttering an oath in Spanish. We waited to see what would happen next, to see how the *Bird* responded, while Joe cursed all the saints in heaven along with: "Jesus, Mary, and Joseph." It didn't seem to help.

After several minutes the wind pushed the hull around, causing the boat to tug on the net and the whale, but the *Bird* felt stable. Frank and Beetle had their heads together. Frank spoke first.

"We need to get this net up high enough on deck to cut it, and to do that we'll need two grappling hooks. Calvin, get the hack saws. Joe and I will haul on the net and tie down the hook lead so Joni and Calvin can get at it with the saws. Ellie and Beetle will make ready the main sail. When I give the word, hoist the sail even if we're still fixed. We may need to have some power to bust free. Be careful with that boom. We don't need anyone falling overboard."

I ran to get the two saws from the engine room and managed to fasten a new blade on the old rusty hacksaw while

Joe and Frank got ready with the grappling hooks. These small homemade weighted steel hooks, about the size of a beer bottle, were perfect for throwing short distances, the four tines small enough to grab the net's mesh. Everyone got into position as if we had done this before. Frank made the first throw, managing to get hold of the net, while he pulled, Joe tied the rope off and threw the other hook. They repeated this maneuver at least four times before we got the first clump of net within reach to start cutting. It was then that we realized how much net there was and how much we would have to cut free. Joni and I went at it with the saws, stopping to hold on as the swells passed, as the boat leaned way over on its side. Frank would give us the okay after he tied the hook line off on the stern cleat, while Joe threw out the other hook to gather more net to haul in. We worked together frantically, knowing we weren't in any eminent danger but felt unsure what could unfold while in this predicament. No one likes being tethered to a dead whale.

Working the saws intensely I could tell Joni felt badly about what happened and was probably blaming herself. I spoke with an easy and steady voice.

"Okay, you got that piece. I'll pull up on this bunch. You hold it and I'll cut."

We took turns cutting and twisting. The rough poly line was hard as wire in some places and did a number on our hands. We were going at what looked like the last section of net when Frank gave the ready signal to Beetle and Ellie, who were waiting patiently at the main sail.

"I think we got it, Frank," Joe said, and you could hear both relief and desperation in his voice. "We'll sail out of here far enough and I'll get down there myself and get that prop free. Goddamn. Woods Hole will never look so good."

Frank gave the go-ahead to Beetle, who immediately started to haul up the main sail. Joe ran to the cabin to man the wheel, and Frank went forward to help the others while Joni and I sat on the stern, our hearts pounding from the exertion. It took a moment to catch our breath.

"Hey, we're free. It's okay. We'll be going home now," I said with reassurance.

Her face softened and she took my hand. "That was a little crazy. Everything happened so fast. Did you see the size of that shark?"

Just then the main sail flapped with a snap as the wind took hold and made it billow halfway up, pushing the *Bird* over on its side and away from the net. The boat began to pick up speed immediately, but then it pitched forward hard like someone slammed on the brakes, catching everyone off guard. The stern rose up exposing the net's steel cable that remained tangled to the boat's running gear. Then the wind took a stronger hold on the sail, pulling the wire higher out of the water.

"Christ almighty," I yelled forward to Frank. "We're on a cable – there's a wire, a wire."

Joe started shouting from the cabin as Frank worked to get the sail down, fearing the strain from the cable could really do some damage to the prop or the rudder.

Joni and I watched the cable as beads of water whipped off the steel coils, the strain suddenly pulled the wire harder and a terrible metallic sound passed beneath us. She picked up one of the grappling hooks as I went forward to help the others. At first I thought she was clearing the gear from the deck, but she threw the hook out over the side. She must have caught the net because she started to pull. I was halfway to Frank and halfway going back to help her when I saw the end of the grappling line she pulled on had tangled itself on the other hook that lay on the deck.

Then things started happening really fast. I yelled to Joni just as the cable that was holding the boat let go, the grappling hook popped up off the deck, grabbed her under the right arm and pulled her overboard. She screamed as she flipped over the side, and then the next thing I knew my body was in mid-air as I jumped in after her.

Flying through the air, hitting the water, the thick rancid smell of it, the figure thrashing almost within reach, all became a blur, as I desperately paddled to get to Joni. Head down, the back of her flotation vest barely above the water, when I finally reached her, she thrashed wildly, I pulled her head up and she let out a desperate cry.

"Help me. I'm caught." It was difficult to understand what she said. "My feet, the rope, it's twisted."

I went for her legs but the rope had fallen free. When my head came out of the water, she was still coughing, trying to get her breath, as the first swell came upon us, lifting us like the dispassionate hand of God.

"I'm hurt," she managed to speak. "The boat?" Her eyes looked wild and frantic. "Where's the boat?" She twisted around with a moan to see the boat rapidly moving away under a half sail, part of it draped into the water, the crew standing on the stern staring at us in disbelief. That's when the first shark passed within arms reach.

"Calvin, the boat."

"Are you okay?" I shouted.

She coughed. "I'm hurt, my side. We need to get back to the boat."

"It's sailing away," I said, taking hold of her work vest.

She cried out in pain and tried to speak but coughed up some pinkish fluid instead. "I can't get my breath, Calvin. The sharks, watch for sharks."

The boat continued to sail further away. Another shark, slender and long, passed behind Joni, its tail higher than our heads.

"Kick the sharks, Calvin."

"What?"

"Kick the sharks if they come near."

"The boat's not coming."

Her right arm seemed useless. "Get the hair out of my face, damn it!" Clearing her face she winced. "My right arm's not working."

"The boat's not coming Joni. Something's wrong." A large black fin headed straight towards us but veered off. We needed to move.

"The net Joni, we're going for the net."

"What?"

"It's our only hope."

The net lay within easy reach, its green matting floated like a sickly weed amongst the sharks. "I'm hurt inside," she said again.

"How bad?"

She tried to catch her breath. A fin came straight at her and then went down, passing beneath us.

"Something rubbed against me," she said, startled.

"We have to move. I'm going to pull you."

"Okay." She sounded weak, her voice trailing off.

When I put my arm around her, she yelled out, but I managed to turn her around and pull from the strap on the back of the work vest. I kicked and stroked as the next swell picked us up, and looked back to see the boat now under full sail, attempting to turn around into the wind. We were getting close to the net; the whale's black bulk looked huge from this new perspective. The green mesh, close now, lay flat in some places, and I couldn't see any fins where it lay.

"Almost there, Joni. Almost there," I yelled. "Hold on."

She moaned something and kept coughing.

The next swell swept us up as I managed to catch a piece of the netting, to hold on and pull further in, but doing so made it harder to kick, so I just kept on grabbing more net.

"We're on the net now. We'll be okay."

As we got further in, it became difficult to move, the mesh snagged my shoes and Joni's vest. I kicked and pulled the snags, we bobbed there waiting for the boat to come. Just below us lay the white underbelly of a dead shark, its head and pectoral fins tightly wrapped and twisted in the net. All around the perimeter, dorsal fins rose up from the gray choppy water, while we lay in the slick of blood and goo. The next swell washed over the whale and converged lifting the net up around us. I could see then that the net was a bad idea, as the wave passed closing the mesh up to our shoulders.

"Calvin, I can't move," Joni cried. "Where's the boat?"

"The boat's coming. It's coming," I said, although now I could only see the top of the mast as we hung in the trough of the wave.

Something pushed hard against us from under the net, whacking our legs as it passed.

"Calvin, this isn't good."

We floated there face to face.

"They'll be here soon." I tried to sound reassuring, but could now see blood wash up from under her shoulder. Then the next wave passed, this time pushing us down and twisting the net around our legs. I pulled and kicked to get free. Joni came up choking.

"We have to move. If we stay here, we're going to get all tangled up," I said as I pushed the hair out of her face.

She looked me in the eye with a desperate plea, "Don't leave me." She coughed, spitting out water, trying to get her breath back. "Don't leave me, Calvin."

"I won't leave you."

"I can't swim. Calvin, I'm going to go into shock. I'm losing it."

"Hang on. They'll be here soon." But now I couldn't see the boat at all, and turned to face the whale, its bulk rising with the oncoming swell. It was our only chance. "We're going for the whale, Joni. We have to get on the whale."

Not waiting for an answer I pulled on the net hand over hand with my legs wrapped around her waist, trying not to squeeze. It took all I had to get to the whale, pulling and praying as we went. "Please God, help us, please"

As the swell washed over us I held on for dear life and pulled harder, parts of the mesh were encrusted with the whale's oily flesh, and other parts were coarse and broken where it draped down from the whale's back like a rope ladder. Just outside the netting, the dark fins rose ominously in the waves. I waited for the next swell, to help lift us along the whale's side, where the water became a thick layer of oily slime, the birds flapped over us jealously grabbing at bits of meat with a cacophony of calls making it difficult to hear.

"This is going to hurt," I yelled into her ear, "but we need to get out of the water."

"Okay, hurry," she said, spitting out blood.

We were alongside the whale when the next swell came and I started to pull us up, but Joni started to scream again. Thinking I was hurting her, I turned to see the head of a white shark come straight up out of the water next to her, the huge triangular teeth exposed and the mouth wide open to clamp onto the side of the whale, ripping at the net and blubber, thrashing wildly. Joni kicked at the head as the shark's black eye rolled back and the water churned with the strange sound of ripping meat. The swell passed, lifting us higher along the whale's back as I desperately reached for more net.

"Calvin!" she shouted as she kicked the shark's head.

I turned and pulled on the net as somewhere low in my belly a force came that gave me the strength beyond anything I thought possible. "Come on, Joni. Come on!" I pulled and pulled, dragging our bodies up the long sloping back of the whale until we were on top.

The next wave came upon us, but it washed by leaving us unharmed. I turned and put her between my legs. She heaved in short measured breathes, her head hung down, the hair covered her face, bits of meat stuck to her clothes.

"Okay, we're on the whale. They'll be here soon." She barely opened her eyes. "Come on, stay with me," I pleaded, trying to catch my breath.

She coughed again, crying out in pain. "I think I'm bleeding inside. I think something's broken."

"I know. I've got you. They're coming."

She mumbled between her labored breaths, "Don't leave me."

"I won't leave you," I said, waiting for the next swell to pass. "I'll never leave you."

The boat was making headway into the wind and it looked like they planned to come alongside the whale. I pushed the hair away from her face; she was trembling all over, and then realized I was trembling as well.

She looked up at me again. "Are they coming?" she said from far away.

"I won't leave you!" She gave my hand a squeeze.

With her body between my legs, and my left arm tucked around her waist, I twisted my right hand into a bundle of net that lay tightly across the whale's back. White whale lice clung to the dead body, and the gulls landed after each wave to peck away, unconcerned with our plight. As the boat drew closer, it felt like rescue was possible but I couldn't picture how it could happen, and it became apparent that our situation remained precarious. Frank and Beetle were on the bow, and when they got within hearing distance they began to yell. I couldn't make out a thing they were yelling with all the birds screeching. Beetle had a rope ready to throw when they approached ahead of the whale, hoping to fall off with the swell, but as the wave reached them, it picked the boat and whale up at the same time causing the boat to career into the whale. He threw the line across its back, and as the boat veered off the line crept toward us. The next wave approached, if I let go we would be swept off the whale and back into the net. If I grabbed the rope, we would be pulled over the side between the boat and the whale, where we'd be crushed by the hull, and back amongst the feeding frenzy. I let the line slip away. Frank was yelling something but I couldn't make it out.

After the boat hit the whale, it started to roll slightly, and I shifted our position to get further on top. The thought of going over topsy-turvy, being pulled under as the whale rolled, tangled with the net below the water with the sharks made me cringe. We wouldn't have a chance.

Joni coughed now with a cry after each convulsion, a stream of blood pooled on the wet blubber by her leg.

"Calvin, I think I passed out," she said with a raspy voice.

When they got within range, I could see Beetle had the rope ready but now they couldn't get up on the whale. Frank was on the bow.

I yelled, "We need to get off now!"

Then the next swell, a big one, passed over us, pushing hard against our bodies, and the whale rolled a bit more. With the swell passing, the boat veered off again, but now I could see they must have had the little diesel running. The exhaust pumped out the port side, billowing white smoke. They made a tighter turn, this time coming on fast with Frank on the bow holding something long and black.

"Good Lord," I said aloud. He had the harpoon rifle and I knew what we had to do.

"Joni, we have to go back into the water."

Her head fell down and her chin rested on her flotation vest. "We have to go back into the water," she said, part affirmatively and partly as a question. She lifted her head as I cleared her hair away, and she saw the boat. "Okay," she said in a slow wavering voice. "I'm ready when you're ready."

As she said this, the report of rifle fire startled us both. I turned to see the harpoon line trailing across the body of the whale, rolling toward us along its back. I let loose the net and reached for this quarter inch thin white nylon rope that could save our lives.

"Next wave, Joni. You hold on to my arm."

I wrapped and wrapped the soft nylon line every which way around my hand and right arm – there was no way I intended to let this go. The boat moved downwind as the next wave came upon us, leaning to one side it swept us off, holding on to each other we slid down the side of the whale into the sea.

We fell into the foul bloody water and immediately our bodies began to move, pulled under, and dragged, I twisted to get righted. We slid along what had to be a large shark, riding over the slope of its body, which by now did not seem surprising. With my right arm stretched out ahead of us, we searched for the surface and air, and after several desperate moments, I managed to turn my back in an attempt to get our heads out of the water. I had Joni close to me, her head under my chin, my hand tucked around her belt, and my legs locked around hers. All I could hear was the sound of water rushing by, turbulence and flashes of light. Joni made a strange gurgling cry, and then she lay limp in my arms. We seemed to be moving very fast. I gulped for air whenever I could, slowly letting it out and then waiting for the next opportunity. And then we slowed and I heard voices.

We were bobbing next to the hull, and suddenly Joe's face rose before me. He was talking to me. They had Joni. Someone was in the water holding her. It was Frank. He looked different with his dark hair all wet and matted. Joe was saying something. He had a knife and cut the line free. Then they had a sheet or a sail around her, and as they lifted her, blood ran from under her body. I looked at Joe. He spoke slowly. "Can you climb the ladder?"

I don't think I said anything and couldn't stop coughing. He turned me to face a ladder as someone else managed to get a line under my arms, and then the next moment I was lying on the stern deck like one of the many fish we had landed, looking out at the gray-green sea, and the dark body of the whale amongst the birds in the distance.

Someone knelt next to me and unwrapped the line from my arm, turned, and touched my body. "He looks okay!" Beetle yelled.

The boat was underway now, my body rocked with the motion as I kept coughing up seawater, someone had the radio turned up loud. Beetle covered me with a blanket and I managed to get up on one elbow before he came back to prop me up against the bulkhead. He knelt by me, unfolding my right hand to remove the last remnants of the rope and wipe away the blood, but it kept bleeding. He gave me a rag to squeeze.

"That will have to keep you until we get Joni squared away."

My heart was still pounding hard, and I couldn't stop coughing. "Where's Joni?" He was holding something back. I could see it in his face, and tried to get up but couldn't. "Bring me to her," I pleaded.

"There's no room."

"Bring me, damn it."

He bent down and dragged me under the shoulders to the cockpit area where they had Joni laid out. Frank knelt over her prone body and was pumping her chest while Ellie caressed her head. Tears ran down Ellie's face as she counted for Frank. She was sobbing while she counted, and then she stopped to put her mouth to Joni's and pushed in air.

The limp body, lifeless, jogged after each thrust. The blood rushed to my head, and I gasped for air to scream but gagged on seawater. I reached out to grab Joni's cold bare foot.

As Frank pumped her heart, he spoke to her. "Come on, Joni. Come on back, another day – come on girl."

Beetle grabbed her by the leg and now we all had a piece of her when a convulsion wrestled her pale body and water poured out of her mouth. She coughed once, spewing water into the air.

"Her pulse is back again, Frank."

"Another breath," he said desperately.

She pushed more air in, and Joni's chest rose under the pressure. Another convulsion of water came out, and then she coughed repeatedly with her head to the side, spitting out water and choking, reaching for air. Her eyes flickered and fluttered open as Ellie wept and laughed, running her hands over Joni's face. Joni moaned when Frank turned her body to the side, and more water came out pink and thick. Her eyes held a distant gaze.

"Beetle, get the medical kit from under my bunk," Frank said steadily.

Then Joe came out of the house for an update. He looked grey and old.

"She's back. Where are they?" asked Frank.

"They just passed the Vineyard and estimate at least 20 minutes."

"When you feel it's safe enough, I want you and Beetle

working to get that prop cleared."

"Roger that," he said and got back on the radio.

I could hear the Coast Guard Air Rescue operator calling in: *"Bird of Passage. Bird of Passage. This is Coast Guard Air Rescue requesting your status."*

It turned out Joe had the Coast Guard in the air before we got off the whale, he responded with the news. Joni appeared half awake and half delirious. Her body trembled and shook as Frank opened a small stainless steel medical kit containing an assortment of vials and syringes.

"Joni, I want to give you a shot of morphine. Is that okay?"

"Okay, Frank," she whispered.

He looked at Ellie, who nodded in agreement before he administered the shot into her thigh.

"That should help, and the Coast Guard will be here soon. We are going to put a splint on your arm, and we are going to put a work vest back on you to protect your ribs. Ellie, get some duct tape."

"Where's Calvin?" Joni spoke so softly I barely heard my name.

"He's right here, holding on to your big toe." Frank smiled. "He's okay."

She feebly lifted her left hand, and I crawled to her side like a cripple. She whispered something as blood ran down her lower lip. I leaned closer.

"You didn't leave me," she sighed.

"I didn't leave you."

Our good hands joined, I sat there watching as they worked to stop the bleeding from the side of her ribs. Her chest bare and breast bloody, she squeezed my hand hard, squinting and clinching her teeth, her eyes shut until they were finished. When she opened them again, she looked dreamily at me.

"Don't worry. I'm not going to die."

"I know. We won't let you."

She tried to move but cried out. Frank covered her with a blanket.

"Hold my hand," she said with a faint smile.

"Don't talk now," I whispered.

They lowered the sail as Ellie and I sat with her and they went to the stern with saws and knives. I was glad I didn't have to go back into the water, and didn't know if I ever could. In the background, the Coast Guard radio dispatch called in again. Ellie jumped to the call and gave them an update on Joni's condition and on the boat's condition as well.

We lay there together hand in hand, as the world began to open up, the gray sky, the dark water, the enormity of it all. Overhead the dark silhouette of a bird passed slowly without a flutter of its wings, and I thought about something Joni told me that night on the beach, something her dad had said before he died, a verse he wrote in a letter that she always carried with her, an excerpt from a book, about the human spirit, about our death being the eternal companion, always watching you within arm's length. The immensity of what just occurred settled upon me.

"They'll be here soon," I said. She gave my hand a faint squeeze.

Then there was a lot of hollering and banging, Joe swearing about fishermen and nets and goddamn dead whales. He and Beetle appeared each with a hacksaw in hand, cuts on their arms, masks and snorkels on their heads. Seaweed clung to their clothes and they looked like they had just fought off Davey Jones himself. Joe whipped the saw overboard and then fired up the big diesel, which came to life with a roar like it knew what needed to be done. He swung her around to the north and put the pedal to the metal. The boat vibrated like a car with two flat tires but he didn't back her down. Frank came and sat with us.

"How's she doing?"

"She's quiet and drifting a lot."

"We need to get ready – they'll be here soon. We need to get away from the boat. They can't drop the basket here."

Then Frank, Beetle, and Ellie pulled the Zodiac off the roof and devised a makeshift stretcher. This took a while, but then Joe gave a wrap on the window and pointed to the north. On the horizon and just above the water line, against the deepening evening gray light, the white strobe of the rescue helicopter flashed.

"I have a visual. This is *Bird of Passage*," Joe shouted into the mic. He reached out of the cabin and fired a red flare. Joni opened her eyes, startled as the flare arced and sizzled above the water.

"It's okay. They're almost here. We have to move you one more time. Frank and Beetle will help you. I'm no good. My hand is shot. I'll be there as soon as I can."

She tried to say something, but the radio was too loud. *"Bird of Passage. Bird of Passage. We have your signal. Rescue swimmer is standing by. We will stand off until you are ready for transfer."*

Joni looked panicky as the helicopter approached. The deafening whack of the rotors sounded like the pounding heartbeat of the earth itself as the helicopter came upon us. She mouthed something to me. I couldn't make it out but could see what she needed to tell me in her eyes, and then they lifted her onto the stretcher and took her away.

By the time I got to my feet, they had her in the Zodiac with Ellie tending the line, paying out as Joe kept the *Bird's* nose into the wind. The noise from the helicopter was frightening. When the raft got back far enough, the Coast Guard pilot gave the signal to tie off and await the basket. The copter then moved in pushing the water into a torrent of spray so thick you could barely see. Up in the cockpit, the crew sat suspended as the basket descended, their white helmets all that were visible and I had to wonder what we looked like to them. The helicopter slowly turned to reveal the winch crewman leaning out, nursing the basket down to the raft, letting the ground lead drag across the water as they gently lowered the cage like an angel gathering lost souls. Within a matter of a few heartbeats, Joni was away, rising up on a wire into the waiting hands of the United States Coast Guard.

The rescue team patiently waited until Beetle and

Frank got back onboard and then pulled up alongside. The crew had been talking with Joe, who came out to wave a thank you. We all waved. Then the pilot gave a snappy salute and pulled out in front of us, making a wide fast turn to the north, the nose dipped, and the copter sped off to suddenly vanish with only the red flashing strobe marking its trail. We watched the flash fade into the night.

"Holy Mother of Mercy!" were the first words spoken by Joe. Then everyone turned to me and nearly attacked me with questions, which Frank said needed to wait until they got me squared away. This required removing all my clothing to discard over the side, and when Beetle was ready to toss the work vest I tried to stop him.

"That thing saved our lives."

"It smells like death, and besides, the whale saved your lives."

I couldn't argue with him, and over it went. They hosed me down naked while Ellie excused herself to go below and rustle up some soup for us all. They wrapped me in a blanket while Frank tended to my hand and mangled arm, which had swollen and sprouted welts with corrugated dark lines.

"Christ, Calvin. Maybe we should have sent you along with Joni."

"I don't think anything is broken, but my arm hurts like hell."

He gave me some medication while Ellie wrapped it in ice and applied clean dressing after the bleeding stopped. She had that totally wired look and didn't speak. After wrapping my hand the first time, she undid the whole thing only to wrap it in the other direction, excusing herself for doing so as I tried to figure out what she had overlooked. She got me bandaged up and comfortable in the wheelhouse with a bowl of soup cradled in my good hand as I stared off into the darkness to the north, worrying about Joni and awaiting the news as we limped slowly back to Woods Hole.

Frank retreated to the aft cabin in order to make the call into the Port Office emergency number. It sounded like there was a lot of explaining to do, and he remained there for some time. The VHF radio buzzed with the story. Some of the fishing fleet had the rescue dialed in on channel 81. Having heard the whole event as it unfolded, they now wanted to know how the young marine biologist was faring, and every fisherman sounded like the good grandfather genuinely concerned about Joni's condition. They even offered to have their wives pay a visit and bring some homemade soup.

"My wife makes a fish chowder that could bring a man back to life, and we're happy in this case we don't have to try," came a call from the *Carl Rice,* which was fishing on Georges Bank. *"And tell that young fella that jumped in and saved that girl that I intend to name my next kid after him."*

"Will do, Cap," answered Joe. There was a pause.

"So what's his name, damn it?" asked the voice.

"His name is Calvin," responded Joe.

In the background we could the guy swear, *"Jesus, can't picture a guy named Calvin jumping into a pack of sharks."*

Joe turned to me and shrugged his shoulders.

"Tell 'em his middle name is Bud," said Beetle.

Joe relayed this to the fishermen and that seemed to help. We had several calls like this, and after a while I drifted off thinking of Joni and prayed she was safe and sound. No one went below, we all remained in the wheelhouse, nodding off now and then. Ellie, half asleep, leaned up against me and would pat my shoulder, checking my ice pack, giving me a reassuring smile. It was after midnight when we finally got the call. Frank came up into the cabin, and Joe throttled down so we could all hear the news. They took her straight to Mass General in Boston.

"She's okay. I guess they had a little trouble on route, but she's okay and stable. She lost a lot of blood, has a fractured arm, a couple broken ribs, and a collapsed lung. They contacted her mother, who will be there as soon as she can."

We all heaved a sigh of relief, and Ellie wept. "I

can't wait to see her," she said. "As soon as we get in, we're going."

"I'm with you on that," said Beetle.

After a long pause, Frank continued. "I'm afraid I'll have to wait a bit before I can make it to Boston. I'll have a little explaining to do when we reach port." He asked me to come below and sit with him and Ellie.

"When we get in, I want you to go straight to the hospital and get that hand and arm checked out. I have a bad feeling that there may be a party waiting for us when we arrive. One of the calls came from a news channel at the Port Office. I don't know how they got the number. They want to get pictures of the crew. Just get off the boat and go."

"I'll get him out, Frank," said Beetle in earnest.

"I'll be running interference," said Ellie.

"I'd rather have the emergency room at Mass General look at it," I said.

Frank gave me a long look. "Calvin, none of us will ever forget what you did out there. I'll never be able to thank you enough. We are all grateful, and personally, I'm still reeling from the whole thing."

"We all are," said Ellie. "I mean, Calvin, weren't you scared shitless?"

"I was beyond scared. It was very strange. Everything looked very bright, overexposed, like we were surrounded by this bright light, but everything was dark – I can't explain it." I didn't want to go back there in my head. "All I could think about was helping Joni. I don't even remember jumping off the boat."

We were all silent, wrestling with the thought of it.

"Well, you're my hero now, Bud," said Beetle with a smile, trying to make light of it.

We all laughed. Again, the marine phone rang. Frank spoke seriously to what sounded like an administrator while Ellie wrapped my arm in a fresh ice pack. We sat there for a while listening to one side of the conversation. Somehow I fell into a shallow troubled sleep but awoke not long after to find

Ellie asleep next to me while Frank was still on the phone, going through a long explanation. Beetle sat on the side of the bed with a cup of coffee. He turned to me. "She's okay. Go back to sleep, and I'll wake you if anything happens." There was the smell of death on my hands, a wretched reminder that wouldn't wash off. Somehow I wrestled myself back into the escape of sleep.

THE NEXT MORNING, I found myself alone in bed with the sun shining brightly through the starboard porthole. Consciousness arrived with a throbbing arm, pain and worry. I ran the past 24 hours through my mind, there was too much to think about.

Up on deck I found Joe behind the wheel looking serious and tired, with the rest of the crew sitting in the cockpit bedraggled in the morning sunshine. We were just south of the Vineyard. The heavy damp morning air filtered the summer light, making the Gay Head lighthouse appear to float on vapor. As we approached Nomans Land, the thoughts of the past three trips rolled around so much I couldn't remember who I was before setting foot on this boat, but knew a different person now returned.

I joined the crew and sat next to Frank, who just put his arm around my shoulder and gave a good moan like my dog does when he's happy.

"Joni's doing fine; she's out of intensive care."

There was a moment of silence as they looked at me and I assumed to assess my condition until Beetle announced: "Calvin Landry – Shark Tracker! Frank we need some Shark Tracker tee shirts."

"It might help fund my next trip because I don't think the NSF will be too happy about this one," he replied.

"Trolling for sharks with the crew for bait. Tell them it was meant to be a creative approach to cost savings."

He laughed. "You can be my publicist."

"Frank, we collected some good data on this trip," said Ellie while she tended to my pathetic looking hand. She leaned close and whispered, "Joni's resting, and asked when we could come and see her."

I smiled as she gave my good hand a squeeze, and then she and Beetle went below to get our gear ready.

Frank turned to me with a look of concern. "How's the hand feeling?"

"It's swollen like a tick with fingers, but actually feeling a bit better."

"I presume you're heading to Boston with the rest?"

Trying to think of what to say, attempting to put into words what words couldn't express, what the past three weeks meant, not knowing how to thank him, I wrestled with a multitude of emotion.

"Joni's going to be alright, she's a strong woman." He paused. "Ashley likes to quote Nietzsche: That which doesn't kill you makes you stronger. Maybe you can convince her to stick around for a while."

He stared off into the distance as was his nature, always looking for any sign of fish.

"Frank…" I stopped short, not knowing how to say what I wanted to say.

He turned and gave me that look that let's you know.

"It's a beautiful world out there, a beautiful wild world. I'm glad you got to see a piece of it. And I'm thankful we're all in one piece."

We sat there under the rising sun, watching as signs of life moved about the coastline. Lobster boats swung about near the east side of Cuttyhunk, a couple of bass fishermen trolled the shore off Nashawena Island, an old wooden cutter sailed out of Quicks Hole. It was good to be heading home.

"Did you get any pictures yesterday?"

"Just of the whale and a lot of fins – I missed the good part."

We both laughed.

Soon we were off Pasque Island when a familiar Woods Hole skiff closed the distance and came alongside. Joe sounded the horn. It was Ollie.

"Welcome to Cape Cod," he yelled. "Is all well?"

We were all happy to see Ollie.

"Boy, did you miss a fun trip," Ellie shouted out.

"So I heard. Here." He gently tossed a brown paper bag on deck. Beetle opened it to find a bag with a dozen doughnuts.

We all cheered: "Doughnuts!"

"See you on the beach." He waved and off he went ahead towards Woods Hole.

Inside the bag we also found the morning's Boston Globe. On the front page in bold letters was this headline: Marine Biologist Rescued from Man-Eaters. The article told the story of Joni falling overboard into a feeding frenzy of sharks and of the crewman who heroically saved her by climbing on top of a dead whale and blah, blah, blah. The cover photo showed her being carried off the Coast Guard helicopter in a stretcher.

"Oh, boy." Frank moaned.

Beetle held the paper bag so Frank could read the following in dark letters along the side: "Richards says use Dyer's Dock."

"Good for Richards," said Frank. "Always thinking."

By the time we got to Lucas Shoal, one of the small Coast Guard boats from Menemsha approached as if they had been out there to greet us. Joe had a short conversation on the radio with them, and we wondered why we needed an escort. When we got further up the Sound, a news helicopter appeared overhead, and it became clear to us all that someone would be awaiting our arrival. We assembled in the wheelhouse one last time.

Frank looked exasperated. "I expect to see a zoo on the dock. The port office has succumbed to media pressure and there are reporters. They expect us to land on the main dock, which I told them we would be doing. However, thanks to our friend Richards, we will land on the far end of Dyers Dock, which will give you a good five minutes to make a getaway. I'll deal with the media. You get to Boston and see how Joni is faring."

Joe gave us a sardonic smile. "I'm staying with Frank. I know how to handle the media. My dad used to work for WCAL in Santa Monica, so I know the territory. Besides, I'm from California." I think Joe found his way into our hearts. Beetle offered him a doughnut like they were now blood brothers.

We entered the waters of Woods Hole under sail and power, steaming along as best we could. It was the height of the summer season, and the steamships to the Vineyard were stacked with vacationers coming and going. We passed the channel of Woods Hole Passage, with the current pushing hard to draw us away from Great Harbor. Ahead we could see the WHOI dock crowded with a number of suited figures milling about and vans with news logos. Joe pulled a hard bend in our path to the old wooden dock across from the inlet to Eel Pond and nudged the *Bird of Passage* up alongside, where we were greeted by our friend Richards waiting to lend a hand.

"Glad to see you all back safe and sound." He smiled. "Frank, they're like killer bees over there. You have my sympathy. I have a WHOI van waiting if anyone needs to use it."

We didn't wait to grab our chance. Ellie and Beetle were making plans on how to hook up with Frank later, while Richards stood on the dock with arms akimbo looking down at me.

"You the one who saved that girl?"

I didn't know what to say and held out my bad hand and offered him a doughnut with my good one. He smiled, took the pastry and while holding the offering he looked seaward in the direction we had come.

"You ever going back out there?"

Before I could answer, Beetle and Ellie got a hold of me and off we went. "Come on. We'll see Joe and Frank later."

We thanked Richards and rushed down the dock, stumbling against the old heavy planking and the gravity of dry land. I fell into the back of the van as Beetle pulled out onto Water Street where we could see a crowd of reporters, WHOI administrators and staff crossing over the Eel Pond Bridge rushing toward the dock as we made our getaway.

As we sped out of Woods Hole, I could see the waters of Great Harbor shimmering with the morning sunshine. Out beyond the Hole, beyond the islands and the horizon, was a place now carried, a place where a golden star rises above blue water with the promise of endless sun-filled days, where the light of this world and the green eyes of another did illuminate the heart of a man who would carry this light within his flesh and bone, by fair wind and following sea, home.

Acknowledgements

I am greatly indebted to the following family, friends, and colleagues for their support and their unstinting help in the preparation of this book: Valerie Tomasselli, who first laid eyes on the manuscript and didn't turn away; Brian Carey for his encouragement; Dave Masch for his insightful comments; Jim Broda for his lifelong enthusiasm; and Geraldine Camilli whose final blessing gave me the ammunition to pull the trigger. Many thanks to the NOAA Image Library for the fish images, and Sparkman and Stevens for the ship drawings.

This book is dedicated to the memory of Frank Carey, a hard-working man of science with whom I labored for many years, a man who loved art, music, and the sea; and to Ollie Brazier, a lover of the water world, friend and fellow shark tracker.

Although many of the events in this book are true to life, the characters are fictional. The depictions of life in Woods Hole are of days gone by when charmed men walked the streets, beautiful women swam naked at the shore, and dogs roamed free.

This book could not have come to be without the inspiration of my son Owen, and the love, patience, and support of my wife Frances Johnson.

April 2010   e. k. king
Falmouth, Massachusetts